300

"CONFIRMATION?" PRICE QUERIED

"Homeland isn't going to give him confirmation, and you know it."

"I do know it, and I told the President."

"We're way ahead of Homeland and everybody else on the learning curve, Hal," Price insisted, feeling the heat rise to her face. "We've been a step ahead of Homeland, the Bureau and Langley since this thing started. Now we're allowing our men to go into unnecessary danger because of it?"

"The President isn't convinced there is danger—"

"What's going to convince him we know what we're talking about?"

"You know how politically delicate this thing is," Brognola replied.

Barbara Price felt the heat come to a boil. "The Man's in denial, and more people will die because of it. We put Able at risk twice and we're doing it again, this minute."

First edition June 2004

ISBN 0-373-61955-3

TERMS OF CONTROL

Special thanks and acknowledgment to
Tim Somheil for his contribution to this work.

TERMS OF CONTROL

CHAPTER ONE

Pacific Ocean

The sailor held the old shotgun away from his body, as if he were holding on to someone else's stinking laundry. He'd fired the weapon twice that afternoon off the rail. Emergency training, the captain called it. The sailor was twenty-two years old and this was only his second Asia-to-America voyage; he didn't feel as if he had been adequately trained for anything, let alone combat.

"Don't worry about it," the captain had said. "With this kind of gun you don't even need to aim. Just point it in the general direction of the bad guy and pull the trigger."

The young sailor, a merchant marine named Shin Un-sok, hoped he never had to fire the thing at all. In fact he had been telling himself over and over that there was no need for all this heightened security. The *Eun-Pyo* wasn't an oil tanker, just a container ship. Only the oil tankers were in danger, right?

Not that the *Eun-Pyo* was a shoddy piece of work. She was modern and sleek for a container ship. Her deck was devoid

of cranes and other equipment for handling the cargo, since
like most container ships she used cargo-loading gear at her
shore terminals. Her hatches were huge, enabling her cellu-
lar cargo grid to be efficiently loaded with standard twenty-
foot or forty-foot containers. Once the interior compartments
were loaded as high as the upper deck, the hatches could be
closed and a double layer of containers loaded on top of the
hatches, if the weight-load ratio allowed it.

Even burdened with all that cargo she was still somehow
an elegant sea beast, or so Shin Un-sok had thought during
his enthusiastic early days as a merchant sailor. The ship's
compact, powerful diesels could propel her on calm seas at
twenty knots, so she could make brisk work of the Seoul-to-
Seattle run.

Shin's love affair with the *Eun-Pyo* had grown cool in the
past twenty-four hours. She had begun to look more brutish,
even merciless, and suddenly Shin was wondering if he
should have pursued his dream of being a sailor. Factory jobs
were boring, but safer.

Something clanked and Shin jumped, cursing under his
breath. What was that? He moved into the shadows alongside
the wall of containers and moved cautiously to the starboard
side of the ship. The clank came from there. Now that he
thought about it, it had sounded like the heavy chain that was
used to lash down the huge tarpaulins sometimes needed to
cover damaged containers. None of the tarps were being used
on this trip, so maybe one of the chains had tumbled off a tarp
roll. It was a weak explanation, but it relieved Shin.

Anyway, there was nothing to be worried about. This ship
carried consumer goods, not oil. The ships that were in danger carried oil.

Shin was trying to convince himself. The *Eun-Pyo* was
filled with televisions and microwave ovens. Its value was a

fraction of a supertanker cargo. There would be no reason for anyone to come after this ship.

Then, at the end of the narrow passage between the containers, the stranger stepped into view. His face was blackened with paint, and Shin knew instantly that he didn't belong on the vessel.

Shin turned to find another figure blocking the way behind him.

The sailor didn't know why this was happening and he realized now it didn't matter. Not to him. I'm a dead man, he told himself. It was the first thing he had said to himself all night that was right.

He might as well go out shooting. He brought the shotgun barrel to his shoulder just like the captain had taught him to do. That was as far as he got. There was a sharp cough that seemed to come in stereo from behind and in front of him, and his finger stopped working before he could yank the shotgun's trigger. Then his arm wouldn't hold the weapon any longer, then his legs wouldn't hold him up. As the darkness became complete, Shin thought philosophically that his worries were over.

SANG BIN FELT the cold barrel of a weapon touch the back of his skull and his hands froze above a bridge control panel.

"Put them up."

The intruder spoke English and sounded like an American. Sang raised his hands, which were cold despite the oppressive heat of the tropical night.

"One of your guards is dead," the man announced emotionlessly.

Sang started to turn his head in surprise, but then caught the window reflection of a second intruder, also aiming a handgun at his back.

"Move again and you'll be dead, too."

"What do you want?"

"How many men on guard?"

"Two on deck aft of the bridge castel and one in the rear. Plus myself." Sang was glad he was fluent in English. This wasn't the time to be misunderstood.

"The rest of the crew?"

"All in their quarters as far as I know."

"Engine room staff?"

"Our engines do not need round-the-clock maintenance but there is probably some crew in the engineering room."

"Total crew?"

"Sixteen. Fifteen if you've murdered one of my men."

"Make it fourteen," said the unseen American before Sang's head exploded.

The American watched the dead Korean collapse to the floor. The window dripped blood and gore, but hadn't shattered because the gun had been aimed up to imbed the round in the ceiling after performing its function. The American pulled his radio to his mouth and spoke quietly. "Bridge is secure. We've got a second guard on duty up front and one in back."

"Team Two here. The aft guard is taken care of."

"Team Three here. We'll find the second guard up here. He'll probably be at the shiplight mast in the front."

The American didn't reply to these announcements, but said, "Team Four, engine room occupancy is unknown."

"Team Four here. We'll deal with it."

The American stepped to a communications console and pulled open the access panel underneath the controls, quickly snipping out six-inch lengths from what he knew were vital connecting cables. The radio was now unusable. Not that any member of the crew was going to live long enough to get up here to send a Mayday, but it was insurance.

The American's companion stood easily in the open doorway, keeping an eye out in case other crewmen unexpectedly strolled onto the scene.

"Only one engineer in the engine room," his radio announced quietly. "He's out of the picture. We're ready to take out the power."

"Go ahead."

The bridge lights died, leaving the room black. The floodlights that illuminated the deck and its acres of containers dimmed and were gone, as did the warning beacons on the sixty-foot mast on the front of the ship. For a moment there was complete darkness.

Then the emergency lights in the bridge came on, white and glaring. The mast beacon flared back to life, powered by its dedicated emergency generator.

The two bridge occupants stood waiting, saying nothing, and the commander counted from fifteen down to three before the emergency lights in the bridge also died.

He nodded and even grinned a little. Freaking flawless. And to think his Army CO had once called him a piece of shit loser. He was going to take his fee from this job, buy a Ferrari and show up at the colonel's trashy little house in Winston-Salem. That would show him who the loser was.

"Team Three here. The fore guard is keeping low. You want us to keep after him?"

"Yes." The guard wasn't going to be causing any trouble if he was busy evading Team Three. The American commander didn't want any problems. Diligence, combined with the operation's extensive planning, meant there would be no surprises.

He hated surprises.

"BLOODY HELL," said the man falling through the night sky. He hated surprises. Plummeting earthward a half mile above the planet, with a black, cloud-swollen sky above and black ocean underneath, the only thing he could see was the distant glimmer of the container ship's lights. Then the ship lights went out. With the protective helmet covering his head it was oddly quiet, like being in a darkroom all alone.

"Stony, we've got a problem." Even as he spoke into the radio, he saw the lights reappear and flicker, then dissolve to leave just a single red beacon.

"Go ahead, Phoenix One," said the female voice in his headset. Even amplified above the rush of the wind, she sounded cool and calm.

"The ship just lost power," he reported. "Her emergency lights came and went. All that's left is the aft beacon."

"The ship's plans say the beacon has an emergency generator independent of other ship power grids," she said calmly.

"That beacon will get hit soon enough," the man called Phoenix One observed in a distinctly British accent.

"Phoenix Five here," came a reply. "The screws stopped."

"We'll have that going for us, at least," Phoenix One replied. Then it occurred to him it might not be a good thing at all. "Phoenix Five, how's your targeting?"

"Shot to hell."

Phoenix One swore again and craned his neck to look down between his feet. He couldn't see Phoenix Five, of course.

"Can you still make it to the boat?"

"I'm going to try."

"Don't kill yourself in the process."

"I'm going to try."

Phoenix One attempted to fix the odds. They made the jump when and where Phoenix Five estimated they had the best chance of hitting the moving target that was the Korean container ship *Eun-Pyo*.

The trick was to get all five commandos onto a moving ship in the dark without killing any of them. Phoenix Five was the man with the best experience, so he was the natural choice to lead the insertion and to make the critical dark touchdown to set up markers for the others to follow.

Phoenix Five had stepped out of the aircraft well ahead of the others, to give him the time he needed to set those markers. The jump was the riskiest for him. There was no room for deviation, and now they had a deviation.

Phoenix One had no way of even guessing the outcome, let alone making odds. "No bullshit, Phoenix Five—can you make it or not?"

"It's going to be close."

"That's not a precise answer."

"That's as precise as I can get, Phoenix One."

"How's our arrangement, Phoenix Four?" he radioed. The last commando to make the jump was keeping an eye on their grouping during the dark descent.

"We're sticking close together, Phoenix One."

"Okay. Talk to me, Phoenix Five."

"We'll open up in a few seconds," Phoenix Five replied. Anyone eavesdropping on the encrypted radio exchange would have been confused to hear an accent that didn't match that of the man called Phoenix One. In fact, it was pure Texas.

Leading the free fall, Thomas Jackson Hawkins was the youngest of the five team members. That didn't mean he wasn't an extremely competent commando, and he brought skydiving expertise that started with a set of paratrooper wings and a stint with Airborne.

He had been on so many jumps he couldn't keep track, but this one would stick in his memory. Hawkins eyed his altimeter and squinted into the blackness of the vast Pacific Ocean with its one tiny dot of illumination. He was diving through the atmosphere, trying to propel his body toward the tiny beacon. The ship was getting closer, but not close enough. He had timed the jump to hit the ship where it would have been if it had maintained its chugging pace through the South Pacific Ocean. When the engine stopped, the ship slowed quickly, and Hawkins found himself fighting for distance. He not only had to reach the ship, he had to reach its aft end to touch down with the best chances of remaining unseen.

Above him, the others waited for his signal. They would deploy at the same time and their extra few thousand feet of slow descent would allow them to steer themselves to the vessel—but only if they had a good marker to aim for.

Hawkins couldn't fail.

He ignored the altimeter when the ship got close. This one was too hairy to trust instruments. He'd have to go on instinct or they'd never hit their target.

His altimeter didn't ignore him. It started its shrill beep in his headphones as the planet approached. It wouldn't force his chute to deploy, unlike most free-fall packs, but its warning was shrill. And all the others were hearing it, too.

The beep became faster and louder. The air was like the roaring of monstrous flames even through the protective helmet. Hawkins watched the red beacon grow.

The beep became a piercing electronic scream.

Phoenix One radioed, "Uh, Phoenix Five…?"

Phoenix Five cut him off. "Deploy in five, four, three, two, one."

Hawkins pulled his release and felt his rushing fall stop with an abrupt jerk, and then he was gliding, the wind dying to a rush. He steered the invisible black parafoil into a controlled dive just as the beacon dimmed and disappeared.

He was flying in blackness.

CHAPTER TWO

T. J. Hawkins was a small boy when his father took him on a walking tour through Carlsbad Caverns. At one point, just for effect, the tour guide turned off the lights. It was unlike any darkness Hawkins had ever seen—blackness too total for the mind to accept.

That was the kind of blackness he saw now. No moon, no stars, no detail of light anywhere on the surface of the black Pacific. Even his tiny headgear LCDs were off.

He flipped the night-vision glasses into place as he simultaneously snapped on the altimeter display. The Korean container ship appeared on the flat, featureless blur of thermally neutral ocean water. She was nearly stopped, but Hawkins refused to trust the depth perception of the thermal image. He steered toward her and made rapid calculations with the height of the top container level on the deck and the altimeter readings, and homed in on the rear containers.

He was thankful he had decided to go in using the standard, square MC-5 ram-airs instead of the newly available canopies based on the XT-11 prototypes. The new chutes allowed for slower landings with loads up to four hundred pounds, so a heavily equipped soldier could touch down at a soft five miles per hour. But the new chutes weren't as maneuverable. He'd decided maneuverability was key, and his executive decision had forced Phoenix One to cull the equipment load. But it now proved to have been the right decision. With the heavier-duty chutes, Phoenix Force would have been destined for a water landing.

When he was close enough he switched from altimeter to a handheld LIDAR device. The Light Detection And Ranging laser allowed him to determine his distance and rate of approach to whatever target he aimed at. He directed the laser-measurement device at the top of the rear container.

He leaned all his weight into the canopy, pulling every inch of height out of it as he passed over the front end of the dark vessel. He had no time for reconnaissance of the ship deck while he was busy finessing the lines for another few inches of angle to the right. He found himself sailing over the top of the deck castle, close enough to touch.

The aft end of the deck behind the bridge was shorter than the fore and didn't give him much distance to work with. Hawkins urged the canopy into a fast dive and found himself swinging recklessly toward the gray outlines of a deck-stacked container. He was a heartbeat away from slamming into a steel wall at highway speeds when he dragged on the guide ropes to create a sudden steep ascent. Hawkins watched the sudden approach of the corner of a container and twisted hard, yanking a guideline with all his weight. The spastic movement maneuvered him away from the container—but not far enough. The steel corner slammed into his side as he twisted back to center. Then he plummeted, catching the steel surface of the container top, rolling and using the momentum to propel himself onto his feet. He fought for balance on the edge of the container, trusting the drag of the parafoil to prevent him from going over.

With an effort he began balling up the collapsed parafoil, quick-disconnecting the lines, then he stooped and snatched a plastic sphere, as big as a golf ball, out of the pocket on his front thigh. He squeezed it hard to crack the twin plastic capsules inside, shook it to mix the contents and quickly rolled it toward the far end of the container. Nothing happened.

At least, nothing Hawkins could see until he snapped the thermal eyepiece back into place.

Inside the sphere, the broken capsules mixed and reacted, spewing a heavy cloud of black, hot particles through the sphere's perforated wall. The particles settled to create a half-inch-deep layer of hot fog within the lip of the container roof.

Hawkins, having already made a quick recon of the aft end of the ship and finding it devoid of life, stepped onto the top of the adjoining container.

That was the moment the dull ache above his hip became a flash of white-hot pain. He grunted and his foot landed poorly on the container roof, even louder than his parafoil touchdown. He found himself on his hands and knees, every inhalation an agony.

Hawkins lambasted himself, pushing himself to toss another sphere and forcing his mind through the mental calculation of his deployment time. Had he been quick enough?

"Phoenix One here. Good work, T.J. Coming in on portside runway."

Hawkins pushed himself to his feet and monitored the landing. The Phoenix Force leader came in fast but on target; he slowed during his last few seconds until he could touch down on the container top in a controlled jog. Out of his bare eye Hawkins saw only the fleeting shadow of a dark figure, but through his thermal lens he had a clear view of the man making a near-perfect landing, sending up swirling clouds of

brilliant particles with each step. The hot fog was already set-
tling by the time David McCarter wadded his parafoil into a
ball and abandoned it in the corner of the container roof.

"Cal, how's our spacing?" Hawkins radioed. He sounded
strained, and he hoped the transmission would mask it.

"About perfect," Phoenix Four replied. "How are you,
Hawk?"

There was no fooling these guys. Already McCarter was
coming to his side. Before McCarter could start the mother-
hen routine, Hawkins reported, "I raised a racket. Watch for
signs of alert."

McCarter went on the prowl around the container edges
as Hawkins monitored the incoming commandos, who
touched down one after another within two minutes of himself.

The Phoenix Force leader was keeping a wary eye on the
faint glimmer of the bridge windows. His thermal imaging
showed him the head and shoulders of a man standing there,
warm in the open window. Probably one of the boarders,
therefore quite possibly equipped with his own night-vision
system. All the man had to do was to make a quick look over
his shoulder to discover the intruders.

With a hand gesture he sent them crawling over the back
end of the container on a rappel line. The Phoenix Force
commander was the last to go over. The man on the bridge
hadn't moved a muscle. McCarter's second concern was the
markers. The hot fog devices, custom-made by the Stony
Man Farm armory, had enabled this insertion, but at a risk.
That risk was almost gone as the temperature of the chemical mist approached ambient and the glow faded on his ther-
mal-imaging LCD.

His third concern was his youngest team member.
Hawkins was hurt and the wound wasn't obvious. No matter

how bad it really was, Hawkins would say something like, "I've had armadillo bites worse'n this."

Even after many missions together, McCarter still couldn't wade through the Texas-size bullshit when Hawkins started shoveling it.

Two of the commandos were guarding the possible approaches while Hawkins endured a quick examination from Calvin James.

James was a tall, lanky black man who sported a pencil-thin mustache and close-cropped hair. If you didn't know him, you would say he looked too neat and too thin to fit into the role of a special operations commando. The truth was that ex-SEAL James was a highly effective warrior, not to mention a skilled field medic.

"How bad?" McCarter asked.

"No way to tell," James replied.

"T.J., be straight, mate. How do you feel?"

Hawkins looked him square in the face and said, "I feel like my guts are busted."

McCarter wanted to shout something profane. How bad did it have to be for Hawkins to actually admit he was in pain? "Stony One, we're down," McCarter said into the radio. "Five was hurt during landing."

"Phoenix Four here," James said into the radio. "T.J. took blunt-force trauma to the middle right abdomen."

"David?" For the first time the emotion showed in the voice of the mission controller. She knew that the team commander was about to make a hard decision.

But there was no decision to make, really. The mission had to proceed, and for very practical reasons. The team was on the ship. The ship and everyone on it would be destroyed if they didn't stop it.

There was another option, of course: jump into the ocean,

deploy the emergency flotation devices and radio for a
pickup. Hawkins could be air-lifted by Medevac to the nearest Navy doctor. But then the ship's crew would have no
hope of survival.

"Patch him into the doc, Stony One," McCarter radioed.
"Keep me posted."

"Affirmative."

"T.J.," McCarter said.

"Yeah?" Hawkins's forehead shone with sweat.

"No sleeping on the job."

"Understood."

McCarter moved to one of the figures standing guard at
the corner of the container.

"Anything?" McCarter whispered.

Rafael Encizo didn't turn away from his watch. "Nothing."

Encizo was Cuban-born, although his light brown complexion was now hidden under streaks of battle cosmetics.
His short-cropped, once-black hair was now grizzled. His
face was slightly squared, hinting strongly of some native
North American Indian ancestry.

The strong forehead, combined with the muscular shoulders and arms, gave him the look that some people interpreted
as slow, both physically and intellectually. He wasn't. Under
the bulk were a cat's quick reflexes and hunting instincts, and
a mind as sharp as the cat's claws.

"We're going ahead as planned, but T.J.'s gonna sit this one
out," McCarter said.

Encizo nodded slightly. "His loss. Cal and I can handle it."

"All right," McCarter said. "Let's move out."

CALVIN THOMAS JAMES and Rafael Encizo moved along the
port rail of the container ship, needing no discussion. They
had studied the vessel's schematics, so they were confident

in their position, but more important they had the confidence that came with having fought side by side for years.

With one eye covered by a thermal lens and the other bare, Encizo watched through the narrow gaps between the containers and glared into every shadow and niche that could hide a person. By the time they reached the bridge castel, the silence was thick.

Encizo brought them to a halt before they reached the deck-level doors into the castel, pointing out the pair of human shapes sprawled against the rail behind a plank davit. A quick check confirmed they were corpses. The Korean crew. One of them sprawled on top of an unfired hunting rifle.

They had armed themselves against just such an attack, but these were merchant mariners, not soldiers. They weren't trained to defend themselves.

They hadn't slowed the intruders, let alone challenged them.

The bridge castel was essentially a five-story building built one-third of the way from the back end of the container ship. The bridge dominated the top floor, windowed on all sides for visibility in all directions. On lower floors would be found radar and communications gear, crew and officer quarters, galley, lounge, maybe even an exercise room. Every function and piece of equipment that could be packed into the bridge castel freed up cargo space elsewhere, and maximizing cargo space was the whole purpose of a ship like the *Eun-Pyo*.

When Encizo put his hand to the door and listened, he heard nothing.

It was bizarre. Too dark, and too quiet. On a ship like this it was unnatural not to feel the hum of distant engines and generators. But the deck was dead. She had drifted to a stop and she was too big to rock gently in the waves of a calm sea. The wind was motionless, and even under the oppressive mantle of clouds it was above ninety degrees. The effect was unnatural.

"Phoenix Two," Encizo announced quietly into his headgear microphone. "We're at the wheelhouse door. We're going in."

Encizo swung the door and Calvin James stepped inside, sweeping the room with the business end of the Heckler & Koch MP-5 SD-3.

The room was empty. The entryway had storage for foulweather gear and portable tools. Beyond it was a spotless galley. Breakfast preparations hadn't yet started. An orange light glowed on a coffee urn bolted to the stainless-steel counter, but the bitter smell told them it was hours old.

A recreation room across the hall was dark and empty. Encizo put the backs of his fingers on the cabinet of the wide-screen TV, finding no residual warmth.

One floor up they found three rooms for officers and two dormlike crew quarters. Their flashlights illuminated some unmade bunks, while the bedclothes on other bunks were so neatly made Encizo was sure they'd pass the quarter test. The captain of the *Eun-Pyo* ran a tight ship.

Well, he used to. The captain was probably dead.

"Phoenix Two, find any crew?" McCarter prodded over the radio.

"Not a soul," Encizo reported. "The wheelhouse is deserted up to the second floor."

"Watch your step," McCarter replied. "You've got at least one man on the bridge, unless he's left in the last few minutes. I spotted him when we landed."

James and Encizo ascended again, emerging into the dark, silent upper floor. Encizo covered the man at the window while James swept the bridge and the adjoining equipment room. In seconds James was back at his side. He and Encizo watched the man, who stood staring out through the open windows into the silent black night.

The Cuban lowered his weapon.

James gave him a sidelong glance. The question was asked silently and Encizo answered silently, flipping on the flashlight to show James the man who stood watch on the bridge of the container ship.

"STONY TWO. The wheelhouse is clear."

McCarter pulled into the shadows at the starboard rail, glancing up at the bridge windows fifty feet above him. The commando at his side joined him.

"What about my sighting?" McCarter demanded.

"He's still here," Encizo reported.

Gary Manning watched the interesting thermal imaging display of David McCarter compressing the flesh of his forehead into a high-contrast frown.

"He got it right between the eyes," Encizo added. "Looks like sixty, seventy percent of his skull mass went out the front of the bridge. They propped him up at the window."

Gary Manning frowned, too.

"Any clue why they put him there?" McCarter asked.

"For laughs?" James suggested.

"To draw out crew," Manning said. "Some sailor is in hiding and looks up and sees the captain or mate standing on the bridge as if nothing is wrong, maybe he'll think the crisis was a false alarm."

"He'd have to be bloody stupid to go barging into the bridge castel as if nothing's happening," McCarter replied.

"Maybe all he has to do is make an approach across the deck to spring the trap," Manning suggested.

"That's right, Phoenix One," James added on the radio.

"Our man here would be visible from somebody on the deck level aft of the wheelhouse. Could be they have an ambush in place."

McCarter stared into the blackness and then nodded, deciding the possibility made sense. Manning thought so, too, even if he wasn't sure why the intruders would go to the trouble after they'd already had the ship under control.

"Okay, we've spotted them," James reported. "Two nests of two, showing up on thermal. They've got radios on their belts. Maybe we can take them down before they get the word to their friends belowdecks."

"Rafe, what can you do from there?" McCarter asked.

"I'm not equipped for sniping, but Cal and I might take down the nearest pair," Encizo said.

"What's 'might' mean, mate?" McCarter asked.

"It means I'm not making promises."

"What's your confidence level?"

"In taking out the nearest pair? High. It's the behind-the-curtain actors who're the worry."

McCarter issued his instructions, then he and Manning waited. They heard brief dual bursts that originated from the bridge above them, then shouts from the deck.

Two figures emerged from the shadows, sprinting in their direction while keeping a close eye on the bridge above. One of them dropped before his third step. His companion didn't look back until he had flattened against the wheelhouse in the darkness, breathing hard and snatching at the radio in his belt.

He never saw the hand that came out of the darkness to snatch the radio. But he was trained and he was fast, and he made exactly the right move, stepping away and raising the mini-Uzi in a single fluid motion.

Manning was faster and stayed close enough to land a palm against the man's skull, sending it into the steel wall with a resounding crack. The mini-Uzi clattered on the deck and its owner slumped beside it. Manning had the man trussed in plastic handcuffs in seconds.

The figure who had fallen on the deck was moving his arms and legs mindlessly but slowly. McCarter didn't approach, but glared into the blackness.

Manning kept one thermal lens on the wounded man, now in the middle of a lake of warm but cooling liquid. The wounded man's head hit the deck with a heavy sound, but his hand still moved, groping for his belt.

He managed to extract the radio from its hook, his hand falling with it to the deck, the remainder of his body limp. It was as if the man were already dead except for the one animated limb. The hand with the radio dragged itself through the expanding pool of warm liquid, leaving cooling streaks in its wake.

Manning lined up his handgun.

He never had to use it. The arm's fading strength was only enough to bring the radio to the man's face before his mouth opened and his life issued out in a long groan.

"Come in." The tiny buzz of the voice was audible even to Manning and McCarter, five paces away. "Who's this?"

McCarter made a movement and Manning saw two more shadows stirring in the darkness. One was talking. As they stepped around the end of the rows of containers the words became audible.

"So maybe one of the crew went rogue."

"None of these bastards have the balls to fight back," a second voice said.

"I don't think—" His words died in his throat when he almost tripped over the corpse and his companion stumbled into him.

"What the fuck, man?"

The first man didn't answer but flipped on a penlight. The tiny beam was brilliant in the pervasive darkness, and the gunners instantly found themselves standing in a lake of blood, in which lay the slack-jawed cadaver.

"Jesus! That's Worth!"

"Shut the fuck up," his companion ordered, snatching his radio from his belt as he flipped off the penlight.

Manning triggered a 3-round burst from the Heckler & Koch MP-5 SD3 submachine gun and through the factory-installed suppressor came a sound like the ripping of heavy fabric. The radio and the hand that held it disintegrated, sending the radioman stumbling away. His companion reacted with a lightning move that brought his Uzi toward the source of the shots. Manning triggered another 3-round burst that cut open his chest at the same instant a burst of fire chopped into him from above. His legs folded and he flopped alongside his companion.

"Phoenix Two, anybody else?" McCarter demanded.

"Looks clear," Encizo answered.

"Cover us," McCarter ordered, then said to Manning, "Come on."

They sprinted the distance between themselves and the wounded man, already on the verge of hyperventilating as he stared in shock at the ruined mass at the end of his wrist. His wide eyes rolled up at them and he recognized the enemy at the last second. He had to let go of his wrist to snatch at the shoulder-holstered handgun with his good hand, but he was already weak from blood loss and McCarter removed the weapon from his fingers before he could make it work. The Phoenix Force leader tightened a plastic handcuff loop on the wounded hand as an impromptu tourniquet, securing the good wrist alongside it. He cuffed the man's ankles for good measure.

One Hand struggled briefly and rolled his eyes helplessly as his shallow breathing became more rapid. McCarter slapped the side of his face hard enough to snap him out of it momentarily.

"Listen to me, mate. You struggle any more and you'll rip off the cuff. Then you'll bleed to death. Understand? It's keeping you alive."

The man nodded.

"How many of your men are abovedeck?"

The wounded man looked confused. "There were six of us."

"How many below?"

"You gotta get me off the boat. It's going down."

"Answer the question. How many more?"

"Ten more down below. You gotta take me!"

"We'll try to catch you on the way back."

McCarter radioed his upstairs pair. "Rafe, Cal, we've still got two shooters sharing the deck with us. Any sign of them?"

"Maybe," James reported. "I think I saw somebody moving between the containers, but it was way up front. Too far to be sure."

"We've got to get belowdecks in a hurry," McCarter said. "I hate to leave a pair of blokes unaccounted for, but we don't have time to flush them out."

"Understood," James replied. "We're on our way down."

"Phoenix Five, what's your status?"

"Just sittin' here with my thumb up my ass," Hawkins reported.

"Remove the thumb from your arse and use it to hold on to your weapon. We're leaving you up here on your own. You're your only defense."

"I'm tucked away like a carcass in a gator meat locker. Nobody's getting at me."

"Then stay there."

As the shadowy, silent shapes of James and Encizo drifted into visibility at the base of the bridge castel, McCarter made a quick evaluation of the probe so far. It was proceeding as well as could be expected, excepting Hawkins's injury, which was bad enough.

He hadn't much of an idea of what they would be dealing with when they got below. They didn't know who, or why, or even how. All McCarter knew was that the goal was critical sabotage. He wasn't happy to be leading his team into this mess with so little intelligence.

But it was far too late for misgivings.

With a jerk of his head McCarter ushered his teammates to the hatch and led the way down.

CHAPTER THREE

Stony Man Farm, Virginia

The small medical facility was compact but extremely well equipped. State-of-the-art and then some. Too bad he couldn't use any of this great equipment, the U.S. Army doctor thought as he performed remote diagnostics with the help of long-distance sensor input.

At least, he had been doing that a minute ago. He raised an eyebrow, then asked again, "You with me, Phoenix Five?"

The Army M.D. was experienced in special operations medical support and his exemplary record had brought him to the attention of Stony Man Farm principals. He'd been convinced to serve a rotation at the Farm. He found it fascinating when he actually had work to do, which was maybe ten percent of the time.

At the moment, he was carefully trying to get a read on his patient, whom he understood to be somewhere in the equatorial South Pacific. The sensors his patient had self-applied fed him readings of basic vital signs as the doctor led the man through a set of diagnostic exercises in the hope of receiving more good information. But the nature of the injury meant heart rate, respiration and blood pressure weren't going to tell him what he needed to know.

He had been questioning the man about notable physical symptoms, but the patient was now giving him the silent treatment.

"Talk to me, Phoenix Five."

Phoenix Five was called Hawk or T.J., but the doctor didn't know his real name. He'd been instructed to refer to him only by his team designation.

The commando's suit was equipped with quick-application diagnostic sensors for field use. The man had simply pulled the tab to expose the adhesive on the sensors already wired into his outfit, then the data relayed to the doctor's system over the commando's existing communications link.

Nothing. The doctor wrinkled his brow and leaned closer to the diagnostics displayed on his monitor.

The data, for a man who had suffered abdominal trauma during a bad parachute landing, wasn't worrisome. No dramatic blood pressure changes, no reported weakness or other symptoms to indicate internal bleeding. The sensor feedback was not, however, a replacement for a medical examination. That man needed to have his guts X-rayed.

The readings were still there but altered slightly. Heart rate increased marginally. Breathing actually slowed and steadied.

"Silent running, Phoenix Five?" he asked.

There was a single beep, which the doctor knew came when the commando responded with the press of a button on his headset, allowing him to answer noiselessly. One beep for Yes.

The M.D. sighed. So much for his diagnostics. He called the mission controller.

THE STONY MAN FARM mission controller had honey-blond hair, but she didn't fit any blonde stereotype. First of all, she had the intelligence of a great strategist.

The woman was attractive, even beautiful, but her beauty came without the makeup, without the stretched-skin look of cosmetic surgery. She wasn't a woman attempting to hang on to her college looks, and she was far more attractive for it.

In an embroidered cowboy shirt and old jeans, she would have been at home on a Montana ranch. But her eyes flashed with piercing intellect that told any casual acquaintance she was far more than a ranch hand.

Barbara Price sat at a desk with a collection of monitors, charts and paper. She spoke into the wireless headset. "Stony One here. I'm on the line, Phoenix Five. Update me when you can."

A beep was her only answer. She tapped into the video feed, which Hawkins had been equipped with for the risky air drop. His night-vision set was specially made to pick up a long-distance thermal-IR signature. Without it he might never have been able to drop himself onto the Korean container ship, but the video pickup was doing nobody any good now. The image feed back to Stony Man Farm showed blackness and nothing but.

"Phoenix Five here," Hawkins said finally. "I just got a visual on our top-deck pair. All three of them."

"Phoenix One, did you catch that?"

"Got it, Stony. We'll keep an eye out for them. Phoenix Five, we can handle it. Understood?"

"Understood."

Price broke in. "Tell us what you see, T.J."

"Two of them are the guys who were guarding the front end of the ship, I'm guessing. Automatic weapons and face paint. The other guy's unarmed as far as I can tell. Hey, he's going over the side."

"Voluntarily?" Price asked.

"Yeah. He's one of them, Stony," Hawkins said. "Looks like there's a boarding ladder there, maybe ten yards from the container we landed on. They must have one of their boats down there. We're pretty damn lucky that guy was below when I landed or he'd have had every top-deck gun ready when the rest of us came down."

"They know you're there now," Price said.

"They must," Hawkins agreed. "They're stalking around like bobcats. Maybe they don't know everybody's in the basement."

"Maybe they know there's one of you still hanging around up top," Price said. "Keep your head down."

HAWKINS STARED into the blackness and didn't answer. Price might be right. One of them was headed for his hiding place and, even worse, the other was pretending to wander off in another direction but keeping a direct line of sight on his companion and Hawkins's niche.

"Phoenix Five?" Price asked.

The first gunner was trying to look as if he were performing a general sweep of the aft end of the container ship by following the open trail between the deck rail and the containers. At the very end of the ship there was a collection of equipment, including a winch box filled with a six-foot-diameter roll of inch-thick, metal-fiber rope. Hawkins's hiding place was inside. Since half the rope was missing, there had been enough room for him; he could peer out through the closed access panel via the wide vents.

A pretty good hiding place. But hiding sucked.

The gunner was closing in and Hawkins watched as the

second man vanished from sight with a burst of speed. He was heading behind the cargo, moving to the starboard side of the ship so he could cover his companion from a better angle.

Price was asking for a report, and he put her off with a beep as he considered his options. But did he have any options? He could take out one of them easily enough, but then the other guy would call in reinforcements. And a gun battle of any kind would bring someone scrambling up from the boarding craft—after *he* made a radio call for help.

Hawkins felt his body tense as an unexpected blossom of pain flowered in his stomach. He clamped his teeth on his lower lip to keep himself quiet. The breath labored out of his nostrils like a winded horse. The pain felt big enough for a damn horse. Like a pain that couldn't have fit into a body as small as a human's, and it peaked in just seconds, so intense it turned his hearing and vision to star bursts on a backdrop of blood. His mind reeled for an explanation. Had he taken a bullet without even hearing the shot? Had there been an explosion and shrapnel?

The pain faded again and the rush of noise and lights went away a second later. Hawkins found himself standing exactly where he had been and amazingly the situation hadn't changed, although he'd been virtually helpless for what seemed like a good ten seconds. He concentrated on sighting the gunners through the vents.

Adjusting the thermal low-light mix of his night-vision glasses allowed Hawkins to spot the cover man, crouched in the blackness at the base of the rear starboard cargo stack. Just one-third of his body showed around the corner of the container, but his head protruded so he could stare intently in Hawkins's direction. So where was the front man?

Hawkins heard a scrape of metal just inches away and realized the gunner had reached the winch box and was fiddling with the latch. Hawkins sank into a one-legged crouch, his back pressed against the cold coils of steel rope, raising his handgun in front of him in two hands and finding he just barely had room to make the full extension in the tight quarters. The flower in his gut was opening again, red and fiery, and Hawkins ignored it. Not again. He wouldn't let it happen.

The access panel creaked slightly as it was nudged open, then a foot kicked it quickly. The panel swung all the way open on creaking metal hinges, and Hawkins smiled through the agony as he strategized his shots. Just as he expected, the door slammed into the side of the winch box with a clang loud enough to mask Hawkins's shot from the suppressed handgun. The head that had peered around the container vanished.

Hawkins didn't hear the body fall, but he saw one motionless leg protrude from the corner and knew he'd been on target. The lead gunner didn't even know his companion was out of the picture.

The point man stepped bodily into the opening, perfectly positioned in Hawkins's target zone. It was a barn-door shot, and Hawkins didn't finesse it as the fresh pain wave ramped up—he just triggered the Mk 23 into the big dark shape. The man took the .45 round full in the chest and collapsed in a lifeless heap.

Hawkins breathed steadily, riding out the next wave of pain. Less intense than last time. Was that good or bad?

"Phoenix Five," he said. "Sorry for the cold shoulder, Stony. The pair of guards got a fix on me. I got the drop on them."

"Phoenix Five, are they out of the picture?" Price asked.

"Hold on." Hawkins was very sure of the lead man, but not the cover man. He made a silent approach on the leg that stuck out from behind the container. When he got close he saw that his shot had taken the cover man in the face. There was no need to check for a pulse.

"They're out, Stony," he reported. "That leaves my friend down the ladder."

"Find new cover. Forget him," Price said.

"Negative, Stony," Hawkins replied. "He witnessed us at some point. He's the one who knew where I was. Too loose an end to leave dangling."

Hawkins made a slow trek around the aft end, stepping gingerly in case a wrong move should make the throbbing in his belly go nova again. When he reached the right spot on the rail, he listened, hearing nothing but the distant lapping tongues of sea against the hull. Then he peered over the rail.

The man on the ladder gaped at him from twelve inches away.

CHAPTER FOUR

Hawkins lashed out with his gun hand before the man clinging to the ladder had time to get the radio to his face. The blow turned his shout into a yelp, and the radio plummeted into the blackness. Hawkins smashed down at him again, fast, and his weapon crunched into the man's cheekbones.

The figure gagged and one of his feet lost its purchase on the ladder. He pirouetted wildly, five stories above the ocean, and Hawkins's backswing slammed the handgun into the fingers that gripped the rung, mashing them like sidewalk worms. The man issued a curious cry and sent his other arm out in a wild flail that managed to connect with a lower rung before he plummeted.

He should have stabilized himself before going on the offensive, but with a hiss of rage and pain he snatched at the handgun in the shoulder holster. He unleathered the gun and pointed it up, but by then Hawkins had noticed the state of the ladder. He grabbed one of the wobbly steel hooks and yanked it to the side, then withdrew behind the rail just in case.

The shot never came, but Hawkins heard an intake of

breath. When he looked over the rail again, the gunner had lost his purchase with both feet. The gun was gone. The man clawed at the rungs for another handhold. Hawkins used a fist to knock away the climber's one good hand.

The gunner made another throaty sound as he started his long, long fall. He somehow managed to miss the thousands of square miles of Pacific Ocean and instead impacted on a three-foot-square boat-landing platform with a crunch.

Hawkins descended cautiously, finding the unsteady platform to be a square of corrugated aluminum on flotation cylinders. It was affixed to the hull with chains that could pull it flat against the hull above the waterline. He shoved the body into the ocean with his foot, then made a quick examination of the watercraft the boarders had used to get to the Korean container ship.

The power was on, so he made out the control panel displays. He opened her up and found he could even make out enough of the power plant to know what he was looking at.

It was one sweet piece of work.

"ARE YOU TELLING ME THEY attacked a twenty-five-thousand-ton cargo ship using personal watercraft?" Price asked. The door opened and she waved in a smiling John Kissinger, whose muscular bulk stressed the hydraulic lift on the desk chair when he sat in it. He slipped on a headset of his own as Aaron Kurtzman shot through the door in his wheelchair and sped into place at a workstation like man on a mission.

"Cowboy just got here, T.J.," Price said. "Repeat that, please."

"I said I don't think these are the kind of watercraft you go rent at the marina in Miami."

"Cowboy here. How about some details, Hawk?"

"On the outside it's looks like your typical Yamaha Wave

Runner GP1200R. Under the hood, as best I can see, is a stock block but everything else looks custom, high performance. I'm even seeing a nitrous oxide booster."

Kissinger frowned. "I could use more information."

"Cowboy, I'm bobbing like a cork and I'm using a freaking penlight. You want the full specifications you can call the guys at *Personal Watercraft* magazine."

"Tell me this, Hawk—how big is the nitrous tank?"

"Small. I know what you're thinking, Cowboy," Hawkins replied. "The booster is there strictly for use as a last resort. The engine's not made for handling any sort of sustained nitrous boost. I'm telling you these are stock blocks."

"Blocks? Plural?" Kissinger asked. "Can you take a look at another one and tell me if it's similar?"

"Negative," Hawkins replied. "This is the only one I have access to."

"Stony One here. There are more watercraft, Phoenix Five?"

"About a dozen, rigged for running without lights. I just spotted them. They're about 150 yards away."

"Approaching?" Price demanded.

"Negative, Stony One," Hawkins replied. "They're just kind of sitting there."

ENCIZO HAD ENCOUNTERED betrayal after betrayal. Virtually every alliance he had made through the years had ended with him being stabbed in the back.

Encizo had now served many years with Phoenix Force. On the surface it seemed unlikely that he would ever find a reason to sever the association, but understanding the complexity of the man told a different story.

Rafael Encizo was biding his time.

He knew that the people who had influence over the workings of the Farm were politicians and bureaucrats. That made them inherently corrupt and prone to be devoid of ethics. It was inevitable that Stony Man Farm would become a tool of the politicians.

When—not if—that happened it would be time for Encizo to make his exit.

That grim reality contrasted sharply with his relationship with the people of the Farm and Phoenix. Encizo had measureless faith in those people, his family. The men of Phoenix Force had become, well, brothers. This was a bond forged only by those who walked together into the beast's mouth again and again, and depended on one another to help kill the beast from the inside.

At the moment Encizo was thinking that this was less like the beast's jaws and more like the guts. At Encizo's feet were those that the beast had devoured. They were sprawled in a small utility corridor several stories belowdecks.

"TIED THEM TOGETHER and shot them dead," Gary Manning muttered. "Poor bastards."

The twelve Korean sailors, guilty of nothing, had been executed for the crime of being inconvenient to those determined to sabotage this vessel.

Rafael gazed at the corpses and wondered why. But nobody knew why yet, and it didn't even matter. Not to Encizo. Not to the twelve Korean sailors, that was for sure.

Murder was murder, the Cuban commando thought, and retribution could be sweet.

He stayed two paces behind McCarter as the Phoenix Force commander moved them along the next narrow passage, leading them into a container hold to commence the search.

The hold was vast but stuffed with stacked containers.

The space between the walls of the hold and the steel boxes was too narrow for Encizo's shoulders and he had to twist his torso to go through. Overhead, the containers vanished into the darkness, which wasn't black but sickly green in the light of their glasses.

He had to squeeze himself through tight spots where the containers had shifted a little too close to the wall. It was in one of the tight spots that he stepped too heavily and heard a hollow metallic clonk that made him wince. The solid floor had changed to a reinforced steel hatch. He almost didn't have enough room to bend for a closer look.

Some sort of a utility access. The cover, a rectangle of small diameter, was reinforced steel, half an inch thick and very heavy. Encizo lifted it so carefully it made no noise. Inside was the glow of electronic devices.

Encizo emerged at the other end of the hold and rendezvoused with McCarter and the others. Each had taken a path around the exterior of the vast hold and the one adjoining it. Only Encizo had a report to make.

McCarter and James stayed behind as Encizo led Manning to the hatch. The burly Canadian had his own troubles squeezing through the tight passage, but he wriggled into a crouch when he reached Encizo's open utility hatch and made a low, wordless sound.

"Phoenix Three here," Manning said in a low voice that still came through clear enough in Encizo's headset. "We've located explosives."

"Stony One here. Go ahead."

"We've got conical-shaped charges. They're marked to meet TK GW specs, UN designation Oh-Oh-Five-Nine. That's 144 mm in diameter and 214 mm in height."

"Any idea what's inside?" Price asked.

"It's clearly labeled 2.54 kilos of EDC1A per charge.

They're tucked deep in some sort of an access cavity under the hold, dead center of the ship. I'm trying to count them—Christ, I think there's at least eight rows of five."

"Do we know what forty charges of this type can accomplish?" Price asked matter-of-factly.

"Yeah," Manning said. "They're rated to puncture 650 mm of RHA."

"And that means?"

"They'll put a hole in two-foot-thick-rolled homogenous armor. One of them will. Forty of them will tear open the bottom of this entire hold, probably split the ship in two. The detonators are timed for eight minutes from now."

"Phoenix Three," Price asked in a level voice, "can you disarm them?"

Manning squinted into the cavity, flicking his penlight around the electrical connections and wires. He snatched off one of the wires, and the glow of the LEDs darkened. "Yeah, I just did. These guys weren't planning on somebody coming around to undo their work, so they didn't put any security in place on the detonation system. All I had to do was pull the plug. That's not the problem."

"The problem is the other staged charges," McCarter interjected over the radio.

"Yeah. Assuming they're timed to go off simultaneously or close, we've got eight minutes to find them all, disarm them all and be really goddamned *sure* we've found them all—or jump ship."

Encizo considered that. "Not enough time," he noted. "Even if we make a fast retreat right now, we don't have time to get to the deck, get over the side and get the inflatables far enough away to ride out the suction when this ship sinks."

"So let's go the other way," McCarter said.

Encizo took the point as they passed through the short

tunnel under the heavy bulkhead. As he stepped into the next hold, a glare of dim light created a sunburst in his night vision.

"They're here," he announced.

"Spread out and take them out from all sides," McCarter ordered. Encizo moved as fast as silence allowed to the front of the hold, then crept along the front of the container rows to the access passage to the next chamber.

"Phoenix Two. I'm in position and I can't see a thing."

"We're at six minutes and counting, mates. We don't have time to finesse this thing. Move fast and play it smart."

That was all Encizo needed to hear. He was tired of skulking in the shadows. He made a rapid advance, spotting the light source in a center aisle in the containers of the next hold. Two men, working by the light of a battery lantern, hunched over another open access panel, their hands busy in the subfloor.

"It's Phoenix Two," he announced. "I'm moving in on a pair in the center aisle of hold three. Everybody else stay out."

They never heard his footsteps. Encizo stopped within two paces, elbows rubbing the containers on either side as he leveled the MP-5.

"Hands up."

Back to Encizo, the closer of the two men froze in a half crouch, his right hand snaking quickly under his left. The Phoenix Force warrior saw the black shape of the handgun materialize in a flash and responded by triggering the MP-5. The man sprang to his feet, then flopped against a container wall and toppled as the second man triggered his weapon wildly, the rounds tearing into the corpse. Encizo witnessed the grisly image of black rain bursting from the body, backlit by the lantern. He put another burst into the wild man, sending him to the mat before he got his aim corrected.

The damage was done. The thunder of the large-caliber rounds echoed through the bowels of the ship. In one clap of gunfire Phoenix Force's clandestine activity was exposed. Encizo heard the shouts of alarm from the next cargo hold.

"Phoenix Two here. There's more of them in the next hold. I'm going in."

"Right behind you, Rafe," McCarter said. "Phoenix Three, pull the plug on this one."

Encizo raced ahead to the short corridor that opened in the next hold, triggered his weapon and raced after his burst of 9 mm rounds as if he were trying to catch up to them. He emerged into another hold and aimed a sustained burst of submachine-gun fire at the fleeing shadows in the narrow central alley between containers.

He put himself behind the stacks as one gutsy gunner stayed in the open triggering an automatic rifle, the rounds carooming off the containers just inches away. Encizo felt for the pause in the fire, then twisted himself bodily into the open, squeezing out a quartet of rounds that chopped the legs out from under the gunner, who went down with a scream. Encizo emptied the remains of the 30-shot magazine into the fallen figure, then pulled back as more shadows stepped into the open at the far end of the hold to return fire. There were at least two or three of them.

As Encizo switched out the magazine on the MP-5, McCarter exclaimed in his earpiece, "They're keeping us pinned down in this bloody hold! We can't get through the tube."

"There's a handful of them, can't be sure how many," Encizo responded. "I don't think I can outgun them on my own in the dark."

"Get clear, Rafe. We'll light the place up a bit."

The Cuban moved along the aft end of the hold in a hurry, found the corner and balled himself up in it, his fingers plugging his ears.

Even with his eyes squeezed shut, Encizo saw the interior of the dark hold light up like high noon and he felt the shriek of noise resonate in the metal walls. Then he was on his feet again, even before the blinding light and deafening shriek from the flash-bang grenades had dissipated. He jogged along the port bulkhead and twisted around the front, finding a space so tight he was forced to move sideways. He flipped on the barrel-mounted light and the brilliant beam made the wriggling bodies visible. Temporarily blinded and deafened by the grenades, they were all but helpless.

But one of them had avoided the flash and rose to his feet at Encizo's arrival, shouting wordlessly and triggering his automatic rifle at Encizo's light. He wavered on his feet—the grenade had stunned him if not blinded him. Encizo placed a triburst in his gut, sending him back down, only to have one of the blinded men get to his feet, wobbling like a bad comic drunk. He brought his weapon to gut level and swept it in Encizo's direction. He never got off the shot. Encizo didn't, either. There was a burst from stage right and the gunner collapsed.

"Rafe?" McCarter shouted.

"It's all clear," Encizo reported as he disarmed the only survivor with a quick kick. His Uzi clattered into the darkness. The survivor looked up, squinting into Encizo's light until he was abruptly flipped onto his stomach and trussed up, wrists and ankles, in plastic handcuffs.

"Let me up," the hardman grunted. "The ship's going to blow."

"Plans may have changed," McCarter said as he approached. "Gary?"

"Same as the others," Manning said behind him as he bent over the exposed subfloor cavity and extracted the ignition wiring with a jerk. "Disarmed."

"How many explosives packs did you plant?" McCarter demanded.

The prisoner's eyes were clenched shut, but he turned his face toward the Phoenix Force leader. "Are you guys Brits or what? Are you the fucking SAS?"

"How many?"

"Four."

"We disarmed one in each of the three holds aft of the wheelhouse, so where's number four?"

"I'll tell you when you've got me off this boat."

"Is the fourth one timed the same as the three in the holds?" Manning said over McCarter's shoulder.

"Yeah. So you don't exactly have time to stand around blabberin'."

"Gary?" McCarter said.

"I took the timer this time," Manning stated, and displayed a small, black plastic device trailing a few dangling wires.

Encizo watched the small red LED digits change from 3:00 to 2:59.

Then to 2:58.

CHAPTER FIVE

"Shit!" yelped the prisoner, squinting at the timer, his vision apparently starting to return already. "We gotta get off the boat, man!"

"Where's the fourth charge?" Encizo asked in a level voice.

"It's in the damn boathouse! You walked right over it."

"Where in the boathouse?"

"Under the floor. It's supposed to knock out some support girders and bring the whole deckhouse down."

"Let's go!" McCarter said. "Rafe, bring him."

Encizo sliced off the ankle cuffs and hauled the prisoner to the narrow flights of dark steel stairs. They ascended in a careless rush, James leading the way at a sprint. The short flights of clanging steps seemed to be endless, and the prisoner complained bitterly as he lost his footing again and again and was dragged bruisingly along. Encizo ignored his complaints and didn't allow their pace to lag behind the others.

McCarter made a terse radio call to their transport aircraft, a Navy jet making wide circles above the ocean and retransmitting their radio signals to the satellite for communications with Stony Man Farm. But there was no way it could get help to the scene before their time ran out.

James was the first to burst onto the deck. He made a rapid revolution, finding the place deserted.

Encizo was the last out, hauling his prisoner onto the deck at the front end of the container ship. The night was brighter now, the overcast beginning to break up and to reveal great slashes of starry sky. A moon sliver was bright enough to silhouette the bridge, which seemed miles away.

"We're not going to make it," the man gasped.

"You'll be there to help us find it," Encizo reminded him.

"There's not enough time!" The man was pleading now.

Encizo was wondering about that himself, but Manning was the one with the timer. Let him and McCarter make the tough decisions.

"Gary?" McCarter said.

"A minute ten."

"We're not gonna make it!" the prisoner wailed.

"Down!" The order came from point man, James, and the group flattened as a torrent of automatic rifle fire erupted in the night, clustering at chest height above the deck like an angry bee swarm, the rounds ricocheting off the abovedeck container stacks. In the narrow, open aisle between the port rail and the containers the commando team was totally exposed. Encizo returned fire from a crouch, targeting the figures that were now bolting from their own hiding places between the containers and the bridge, and heading for the rail. He emptied the magazine, taking down a pair of runners. When the MP-5 cycled dry, he snatched at his handgun holster.

By then the others were getting back to their feet, but before any of them had a chance to get off another shot, a new, distant echo of suppressed machine-gun fire flew over the deck, and they watched three more of the fleeing gunners collapse abruptly, one of them throwing his arms up and flopping over the rail where he had been about to climb over.

"Phoenix Five here to clean up your messes," Hawkins said in their headsets.

"Hawk, where are you?" McCarter demanded angrily.

"Here I am." They could see him now, stepping out of the darkness from behind the bridge castel and waving.

"Time!" McCarter demanded.

"Oh-two-nine," Manning replied.

"Phoenix Five, get out of there—that wheelhouse will blow in twenty-five seconds."

As if he'd been waiting for the go-ahead, the dark shadow that was Hawkins bolted for the rail and slid over without hesitation.

"Hawk," McCarter started, then he was interrupted, a feat that would have been impossible using the old half-duplex, "push to talk" two-way radio mode systems.

"Phoenix One, exit the ship at the aft port anchor winch," Hawkins said. "I'll meet you there with water transport as soon as I can."

McCarter didn't bother to ask for an explanation, and they headed up front. Encizo heard his prisoner mutter something like, "I told you you weren't gonna make it in time."

"Time!" McCarter said as they reached the aft port anchor winch.

Encizo didn't need to see the LED display. The countdown had continued in vivid mental images in his head. "Four," he retorted. "Three. Two."

They all turned back, and with the giant containers towering in front of them they could only see the port side of the bridge castel. It seemed to swell, then burst open as its walls were obliterated by the cloud of explosive gas expanding from inside. The bizarre, pervasive darkness of the night was replaced by the strange, high-contrast shadows of orange firelight, and the deck rumbled under their feet.

"The first hold—how long until they'll detonate?" McCarter demanded.

"The fire won't reach it, unless and until the bridge collapses," Manning said.

"Let's not wait for it!" James declared. He had ignored the spectacle of the blast to make a quick deployment of the Kevlar line in his pack. It was secured to the anchor winch, and he gripped the line as he walked over the rail and plummeted out of sight. Manning jumped onto the rail and grabbed the line, sighted James, then dropped after him.

"Undo my hands. I can rappel."

"No time for that," McCarter said.

The prisoner felt himself being hoisted off his feet by Encizo's powerful arms.

"Don't do it! I'll drown!"

"Like I care," Encizo said.

Then he stepped to the rail and sent the handcuffed killer flying out into the blackness of night, with sixty-eight feet of empty air between himself and the concrete-hard surface of the Pacific Ocean.

MCCARTER LAUNCHED himself over the rail just seconds after Encizo and felt the ship heave, bucking him like an irate metal horse. He tightened his grip and swore under his breath, twisting his body just as he swung into the hull. His backpack took the blow, and the electronics gear inside flattened. Combat-hardened or not, they weren't made to take wrecking-ball treatment. McCarter's body felt as if he'd endured a bad body slam without the benefit of a gym mat.

Below him Encizo was still descending as if nothing had happened—he'd been far enough from the hull so that he hadn't been slammed. McCarter followed him down at a SEAL-pace rappel, only to find his world perspective shifting maniacally.

"It's going down!" It was Hawkins, shouting up at him from miles away. McCarter's radio was defunct.

Now he understood it. The front end of the container ship was rising out of the water incredibly fast. The middle of the ship had to have had her guts blown out.

"Go!" McCarter shouted with an exaggerated wave of his arm. Any boat in the vicinity when the ship went under would get pulled down with it by the tremendous suction.

"Jump!" Hawkins called back.

"Leave now and that's an order," McCarter shouted over his shoulder.

"Can't hear you!"

That was Encizo! The Briton expected that kind of sass-back from Hawkins, but that son of a bitch Encizo had to choose a situation like this to turn rebel. McCarter knew all their lives depended on him getting into the ocean *now*, or they'd never reach a safe distance.

There was another bang and the slimy surface of the ship crashed into him again and *lifted* him. Christ, he was getting carried skyward by the slopping hull of the ship. He flopped onto his back and scooted along it, sliding, barely controlling his descent with one desperate hand on the rappel line. Ahead of him he saw the end of the hull. It was the keel, and he was going to slide off it like a kid at the water park slide.

Then he was airborne, throwing away the rappel line and twisting his arms violently for some sort of midair stability during the fall. He didn't even know how far he had. He tried to get his bearing on his relationship with the ocean—then the ocean smacked him in the face.

He clawed his way to the surface in seconds and there were hands on him before he blinked the salt water from his eyes, yanking him out of the ocean and dropping him on the floor of a small boat.

"Go!" shouted more than one person. As McCarter struggled to his knees, coughing up rancid seawater, the boat lurched into motion and sent him flopping back to the floor again.

The Briton wondered what everybody was looking at. He pulled himself onto the bench seat, sluicing his dripping hair, and saw it.

The Korean container ship had been transformed into an ugly pair of wrecked hull sections, still hinged in the middle as the interior holds flooded. The massive pressure of the water was pushing streams of compressed air and smoke out of every gap and vent in the hull sections, creating hundred-foot plumes of fume. The hull pieces were sinking fast.

Very fast. The calm Pacific was now a stormy sea, battering their small boat from every side, and they seemed to be barely making headway. When McCarter turned to the front of the boat to see who was driving, he was shocked to see there was nobody. The craft wasn't even equipped with an engine. It was being towed behind a revving Wave Runner.

He didn't have time to ask what was going on. The steel girders that had been straining to keep the halves of the dying container ship connected began to snap. The starboard side of the front end of the ship tried to rise back to the surface under the immense buoyancy of trapped air while the port side remained tethered to the heavier aft end.

McCarter thought he had entered some sort of ridiculous monster movie when the massive front end of the upended

ship twisted ponderously in their direction, poised over them
shuddering and enraged as the aft end tried to drag it down
then jerked to life as the final strands between the two ends
parted. The front end turned to face them as if determined to
take them down with it. It was literally a twenty-story building collapsing on top of them. Over the tremendous roar of
noise McCarter heard the dismal whine of the little watercraft
struggling to pull them to safety.

CHAPTER SIX

McCarter felt the sea rise under the boat as thousands of gallons of displaced water pushed away from the descending bulk. With a jerk, the escape raft picked up speed and began riding the rising wave. He didn't know how or why, but the little watercraft had come up with enough muscle to drag them from under the crashing hull and then race to stay ahead of the churning chaos of waves and froth.

An exploding white wall of water hid the ship before the air was filled with hurricane-force rains. But the rainstorm was over in seconds and by then the front end of the ship was just a hill of deflating blackness in the dark Pacific. Soon it was gone.

The Briton marveled to realize Phoenix Force hadn't been snuffed out. For a moment there, he had been convinced there was no escape.

He snapped back to the here and now, counted heads, then sought out the hand pumps that ought to be in any marine raft. He yanked open the compartments until he found a pair of them, tossing one to James, and they quickly began pumping out the bottom of the raft.

"Alive or dead?" McCarter asked with a nod to the limp, handcuffed figure sprawled between the bench seats. In answer the figure writhed and hacked up seawater. "I guess we gotta keep him," McCarter added.

The watercraft sputtered and belched smoke, then with a jolt and a metallic screech it died.

"The booster killed it," Hawkins said with a hand to his ear as the escape raft bumped into the rear end of the drifting Wave Runner.

"Can't complain," Manning said. "It saved our butts."

"Maybe, maybe not," Hawkins said. "Company's coming. They're trying to get us to respond."

"How many?" McCarter asked.

"I saw maybe ten or twelve more Wave Runners while you guys were belowdecks, but only three of them were manned," Hawkins explained. "I think that's what they came in on. They inflated the raft to ferry in the attack team after they'd brought the ship to a stop. They were port and aft of the ship." He wrinkled his forehead as he listened again. "They saw us try to get away when the ship went down, but I don't think they know we made it clear."

"But do they think we're their guys?" McCarter said.

"That's how they're playing it," Hawkins said.

BURT ROLLING DRIFTED out of consciousness and into a world of pain. There wasn't a single wound that he couldn't have handled. He'd been shot in the ribs in Bosnia and never stopped grinning. He'd broken a wrist bone in a training accident and finished the exercise before mentioning it to his CO. He was a tough piece of work.

But right now he wanted to cry like a baby. He'd been bruised when he'd flopped down to avoid the light-and-noise grenade, and a shoulder had come out of its socket as he was being dragged onto the deck by the Cuban gorilla—he'd swear to God the guy talked like a freaking Cuban. He'd known better than to fight against the plastic handcuffs but he'd done it anyway, and right now his hands had no feeling. They'd die and have to be amputated if he didn't get circulation back in them soon.

The worst had been the fall. The Brit—now what the hell were a Cuban and a Brit doing in the same outfit? It had been the Brit who'd told the Cuban to launch him into the water. The impact had been the worst belly flop in history. Ribs broken, Rolling's skin was flayed through his clothes, and his head had been snapped back, hard, with a crack. He could still make his body work, but he was sure there was damage to his vertebrae. One false move and the crack could become a break. Instant paralysis. Then Rolling would be nothing but a talking head in a wheelchair.

He'd rather die.

New pain made him suck in air. It was his hands! The cuffs were off and the blood was flowing back into them. He concentrated on his hands. If they hurt, it meant he could keep them, and that was good news. Because he was going to need a new career path pretty soon. This wasn't the easy money he'd been promised.

He forced himself to raise his head and found himself slumped over the handlebars of one of the Wave Runners. He wasn't sure how he got here. There was a vague memory of lying in the bottom of the inflatable raft and half drowning in a couple of inches of slopped-in seawater. The enemy commando outfit had to have propped him up in the Wave Runner—but why the hell had they done that?

More Wave Runners. Rolling could hear the engines and saw a headlight closing in from the front, another from the right, and one from the left. Three. Was all the rest of the team dead? Probably——the commandos had been effective. Very, very effective.

So where were they now?

He felt a grinding of bone on bone at the base of his neck and froze with his head raised inches above the handlebars. He saw the lights of the approaching watercraft, and in the rearview mirror he saw their headlights playing over the inflatable that floated in the water, one end rubbing the rear of his Yamaha. Five stealthy bodies ducked low behind the plastic sides of the raft.

"You should probably keep your mouth shut at this point, mate."

It was the Brit. It was sage advice, and Burt Rolling had a healthy respect for the guy. Maybe if he'd had some role models like that in the Army he would have reupped.

All the commandos were toting heavy hardware, but it was the black guy who'd armed himself with what had to be an M-79 grenade launcher, this one fitted with a thin frame of metal to replace the heavy wood stock of the units that Rolling had trained on. The Cuban was toting some sort of sniper rifle.

Rolling was sweating as he'd never sweated an operation before. The commandos would be hard to kill, but Rolling's teammates were well-trained, well-equipped and homing in on them from every direction.

Rolling was sitting right in their line of fire.

"ROLLING, IS that you?"

The prisoner on the watercraft moved his hand in a slight wave, then lowered his head again to the handlebars.

"Rolling, you hurt?"

McCarter felt the water swirl around him and strained to hear more. There was a rumble from one of the engines, and then the front watercraft began a slow approach.

From the front he'd have the toughest time seeing the team of five men hiding inside the inflatable.

But the approaching craft veered to the side and came in slow, pausing forty feet away, the engine throbbing. The driver called the prisoner's name again, but the prisoner was slumped on the handlebars and didn't move a muscle.

There was a frustrated curse and the engine thrummed to life, then approached.

"Now," McCarter said just loud enough to be heard inside the raft.

James sat up fast and fired the M-79 grenade launcher in an eye blink, aiming past the approaching watercraft at one of the more distant parked Wave Runners. Encizo inserted the butt of the sniper rifle into the ball of his shoulder and triggered a round at the headlights of the second sentinel, a hundred yards off to the other side of the inflatable while Hawkins, Manning and McCarter were cutting into the figure on the nearest watercraft. He toppled into the ocean as the high-explosive round blew his partner's craft out of existence.

Encizo's sniping had killed the headlights on the last watercraft and it throbbed to life, spinning in a tight circle of spraying water until the weapons of the Phoenix Force warriors turned on it. Encizo's next round chopped the driver through the middle and a barrage of machine-gun fire managed to reach the distant target well enough to pepper the body with rounds as it collapsed.

James had hastily loaded the single-shot M-79 with another HE round, but the battle was decided. He extracted the round, then looked up sharply.

The prisoner was moving, but it was the limp collapse of dead weight, and he slithered into the ocean without a sound. Encizo snatched him by the collar and pulled his head and shoulders out of the water.

"Did he take a round?" Hawkins asked.

James glanced over the body, then put the fingers of both hands at the back of Rolling's neck.

"There's a fracture. It was just a matter of time before he moved it wrong and severed the nerves."

"He might have provided some answers," McCarter said bitterly. "Let's go see what else we've got."

IT WAS AN EERIE, surreal place now. The surface of the ocean was uncannily smooth, placated by the growing slick of oil. The cloud cover had mostly cleared, opening a sparkling vista of stars and a sliver of moon that reflected brilliantly off the Pacific. It was an immense, empty silence on a sea that should have contained a massive, chugging structure of steel and aluminum.

They paddled the inflatable to the nearest watercraft and found it bullet-scarred but functional, then used it to tow the raft to the other watercraft. Ten more identical Wave Runners, tethered together, floated unmanned on the ocean.

McCarter, who had appropriated Manning's radio, gave a terse but complete report to Barbara Price.

"Now it's my turn to bring you up to date," she said. "There were five more attacks against merchant marine ships within the past hour, all within eight hundred miles of where you are now. Three of the five ships are on the bottom already, with one hundred percent casualties on all five ships."

"What!" McCarter exclaimed. "I thought we'd convinced the Man to have the military ready to respond."

"But he couldn't be convinced to move men and equipment. He didn't have a lot of faith in our radio traces. They didn't put men in the air until their radio checks started going unanswered, and by then it was too late. The ships were blown and the perpetrators gone before our military arrived on the scene—in fact, they are still en route to one ship. It's gone from radar and you can guess what they'll find there."

McCarter pondered the news, thinking bitter thoughts.

"There's something else," Price added. "There's been a catastrophic explosion at a shipping and distribution facility in Houston. It happened less than forty minutes ago. We're still thinking it through on this end—we can't figure out if it is connected."

"Were any of these ships destined for that center?" McCarter asked.

"No. It took in mostly Chinese-made consumer goods," Price explained. "Clothes, housewares, electronics, toys, that kind of thing."

"Stony, that's not the kind of stuff that would feed a big explosion," Manning commented.

"Exactly," Price said. "But something did. The facility is gone. Leveled. There were upward of twenty people inside, but investigators are saying they don't even expect to find body parts."

"Is there any idea *why?*" McCarter asked, exasperated.

"No. There isn't."

"What about all this—did any of the Navy response teams get a clue about where the strike teams came from and went to?"

"No. We're working on that ourselves, Phoenix One," Price replied. "I wish I had an answer. Any answer."

Stony Man Farm, Virginia

KISSINGER AND KURTZMAN huddled at a pair of workstations. As the Stony Man Farm armorer, Kissinger had an in-depth understanding of weaponry, from nonlethal, handheld defensive devices to large weapon systems. Tinkering with just about anything that could be engineered or mechanized was a kind of sideline hobby. Personal watercraft wasn't one of his areas of expertise, but the thing had an engine.

"This is the breed of watercraft they use for setting world records," he explained to Kurtzman. "Even the average model is damn fast, so you don't have to invest in exotic hull materials or a specially machined block to customize it into a real monster."

"How fast are we talking, Cowboy?" Kurtzman asked as he assembled geographic and meteorological data.

Kissinger jabbed at his own screen. "World records are topping one hundred. That's mph, not knots."

"In a Jet Ski?" Kurtzman asked.

Kissinger grimaced. "Personal watercraft. It's only a Jet Ski if Kawasaki makes it. Whatever the brand name, they're small enough to evade merchant marine radar, not to mention spy satellites that aren't looking for them, and they're fast enough to catch up to a container ship going full throttle."

"What we need to know is where they came from," Kurtzman said. "So how fast do these things travel over distance."

"The answer—on a flat lake and going in a straight line— it might sustain sixty, even sixty-five miles per hour. But that's a guess. I could do better if I know more about those specific machines," Kissinger said apologetically.

Kurtzman said nothing as he fed the numbers into his PC and watched the plotting materialize on the grid map on his screen. He shook his head and his fingers flew in another quick burst of keystrokes. The next plotting didn't satisfy him, either.

"It's not working," he said, then tried again.

"I told you, my numbers could be way off, Aaron."

"I'm going way off. It's not making sense." A final screen came into being. Kissinger moved in close to look at the digital chart.

"This blue icon is the container ship," Kurtzman said, tapping his finger on the monitor. "The green dots are islands. The red lines are possible sea routes for the watercraft."

"The red lines all end in open ocean," Kissinger said.

"Not even close to a landing point," Kurtzman agreed. "If we double their tank capacity, give them unrealistic fuel efficiency, push their speeds past your world-record levels, it still doesn't work. There's no ship close enough to have launched them, and there's no land nearby that could have been a staging ground."

"So where'd they come from?"

Kurtzman folded his arms on his chest and glowered at the screen. "I have no idea."

"Barb here, and I'm conferencing in T.J.," said the mission controller's voice from the phone on the desk.

"Phoenix Five here," Hawkins said a moment later. "I've been poking around in the electronics, and I've got what I think is a trip computer mounted in the dash. I turned it on and it started giving me GPS coordinates. Current position and a destination."

"Good," Kurtzman enthused. "Let me have the destination."

Hawkins read it out, and Kurtzman wrinkled his brow at the screen.

"Well?" Cowboy said.

"What's the verdict, Bear?" Hawkins asked.

"Well, it's doable with the fuel you've got, but it leaves you sitting in the middle of the Pacific Ocean," Kurtzman explained. "Not so much as a sandbar in the vicinity."

"Phoenix One here. It's got to be a water pickup, then," McCarter said.

"Negative," Kurtzman replied. "We'd see the pickup ship from the sats."

"I thought the NRO eyes were off-limits," McCarter said.

"The Man changed his tune the minute I was able to confirm we had a hit on our hands," Price said. "He put through the order to NRO and we've got very high-res eyes on that part of the ocean."

"There's not a damn thing going on," Kurtzman added. "No ships anywhere near you. No aircraft capable of making a pickup."

"I guess we might as well go check it out," McCarter said. "We haven't got any other ideas to follow up on at the moment. And I for one would like to know what the hell is going on around here."

CHAPTER SEVEN

The world had witnessed many catastrophes in recent years, but this time the events were so strange it made them seem unreal. Even taking a terrorist's point of view, it was tough to understand why.

Barbara Price and Aaron Kurtzman were having a cup of coffee together on the front porch of the farmhouse when it started. It was a sunny, crisp morning in the Virginia mountains and they were enjoying the fresh air while they could.

Their opportunity ended with a bang. It was the screen door, swinging open and slapping against the house. Carmen Delahunt was there, a beautiful, fiery redhead and a cybernetic detective of rare talent. Her skills were the linchpin in many Farm electronic intelligence searches.

Her eyes swept over them, dark and hollow. All she said was, "Come on."

The huge wall-mounted monitor in the War Room in the farmhouse was playing BBC News, where a harried British anchor was trying to make sense of fresh copy. "I am asking for confirmation on this now. Yes? A third? A third vessel? I hesitate to say this—we are now getting reports of a second oil tanker burning in the Atlantic Ocean. They join a report of a tanker in the Indian Ocean that is on fire as we speak. These reports started coming in to us in just the last few minutes, and there may be confusion among our sources. Yes? We are getting video of our first reported fire."

"Is this for real?" Price asked.

"Two minutes ago CNN's doing a recorded piece on the Japanese economy, then all of a sudden this," Delahunt said. "I surfed the networks, but they're all getting the same news."

"We're going to video," the BBC anchor said.

The huge screen transformed from the shot of the newsroom to a video feed from the ocean. A camera on a ship's deck was recording the image of the tanker sitting on the sea and billowing black smoke from a dozen places, stem to stern. The tanker had to be miles from the camera, but its length filled half the screen.

"What we are seeing is an oil tanker somewhere off the west coast of Africa, where the as-yet-unidentified vessel is burning out of control. This video is coming from a British ship that is en route to the vessel in an attempt to rescue survivors—oh, good Lord."

The video went from slate-blue sea and thick black smoke to orange and white. The tanker's midsection seemed to burst like a bomb, and the previously uniform outline of the ship disintegrated. The rear end slid away. The short front end rose out of the ocean slightly, then burst apart, as well. The orange flame and the black smoke swelled across the ocean, and the tanker pieces were swallowed up in fire.

When the image cut, the anchor looked even worse, more confused and hesitant. "Apparently we have video coming in now from the Indian Ocean. This would be the second burning tanker that we can positively confirm, but we are now getting reports of more oil tankers burning in the Indian and

Atlantic oceans. There is confusion about this, but as near as we can tell there are six total. I will repeat that. We have reports of six oil tankers burning. We're going to video now."

The shot was closer, but shakier, coming from a handheld camera in a small aircraft. The audio feed came through the BBC channel, as well, and they heard someone speaking French, shouting over the aircraft engine noise.

The tanker was a gray behemoth with a ragged crater in her decks that issued black smoke and hundred-foot tongues of orange flame. The outer fringes of smoke whisked past the camera, and Barbara Price suddenly felt her throat close. She knew what was going to happen. She had just seen it. And she knew that the aircraft...

"Get the hell out of there!" Delahunt pleaded with the pilot of the tiny plane.

Then Price heard the BBC anchor shouting, "Are we in contact with them? Get those bloody fools out of there before it's too late."

The orange mass expanded from within the billowing black smoke and the ship swelled like a balloon and burst apart. The clouds of superheated orange fire reached out, and up, and smashed into the lens of the video camera.

Maybe, when he saw the explosion, the French-speaking cameraman knew he was doomed. Whatever the reason, he kept the camera trained on the fire until it engulfed him.

Price, Kurtzman, Delahunt and the BBC news anchor, were all too stunned to speak.

Somebody waved something at the corner of the screen and the anchor was the first to snap out of it. He looked at the TelePrompTer.

"We're getting reports now of two more ships burning in the Indian and Atlantic oceans. That makes eight total tankers reportedly on fire."

The BBC anchor seemed to run out of words.

"Let's get to work," Price said quietly.

IT SEEMED AS IF just minutes had gone by, but the efforts that went into the logistics of the meeting were tremendous. The big room was filled with a gathering of men and women who together formed the most effective antiterror organization on the planet. The man who made it possible, the one who interfaced directly with the President of the United States, was the last to arrive. When he came in, it was like a harried, burned-out business executive coming home at the end of a very bad day—to an empty apartment. He didn't greet anyone. He didn't even look up until he slumped in his seat and popped a small handful of antacid chewables into his mouth.

Then he did look at them, every one of the faces at the table, as the conversations gradually died. His gaze finally rested on Aaron Kurtzman and Barbara Price, huddled together over a tablet PC.

"I hope you've got something," Hal Brognola said wearily. "Because nobody else in any federal agency has one damned clue."

"We have something," Kurtzman said. "Maybe."

"Thank God for a maybe."

Hal Brognola, director of the U.S. Justice Department's Sensitive Operations Group, was Stony Man Farm's White House liaison. He was the one who procured official presidential sanction for the Farm's covert activities. But the sanction wasn't truly official, since it would probably be denied if made public. Stony Man Farm's modus operandi did, after all, violate the sovereignty of other nations, not to mention the Bill of Rights.

The President had used the SOG, and the SOG had handed him several successes where CIA, military and other security tools in the federal government's belt had failed. Those successes gave rise to higher expectations and more weight on the shoulders of the Stony Man liaison.

"We've seen the latest intelligence reports," Price told him. "I'd have to agree with your assessment. They're clueless. I'd like to start with a summation. Some of us were en route and need to get up to speed."

Brognola nodded.

She rose. "Eleven hours ago, 9:03 a.m. here, explosive devices detonated on eight oil tankers. All vessels sank within an hour." A map appeared, showing a series of dotted lines emanating from the Middle East and terminating with a tiny orange flame icon. There were several in the Pacific, one in the Mediterranean, one in the Mozambique Channel and another in the Indian Ocean near the southern end of the African continent.

After a moment in which the gathering stared silently at the map, and the tiny flame images and what they represented, Price touched the table in front of her. A cutaway image of an oil tanker appeared.

"I'm not sure how much you all know about the construction of an oil tanker. Suffice it to say that the interior is divided into compartments that allow the ship to carry multiple types of petroleum products and reduces the potential impact of a spill. Blowing a hole into a single compartment, no matter how catastrophic the breach, won't sink the vessel. Many or most of the compartments have to be compromised. That's what was done today. We estimate there were ten to twenty-two explosive devices on each of the eight vessels."

"That's what I don't get." It was David McCarter, the Briton who served as Phoenix Force's commander. "They planted all those explosives on all those tankers. How could that have managed it?"

"Putting them there wasn't the hard part," answered one of his teammates, explosives expert Gary Manning. "All they had to know was where to place them. Whoever it was, I'd bet that getting the hardware was the real challenge. They needed to procure the explosives, igniters, controls, all that stuff. Then they needed some waterproof packaging for the devices. Next, underwater gear and a trained scuba team to do the work."

"What kind of waterproof packaging?" Kurtzman asked.

"Could be just about anything," Manning said with a shrug. "If I was going to do this, I'd put together double-hulled containers, probably some sort of fiber-reinforced plastic for flexibility and strength. I'd shape it so that water flowing past it would apply pressure to actually strengthen its adherence to the hull."

"Placement would be how difficult and slow?" Hal Brognola asked.

"Not difficult or slow." The new speaker was a man with light brown hair and brown eyes, and a notebook in which he had been doodling a vaguely technical-looking rendering of the container. His name was Hermann Schwarz, but he was usually called Gadgets. "All the explosives can be installed in the container ahead of time. Days or weeks ahead of time, so the containers can be dropped into the water at the dock when it's not being guarded. Before the ship even gets there. Then, when the ship is on the scene, a single man in scuba could actually attach the devices. Find them, open a release valve to flood the hollow hull of the device with seawater until the buoyancy is neutral, release the weights and guide the thing up to the underside of the tanker. Then all they'd have to do is adhere it to the tanker hull."

"You make it sound easy," Brognola growled.

"Placing the units would be easy," Schwarz said.

"Gadgets is right," Manning agreed. "Placing the units would simply require a lot of man-hours underwater, but nothing complicated. Not as long as the preparation was good."

Brognola frowned. "They simultaneously destroyed eight oil tankers. I think it's safe to assume their planning was good."

"And well funded," a blond, scowling figure said, almost to himself.

"Yeah," Manning agreed. "That's a lot of explosives."

"It's a lot of manpower." Carl "Ironman" Lyons wasn't looking at the display, or at anybody, but frowning into the tabletop as if to intimidate it into giving up its secrets.

"Not necessarily. Not if they used a strategy like we're talking about," Manning said. "One team of just a few divers at each docking facility could have submerged the devices, then placed them as the ship came and went."

"The ships originated from the same facility?" Lyons queried.

"No," Price replied, nodding at the display, which switched to a map of the Arabian Peninsula. "Four originated from Persian Gulf tanker terminals. Two came from a terminal at Yemen. Two more originated in the Med."

"Any chance this was an elaborate insurance scheme?" McCarter asked. "The payoff would be in the tens of millions at least."

"Probably in the hundreds of millions," Kurtzman agreed. "I thought of that one myself. It could be a way for a cash-strapped oil company to restore themselves to solvency, if they got away with it."

"Which doesn't seem likely," Price said, shaking her head.

"There's other reasons why this probably isn't insurance fraud," Kurtzman added. "One, this can only be deemed an act of terrorism, and insurance coverage on terrorism has been slashed since the World Trade Center attacks of September 11, 2001. Also, ownership wasn't common for all the ships. Three were oil company tankers. The rest are owned by shipping companies. We're following the paperwork trails to find any sort of a behind-the-scenes link to tie the ships together, but we've got zero so far."

"That's no help," Brognola growled. "What about the ownership of the cargo—whose oil was it?"

"Yemen," Price said. "Qatar. Syria, Kuwait, UAE, Egypt and Oman."

"Huh," someone said.

"What?" the big Fed asked. "What could that possibly tell you, Rosario?"

The man was examining the map on the display, rubbing his chin. He was big. He looked tough, even sitting casually at the meeting table. Somehow, Rosario "Politician" Blancanales also managed to come across as perceptive and intelligent. And he was.

"Saudi Arabia is conspicuous by its absence from the list," Blancanales said. "Just about every other nation on that map lost oil except Saudi Arabia."

"Hey. Hey, yeah," Hermann Schwarz said. "That seems a little too odd to be unplanned."

"So the finger points at a Saudi entity," Brognola said.

"Seems to me someone is *trying* to point the finger at Saudi Arabia," Blancanales said. "It's too obvious. I think it's a decoy."

"Barb?" Brognola asked.

"I came to the same conclusion as Rosario," Price said. "It's too easy to look at the facts and place the blame on Saudi Arabia."

"We have anything else to go on?"

Price touched her hidden tabletop controls again. She didn't look at the display, but every other pair of eyes locked on the new image. It was a map of the world, just like the first graphic they had been shown. In this image the dotted lines of the tanker routes didn't terminate with the little flame icon, but extended farther to illustrate the complete route each ship had planned to take and where it would have ended up.

Every one of the dotted lines converged on North America.

"Sons of bitches," Schwarz complained. "That was our oil they blew up."

CHAPTER EIGHT

The door opened and the young Japanese man jerked his head in time with a rhythm only heard in his tiny headphones. He froze when he found himself in a room that was uncannily silent for having such a large number of people inside.

They were staring at the wall graphic. He'd seen it earlier. Every one of those tankers had been headed for the U.S. Just one more compelling and inexplicable piece of the whole bizarre puzzle.

"I can't believe this was kept under wraps," Brognola said, breaking the silence. "I wonder if anybody on our side has figured this one out yet."

"It wasn't as easy as you'd think to track down this information," Price explained. "Half of these trips were unscheduled, to fill special orders or take the place of disabled vessels.

"Somebody was pulling strings to make that happen," Lyons declared.

"We're trying to trace exactly how it all came about," she answered. "It will take time to do so. We have a more promising lead that *might* be about to bear fruit.

"Akira, what do you have for us?"

The young Japanese man, Akira Tokaido, found every eye turned on him. He grinned and waved a half-page printout. "I've got fruit."

Price made a brief gesture with her hands at the gathering, and Tokaido dragged the headphones off his ears. "When the tanker attacks started, we initiated a scan-and-archive function of any and all communications we have access to in the region of the attacks. It's a big job, but we make it work through all sorts of digital network spiders you don't want to hear about. We just dump everything on the drives as fast as we can and start searching it for anomalies."

"You talking satellite feeds?" T. J. Hawkins asked.

"Well, yeah, every kind of sat feed there is, including commercial, military, scientific, the networks, the global phone systems, everything. Lots of radio stuff gets shuttled digitally at some point, so we tap into the public and private networks and the Internet, which carries a lot more audio communications than anybody realizes."

"You'd end up with a *huge* junk dump," Schwarz said. "Even if you know what to look for, wouldn't it be almost impossible to find in all that chaff?"

"First of all, our spiders kick ass, Gadgets," Tokaido enthused. "We've been databasing communication protocols and content samples and the system gets almost exponentially better every time we make a full-scale run of it. But it does take three or four hours for the system to flag suspicious data in just ten minutes of real-time communications when we do a dump from territory that big."

"And?" Brognola prompted impatiently.

Tokaido was simply too laid-back and cheerful to be intimidated, even by Brognola. "Yeah, well, *and* we found hidden voice and data inside a set of satellite telephone signals. It looked as though somebody was transferring his collection of topless beach videos over a satellite data modem, but the video had quadraphonic sound and all four of the audio channels were encrypted voice communications. The system decrypted the voice and matched the time codes to the events, and when we took a listen it was pretty obvious we had observers reporting back to the perpetrators."

"The communications didn't tell us anything," Kurtzman added. "But once we knew what we were looking for we started hunting for more communications coded the same way. Akira's come to tell us that we've found it."

"Yeah, Hunt's back there listening in live, and this time it's not observers," Tokaido said excitedly. "Now it's the guys who're actually planning the next stage of the operation."

"What?" Brognola exploded and half rose from his seat. "Couldn't you have got to the point a little sooner? Let's get this information out to somebody who can do something about it!"

"We don't know where and what it's going to be yet," Tokaido said evenly, losing the grin. "We've got six teams, unknown numbers in each, staged for the next phase of the operation. The feeds are jumping to and from terrestrial and satellite almost at random, and it's a hell of a trace."

"What else do they tell us?" Brognola demanded.

"That's about it, so far," Tokaido said. "Hunt's analyzing every word."

"Dammit," Brognola spit. "There's nothing worse than sitting down with the President with a report like this one. Just enough to raise his expectations, not enough to do a damn thing about. It pisses him off."

"Been there," Kurtzman shot back.

Brognola's glance targeted Kurtzman like a blowgun dart, but bounced off as if his face was made of steel plate.

"Yeah," Brognola said wearily. "I guess we all have."

THE MEETING disintegrated slowly. It was the worst kind of
Stony Man Farm gathering, with almost every top-level SOG
member in attendance but concluding without a course of action. Only the cybernetics and communication teams hurried
out, leaving the commando team members staring at one another.

These weren't men who liked being directionless.

It was Hawkins who had the bright idea. He strolled over
to one of the compact workstations and roamed the internal
network until he found the file he wanted and pulled it up.

Schwarz got curious and leaned over his shoulder, staring
at the screen and nodding as his forehead grew heavy with
concentration. Manning joined them next. It was Carl Lyons,
stretched out in his chair and drumming the tabletop, who finally asked, "What are you doing?"

Hawkins looked over the fold-down screen. "Intelligence
analysis."

Lyons frowned. He turned to Rosario Blancanales for an
explanation. Blancanales would have figured it out.

Blancanales shrugged and said, "Topless beach videos."

The Able Team leader closed his eyes as if in great pain.

THE MEETING RECONVENED with unexpected swiftness as the
entire cybernetics staff poured back into the room, Brognola
on their heels, the Farm communications head and the blacksuits commander hustling in seconds later.

"All right, what is it?" Brognola demanded.

"We've traced the new communications to a satellite up-
link coming from the Pacific," Kurtzman reported as his
hands flew into action on a tablet PC he tossed on the table.
"Micronesia," he added. A map of a vast expanse of the Pacific Ocean blinked into existence on the wall screen.

"What's in Micronesia?" McCarter asked.

"I've been doing a quick check of the shipping routes," Carmen Delahunt reported. "There's plenty of traffic in the area—close enough for one of the islands of Micronesia to serve as a staging point for an attack."

"Not if they're shipping oil," Lyons stated.

"You're right, Carl. Especially not to the United States. There's some Latin America–bound tankers taking the route to the west coast of the continent, but they're few and far between. The South American countries mostly get their oil from the Middle East via the Atlantic crossings, just like North America, or from other South American nations."

"So what's the target?" Price asked.

"Lots of cargo passes over that part of the ocean," Delahunt said. "Anything and everything that's made in India, Pakistan, Malaysia, whatever. Everything from clothes to cars to electronics to factory equipment."

"Something is not making sense here," Brognola complained. "We sure these are the perpetrators?"

"Yes, we're sure about that, Hal," replied Huntington Wethers, a tall, distinguished-looking black man who was a former cybernetics professor. "The digital ID match we made on the source can't be wrong, and their method for encrypting audio in the soundtracks of a video file is sophisticated and unique. That uniqueness is their flaw. We'll ID them anytime they use this technique. Our spiders haven't found any samples of it used elsewhere. Anywhere. Ever."

"Okay, I'll buy it," Brognola said uncertainly. "What do we know?"

"Very little," Wethers said. "I've been transcribing every word and there's little to tell us when, where or why. They—whoever they are—are careful and professional."

"What's in the manifests for the current shipments en

route across that stretch of the Pacific?" Kurtzman asked. "Anything that stands out?"

Delahunt shrugged. "I've just scratched the surface here, but a computer collection lists nothing surprising. All kinds of consumer and commercial goods, but no special military shipments. No cargoes that would create the kind of environmental catastrophe like they're fighting to avoid from yesterday's oil spills."

"What about financial losses?" Manning asked. "Any one company or industry poised to suffer losses if a bunch of the en route ships go down?"

"Again, no," Delahunt said. "There are hundreds or thousands of companies with goods on the seas at any one time. Sometimes a single container ship will carry many cargoes from a handful of countries—that's the flexibility offered by standardized ship containers."

"There's got to be a common thread," Brognola said.

"The destination," Blancanales stated. "There'll be all kinds of ships on Carmen's list that are headed for the U.S."

Brognola shook his head. "Who'll benefit if all kinds of different imported goods never reach the United States?"

"Those who don't want the United States to import goods," Lyons pointed out.

Blancanales nodded.

"That's a pretty simplistic solution," Manning commented.

"Which puts it at the top of my list of likelies," Huntington Wethers declared. "The U.S. has seen a resurgence of nationalism and isolationism since the 9/11 terrorist attacks and the Afghanistan War."

"How much of a resurgence?" Brognola asked. "I've seen a few demonstrations but nothing I would have been worried about."

"We've got files on some enthusiastic fringe groups, but

they're small and most of the followers are transients," Tokaido said. "They find a cause and follow the fad for a while, then lose interest."

"Any of those fringe groups dangerous?" Kurtzman said.

"They never have been," Tokaido said. "They're usually just a few mad-as-hell guys with cause and a Web site. No resources or strategy."

"That's where this theory stops holding water," Brognola said. "But I guess we don't have any better ideas. So what happens when they prepare to attack?"

"We track their communications until we home in on the perpetrators," Price declared matter-of-factly. "Whom we stop."

"So we need a team in the vicinity to chase them down," McCarter stated.

"We need more than one," Carl Lyons said.

"We're ready to move," Price added. "Phoenix and Able can be on their way right now. The blacksuits are on alert and can be mobilized in ten minutes."

Brognola looked at her. "Need I ask?"

"Striker's whereabouts are unknown," she replied, her voice without inflection.

"When did we last hear from him?"

"I think I had most recent contact with Striker. He called in five days ago," Kurtzman said, then added, "from Aberdeen."

"He was that close and he didn't bother stopping in for a cup of coffee?" Brognola growled, and hoped nobody thought he was being flip. He was dead serious.

Kurtzman shrugged, and somehow Brognola knew it was a disingenuous gesture. Kurtzman confirmed the big Fed's suspicions by adding lamely, "He had a lot going on."

Brognola frowned and leaned over the table, staring his friend straight in the eye.

Kurtzman did something he almost never did.

He fidgeted.

Brognola said one word, but dragged it out as long as a sentence. "Yeah."

What Kurtzman *heard* him say was, "I know there's something else going down. I know you know I know it. I don't have time to deal with it now but when I do, you *will* provide me with a complete report."

"Tell me this," the big Fed asked. "Can we, or can we not, count on Striker being available should he be needed."

"I would have to say 'Not,'" Kurtzman replied carefully.

"Fine." Brognola's tone made it clear that there was absolutely nothing that was fine. He got to his feet. "I meet with the President in less than one hour. He demanded a face-to-face on this one. I'll be in touch."

BROGNOLA SOUNDED no happier when they heard from him an hour and twenty minutes later. "The Man said something about 'a waste of taxpayers' hard-earned dollars,' and then he told me to go ahead and do it anyway."

Price wasn't quite satisfied with the answer. "Are you saying we're going?"

"Phoenix is going," Brognola answered from the speakerphone. She and Kurtzman were in her office, situated in the basement of the farmhouse just a few steps from the War Room. "I think the Man just wanted me to know he didn't trust our conclusions. But he's low on options."

"We've been down this road before," Price retorted. "Even when he thinks we're wasting time and resources we deliver results."

"Usually," Brognola admitted.

"*Most* of the time," Price retorted, a slight rise in her voice. "Tell him to weigh our results against any bureau in the federal government."

Kurtzman said nothing, and neither did Brognola, for an arduous ten seconds.

"You are absolutely right," Brognola said. "I didn't mean to cast aspersions on Stony Man. I was just relaying some of the Man's frustrations."

Then came a five-second silence that was even worse.

Price ended it by asking, "Why not Able?"

"He wants somebody here to react if and when our South Pacific wild-goose chase—his words, not mine—prove to be a bust."

"I hope he's planning on having other agencies on the scene," Kurtzman said. "The one fact we did gather was that there are six teams involved and that means six targets. Phoenix doesn't stretch that far."

"He's looking into it," Brognola said. "What's our ETA?"

"Phoenix can be on the scene in twelve hours or less. We're loaded and prepped to get them to Micronesia. Jack's got an aircraft checked out and ready to go."

"I hope we can figure out a more precise target than just Micronesia within twelve hours," Brognola said. "The dry land doesn't add up to much acreage, but it covers a whole lot of square ocean miles."

Price had been thinking the same thing. Would she have something to do with Phoenix Force after flying them halfway around the world? Or would this be a tremendous waste of time and resources?

"We're working on it," she said.

Brognola hung up without comment and Price dialed upstairs, then to the old barn. She spoke for just seconds, but it was enough to send Phoenix Force running for the waiting jet, which would be towed from the disguised hangar, ready for takeoff in under a minute.

Then she hung up and looked thoughtfully at her old friend. "Well, Bear?" she asked gently.

"We're working on it," Kurtzman said.

CHAPTER NINE

"We've stopped at another gas station," McCarter confirmed. "We're refueling, Stony. What's our situation?"

"I think we're closing in, Phoenix One," Price reported back. "On full tanks there are no less than fourteen islands within your range."

"I sure would like to get off this seat," Manning said. "Somehow I don't think the designers intended for it to be used for an eight-hour stretch. I've got severe ass-itis."

McCarter felt the same way. His backside hurt, and his entire skeletal system was vibrating from the hour after hour spent driving the Wave Runners. When they made the decision to take the personal watercraft out into the empty Pacific Ocean to find where the container ship attackers had come from, he'd never thought he would spend the entire night on the thing.

They had assumed the GPS coordinates on the Wave Runner's augmented control system would take them to a rendezvous with whatever transport had brought the saboteurs into the middle of the ocean. Since nothing showed on radar or satellite, McCarter hadn't known what to expect.

What they found at those coordinates was a big floating plastic sack of fuel suspended in a frame of interlocking plastic tubes. They started the battery-powered electric pump, refueled their personal watercraft and continued on to the next set of GPS numbers.

McCarter had to admit it was an effective method of sneaking a large number of armed men onto any given point in the ocean. Stony Man Farm and the rest of the world had been watching for oceangoing threats with spy satellites and radar and the personal watercraft were invisible to them under typical operating conditions. The plastic, low-profile fuel tanks, floating on inflatable pontoons, could have been placed there weeks ago.

The only drawback to this insertion method was operator comfort—there wasn't any.

"We're not going to have to tour all fourteen of those islands, are we, Stony?" McCarter asked.

"Negative," Hawkins answered. "Somebody's trying to reach us via radio."

"Radio?" Manning asked. "Regular, real, nonsatellite radio waves?"

"Yeah, and pretty low-powered, too. I heard just a short message and then it was gone. It said, 'Base remains secure.'"

"Where from?"

"It was too quick to track," Hawkins said. "Stony, did you hear it on my feed?"

"Affirmative, Phoenix Five," Price reported. "Aaron's isolating the message."

Hawkins had taken the personal watercraft that was rigged for communications. A waterproof compartment bolted near the handlebars contained the preprogrammed GPS and the radio gear, not to mention a satellite telephone. Hawkins had made a few quick connections to hardwire his Stony-supplied communications gear into the watercraft electronics. The signals would go through Hawkins's compact communications computer and piggyback on his comm feed as a separate data stream. All their communications were being sent back to the Navy aircraft that shadowed them, too high and too far back to be seen or heard in the night.

They were now on their third USN escort—there had been shift changes when the fuel tanks grew low.

Kurtzman came on the line. "I did what I could with the message."

"Get anything from it?" McCarter asked. He was the last of the team to refuel his vehicle using the small pump device on a hose trailing into the underside of the floating sack of fuel. He really wasn't looking forward to burning that entire fresh tank in the saddle of this vibrating sea beast.

"Not a thing and I don't think it matters," Kurtzman said. "I suspect the message was transmitted from the closest of the nearby islands. If so we have a destination."

"I'm sending you the coordinates," Price added.

"Got them," Hawkins said.

"Then let's get there," McCarter said. "The sooner the better."

The brilliant orange sun came up behind them, and they chased their stretched shadows over the ocean for half an hour until they spotted the strip of green that fuzzed up a spot on the Pacific. McCarter called for a reduction in speed. Without the high-speed breeze, they were enveloped in sticky heat. At just past dawn, the temperature was already in the nineties.

"What do you expect when you're straddling the equator?" Encizo asked, examining the land dot through his binoculars.

McCarter's field glasses showed him nothing of value.

Palm trees in white sand. Maybe a half mile wide. No sign of human habitation.

"Looks like Gilligan's Island," Manning commented.

"Whose island?" McCarter asked.

"Everybody knows who Gilligan is," Hawkins said.

McCarter frowned and struggled to identify the name.

"The millionaire and his wife, the movie star?" Hawkins demanded.

"And the rest," Manning said.

"I'm pretty sure that when you explain it I won't care, so don't," McCarter told them. "Let's move in slow. No wakes. We'll reassess our approach closer in."

"Aye-aye, Skipper," Hawkins said.

McCarter shot him a dark look, not sure if he was being insulted, then led the approach to the island. He had taken them to within a few hundred yards when he brought them to a halt again. Now he made out buildings tucked into the palm trees. As he examined them through his field glasses, a second radio alert was transmitted.

"Same as the first message," Hawkins said. "Exactly the same. Must be a recording."

"Stony, we have any data on this pile of sand?" McCarter asked.

"Nothing of value," Price replied. "It's listed as Temaru Island, inhabited, privately owned, falling under the jurisdiction of the Federated States of Micronesia."

"You're right. That's of no value," McCarter said. "We're making our approach from the east, and we're seeing a small bay on the northeast side of the island. There's a dock and a slick-looking cabin cruiser. We've got a pair of buildings on the island itself. This place looks like some rich bloke's private resort."

"You're probably right on the money," Price agreed.

"Yeah," McCarter said. "Did you all catch that? This could be nothing more than a bunch of rich people on holiday. We'll not be using deadly force unless and until we find out these are the people who sank the container ship. Got it?"

There was a flurry of affirmative answers and McCarter steered his watercraft for a beach landing.

Stony Man Farm, Virginia

"THERE'S GOT TO BE archived satellite footage of this damn island," Kurtzman muttered as he riffled through hundreds of military satellite image directories.

"I've found something," Carmen Delahunt reported from across the Computer Room. "Oh, but they're crap. These must be ten years old. Here they come, Aaron, but they won't do you any good."

Kurtzman opened the images and found himself staring at an egg-shaped blob of land with a small bay. Delahunt came to stand at his shoulder, and she jabbed a pen at a fuzzy pixilation on the landmass.

"Those could be buildings," Kurtzman commented.

"Or woolly mammoth for all we can see."

"You're right. They're worthless. Akira? Hunt?"

At other workstations, Tokaido and Wethers were making their own cybernetic probes, each approaching the investigation from different angles. Each man responded with a shake of his head.

Kurtzman frowned again at the messy blob on his screen. It told him nothing, and somehow it was symbolic of this entire operation. An unfocused picture without any real detailed intelligence.

Delahunt was reading his mind. "We're pretty slim on facts this time around, Aaron."

"Yeah. We don't know who. We don't know how. We haven't a clue as to *why*."

"We've got Pol's nationalist-slash-isolationist theory," Delahunt offered.

"Just a theory. It's not taking us in any good direction. Even with this little island we've got nothing but a fuzzy understanding."

"It feels like we're missing a linchpin piece of data," Delahunt agreed. "There's some basic component of information that we haven't latched on to yet. We just need to figure out what that component is and the whole picture is going to pull into focus." She tapped the monochrome pixilated graphic. "Temaru Island and all the rest of it."

"Got any ideas where we'll locate that linchpin?" Kurtzman asked.

"Sure. A hundred ideas. All of them long shots."

Temaru Island, Pacific Ocean

CALVIN JAMES WAS so sharp he almost—but not quite—came across as a pretty boy. Chances were if you passed him walking down the sidewalk you'd think he was a high-priced attorney or even a successful stage actor: a little too clean-cut, a little too neatly groomed. A little too thin to be tough, let alone dangerous. The image was a lie.

Few men on the planet were more dangerous than James. Take away his gun, and he could best you with a knife. Take away his knife and he would snap your limbs with his bare hands. Tie his arms behind his back and he'd dance in close, kick your feet out from under you and deliver a fatal kick to the throat.

His hands were his weapon of choice when he made the attack on the guard, who was stationed just a few paces in-

side the palm tree cover on the southernmost end of the island. They'd come across him while on a perimeter check,
discovering him lounging against a curved palm tree trunk,
bored and inattentive. He was idly watching the ocean, occasionally strolling to the edge of the sand to look up and
down the beach, and talking to himself.

James didn't catch much of the conversation before he
sprinted to the guard and rapped his skull into the palm tree
trunk with a crack. The guard slithered to the ground, his
weapon landing next to him. Forty-five seconds later he was
in shackles.

McCarter checked the prisoner, relieved to find a pulse.

"So much for pulling our punches," he muttered.

"You think we should have negotiated and hoped the M-16
was for show?" James asked. "If I find this is the wrong place,
I'll deliver a sincere apology when he wakes up."

They circled the island, avoiding periodic video cameras.

"There must have been surveillance when we landed,"
Manning stated. "So why haven't we raised a ruckus?"

"Let's go figure it out," McCarter said as they took up positions at the edge of the sparse stand of palms. In front of
them were a few acres of green, manicured lawn, totally out
of place on the island, and a low building that had to cover a
couple acres of ground on its own.

Encizo put the only visible video camera in his sights and
obliterated it with a quick shot, then the five men crossed
the manicured lawn and reached planned points along the
exterior of the building. The walls were rough-hewn native
timber, but it was just for show. Underneath were typhoon-
resistant concrete walls.

McCarter and Manning flanked a wide set of glass doors
leading onto a brick patio the size of a baseball diamond.
Manning waited for a heartbeat, then stepped in front of the

glass and yanked on the handle. The door slid wide, and Manning leaped out of sight.

No shouts of alarm or hails of gunfire emerged. McCarter took the next risky step by leading the way inside, covering the rear great room to the left as Manning entered and swept the right. They were alone.

"Phoenix One here. Come on in."

The team gathered wordlessly in the great room, ears seeking signs of life in the heavy stillness of the resort. Hawkins and Manning gravitated to a small electronic panel alongside the sliding door while the others fanned out to investigate the entrances to the room.

Encizo found a tiny office adjoining the great room. Rough-hewn wood paneling, wicker chairs with hand-carved legs and a man-size Maori teko-teko standing patiently in the corner. In the desk was a leather-bound guest register, but the last checkout date was eight months earlier. He slipped the register into his pack.

Manning and Hawkins abandoned the security system panel without bothering to screw the cover on again. The small LCD panel McCarter had discovered was much more interesting. It was on the wall alongside four paintings in frames of polished bamboo, matching the LCD display, showing an image similar to the paintings until McCarter zeroed in and touched a button camouflaged in the woody frame. Now there was a meteorological radar display.

The Briton flipped down a section of the bamboo to reveal more controls and he began flipping channels. All were static.

"This get anything except the Weather Channel?" he asked under his breath.

"Local cable access," Manning replied when a view of the beach appeared. They saw the big cabin cruiser, lifeless and rocking gently on the water. There was a distant figure, under a small leafy shelter at the farthest end of the palm tree forest.

"I don't see a way to zoom from this display," McCarter said. "I'd bet you the queen's jewels that guy's sleeping like a baby. Guess that's why he didn't spot us coming in."

Manning nodded, then McCarter cycled to the next screen. It was the zoom image they had been looking for, focused on the ocean beyond the northern end of the island but showing the guard in the lower right corner. He was in a wooden chair, leaned back against the base of a tree, the M-16 on his chest rising and falling slowly.

"I'm surprised we can't hear him snoring all the way down here," Manning said.

"His catnap is just about over," McCarter added. "Look who's coming."

Manning squinted into the display, then caught the glint of metal on the surface of the ocean. A ripple on the water added enough contrast to show him the outlines of more watercraft.

McCarter gathered the team with a gesture as Manning clicked through the other security camera displays, stopping on the final screen.

"This is it," Manning said. "This is the only other living soul I can find in the whole place other than the guard out front."

It was a young, muscular man in a loose cotton shirt that matched his khaki shorts. He was stretched out on the colorful flower print of the oversize cushions of a chair in a sitting room, but he was anything but relaxed. His arms were folded tight on his chest and he vibrated his foot nervously. The low table at his side held an oversize suitcase, propped open to reveal a computer and radio equipment. Wires fed into wall sockets.

"He'll have the feed from the cameras," Manning said quickly.

"I put this one out of commission," Encizo reported with a nod to where a small wire dangled from a tiny ceiling-mounted device.

"He's on the second floor," McCarter observed. "Facing north. You can see the top of the yacht out his window. Let's take him and the hardware intact."

"He's on to us," Manning reported as the figure jumped up with a frown and began working his computer.

They separated into two teams that found two ways upstairs, finding themselves on opposite ends of a fifty-foot corridor that stretched the length of the second floor. Just three doors allowed access to northside rooms. McCarter's gut pulled him to the central door and he kicked it open, sweeping the parlor. It was the right place. But the suitcase was gone, just a couple of empty wires slack on the table. As Encizo and James sprinted left and right to check the other rooms of the suite, McCarter went to the balcony and spotted the young man in beige limping away in a hurry.

The Phoenix Force commander stopped him with a burst of machine-gun fire. The man stood there, breathing harshly, and turned slowly to face him. When James and Encizo were there to provide cover, McCarter hopped the wooden lanai, hung for a moment from the deck and dropped several feet to the ground.

"Don't come any closer," the young man wheezed. His face was constricted with pain. His ankle had an impossible bend to the instep that showed that he had executed a less successful leap from the balcony.

"Yeah, or what?" McCarter asked.

"I'll burn it." The young man held up the suitcase, his thumb poised shakily over a red plastic circle. "I press this button and everything inside melts."

"But we'll have you."

"Huh. I'll tell you all I know, soldier boy, and I know nothing."

"I doubt that," McCarter said.

"Listen, if I screw up, I don't get paid," the man gasped, grinning sardonically. "But if I do get paid it's a *lot*. So just let me get into the boat and get away. I'll toss you the suitcase when I'm on my way, and nobody'll know."

"I'm not making deals with you, mate."

"Have it your way," the young man said as he made to bring the suitcase down. But before he could there was a single shot and the suitcase dropped to the earth. The young man's hand was a mass of blood and broken bone.

"Make another move for that suitcase—" McCarter never finished the threat. The young man twisted and grabbed at the suitcase with his good hand, slapping the red button, then he dived in the opposite direction to avoid the burst of gunfire and the flash of fire from the inside of the suitcase. In the sudden quiet that followed, the young man sneered at them as the smoke sizzled from the seams of the suitcase.

"Now arrest me and get me to a frigging hospital," he barked.

The suitcase released a trumpeting hiss and McCarter tossed himself backward, onto his face, but not before he witnessed the expression of shock on the face of the young man. There was a metallic burst, and McCarter felt a wall of fire embrace him and slam him into the earth. Then it was gone and it seemed as if the rest of Phoenix Force was slapping at his clothing simultaneously.

"I'm okay," he protested as he pushed himself up and was helped to his feet. He could smell the stink of burning hair. His. And the reek of cooked flesh, which wasn't his.

The young man had gone fetal on his back, his mouth still wide. Still surprised.

"Guess he didn't know what was coming," Hawkins muttered.

"Guess not," McCarter agreed.

CHAPTER TEN

The killers on the Wave Runners heard the commotion on shore and made U-turns offshore, heading back out to sea. They'd traveled less than five hundred yards before they began to burst apart with a series of lightning flashes and a half second later the sound of the explosions cracked against the island shore like an exploding brick of firecrackers. By the time the cracks faded, the ocean was empty. There was nothing more than an oil slick and slivers of debris to show where there had been a team of more than twenty mercenaries.

The explosions stunned the guard at the north end of the island into immobility. He stared at Manning like a simpleton. There was no fight in him as he was disarmed and cuffed.

"This guy isn't the sharpest tool in the shed," Manning explained. "McCarter's still working on him but I'm telling you now he knows nothing worth hearing."

"What about the first guard?" Price asked on the headset.

"Cal?" Manning prompted.

"I've got nothing or almost nothing, Stony," James replied. "Both guards were just hired hands, and they were recruited for their firearms skills more than anything else. They say the one who got fried, the communications guy, was called Commander. Sounds like he was more of a middle manager to me. He was essentially charged with keeping the teams organized. Here's another news flash—they were confident they'd never be tracked back to the island so they had just token defenses."

"Sure he wasn't playing dumb?" Manning asked.

"He's just some Army grunt, and he was just about scared enough to soil his drawers," James said. "He knows he's in deep trouble, and he's trying hard to be Mr. Cooperative. Now that's where my one potentially useful last factoid comes in. He claims to have overheard a name, and he thinks it was the real commander, the actual guy in charge of the whole operation. He says Colonel Coral."

Hawkins had joined them and he said gently, as if breaking bad news, "Cal, I hate to burst your bubble, but that's a fish-and-chips place in Fort Worth."

"That's what he said," James insisted.

"Well, you're right about the guards, Cal," Price replied. "We've got their military records. Both were U.S. Army enlisted until last year. They were unexceptional MPs, but both scored high marks in special firearms and sniper training. They didn't know each other while in the military as far as we know and were based a thousand miles apart. Neither of them opted to re-up and that's when the Army lost interest."

Phoenix Force had gravitated to the patio outside the empty resort, where the exhausted team shed their gear and collapsed in poolside chairs to await the transport chopper that was on its way. They had searched the premises without success for more computers or files. Manning tapped into the security and video system but found nothing more extravagant than a bunch of video cameras and a high-end dish that received exceptionally sharp HBO. The yacht was left untouched, awaiting the arrival of a Navy bomb squad that could sniff out booby traps.

The two guards were now cuffed in chairs under umbrellas, too far away to converse with each other, their clothing drenched with sweat. When McCarter joined the others, he found them chugging tall frosty glasses of something. Manning gave him a tired-dog grin and handed him one. It was pineapple juice. Canned.

"Stony One here," Price said as she came back on the line. "Colonel Coral looks like a bust. There are several Corals in the military, but none of them are likely suspects. We'll go a little deeper on them to be sure but—sorry, Cal."

James shrugged. "Hey, I wasn't personally invested in Colonel Coral."

"What about Rafe's ledger, Stony?" McCarter asked after draining his glass.

"He faxed us all of it, but there's nothing. We see no tie between the folks listed there and yesterday's occupants. We traced the ownership of the island and the resort to a struggling Seattle investment firm. They rented out the island three months ago in a quasi-legal agreement to another company called TV Enlightenment Unlimited, ostensibly to produce infomercials. The deal was for cash and the income probably saved the investment firm, but they look clean. TV Enlightenment Unlimited, of course, doesn't exist."

"Good Lord," McCarter said into his ice cubes. "We're at a dead end, Stony?"

There was nothing, then Price said diplomatically, "We're stalled for the moment, Phoenix."

"So what's our next move?" McCarter challenged her.

"A Navy forensics team will try to ID the body of your middle manager. The boat might yield some clues. Meanwhile, you can sit tight and get some rest. None of you has slept in more than twenty hours."

"Understood, Stony," McCarter said.

He understood just fine. They were at a dead end.

Stony Man Farm, Virginia

CARMEN DELAHUNT wasn't a game player, which was a flaw for any agent trying to climb the Federal Bureau of Investigations seniority ladder in Quantico. The excellence of her work was less important to her career than political maneuvering, which she refused to engage in, so she'd languished. Then her work, and her impressive list of successes, had come to the attention of Hal Brognola and he'd brought the small, vivacious redhead into the Stony Man Farm family.

Delahunt thrived at the Farm, where she was judged by her work, where brownnosing wasn't a required job skill. She respected the people of the Farm, she thrilled at the excitement of the cybernetic hunt. She knew she was a part of what could be the most effective electronic intelligence-gathering entity on the planet. When she unearthed some scrap of intelligence that was critical to the effort—well, *that* was job satisfaction.

At the moment, Delahunt was feeling extremely dissatisfied and she exhaled a long sigh.

It was out there, somewhere. The one critical piece of data that would get this whole thing moving again.

Once Delahunt overheard Kurtzman compare her investigative technique to the work of a very careful terrier who methodically tore at a slipper until there was nothing left except threads and scattered stuffing. She had been complimented—she'd known Kurtzman meant it as a compliment, although he'd turned red when she said thanks.

Well, the slipper was in shreds, the stuffing was spread all over the living room and the terrier had run out of pieces big enough to chew on.

If only she could find the matching slipper…

She looked at the notes on the notebook beside her keyboard. Every useless fact was listed in a few key words. Time to start from the top, do it all again to see if anything fresh popped up.

Plugging in the name of the Seattle investment firm that had rented out the Pacific island, she found her answer in seconds.

"IT'S ELLIOT ANDERSON Investment Realty," Delahunt explained as she plopped down her printout in the War Room with Kurtzman and Price gathering around. "Controlling interest is held by this company, Whiting Realty and Investments. That's a subsidiary of Formation Holdings. The list goes on and I had to tap into three European banking systems to follow it to the source, but the source is here." She poked at the last line of the printout.

"'Jackson American Home Stores,'" Price read. "Is that like Jackson's American Mart?"

"Yes," Delahunt said. "But you may know Jackson's American Mart was bought out by a conglomerate, and that's what caused all the lawsuits that were in the news a few years ago. Jackson American Home Stores is a very small chain of retailers with more high-end merchandise. It's still under its original ownership, and the company owns Temaru Island by way of Elliot Anderson Investment Realty."

Price saw where Delahunt's trail was leading, but she almost couldn't believe it. "Jackson's American Mart," she said cautiously, "is still owned by Franklin Jackson?"

Delahunt nodded.

"Franklin Jackson?" Kurtzman repeated, as if testing the words. "*Senator* Franklin Jackson?"

"Yes."

"Carmen, I can see why this makes sense to you," Price said. "We all know Jackson's views, and it's a suspicious link between the two companies, but we can't go after a U.S. senator without some pretty compelling evidence."

"I've got it," Delahunt said. "I found it in the newspaper."

She flipped to the second page of her printout, from a *Washington Post* subscriber Web page. There was a picture of a U.S. Army officer, fiftyish and buzz-cut. The small item had a small headline: U.S. Senator Hires His Own Protection; Calls Secret Service Inept. The picture caption read: "Senator Jackson's new Head of Security, ex-army Colonel Warren Korl."

"Hal," Price said, "is not going to like this at all."

"EXPLAIN IT TO ME AGAIN," Brognola demanded. "I'm not convinced."

"All right, Hal," Price said patiently. "You know Jackson. You know what he stands for."

"Of course I know Jackson. Any moron who's watched the news in the past two years knows Jackson. His purpose in life is to educate America about his point of view."

"He's a fervent proponent of U.S. isolationism."

"That's putting it mildly, and that's the problem. He's too high-profile."

"He owns the island," Price continued, "and he's tried very hard to cover that up. There's at least three illegal corporations set up to hide that fact."

"So impeach him. That's not damning evidence."

"Our one piece of intelligence from the guards on the island named a Colonel Coral as the mastermind of the attacks.

We were thinking coral as in ocean, but Senator Jackson has just hired Colonel Warren Korl."

"It's a publicity thing to embarrass the federal government and draw more attention to himself," Brognola protested. "This is all circumstantial evidence."

"We're not preparing a judicial indictment, Hal," Price said. "We're looking for a course of action."

"It's a risky course of action," Brognola shot back. "We're playing with fire once we start hunting down U.S. senators."

"I know for a fact that the President isn't on friendly terms with Senator Jackson."

"'Course not! Nobody is! But Jackson's an elected representative of the U.S. people. If we target him, the Man's going to assume he's next. A senator is not an acceptable target."

"It is if it's the correct target." Price's voice contained an underlying chill.

"And that remains to be proved. I say *proved*."

"Prove it how?" Kurtzman interjected.

"You know how to track the perpetrators back to their source," Brognola said. "It's what we do."

"Then let us do it."

"Fine. Do it. But keep your hands off the senator," Brognola said. After a moment he added, "Barb, you have to trust me to know when it's a matter of our survival. We can't get anywhere near the senator unless we have irrefutable evidence. Anything less and we're cutting our own throats."

"Okay, Hal," Price said. "We'll keep our distance from Jackson. But we will get the evidence and it will be so good even the Man will know that taking him down is the right thing."

"The problem is," Brognola said, sighing, "that even if he is guilty, even if we have evidence, taking down a U.S. senator might be the *wrong* thing in the eyes of the President."

CHAPTER ELEVEN

Virginia, U.S.A., 15,000 Feet

"Tell me you got it," Carl Lyons growled when the phone speaker clicked.

"I've got it," Kurtzman replied. "I kind of got it."

"What's that mean?" Lyons asked as he felt a slight shift in the altitude of the Cessna as it changed its heading. The pilot hit the gas and the engine whine intensified.

"We've been able to trace his calls by location," Kurtzman explained. "We still can't unscramble his signals."

"So we know where he is but we don't know what he's planning?" Lyons asked.

"That's right, Carl," Barbara Price interjected. "For right now all we can do is home you in on him and watch for trouble."

"That doesn't sound too promising," Lyons complained.

The problem arose when the nature of the communications hiding improved. Maybe when Phoenix Force hit them in the South Pacific the enemy got a clue. They were still using the technique of hiding their audio signals in what appeared to be a file transfer operation over a satellite phone feed, using phones rigged to pick up just the audio hidden in a data feed while the gigabytes of junk data that was escorting it flew away into the ether, unused.

But now, on top of this method of disguise, they were using 128-bit encryption to make the signals unbreakable. Stony knew when and where they were communicating, but not what.

"It's the best we've got so far," Kurtzman said. "We're also watching traces on the numbers he's been calling. They're converging. Maybe that means something."

"Maybe not," Hermann Schwarz said. He, Lyons and Rosario Blancanales were the only passengers on the Cessna, sitting around a slim conference table with the speakerphone. They had been making hundred-mile-wide circles over Virginia for almost two hours before the expected trace from Kurtzman finally came in.

"So where is it?" Blancanales asked.

"It's the 'where' that makes this a compelling lead—Kentucky, south of Louisville. We think Colonel Korl and his team are heading for a town called Baymont, which means their target must be Poynzsa Automobiles."

"I've heard of it," Schwarz said. "They got all the bad press for not hiring local construction firms."

"Yes, but you've just scratched the surface," Price said. "Poynzsa is funded by a Malaysian consortium of companies all looking for a way to break into the U.S. markets in a big way. They banded together and had enough political muscle to have the Malaysian government strong-arm the U.S. into making major concessions in terms of tariffs, tax breaks, labor regulation waivers, you name it.

"The new car plant is just one part of the picture. They're also putting in a steel service center, plastic pelleting and

molding, controls subassembly plant, you name it. They
brought in their own construction crews and hired locals only
for day labor. The new factory uses mostly Malaysian man-
agers with a few token Americans in high-profile positions.
The workers in the factory are all hourly staff who've mi-
grated from a TV factory that shut down there two years ago,
so they're willing to work at minimum wage. The same labor
scenario is duplicated in the supply plants."

"All the money funnels back to Malaysia and the U.S.
gets nothing but some low-wage jobs," Blancanales said.
"The U.S. was accused of the same thing in other countries
for a lot of years."

"And the U.S. doesn't like it any better than those countries did," Price said. "The backlash is growing. A handful of
elected officials who pushed Poynzsa's concessions were
voted out of their jobs. It was too late to stop the Malaysians,
though. The plant went through startup this week and initi-
ates small-scale production with the midnight shift tonight."

"I guess Pol called this one right," Schwarz said. "What
better target for a fervent isolationist?"

"We're still guessing here," Blancanales warned.

"But if Poynzsa does turn out to be the target, then a lot
of our guesses are confirmed," Price said.

Blancanales shrugged. "I don't know if we should hope
for that or not."

Washington, D.C.

"YOU FEELING okay, Senator?"

The aide was a sweet young woman, pretty and looking
smart in her dark blue skirt and jacket.

Senator Franklin Jackson smiled warmly. She was en-
chanting. A perfect little flower, with straw-colored hair cut

in a conservative, professional style but highlighted with shining silver braids that gave her a touch of flirty innocence. He especially liked the cute naval motif—white trim and brass buttons embossed with anchors. The girl might not even be old enough to vote, and that was just how he liked them.

"Thank you, but I feel fine. It's just that I've been up since three in the morning and I'm bushed."

Maybe she'd been expecting a polite nod or maybe a curt, "I'm fine, thank you." Taken aback at suddenly having the full, beaming attention of a United States senator, she wasn't quite sure what to do with herself, and Jackson allowed the silence to work its magic. After a few seconds she was frantic to fill the silence.

"Anything I can do to help, Senator?" But she smiled when she said it. Maybe she really meant it. Jackson loved it when they responded to him.

"No, thank you." His eyes locked on her left breast for a few heartbeats longer than it actually took him to read the ID tag. "Not tonight, Carla. Maybe some other time."

"I'm here to help," Carla said with a smile that was all white teeth and beautiful skin. She moved her hand slightly as if to touch his arm, but then didn't quite follow through with it.

When Jackson joined his bodyguards in the elevator, the big one, Morgenstern, nodded back at the offices. "Shame to pass it up."

"You better believe it, but I didn't pass it up. I just took a rain check. Tonight's too important for distractions."

"Don't know if I'd have the willpower, Senator," Gerald Maxie stated. He was smaller than Morgenstern, but he was still a mountain of a man at six foot two. With an enormous chest and shoulders, he probably outweighed Morgenstern by fifty pounds, all of it muscle and bone.

Jackson knew it wasn't willpower that enabled him to delay an interlude with Carla the intern, but anticipation of other things. His plans were proceeding, but there was trouble. Somehow one of the teams in the Pacific had been tracked back to the island.

It was a minor issue except for the niggling uncertainty. How had the trace been made? Could it be used against him again?

"There must have been some trained and armed military men on one of the ships and they got the drop on the team," Korl had rationalized. "They managed to call in the Navy before the ship blew, and the Navy reacted fast enough to get a visual trace on our men."

"You sound pretty sure," Jackson said.

"I've run the play over and over. It's the only possibility. It was one of the scenarios I anticipated. The chance of comebacks is zero."

"You sound pretty sure of that, too," Jackson added, but he knew the colonel was right. They had designed the raids and equipped the men with an overall strategy in mind—to make the probes untraceable and the men unidentifiable. As soon as it became clear their cover was blown and capture was a possibility, Korl had blown up every one of the watercraft.

It was brutal. It was heartless. Jackson was a little uneasy about that part of the plan. But the long-term benefits for the people…well, he had thought this all through before. No need to dwell on the ugly reality of it all now.

The truth was, the country needed a slap in the face, or else she would get a knife in the back.

"I'm cocksure that none of the Temaru Island, uh, factors, is still around to be a thing to worry about," Korl declared. "The operation is still free of leaks. Plus, we were one hundred percent successful."

That was the kind of statement that restored Jackson's confidence. "We were, weren't we?" he agreed with a wide grin into the phone. "Neither of us expected to have a perfect success rate in the first two phases. It's better than I could have hoped."

That was good enough reason to rejoice, and Carla the intern would have been a celebration indeed. But tonight the operation made another major advance.

Tonight, Jackson was bringing the message home to America in a very big way.

Arlington, Virginia, U.S.A.

SENATOR JACKSON'S housekeeper had prepared a large porcelain tureen of lobster bisque, steaming on the hot plate, and a still-warm, freshly baked loaf of bread on the cutting board. He finished his dinner in minutes, while Morgenstern and Maxie were just getting started, then didn't have anything to do except pace the room and flip through the channels.

There were brief reports on the news about the *Showdown in Baymont* or the *International Crisis in the Heart of America,* depending on the network.

"Midnight tonight is the deadline given by the Jobs for America coalition," the talking head reported. "Its demands are straightforward but far-reaching. They want at least fifty percent of the managerial staff at the Poynzsa factory and its supply factories to be U.S. citizens. They also want half of the dollars spent on parts and materials for the factory to be spent with American suppliers. They want a promise that one hundred percent of the construction on the second assembly plant will be performed by local firms. Poynzsa management have so far refused to negotiate with the coalition, which called for demonstrations and promises to shut down the plant if the deadline passes without an agreement from Poynzsa. Midnight tonight, in Baymont, Kentucky, we'll be watching to see if and how this gathering of peaceful demonstrators plans to carry out the threat."

"Those Malaysian assholes won't even negotiate," Jackson said, waving at the television. "We break our own laws to let them in so they can leach off this country, and they don't have decency to negotiate over a few lousy blue-collar jobs."

"They're tricky little pricks, Senator," Maxie agreed through a mouthful of French bread.

"They're worse than pricks. They're *foreigners*. They have no business profiting on the United States."

Morgenstern nodded. He and Maxie had been assigned to the senator for just a few weeks but had learned how to behave when the man launched into an America-for-Americans rant. You agreed, you nodded, you mostly kept you mouth shut and looked interested. You never, ever argued with him.

On the mantel over the fireplace was a framed campaign poster, the one that got him elected in his home state: "America First, Global Economy Second."

It turned out there were a lot of U.S. citizens who were uneasy with the increasingly global role their nation was playing. None of the career politicians were in tune with the American people, so they failed to see this new reality, but Franklin Jackson was.

When he announced his campaign for a Senate seat in his home state, there was an immediate media interest. He was, after all, one of the richest men in the country. His court battles and big mouth had made him front-page news for years. Nobody was happier about his Senate run than the media. Nobody expected him to win.

When he began staging speeches, his sound bites were

provocative and edgy enough to garner him nationwide air-play. He was laughed off as an extremist from coast to coast.

Those who laughed, especially the political party candidates, became horrified when Jackson's following grew.

Then his opposition was scarred by a scandal. The people of the state had lost jobs by the thousands since the economic downturn that started with the September 11, 2001 terrorist attacks. They saw themselves languishing in economic limbo, unnoticed by the government. It became clear that Jackson might actually ride that sentiment into a Senate seat.

"We're sending billions of U.S dollars overseas to help rebuild Afghanistan. But I don't see anybody trying to rebuild my part of the country. Congress hasn't voted this state a big new budget to rebuild and bring back the jobs this state has lost. I don't think anybody in Washington even knows there's a problem here. They're too worried about Afghanistan and the rest of the world.

"Where did the jobs go? Overseas. Where are the electronics coming from? Asia. TVs and computers are from Mexico. All our clothes are made in sweatshops in South America and Southeast Asia. You want a job? That's where the jobs are—somewhere else! Anywhere *except* the U.S.A.

"Even when we do make something here in the U.S., we're making it using steel from Europe, where the government has subsidized the production of the steel. The U.S. government tried to slow down imports, but they sure didn't try very hard. Can our steel companies survive against other companies that are subsidized by their national governments? Of course not!"

They called his speeches rambling, deceptive, "inspired by bitterness."

If that meant he had his own personal reasons for hating the way the U.S. was taking care of the world while ignoring its own people, then they were correct. But he was clearly not alone. When the ballots were counted in what had turned out to be a fragmented race, no less than four candidates received a good share of the vote, but the race was won by Franklin Jackson.

The new senator stormed onto the Senate floor on his first day, ready to change the U.S. for the better—and he was promptly ignored. His speeches were cut short. He was seated in the least important committees. When his patience ran thin and he erupted in a Senate floor rage he was removed, the laughter following him out.

It was on that day that he came up with the plan that would make the people, and the Senate, see that he was right.

If they didn't believe the U.S. was being subjugated by the influence and preference it gave to foreigners, he would take his own steps to stop the subjugation.

He was a businessman, so he knew that the way to make it stop was to make it unprofitable.

The news channel replayed the earlier segment on the demonstrations at the Poynzsa plant. A perfect example of what should *never* happen to the people of the U.S. But U.S. greed and the duplicity of the Malaysians had enabled it to come about.

Tonight the Malaysians would learn a lesson: operating in the U.S. was going to be far more costly than they ever dreamed. They would be uninsurable. They would be incapable of producing their product.

Poynzsa Corporation's business plan called for its U.S. operations to begin generating revenues as of today, but by the next day it would be hemorrhaging hundreds of thousands of dollars daily and have no foreseeable turnaround. Poynzsa would walk away and write off the endeavor as a huge loss, which would be better than trying to ride out the catastrophe and risk miring the entire corporation in bankruptcy.

Jackson had looked at their business plan. Such an outcome would be inevitable.

Poynzsa would be the first high-profile foreign firm to flee, but many more would follow. Senator Franklin Jackson would look like some sort of a genius. Or a prophet.

CHAPTER TWELVE

Baymont, Kentucky

"It's going to be tough getting in here," Rosario Blancanales observed. "They've got SWAT, state police, local police and the Feds inside."

"I think I saw a Mountie," Hermann Schwarz added.

Carl Lyons lightened his touch on the brake and the Land Rover idled a couple of feet forward. "All this law enforcement is overkill. It's too many cooks. They'll be competing against each other, there won't be a single commander, they'll leave all kinds of gaps in the security, and then blame each other when the fallout comes."

Able Team's Land Rover was eighth in line for entrance into the gated grounds of Poynzsa Campus One, the huge central hub of the facility with a main factory, a supply warehouse that handled the logistics of parts for the assembly lines, and a shipping center for finished cars stationed on a fenced, three-mile-wide square of former farm field.

The crowd of protesters gathering at the main entrance swelled hourly as the excitement of the mysterious deadline called out the merely interested as well as the dedicated. The news networks reported four thousand people on-site and projected twice as many before the deadline. Poynzsa legal efforts to keep protesters away had failed when the company found the popular backlash had turned the political tables against them. There wasn't a judge to be found who would block the demonstrations. The hordes were pushing in the police barricades alongside the pavement, the red-faced protesters venting their fury at every vehicle without knowing or caring who was inside.

"The real problem for an intruder is from the media," Schwarz said, smiling and waving at a shouting fiftyish woman with braided hair and a home-sewn sack dress just outside his window. She had the look of a hippie radical now making her way through life as a professional demonstrator, but her anger looked forced. Time had dulled the indignation, but she made the effort for the hovering reporters. "There must be a hundred cameras surrounding this place, and they'll have to get in without getting picked up on video. Check it out." He jabbed a finger up at the bright yellow wing of an ultralight aircraft, carefully staying away from the crowds while a remotely operated camera dangled from the skeletal aluminum frame.

Lyons was silent as they worked their way to the security gate, heavily reinforced with Kentucky state troopers, and were passed through on their Justice Department IDs. They parked in the visitors' lot in front of the elegant brick facade of the small managerial building adjunct to the manufacturing plant. Most of the cars had government plates.

"Guess it's okay to use U.S. law enforcement even if you import all the rest of your workforce," Schwarz observed.

"Why not?" Blancanales said. "It's free."

The curved flight of concrete steps to the reception area

was grandiose and flanked with a pair of statues on granite pedestals. One was the crescent moon and star burst from the Malaysian flag, a full yard in diameter and six inches thick. The other statue was an eagle, so Americana it could have been pilfered from the front of a small-town library.

"I feel like I'm entering the state courthouse," Schwarz said, stopping halfway up and turning to gaze out. The campus was designed for expansion, with several hundred yards of sodded landscape cushioning the existing buildings from the fence. The grounds' machine-made contours and the occasional copse of saplings gave it the look of a new golf course with several years needed to make it mature. It was peaceful and vacant, odd in contrast to the throngs of people pressed against the gates and the blinking lights of news aircraft.

"They'll come in like we did," he declared. "In disguise. No other way. They'd never strong-arm their way in without risk. It's got to be an undercover job."

Lyons nodded. "So they'll come in the front door, just like we did."

"Evening," Blancanales said loudly.

"Help you, gentlemen?" The demand came from a suspicious private security guard who was descending the steps.

"Checking things out." Lyons thrust his Justice ID at the guard and gave him all the time he needed to examine it. "All employees have ID tags like that?"

The guard looked at the laminated card pinned to his windbreaker as if trying to figure out which ID tag was in question. "Yeah. They're coded with an RF serial number."

"Easy to duplicate," Schwarz commented.

"I know it," the guard admitted. "They're a handicap. Nobody looks at the pictures anymore as long as the RF reader thinks it's legit. I tried telling them that we're checking the tag instead of the tag wearer."

"You could turn it off and use humans to check the ID photos, at least for the time being."

The guard grinned. "Common sense, right? But when I suggested it they looked at me like I had come up with some sort of brilliant plan. But at least they started doing it. There's a biometrics ID system going online in a week. In the meantime my company was hired to watch the place and consult as needed. Here's my card."

Schwarz took it and read the details on a security consulting firm in Indianapolis. "Thanks."

"I've kind of been interested in Justice. Maybe you could let me know what you guys are looking for in new recruits."

"Sure," Schwarz said with a polite grin. "I'll send you something."

The guard was Schwarz's new best friend and he hurried to open the front doors, which were two-story glass panels that had a drive assist so they could move with a light touch. "Nice guy," Schwarz said as he pocketed the business card. "Maybe Phoenix could use another name on the roster."

The comfortable, carpeted halls gave way to sterile floor tile and brick walls as they passed from the managerial wing into manufacturing. They went through four checkpoints, manned alternately by Americans from the Indianapolis firm and Malays who were a part of the standard security force. Their bags went unsearched, but the ID tags supplied at the front gate were scanned repeatedly.

"Check it out," Blancanales said, nodding at a ceiling fixture next to a security camera. "RF reader. They can monitor and record the movements of every employee."

"Easy to beat?" Lyons asked.

"Yeah. You just take the tag off."

They emerged through a pair of double doors, plastic-sealed to keep the air-conditioning in the offices, and stood on a concrete landing overlooking the main factory entrance. Teams of guards were milling around in wait for the shift change. Beyond the entrance there was the fifty-foot-tall enclosure containing a vast landscape of machinery, shelving, overhead cranes, autonomous vehicles with blinking red lights, and churning machinery. The dangling overhead fluorescent lights were brilliant but sickly yellow.

The deluge of rumbling equipment and the occasional crash of a 500-ton metal forming press filled the open space with an almost visible haze of sound.

The far wall, hundreds of yards from where they stood, was obscured by the polarizing effect of the lights and machinery exhaust and gave the impression of an unending horizon, as if they had entered a vast mechanical world out of a grim science-fiction film.

"Suddenly I don't understand all the commotion outside the gates. Who would *want* to work here?" Schwarz asked.

"Anybody who doesn't have other options," Blancanales said as they descended to the manufacturing level and moved into the depths of the plant, receiving a nod from a bored-looking Baymont police officer. "I see only three guard posts. They must be pretty confident that whoever gets inside is supposed to be there. Look at us, walking around like we belong here."

Lyons pulled out his mobile phone and touched it. The line was permanently open to Stony Man, but a phone was less alarming to observers than the headset they often used in the field. "Able One here," he said. "What's Korl's status?"

"Nothing yet, Able One," Price said. "We're tracking communications from three of their phones in the vicinity, but they haven't been making calls in the past thirty-five minutes. We can only assume they're in transit and still together. Before you even ask again, I'll tell you we have had no luck breaking their encryption."

The three commandos looked at one another when a per-cussive thump reached them, felt in the concrete floor as well as heard. There was a distinction to it that was impossible to describe, but they knew it wasn't another miscellaneous plant noise. They bolted for the main entrance, where most of the guards and law enforcement had yet to realize something was happening, although it was dawning on them as plant workers who noticed the slight aberration were showing alarm.

Checkpoint security organization disintegrated as guards and staff rushed out of the entrance and stopped to stare at a rising mushroom cloud, stark black against the night sky.

"Stony, we've got an explosion," Lyons reported quickly, his voice low as he moved away from the throngs. "A mile and a half north-northeast of our position and it's big."

"There's nothing at that location, Able One," Price re-ported. "It's undeveloped."

"Are there utility lines or anything?"

"Negative. It's a distraction, Able."

Lyons had already come to that conclusion. But a distrac-tion from what?

Schwarz jogged passed him into the parking lot and looked up and over the building, cupping his hands around his eyes to shield the glare of lights.

"Here they come," he said.

Lyons squinted up and saw the tiny black wings spiraling among the stars.

BARBARA PRICE GUIDED their footsteps using architectural CAD schematics of the plant and they burst onto the roof a minute later, hugging a hook-shaped exhaust vent the size of a backyard toolshed as they armed themselves with the hard-ware from their bags.

A second explosion detonated in the middle of empty land, even more distant from the campus. Price reported that local law enforcement radio communications showed they were concentrating excitedly on the blasts. She couldn't reach the field commanders to alert them to the real danger. All the media attention had gravitated to the explosions, as well, and the second blast couldn't have been missed by any news videographer worth a paycheck.

The small shapes above them moved in fast after the second blast.

"Those aren't parafoils!" Blancanales exclaimed. "They're ultralights."

The first tiny aircraft dived at the roof of the plant, leveled out abruptly and set down after rolling less than twenty feet. The landing took place on the farthest corner of the vast roof, and other aircraft were coming down at various points, buzzing with no more noise than a chain saw.

"Separate," Lyons commanded, jerking his thumb in directions for Schwarz and Blancanales. "Take out the vehicles if you get the chance. They won't deploy their loads if they don't have a way out of here."

Lyons was alone seconds later, and he bolted from the protective shadow of the exhaust vent, scrambling up a short ladder and vaulting onto the higher level before diving to the ground, faltering against the foot-high brick frame holding a network of glazed skylights. Fifty feet ahead of him the ultralight that had been zeroing in on his position touched the surface on big balloon tires that bounced it along for a few paces before the operator brought the low-mass aircraft to an easy stop and the buzz of the motor cut to a puttering idle.

The pilot hadn't seen Lyons, who wormed closer, reluctant to fire for fear of hitting the cargo.

The pilot stepped off the padded seat, which was bolted

to the composite frame. He crouched, then opened a pair of latches under the seat to drop a large cylinder onto the roof. It was thickly covered with corrugated plastic wrapping for cushioning, and the wrapping uncoiled as the pilot rolled it. He stood the cylinder on its end, yanked out three stabilizing legs one after another and tapped at a set of buttons on the top of the device. A pair of red lights came to life on the nose and tail of the device.

The deployment was well rehearsed; it hadn't taken half a minute. The pilot then turned and took a step away from the device and Lyons was free to strike. He ran from behind the nearest air-exchange fan box and targeted the pilot from ten paces. The man grabbed at his own gun and almost had it out of his shoulder holster when he spotted the red dot of the laser-aiming module on his chest and knew he was doomed.

As the bullet ripped his heart, he collapsed to the rooftop.

Lyons inspected the device in a hurry. "Able One here, Stony, check this thing out." He snapped a digital photo from the tiny lens on the handheld PDA and sent it winging back to Stony Man Farm.

"I've got the photo, Able One," Price said. "We're looking into it."

Lyons grunted. "I'm not exactly flush with free time, Stony."

"Cowboy here. Able One, I'm looking at your photo. It's a shaped charge. It's designed to pierce the roof and channel the explosive force into the structure below. The display is simply an on/off. The electronics inside will tell us more about the controls but the lack of a time display leads me to believe it's radio activated. I need to see the innards before I can tell you how to turn it off."

"I've got news for you, Cowboy," Lyons said. "The top is

welded in place. There's no way I'm getting at the innards. I suppose that means there's no way I can turn it off."

"That's right."

"Can I dump it on the parking lot? Maybe it won't kill as many people."

"Don't touch it, Able One!" Kissinger said with uncharacteristic urgency. "Those are self-leveling legs, dammit!"

Lyons swore bitterly under his breath. He should have noticed that. The implication was obvious. "Able Two and Able Three, this is Able One, respond now." He waited a heartbeat. "Respond *now*. I don't care what your situation is."

It was as commanding as Carl Lyons could be. You had to have a hell of a big set of cojones, or be dead, to ignore an order like that.

Able Two and Able Three didn't answer.

CHAPTER THIRTEEN

Rosario Blancanales went through a series of twists and turns before leaping up a three-foot rise in the roof and getting his bearing on an incoming ultralight, which was now directly overhead and descending fast. He had timed his movements carefully, exposing himself only when the craft was directly overhead and the pilot unlikely to see.

He paused long enough to catch a progress report on the first ultralight. The pilot had put some sort of a bomb on the roof, upended on tripod legs. It looked like an oversize sniper rifle shell, it was as big as his thigh. It didn't take great brains to know that the slender tip was designed to penetrate the roof, then the wider body would detonate inside the plant, directing the force down in a funnel-shaped blast.

Very effective. These guys were sophisticated, good at their job. An amateur would have just chucked his charges at the plant from the air and headed home, and the damage might not have even penetrated the roof.

Blancanales waited for the ultralight to bounce onto the roof and came up behind it before it had rolled to a stop. He aimed well above the cargo on the belly of the aircraft and triggered the Heckler & Koch Mk 23 Mod 0 repeatedly, perfecting his aim on the run. The first two shots crashed through shafts of the composite frame and chunks of debris and made a metallic ring when they slammed into the slowing propellers. The pilot twisted bodily out of the ultralight and Blancanales's third shot took him in the side, tearing out his hip. He was still spinning when he impacted the roof surface. When he came up again, he had extracted his handgun and shoved it skyward at Blancanales.

The Able Team commando triggered a final, no-nonsense head shot, and the .45-caliber round painted a bloody V that glistened in the harsh xenon lights.

He heard an angry buzz as a quick burst of machine-gun rounds splattered into the asphalt roof, sending the stocky commando bolting across the surface until he came to a drop-off and plummeted eight feet to a lower level. He flattened his body against the wall and tucked away the suppressed Mk 23. The fact that there was an ultralight-mounted machine-gun blazing in his direction meant he had probably been noticed already.

Blancanales heard the buzz of the craft grow, then alter, then recede. The pilot had witnessed his tortoiseshell retreat and was going to come at him from an unprotected angle. Good strategy. Not much alternative cover in the vicinity except for a small mushroom-shaped steam exhaust that wasn't any taller than his chest.

He took out the Mk 23 again, pressed the rifle against his body to shield it from view, then bolted into the open as the buzz of the ultralight grew to a whine. He fired wildly at the little aircraft, although it was still outside the reach of the handgun, then dropped onto his knees behind the steam vent as the pilot began return fire.

The ultralight pilot didn't bother to put a cushion of distance between them this time, but turned sharp and quick and homed in on the steam vent. Blancanales had him fooled, at least for the moment, and he wasn't the kind of guy to let special moments slip through his fingers. He got to his feet with the M-16 A-2/M-203 combo and triggered a single 40 mm buckshot round from the M-203 grenade launcher. The ultralight had foolishly closed to just 150 yards. The pellets rattled around within the frame for a fraction of a second before they succeeded in tearing it to shreds. The craft was transformed into stringy fiberglass shards, fluttering nylon confetti and spraying blood.

The heavy engine and the bulky cargo separated from the smaller pieces and sped to earth end-over-end. Somebody was shouting from the radio on his belt and vaguely Blancanales knew it was Lyons, but he couldn't respond. All he could do was watch the pieces fall and he was silently talking to the cargo of the ultralight. Or maybe he was praying.

Don't blow, he thought. *Don't blow. Don't blow.*

The cargo cracked against the earth and blew big.

SCHWARZ LOST COUNT of ultralights at six. How were they supposed to take out six of those damn things?

All he could do was all he could do. A stupid affirmation but somehow it made sense, and somehow it made him as mad as hell. He barreled over the edge of a drop-off just as his target ultralight rolled to a stop. Schwarz jammed the barrel of the M-16 A-2/M-203 into his gut before his feet hit bottom and he triggered an automatic burst that cut viciously into the little aircraft, cutting up the frame, ripping through the nylon wing panels and stitching through the chest of the shocked pilot.

Easy enough. He never slowed as he raced across the open roof and realized he had lost track of the next target. Maybe it had seen him and fled. There was a sudden buzz and the thing rose from the edge of the building, ten paces away, like a swamp monster coming out of the murk, then it dipped low and shot down at him.

Schwarz knew the pilot couldn't fire through the prop, so when he bolted, it was directly at the whirling circle of the spinning blades. The pilot panicked and veered to the left, and Schwarz triggered an automatic burst that zigzagged over the ultralight. He never knew what vital part he hit, but the craft descended violently into the roof, smashing its rear end to kindling, then slamming slow-motion into the nearest roof-mounted obstruction. The shed with the ventilation fan took the impact with a dent. The ultralight was obliterated.

The pilot staggered out of the wreckage, his forehead visibly crushed, his vision passing drunkenly over Schwarz before he flung away his stubby machine pistol and veered back onto the ultralight. He half collapsed, half knelt in the wreckage and fumbled at the explosive cargo, which was dented but intact.

As the pilot fought with one of the twisted disconnect latches, Schwarz halted and aimed, not five yards away, and said, "Stop."

The wounded pilot tugged on the latch and the cylinder tumbled at his feet. He gave an almost childlike cry of delight as his hand grabbed at a protective steel panel and yanked it, revealing switches inside, and his fingers went for the switch.

Schwarz triggered a burst from the M-16 A-2 and the pilot toppled to the rooftop, his arm distended into the air for a moment as his fingers still sought blindly for the switch. Schwarz jogged forward and examined the pilot, then the cylinder. There was one on/off switch.

Schwarz swore under his breath, pretty sure what the result would have been if the pilot had succeeded in turning it on.

And there were more of those things being set up right now. Schwarz grabbed the bolted-on rungs on the vent-fan and pulled himself on top, looking for another target.

He saw nothing. The uneven topography of the plant roof made it impossible to scout far and he had no idea even where Pol and Ironman might be. And he didn't have time to make a serious reconnoiter.

No more buzzing motors. All the ultralights were down. A sharp clank from beyond several levels of the rooftop started Schwarz moving again in a hurry.

When he got there, it was too late. The cylinder had already been deployed, and Schwarz felt something like a golf ball come into his throat when he saw it.

"Don't move."

The pilot froze at the sound of the voice and at the sight of the laser dot on his hand. The dot quickly traveled to his torso.

"Turn slowly."

The pilot did as he was told, revealing a handgun holstered under his arm.

Fifty yards separated them, but Schwarz's handgun was the Heckler & Koch Mk 23 Mod 0. The U.S. Offensive Handgun Weapon System—OHWS—was designed to have the accuracy of handguns used in competitive shooting, combined with the durability and operational capability of a combat handgun. It was developed for U.S. special forces units throughout the military, and it had its detractors. But with a few minor upgrades, courtesy of Cowboy Kissinger and the Stony Man Farm armory, the Mk 23 was a fieldable weapon.

The pilot went through a series of emotions in seconds. First he showed surprise at the weapon, then maybe fear when he knew he was irrevocably targeted by a competent man with a competent weapon.

Then he was amused.

"Shoot me. I dare you."

Schwarz's bluff had been called. He didn't dare shoot. The man stood between him and the cylinder, and if Schwarz shot him, he would likely fall into the device, knocking it over. The self-leveling legs told Schwarz there was probably a mercury switch inside, and since the thing was activated it would detonate. How many people were still inside the factory? How many would die?

But the thing would go off anyway when its internal timer counted down to zero or when its RF receiver got the signal. And that would be in minutes or in seconds.

"Pick it up," Schwarz said.

The amusement on the pilot's face soured.

"Listen carefully, flyboy," Schwarz said rapidly. "I have two choices. Shoot you and hope you miss the device when you die or have you pitch it off the roof and hope the switch inside is not too sensitive to make the trip. Doing nothing is not an option."

The pilot's expression became an ashen mask and his mouth went slack.

"So what will it be? Die now or take a chance?"

"You can't make me do it!" the pilot pleaded.

Schwarz allowed the marker of the Mk 23 Laser Aiming Module to waver off the pilot's torso just long enough to fire a single shot. The .45-caliber round slammed into the rooftop less than a foot from the pilot.

"I'll do it, I'll do it!"

"Then do it—very, very fast and very, very carefully."

The pilot turned and appraised the device, then made a gasping sob as he grasped the cylinder in two hands and lifted it off the ground. He took a step, then another. He raised his foot a little higher for the next step to get over a drainage pipe, and then his step wavered.

Schwarz held his breath. Lyons suddenly mouthed off in his headset.

"Able Two and Able Three, this is Able One, respond now."

Schwarz couldn't answer. One hundred percent of his concentration was locked on the pilot as he fought to regain an unnaturally perfect balance. Was the mercury switch set to go off with a topple or just a jiggle?

"Respond *now*. I don't care what your situation is," Lyons shouted.

The pilot took his next two steps more assuredly, and Schwarz was thinking this idiot plan might just work. He thumbed the radio to respond to Lyons, but the words didn't leave his lips.

There was a blast from the opposite side of the factory, but huge enough to shake the building underneath them, and the pilot staggered wildly, shouting, "No, no, no!" to the Fates as he desperately clung to the device.

They fell together as the building vibrated, and Schwarz tossed himself backward off the nearest ledge, not caring what he was throwing himself into but knowing it was better than—

The blast came when he was still in the air, the wall of sudden fire becoming a roof over him before it quickly ate its way down the wall that was protecting him from the force of it. When he hit the next surface Schwarz rolled to his feet and ran. He felt stupid for thinking he could outrun the blast, but he ran anyway.

CHAPTER FOURTEEN

Rosario Blancanales tried the radio. "Able Two here."

"Report," Lyons demanded.

"The first one was one of mine," Blancanales said. "But it went off in the parking lot. I'm in the northwest corner, and the building looks okay."

"What about number two?" Lyons demanded.

"East side of the building," Blancanales replied. "Gadgets went that way."

"Able Three, would you goddamn report?" Lyons shouted from the radio.

Blancanales felt undamaged, although he was chiding himself for being slow to hit the deck. Now he climbed, making for higher ground. There were still other devices unaccounted for. When he heard a cough, he froze on the roof of a ventilation box, then realized it was coming through the headphones. The cough came again and sounded very much like Schwarz on some sort of heavy depressant.

"Able Three here," Schwarz reported, the words coming with effort. "Six total ultralights by my count. I took out three."

"I took out one," Lyons responded instantly. "Pol?"

"I got two. We're in the clear."

"Negative!" Lyons responded. "Mine is activated and can be detonated."

"Where?" Schwarz demanded.

"Southeast quadrant. Why?"

"That second blast you heard is on the west side of the building. Everybody inside it going to be panicking and headed for the exit at the southeast end of the building."

Blancanales grew cold as he listened to the conversation and realized he was standing on one of the highest points on the roof. He could see the black smoke clouds coming from the west end of the building and now he made out the stock-still figure of Carl Lyons standing there, as tiny as an ant, as if he were miles away. Then the ant skittered away and disappeared.

Blancanales didn't know which of the two very bad choices the Able Team commander had just made, but he knew Ironman might not survive his next course of action.

"Pol, go give Gadgets an assist," Lyons ordered on the radio. "I'll see what I can do downstairs."

Lyons had chosen to go down. His course of action was either to get rid of the weapon, and almost surely detonating it in the process, or going into the plant to try to stop a panicking stampede of humans before the bomb on top of him went off anyway.

"Good luck, Ironman," Blancanales said.

LYONS DIDN'T CALL LUCK "luck." To him, a chain of events just happened, and sometimes they happened for his benefit and sometimes not. But right now he could use some luck.

"Did you get that, Stony?" he asked as he tumbled down the steep utility stairs.

"We're calling everybody on the scene to alert them to a device in the southeast quadrant of the facility," Price replied with calm efficiency.

Lyons knew it would take minutes for the official word to filter down to the scene. Minutes he didn't have. He crashed through the doors and found himself on the steel-grate balcony overlooking the factory floor, with hordes of plant workers streaming through the aisles and heading for the main entrance, where they were bottlenecking. There were hundreds of them and they were gathering under the staging site of the one surviving weapon as if the plan had been carefully engineered that way.

Lyons ran along the balcony until he could overlook the entrance, and had the presence of mind to drop his M-16 A2 before he started shouting.

"Hey, get those people back."

A few faces turned in his direction. One was a frowning FBI agent, an elder in the agency's bureaucracy.

"Who the hell are you?" the agent yelled.

"I'm with Justice—there's a bomb right on top of us. Move the people away from here!"

"The whole place is wired to blow," the agent retorted.

"All disabled. Now get these people away from here!"

The agent sneered. "I got news for you, buddy—"

Lyons didn't have any more time to waste on niceties. He grabbed the discarded weapon and thumbed a single 40 mm round into the breech of the 203 and fired. The HE flew over the heads of the crowds and descended into a storage yard for huge coils of steel. It detonated and flung steel rolls up and out, filling the factory with thunder and the ring of warping metal. Lyons allowed himself the luxury of watching the coils collapse among themselves to assure himself there were no casualties. Then he triggered a long burst over the heads of the guards and the screaming crowds. Some were surging toward the entrance, but most were struggling to reverse course.

If only there was enough time.

Lyons ducked to the balcony as the FBI agent and a pair of guards took the initiative and fired at him. Lyons changed out the M-16 A-2's magazine, then jumped to his feet again, firing an extended burst that sent the gunners diving for cover. It was amateur gunplay, but for sheer drama it couldn't be beat as his unstoppable torrent of 5.56 mm rounds smashed through guard-shack windows. The glass exploded and rained throughout the entranceway. Then he targeted the huge fifty-foot-tall garage doors. They were thin aluminum and the gunfire raised a thunderous rattle.

Lyons dropped, slapped in another fresh mag and leaped down the stairs, sending a warning burst on the heels of the crowd, just to keep them moving, then he turned on the guards, sending another crashing burst into the guard shack. A burly young security guard bent at the waist and bolted, and Lyons found the place suddenly abandoned.

Except for the FBI agent, who stepped into the open just long enough to unleash a vicious blast from a combat shotgun. Lyons dodged into a storage bin and listened to the cacophony of buckshot rain against the steel sides. The agent pumped the gun, but Lyons was already out and firing again, and this time he aimed for human flesh. The agent's shins each took a round and he pitched onto his face.

The agent was good; he was a warrior. He grunted with the exertion of raising his upper body on his elbows, gritting his teeth and groping for the shotgun trigger.

Then the weapon flew out of his hand and the agent found himself staring into the wildest eyes he had ever seen. This man was a killer, an execution machine. For the longest second of his life, the FBI agent lost all contact with his skill and his professionalism and thought in mythical, maybe spiritual terms. In his mind came the words "Angel of Death."

Then the bizarre inconsistency of the scene broke the spell. He grunted through his pain, "No bodies."

The grim figure draped his assault rifle on his shoulder and hoisted the agent off the floor. "No shit, Sherlock."

"Where are you taking me?" The agent found himself slumped over the shoulder of the man who'd shot his legs out.

"You haven't been paying attention."

As the agent was carried with powerful strides out the front of the factory, his mind whirled through the tendrils of pain and then he remembered what this man had been trying to tell him. About a bomb. Right above them. He raised his head to look back at the wide gaping entrance of the plant. Soundlessly, his consciousness fading, the FBI agent watched the entrance fill with fire. Maybe it was real. Maybe he was dead and he was witnessing the mouth of hell opening up to swallow him.

CHAPTER FIFTEEN

"Mills," gasped the senior agent on the gurney, "shut up."

"Did you see what he did to us?" The agent in the suit, Mills, was rookie by FBI standards, and he didn't like having his hair mussed. He was flanked by a pair of sidekicks who looked similarly disheveled. "You're under arrest, buddy."

"Agent Mills, go away." The agent on the gurney was wearing pressure bandages on two shot-out shins but was somehow staying in control.

"I believe you're acting under duress and/or coercion," Mills spit back at the senior agent. "I'm removing this man for questioning."

Agent Mills held a fighter's stance and Lyons shrugged. He had roughed up the three agents, still draping the senior agent on one shoulder. They had insisted on seeing his ID while Lyons had insisted on finding the ambulance. "That's how you got into trouble before, remember?" he reminded them.

"Yeah, you're pretty clever. And pretty lucky."

"You're right. This was my lucky day, even before I ran into the Federal Bureau of Incompetence."

"Just back off, Mills," interjected the agent on the gurney, but he was fading as the painkillers from the IV seeped into his bloodstream. His words slurred.

Mills put his hand on his holster under his arm. "Don't make me draw my weapon. If you are what you say you are, it would be bad PR for Justice."

Lyons shrugged. "Looks like the FBI's gonna be the ones explaining themselves to the newspapers in the morning."

Mills had had enough. He groped for his weapon as he grabbed Lyons's shoulder and spun him against the side of the ambulance for a search. Then, unexpectedly, Mills felt himself hitting the ambulance, hard, and he slumped to the ground. He tried to get at the handgun under his arm, but his other hand shattered beneath a heavy stomp. Mills collapsed on his face and grabbed the broken hand with the good one, only to have them both jerked behind him.

Mills sought help from his friends. The handguns materialized in the hands of his fellow agents, then vanished again. There was utter chaos.

Mills found himself handcuffed facedown on the asphalt, alongside the other two agents.

"Let's start over. I'm with the Department of Justice."

The guy with the attitude thrust his ID into Mills's face for the second time. "Got it? You are under arrest."

Mills saw two more men standing alongside the grim, blond guy who had carried in the FBI field commander. It was those two who had subdued the other agents while the grim one trussed Mills.

A scarier trio Agent Mills had never faced. Not when he was a beat cop on the streets of New York City, never during his brief stint with the Bureau. They were bruised and bloodied. One had a face half reddened by heat blast. With their assault rifle/grenade-launcher combos draped on each shoulder, they looked like news video of exhausted Special Forces soldiers on a cave hunt in Afghanistan.

"Feds can't arrest Feds," one of Mills's comrades protested.

"Then what was that guy getting you all spread-eagle for, Ironman?" asked the heat-burned man, whose bloodied face split into a grin.

Ironman? The big one was called Ironman, for Christ's sake? Mills found himself carried into the air and placed on his feet. He was shoved a few steps, but stopped belligerently.

"You can't arrest me."

"Walk or be dragged."

"Where are you taking us?"

"Jail."

"You know what the Bureau will do to us?"

"Yeah," the Ironman said. "I know all about how the Bureau handles agents who make them look stupid."

"But if you work very hard this will all blow over in eight or ten years, and your career will be back on track," said the burned one, who couldn't stop grinning.

Mills looked beseechingly to the third one, who had been silent. Christ, this guy looked as if he ate engine blocks for breakfast.

"Give us a break," Mills begged him.

"No hablo Ingles."

Mills found himself sprawled in the rear of an SUV with his fellow agents, and his heart sank when the vehicle was allowed to exit the grounds of the automobile plant with a wave of an ID. He'd made a big mistake. He had an ego and a temper, and this wasn't the first time he'd got himself in trouble because he couldn't keep his big mouth shut. But even now the excruciating pain in his hand kept forcing his temper to a near boil.

"Look, man, you have got to give us a fucking break," he

called out. He tried hard to sound sincere but it came out as a threat.

"Maybe if you said you were sorry." It was Smiling Boy, who was in the back seat using alcohol swabs to clean the abrasions on his face.

Mills apologized, as loudly and as sincerely as he could, but even he didn't think it sounded very genuine. When he was done he heard a quick, quiet discussion in the front seat. Then Smiling Boy made a phone call.

SAM ZUCKERMAN didn't know what to make of the phone call, but he'd believe anything right now. He grabbed the camera and ran out the storefront offices of the *Baymont Courier*, slowing just long enough to lock the door behind him.

There was nobody left in the office because all three reporters and both photographers were at the Poynzsa campus. Sam was just an intern, a sophomore in the journalism department at Baymont College, but he'd elected to join the overnight vigil just in case something major happened at the factory.

Something major had happened. More major than any of them had dreamed of. Sam had been left at the office to handle incoming calls while the paid staff covered the story.

Could the call he'd just received be for real?

The drop-off point was just two blocks away, and when Sam reached it and jogged around the corner he spotted an SUV speeding away. There, just as promised, were three squatting guys in plastic handcuffs lined up on the curb. Extra cuffs were used to secure their wrists to a sewer grate. Their windbreakers were black and had huge yellow letters on the back: FBI.

Sam Zuckerman started taking pictures.

"What the hell are you doing?" asked the one on the end, his face scarlet.

"What's it look like? These are gonna be great."

"We're FBI, asshole."

"That's not what I was told. I hear you're part of the bunch responsible for the explosions at the plant."

"We're not, kid, I swear!"

Zuckerman paused when it suddenly occurred to him that he wasn't a paid employee of the local paper, and the camera he was using was his private property and he wasn't obliged to give the *Baymont Courier* anything.

"Are you gonna call the FBI or not, asshole?"

Zuckerman grinned at the man with the red face as he thumbed the numbers on his mobile phone, got information, got connected, and heard the machine on the other end answer with, "You've reached the offices of Global Press Syndication."

When Zuckerman reached the photo desk and described who he was, where he was, and what the pictures were, the photo editor laughed.

"Yeah, I'll buy 'em, FBI or not."

"I'll e-mail them in twenty minutes," Zuckerman said.

"What the hell do you think you're doing?" the red-faced prisoner demanded, practically hopping up and down.

Zuckerman snapped another photo and said, "Earning next year's tuition."

Arlington, Virginia, U.S.A.

SENATOR JACKSON'S FINGERS pressed the remote control spasmodically, scanning the channels with increasing speed as if it would help him arrive finally at the news broadcast that was telling him what he wanted to hear.

He gave up on an ABC News feed and sent the remote crashing into the wall.

"Looks pretty bad to me," Maxie commented. "I mean, bad for them, which would be good for you. Us."

On the screen was the nighttime shot of the Poynzsa plant surrounded by emergency vehicles and hazy with smoke.

"Look at that! Look!"

The legend on the screen read *Twenty Feared Dead in Baymont.*

The phone rang and Jackson snatched it up, waving the guards out. It had better be Korl.

"It's Korl."

"What went wrong?"

"I haven't figured that out yet."

"You going to try to tell me that we still achieved our goals this time, Colonel? Because we didn't. That building is virtually intact and casualties are incidental. Did any of your charges go off as planned?"

"One did, Senator—"

"One!"

"Another detonated alongside the building and caused some damage. Another blew up when the ultralight crashed in the parking lot. The last three charges are being dismantled by bomb squads. They were never activated."

"How did this happen, Colonel? This is a huge failure."

"I realize that, Senator," Korl replied quickly. "I'm trying to find out what went wrong."

"What are your pilots saying?"

Korl paused before admitting, "So far none of the ultralights has returned."

"None?" For a moment the senator was too flabbergasted to be angry.

"None, Senator. Somebody knew more than they should have about our plans."

The words echoed in the chasms of the senator's brain. *Somebody knew.*

Nobody was supposed to know.

"Now what do we do, Senator?" Korl asked.

"What do you mean?"

"You may have a leak. Do you want to slow down and plug it before proceeding?"

"No. We're not slowing down for any reason. We can't afford to."

"Then may I make a suggestion?"

"What?"

"Accelerate. If we're not going to slow the timetable, then let's speed it up. If there is a leak, the information they provide will still be wrong."

"That's fine," the senator said. "The schedule can be altered, but not the target. The target can*not* be changed."

Korl rang off without telling the senator the specifics of the new timetable. That was wise, in case the bug was in his office.

The senator called in the bodyguards and ordered them to sweep the place for bugs, top to bottom, It was almost dawn before he finally dozed off in his chair with ABC News still covering the story. By then Jackson had his own name for the story: The Bungle in Baymont.

The next target had better not get bungled. It was the most important thus far, because the next target was bringing his message right to the general public.

It was about time the good citizens of the United States started listening to the voice of Truth.

Chandler, Indiana

ROSARIO BLANCANALES felt as if he'd slept fifteen minutes, tops. The cheap hotel clock radio said his nap had actually been almost a full half hour. He had a sinking feeling that was all he was going to get.

He was still barefoot and buckling his belt when he crossed through the door that adjoined the rooms in the old hotel. Lyons was talking on a headset and tapping the screen on the notepad computer that was now linked up with the rest of the electronics from the communications case.

Blancanales took a cup of coffee from Schwarz and peered into the screen. The mapping software showed the lower half of the State of Indiana, along with parts of adjoining states. Four white dots blinked at various points. One went out. A second later all three vanished.

Where each white dot had been was a small red numeral 2, and a dotted red line joined each 2 with a small red 1.

"You're on speaker and we're all here," Lyons said as he took off the headset.

"We think we've got another attack imminent," Barbara Price said. "Our phone call traces have begun moving together again."

"That's the display we're looking at?" Blancanales asked. "It looks…I don't know, simplistic."

"Because all we know are some very simple data points," Price said, sounding weary. "Bear and his people have been working nonstop to break the encryption, and they just can't get through it. When one of the phones makes a call, we know it. We know what phone they call if it's on the same satellite system, and we know where they are when they make it. That's all."

"These the same phones that got together in Baymont?" Schwarz asked.

"Yes. Then there was nothing until twenty minutes ago. The call you just witnessed shows them on the move, all heading the same way."

"Where to?" Lyons asked.

"The paths more or less intersect in Cincinnati."

"That's not too precise," Lyons said.

"I know. Able, you'll head for Cincinnati and we'll hope to have better intelligence when you get there."

"We're on our way," Lyons told her.

"Wait," Blancanales said.

Lyons stopped with his finger on the button and looked expectantly at Blancanales.

"Pol?" Price prodded.

"Barb, isn't the first Jackson Department Store in Cincinnati?"

"Oh. Maybe. Hold on." They heard the rustle of papers as the Stony Man mission Controller grabbed for a nearby file and scanned the hard copies. "Yes. That's the store that was expanded into the Heartland Mall."

"Oh, crap," Schwarz said under his breath. "If we're right—if it is Jackson behind all this mess—that makes a logical target."

"How so?" Lyons asked.

Price spoke up. "The Heartland Mall was constructed around the original Jackson Department Store. It was his central point of contention during his defamation lawsuit against the French retail conglomerate that bought the chain from him. He convinced a lot of people that the Heartland Mall was a symbol of the subjugation of Americans by foreigners."

"But it means he's raising the stakes," Lyons said. "He's going after the public."

"That's crossing a dangerous line," Price added. "Going after civilians in a factory is one thing. You could make some sort of an argument that they elected to work at the Poynzsa plant. But killing innocent civilians just because they're in a shopping mall will create public outrage."

"Barb's right," Lyons said. "If he's trying to build sympathy for the isolationist agenda he'd steer clear of murdering Sunday shoppers. He's not a stupid guy."

"Maybe going after the Heartland Mall isn't a stupid move if his goal isn't what we think it is," Blancanales suggested.

"He wants the U.S. to be more isolationist and less global—what else would his goal be?" Lyons protested. "That's the motive that led us to Jackson in the first place."

"I'm thinking about this from the point of view of Franklin Jackson," Blancanales explained. "He gets himself elected a senator on his campaign of isolationism. His slogan was something like 'America First, Global Economy Second.' He was kind of a joke. I remember him bragging about how he was going to strong-arm Congress into passing sweeping reforms to close the borders to immigration, businesses, anything and everything from outside our borders. But what really happens?"

"He's a laughingstock," Price said. "The Senate didn't put him on any important committees, let alone a committee relevant to his goals. They ignore him. The running joke on the Hill is that when Jackson stands up to talk it's time for lunch."

"So he's a complete washout as a senator, and his popularity plummets," Blancanales added. "His popularity ratings are at record-setting lows for a U.S. senator. Even Jackson has got to realize he's lost his credibility with the public by now."

Schwarz shook his head. "I think I see your point, but your point refutes your argument. If he creates a wave of isolationist sentiment, he rides it back up the popularity polls."

"Only if he's successful, but he will be if it becomes too expensive for any foreign entity to even consider doing business here. What do you think is going to happen to Poynzsa as a result of the attack last night?"

"They'll rebuild and make cars," Lyons said. "Even if the attack destroyed the complex, they probably would have done so."

Blancanales nodded. "Now, what do you think will happen to Poynzsa if a series of attacks against a whole spectrum of foreign businesses makes any sort of operations in the U.S. or transport to the U.S. uninsurable?"

Lyons and Schwarz thought about it. The phone speaker was silent.

"Look at the oil companies and the transport companies that lease them the oil tankers," Blancanales pointed out. "Once it's clear that the common denominator in all the attacks was the U.S., the insurance premiums for U.S.-bound cargoes will double or triple or worse, and that makes transporting oil to the U.S. too expensive. The same goes for the container ships. It'll be unprofitable to use cheap Southeast Asian labor to make your products because the cost benefits can't outweigh the insurance on the shipping fees."

Schwarz blinked. "Pol, you're talking about changing a business bureaucracy. They move slower than governments."

"Not when they're hemorrhaging dollars," said Price. "Poynzsa's board already announced it's pulling out of the U.S. They estimate that the return on their U.S. investment just went from three years to seven, and the entire corporation will get dragged into bankruptcy before then. They're writing off the entire facility."

"Some U.S. companies are going to get a good bargain on a like-new car factory," Lyons muttered. "If the Heartland Mall is the next target, we shouldn't be wasting our time on a road trip."

"I don't think so, either," Price said. "I'll have transport for you in thirty minutes. And then I've got to figure out how to break the bad news to the politicians."

"Let Hal handle the politicians," Lyons suggested.

"Hal is who I'm talking about."

BARBARA PRICE WAS wrong. Even while she was briefing Hal Brognola on the phone she could tell from his terse reactions that she had underestimated him this time. He had been doubting the assumptions that Stony Man Farm was making, but so far Stony Man had made no false steps. He was convinced.

"Able is en route by air," Price said. "We're flying in the blacksuits. The Heartland Mall opens its doors in ten minutes, and our tracking shows the phone signals converging less than two miles away. If they're going for maximum casualties, they'll strike about twelve-thirty."

"You know I've got to go to the Man with this," the big Fed said. "Send me any visual aids you've got. Anything that looks like evidence. This is gonna be a hard sell."

CHAPTER SIXTEEN

The White House, Washington, D.C.

The Man just sat there. He'd trained himself during his first campaigns to stop and think very deliberately when he stumbled across a question or a situation that required political finesse, but this time he was truly taken aback.

He leaned forward, his elbows on the desk. "*Senator* Franklin Jackson?"

"We think so."

"You knew this yesterday?"

"We had our suspicions yesterday, but it seemed unlikely. However, the details are beginning to line up."

"What evidence do you have?"

"No evidence that would indict the man in the courts. It's all circumstantial."

"So why are you coming in here telling me that a U.S. senator is guilty of terrorism?"

Brognola looked at him and said calmly, "Because I believe he is. My people believe he is—"

"But you've got no proof!"

The head of the Sensitive Operations Group said nothing for a moment, and that was long enough for the President to think about what he had just said.

"I've always been up front with you, Mr. President. I didn't think this was a good time to start holding back."

"Of course," the Man said with an awkward offhand wave.

"And the nature of the SOG is to take action when and where the other agencies can't. Which means we sometimes have to act on unproved charges, without what the courts would call probable cause. Like now."

"Yes!" the Man said. "I know, Hal. Were you practicing this speech on the way over?"

"Yes."

The President gave a wry grin. He and Brognola didn't exactly see eye to eye on every issue, but he knew the SOG liaison was smart, even brilliant. Brognola clearly had had initiative enough to know what reaction he would get to his revelation.

"I can't believe these charges," he said, shaking his head. "Yes, he's a jerk, and he's arrogant, but he is a United States senator."

"We've both known unscrupulous people who've taken a position of power in the federal government," Brognola said, and went on before the President could protest. "If you think about it, sir, it isn't too unlikely for a man like this to get where he is today. He didn't need the finesse of a long-term politician, just a skilled speech writer and an enthusiasm for a cause *célèbre*. Jackson also had the advantage of fortuitous timing."

"Is that your profile on Jackson?" The President nodded at the document in Brognola's hand. Wordlessly the ten sheets of stapled paper were handed across the Oval Office desk.

His eyes skimmed the contents, getting past the introductory sections of the report. Nothing new in the summary of Jackson's career, but there were details on his business dealings that the President wasn't aware of.

In the mid 1970s Franklin Jackson bought controlling interest in a failing five-and-dime store in a small Ohio town outside what was the Cincinnati city limits. He was just thirty, and by forty he had turned the store into a chain of discount department stores that spread throughout the Midwest. Jackson Department Stores had a hard time finding their niche. The other mass-merchandise stores had lower prices. The more high-end department stores in the shopping malls attracted more foot traffic. Jackson had had a tough time finding the funding he'd needed for his aggressive expansion efforts because nobody believed his business model would succeed.

Somehow, the chain did grow to two hundred stores before hitting the wall in 1990, when the serious impact of the mass merchandisers' aggressive pricing began to take its toll. Jackson copied their buying strategies but refused to purchase foreign-made products if any U.S. alternative existed.

Jackson promoted this philosophy in his advertising. People found the philosophy commendable, but not enough to pay a premium for his products. His stores couldn't overcome the pull of the mass merchandisers. Regional price wars began to drive Jackson outlets out of business. When he joined the price wars he lost so much money the store became insolvent and unsalvageable, but when he kept out of the price wars he was undersold dramatically, his foot traffic plummeted and his cash flow dried up.

His stores were driven out of one region after another.

He sued his competitors for violating tariffs, for unfair trade practices and for nonstandard accounting procedures. His advertisements proclaimed that the Jackson Department

Stores was the last American retailer. He told the public that spending their dollars elsewhere was the same as taking food away from the children of unemployed U.S. citizens. Eventually the advertising became too slanderous to be aired or published.

He became known as One-A-Week Jackson, because, like clockwork, he was forced to close about one store every week of the year. His two hundred stores had shrunk to half that number before he finally gave up in disgust. During a grim meeting with his financial officers, he abruptly stood and walked out, never to return to the corporate headquarters. He sold the chain in a deal that he brokered over the phone that evening, keeping only a tiny break-even chain of specialty stores selling American-made handicrafts.

The business world saw it as grand entertainment, and it wasn't over yet. The investment group that bought the chain immediately changed its buying practices to be more competitive, which meant buying imports if they were cheaper than U.S.-made goods. To his horror, Jackson learned that seventy percent of the investment firm he sold out to was owned by a French retail corporation. To add to the debacle, he learned he had signed away the rights to his name for twenty-five years, unconditionally.

The reinvigorated chain opened several new stores before the investment group began development of the Heartland Mall, which would be anchored by a big new flagship store that would be built over and around the little five-and-dime store that had been the very first Jackson Department Store. It was marketed as a tribute to the American spirit, despite the fact that half of what it sold was from outside the U.S.: television sets made in Maquiladoras just over the Mexican border; clothing from sweatshops in Bangladesh, India and Pakistan; a little of everything from China. The investors and management of the mall were all French, tied to the firm that now owned Jackson Department Stores.

It was the last straw. Franklin Jackson sued for his name to be removed from any store that sold foreign-made goods. Legal bills ate up two of the ten million dollars he had been paid for his share of the chain. Another million went into an advertising campaign to promote his cause. Another half million had to be paid back to the investment group after the court not only ruled against him but ordered him to compensate the firm's legal fees and pay slander damages.

The boisterous, outspoken, self-promoting Franklin Jackson went silent. He paid the court-ordered fines and damages and became invisible—for a few short months.

His business career was over, but his political career began. He hired a consulting firm to make a geopolitical survey of the United States and when he found the state where there was a large enough population niche sharing his ideals, he quietly changed his residence, trained himself in speech-making and out of nowhere announced himself as a candidate in the next senatorial race. The political parties were stunned by his appearance and by his aggressive and expensive campaign. His message targeted the niche of frustrated people of either party who saw the U.S. spreading herself too thin around the world.

"It is right for the U.S. to spend your tax dollars to defend you, but is it right to spend your taxes to prop up a government that can't support itself?" he said during his one debate appearance in answer to a question about environmental policy. "What good does that do you?

"Why are we subsidizing the people of the Third World when you can't get a job in America today?" he exhorted a group of laid-off steel workers.

"We spent ten billion dollars to support human rights efforts in Asia and then we cut off your welfare support!" he exclaimed to a gathering at an inner city storefront church.

His posters shouted his message, developed and market-tested by the political marketing firm hired for his campaign: "America First, Global Economy Second." Eventually the message was abbreviated to simply "America First."

Then Jackson gave an especially well-received speech at a gathering of more than a thousand airline workers whose jobs were threatened. "I don't pledge my allegiance to one world," he said in his practiced, resonate speaking voice. "I pledge to one nation, and I will serve one nation!"

The airline workers began chanting without further inducement. "One nation! One nation!"

Jackson never finished that speech. Nothing more needed to be said. Within twenty-four hours every campaign poster, every commercial, every radio spot had been replaced to feature the new credo of the Jackson campaign.

One Nation.

Even when his opponents responded with a biting satirical campaign called One Issue, Jackson was unfazed and his popularity grew, playing on the fears of people who wanted America for Americans. When the polls showed that his followers were still not strong enough to win him the election, his consultant team reinvented Jackson for more broad-based support. The message was this: the U.S. can't afford to be the world's police station and soup kitchen, and Franklin Jackson will help moderate the expansionist attitude in congress. The "America First" slogan reappeared.

Jackson agreed to this shift in the campaign, but only reluctantly. It compromised his message, but the results couldn't be argued with. His popularity squeaked him ahead of his opponent, and Franklin Jackson was elected to the U.S. Senate in one of the closest elections in the history of the state. His opponent's election-night calls for a recount were quietly stifled by the governor, who had just installed millions of dollars of new election equipment statewide and would permit no one to cast doubt on its accuracy.

When he was declared winner, when he knew it was official, Franklin Jackson fired his marketing team and made an acceptance speech that made headlines. All the moderating views he had given lip service during the campaign were forgotten as he declared his intent to ramrod through Congress a series of bills designed to withdraw the United States from the world economy, to insulate her people from the destructive influence of foreign trade, to prohibit foreign ownership of U.S. real estate or businesses, and to put severe restrictions on the total dollars the U.S. government was permitted to spend for any nonmilitary reason outside the U.S.

His electorate was stunned. Jackson shrugged it off and went to Washington.

On his first day as a sitting senator, Jackson struggled to have himself heard. He was never given the floor. By the end of the first week he was in such a fury he shouted down a senator who had the floor and launched into a speech that only ended when he was physically removed from the Senate.

When allowed to return, he was finally handed his opportunity to speak, only to find himself virtually alone as most of the senators left their seats. It became well known that the lunch hour started whenever Senator Jackson had something to say. He became the Senate laughingstock, and he knew it.

Jackson had learned a hard lesson. He began to play ball, making vote trades for unimportant committee seats, but these gains were so marginal that even he knew he would never foster real support for his One Nation suite of bills, let alone get a vote.

He was the ultimate one-issue candidate, and his issue was of no interest to anyone else on Capitol Hill. His constituency felt betrayed and his popularity plummeted until only a small niche of isolationists remained loyal, and even they were migrating to new causes.

THE PRESIDENT of the United States sat back in his chair, staring at the ceiling, the famous forehead wrinkled in thought. The Stony Man profile of Senator Franklin Jackson was an eye-opener.

"You've given me a new perspective on the man," he admitted to Brognola, who was sitting stiffly in a wing chair.

"I felt the same way when I read it, Mr. President," Brognola said. "I have to admit I had severe misgivings when my people named him as a prime suspect. Jackson is a textbook example of how someone with extreme views can reach a high level of power, if he has the funds, the charisma and impeccable timing."

The President sat forward suddenly, pushing the profile back to Brognola. "You've convinced me he has motive, but I still don't believe he's implicated here. You've said yourself you've got only circumstantial evidence. I want better than that before we go after him officially."

"Of course. But what I want from you now is widespread protection for the Heartland Mall." Brognola glanced at his watch. "It opened for business eighteen minutes ago. We need a heavy security presence at least."

"Hal, the only reason you assume this is the Cincinnati target is because of the connection to Jackson. Well, I don't buy the connection, so I can't believe there's about to be an attack on the Heartland Mall."

"There's going to be an attack somewhere in the city," Brognola protested.

"You've got a direct link to the director of Homeland Security—use it."

"We have," Brognola said with forced patience. "But a citywide alert doesn't help mall-walkers caught in the cross fire when the bullets start flying."

"I'm not telling you to keep your people out, Hal. I'm just saying it is premature to panic the public."

"Premature," Brognola repeated. Then he stood, mumbled his goodbyes and headed for the door.

When the door closed behind him, and he was alone in the Oval Office, the President let out a long breath. It wasn't the first time he'd been forced to make a decision like this one, weighing the lives of his people against less tangible considerations.

Every time it knotted his stomach.

God, he hoped he wasn't wrong this time.

CHAPTER SEVENTEEN

"They don't deserve this," Rosario Blancanales said.

"Who?" Carl Lyons asked.

"Any of them."

The security monitoring room at the Heartland Mall was a two-man closet with five men in it. Blancanales was watching the throngs of Sunday shoppers in the six monochrome displays, showing video feeds from twenty-four cameras placed throughout the public areas of the indoor mall. These were Americans, as typical as you could get. All races and colors. Rich and poor shopped here. None of them deserved to be the targets of terrorism. They didn't deserve to have to even worry that they might be.

"What are our chances of this happening?" the nervous mall manager asked in a heavily accented English. He was a part of the management team brought to the United States by the French company that owned Jackson Department Stores and had funded the Heartland Mall. He thought he was dealing with U.S. Justice Department security advisers. In the interest of covering his own derriere, he was more than happy to surrender responsibility for mall security to a U.S. government agency if crisis loomed.

"Who knows?" Lyons asked. "Leave it to us, would you? We'll let you know if we see anything suspicious."

The mall manager and his head of security left the three members of Able Team in the tiny office, and Gadgets Schwarz immediately began plugging in a series of cables from the video system. The cables went into the communications suitcase where they were routed into the notepad PC and miniature wireless modems. The mall's security network had been designed to accommodate only a single video stream, but in seconds Stony Man Farm was receiving output from all six monitors in real time.

"I feel like an asshole," Lyons said.

Schwarz and Blancanales both knew he was talking about the lie he'd been forced to tell the mall manager and security chief.

"Yeah," Schwarz agreed as he opened the main panel with four quick spins of a screwdriver and disconnected controls. "But we're pushing our luck as it is by having this much contact with them. We explain ourselves any more, and there'll be so much panic it'll reach the White House."

"Then we're SOL and we're not doing anybody any good," Blancanales declared.

"I don't know if I feel all that helpful right now," Lyons grumbled.

"All your feeds are reaching us," Aaron Kurtzman reported through their headsets. "I'm testing my control." The images on the screens had been switching from one camera to another at eight-second intervals, but now they started cycling randomly as Kurtzman used his hacked commands to take over the system. "Everything looks okay at my end," Kurtzman said after a minute or so. "I'm recording everything."

"Where's our backup?"

"Stony One here," Barbara Price came in. "The blacksuits are an hour out."

They stared at the screens, watching them cycle rapid-fire. It was too fast for them to get a good look, but at the Farm a host of personnel had been recruited to watch the twenty-four separate video feeds that were being displayed. They could monitor every part of the mall better than Heartland Mall security ever dreamed of doing.

"What now?" Schwarz asked.

Lyons shrugged. "Let's mall-walk."

They had nothing to go on. There was a heightened security alert in the city, unbeknownst to the citizens of Cincinnati, and that made another attempt at penetration by air unlikely. But anybody could walk in with any other kind of portable weaponry inside a shopping bag. The three members of Able Team couldn't even cover the four sprawling wings of the facility, let alone the dozens of entrances.

Dressed in civilian clothing and carrying their hardware in sports bags, they left the long, plain hallway to the business offices at the far end of one wing and headed for the central court, where a dancing fountain and a collection of fast-food counters brought in the lunchtime crowd.

Lyons felt a growing dread as they looked over the food court. There had to be a couple thousand people just within his line of sight, maybe five or ten times that many in the entire mall. How could the three of them hope to do any good if an attack started—any attack? Even when the blacksuits arrived, they would be only a scattering of armed men among the throngs.

"Let's just make an anonymous call to the police and clear this place out on our own," Schwarz said. "I'm not kidding, either, Ironman. What are we supposed to do if the shit hits?"

"I don't know," Lyons responded in a low voice, and he sounded uncertain.

Blancanales and Schwarz looked at him. Lyons was never uncertain.

The Able Team commander grabbed at the wireless phone, which had an open channel to the Farm.

"Able One here. Stony, we have *got* to come up with something better. If we're right about this being the target, then this place is a holocaust waiting to happen."

Price started to say something, but was interrupted.

"Stony Two here," Kurtzman said. "I'm patching you in, Barb. We're monitoring new phone activity. Korl's men are on-site. Getting more signals now. They're inside the mall. They're popping up all over the place."

"I'm seeing it, Bear," Price said.

"Able One here," Lyons said. "We've got no visual—where are they?"

"Able One," she said, "they're everywhere."

CHAPTER EIGHTEEN

The old man in a wheelchair had been sleeping while his daughter and granddaughter ate ice-cream cones, but his head jerked up when he heard the sound.

He stared at nothing until he noticed the three members of Able Team. They had barely heard the rattle over the ambient hubbub of the mall and, aside from the old man, they were the only ones who reacted to it.

A second rattle came as Able Team discarded the sports bags and Lyons met the gaze of the old man, thirty feet away from him.

"Fire alarm!" Lyons shouted.

The old man's daughter started to scream when she saw the guns and more screams sprouted spontaneously around the commandos, but the old man wheeled himself through the crowds and grabbed at the closest red wall switch. As Able Team bolted back the way they had come, the fire alarm whooped. The people ahead of them on the upper level walkways froze at the sound, then began heading for exits, only to panic when they found themselves in the path of three men with machine guns.

The mall manager staggered out of the utility hall into the public areas, his scalp streaming blood onto his face and a tiny, ugly black hole in his red-soaked shirt, just to the side of his clinging tie. His eyes were wild, surprised, but when he recognized the Able Team warriors, Lyons saw only accusation. The man said something in wheezing French, then a rattle of fresh gunfire reached out from within the utility hall and stitched him across the back, dropping him on his face.

The sound of screaming people was growing distant when Lyons stepped into the utility hallway and found himself face-to-face with a man in a U.S. Army uniform, chewing hard on a wad of gum and peering into the magazine of his micro-Uzi submachine gun. It was a stupid time to check his rounds, but his reaction to Lyons was swift and professional. He slapped the magazine into the underside of the SMG without hesitation, and cried out a name as he turned the micro-Uzi on Lyons.

The Able Team leader sneered. He hated this gum-chewing, smart-ass, grinning son of a bitch. The Atchisson Assault 12 shotgun roared before the SMG made a peep, and the buckshot slammed into the phony in the soldier's uniform like a wall of flying glass, ripping him up and dropping what was left. Lyons aimed the Colt Python in his left hand at the end of the hall, and when the next gunner ran into view the big handgun bucked once, twice, and the second gunner went down as he triggered his stubby machine gun into the ceiling panels.

"Stony Two here—we just lost our video feed, Able One," Kurtzman radioed as Lyons dragged on a small headset. Blancanales and Schwarz were close behind him when he burst into the mall administrative center and unloaded a buckshot round at the gunner taking cover behind a steel desk. The close-range shot in the small office flayed the gunner's scalp to the bone and transformed the stacks of paperwork into a cloud of confetti.

The glass door to the security cubicle went from transparent to opaque. Somebody inside had tried to clear them out with a shot through the glass, only to discover it was bullet-resistant. Lyons almost laughed with bitter humor. His sight was hampered by the persistent image of the dying mall manager, who had accused him with a glance as he died. Lyons had lied to him, betrayed him.

Reason told Lyons he hadn't betrayed the man, that he had done what he could, but that didn't make the image go away. He knew he'd be carrying it around with him for a long, long time.

And that made him very angry.

He crossed the room in two leaps. The door to the security room nudged open an inch and he grabbed the bottom of it with his foot, pulled it wide and triggered the Colt Python into the belly of the gunner inside, whose instant of profound shock died with him. Lyons slammed the door shut again and triggered the Python at the floor, obliterating the scalped gunner before he managed to get his shaky hands to trigger his SMG.

Schwarz wanted to say something smart such as, "Why do we even bother coming along if you're going to do all the work." But he knew when to keep his mouth shut.

Lyons faced him, spattered in gore from the bloody blowback of the intimately close-range kill shots.

"Gadgets," he said through teeth that were locked together, "fix it."

Hermann Schwarz had seen more than his share of blood in his lifetime, but he paused when he opened the opaque door to the security room.

"Jesus."

"Problem?" Lyons asked.

"No, other than I gotta wade through an eviscerated human being to get at the control panel," Schwarz complained silently.

The gunners had simply powered down the security system, and Schwarz brought it back to life by throwing the circuit breakers. The monitors flickered, then showed him six different views of the interior of the Heartland Mall.

Schwarz said it again. "Jesus."

"Good work, Able, we're getting video," Kurtzman radioed. "You seeing this, Barb?"

"I've got guns in all wings," Schwarz said. "Tell me I'm wrong, Stony. All levels. The courtyard. Everyplace."

"Affirmative, Able Three," Kurtzman said. "We're counting guns now, but it looks like they've covered every entrance except north wing side entrances and that's a madhouse."

Schwarz watched the monitor switch to the north entrances, where hundreds of people were hurrying through the doors in a steady stream.

"They're letting the public escape?" Blancanales asked.

Price came on the line abruptly. "We can't tell if it's part of the plan or accidental. The blacksuits are still ten minutes away. I've got every kind of law enforcement coming."

"We're headed to the north wing, Stony," Lyons said. "We'll do what we can to protect the civilians."

THEY EXITED the utility corridor to find the nearby side exit being guarded by an imitation soldier. The uniforms were again U.S. Army and the weapons were M-16s. Four bodies littered the floor in front of them. Blancanales saw them first, and all it took was a glance to show him these were civilians.

Innocent people. They were dead because they happened to be there.

The guards weren't expecting to face armed resistance, but their reaction time was uncompromised. Blancanales squeezed a pair of 3-round bursts from the MP-5 and took down the first one as he triggered the assault rifle. Lyons's combat shotgun swept the second gunner off his feet, depositing him in a heap under the torrent of glass raining from the decimated row of glass doors.

They jogged down the short public hall to the main walkway of the upper level, which was abandoned except for a pair of bodies sprawled in front of the wide doors of the department store that anchored the wing. The store itself was eerily quiet.

"Here's one," said a voice from below. Schwarz was the first to reach the rail and observed a pair of gunners in Army fatigues. The one with a list waved at a storefront. His companion lobbed a hand grenade into the small gift shop, then walked on unhurriedly. When the five-count ended, the shop burst apart in fire and shattered glass.

Lyons ordered Schwarz to race ahead as the pair disappeared from their line of sight, and he staged himself to have an unobstructed view of the terrorists. He held back to cover the rear, while Blancanales kept an eye out for more of Colonel Korl's men.

Schwarz heard the metallic roll of another grenade and then a shriek that came just before the blast. A civilian. Hiding in the store. When the rain of glass ended, Schwarz heard the chuckle of the mercenaries.

"Stupid bitch," one of them said, still laughing as he peered at his list, then looked up at the earring store in front of him. "Do this one."

"Consider it done," said his partner, who already had the

grenade pulled out of his shoulder pack when Schwarz triggered the MP-5. The 3-round burst took him in the chest, sending him staggering several paces before he hit a knee-high brick planter and fell into it, crushing the greenery. He was unbloodied, and with a curse Schwarz knew he wore armor. The man scrambled back to his feet, grimacing in pain, and Schwarz fired again before his target could escape. This time the rounds chopped his hand off at the wrist and the grenade dropped at his feet. He was overcome with shock and spent the last five seconds of his life staring at the bloodied stump with a low moan rising from his guts.

The grenade blast turned him to a corpse and deposited his remains atop the counter of a kiosk that had been selling giant pretzels. His sack of grenades failed to detonate and clattered to the ground.

His companion with the list of targets had vanished, and Schwarz was about to make a run down the nearby up escalator to take him out and to secure the bag of explosives.

Then he heard Blancanales's urgent command in his headset. "Down, Gadgets!"

Schwarz dropped into a crouch and looked for Blancanales, finding him standing inside the entrance of a jeans store, pointing in the direction of the courtyard that was the hub of the mall.

Schwarz saw them now—another pair of mercenaries in Army fatigues coming toward them at a quick walk. One of them was lobbing a round object into one of the storefronts, then moving away from it just before it blew.

"I thought I just took out that guy," Schwarz said to himself. Then he hissed into the radio, "Able Three here. I've got them."

"Hold a minute, Able Three," Lyons replied. Schwarz glanced back but couldn't spot the Able Team commander. Why exactly did he need to hold up?

"Hey!" shouted a distant voice, attracting the attention of the pair on the upper level. They went to the rail and looked down at a man shouting below.

"—shot his hand off and he blew himself up!" Schwarz heard the distant voice explaining. It was the fish that got away.

"Now," Lyons said, and simultaneously he and Blancanales stepped into the open while Schwarz stood abruptly and triggered a long, full-auto burst from the submachine gun. Blancanales unleashed his own extended stream of fire. The pair was caught in the open, helpless, and their bodies vibrated under the murderous barrage before collapsing to the floor.

Schwarz raced to the rail and sighted for the mercenary on the lower level, but the man had escaped a second time.

"His luck's gonna run out," Schwarz declared.

"Or ours," Blancanales said, and pointed back the way they had come. There were figures in fatigues emerging from the silent entrance of the abandoned department store that anchored this wing of the mall.

The leader was staring at his wristwatch and shouting, "Let's move. Let's move."

There was a shout of alarm when one of his men spotted the Able Team reception committee. Before the leader knew what had hit him, a barrage of machine-gun fire and shotgun blasts slammed into his group, bloodying most of them and killing three in a heartbeat.

Schwarz saw the leader drop and flatten against the low glass wall; the instant he knew he hadn't been wounded he went for his watch again.

"Twelve seconds!" shouted the leader as he launched himself off the floor, only to be sent reeling when Schwarz triggered a blast that emptied his magazine. The leader moaned in agony over splintered ribs.

"Eight seconds," Schwarz said, his thoughts suddenly dominated by the inexorable countdown.

"They're blowing the store!" Blancanales declared.

Schwarz nodded. "Five," he said as Lyons appeared at his shoulder and triggered a pair of quick shotgun blasts that tore into the group of cowering mercenary survivors. One of them caught a face full of buckshot and cried out. Only one of them had the guts to force himself through the hail of shotgun fire into the cover of one of the stores, but the second blast ripped into the flesh of his legs and he toppled, his lower torso still exposed in the open walkway of the south wing.

By then Lyons had followed Blancanales and Schwarz in a frantic dash down the walkway. The eruption of yellow light seared his peripheral vision just before he careened around the corner into the east wing, then the walkway jolted underfoot, flinging him up, and he crashed down heavily. There was a blast of searing hot air and a wall of sound that pummeled him bodily before it passed over and was gone.

Lyons pushed himself to his feet, watching the almost-ethereal pillows of burning vapor that bulged and bounced against the hundred-foot ceilings over the hub of the mall before they silently burned out.

Blancanales and Schwarz were likewise battered but unwounded. They'd taken less of the blast than Lyons had.

"Able One here," he said into the headset. "You reading me, Stony?"

"Stony One here," Price replied. "We saw it happen, Able."

"Tell me the store was empty."

"I think mostly empty," Price said. "We didn't have access to the surveillance inside the store, but there are a lot of people in the parking lot. Most or all of the shoppers got out."

"Able Three here," Schwarz said. "Stony, did you happen to see what their two-man teams were doing to the smaller stores? What the hell was that all about?"

"We witnessed it happening in all but the north wing," Price said.

"They were the stores with foreign owners or investors," Blancanales said.

"That's our guess."

"What about the department store that just went up?" Lyons asked.

"Toronto-based retail chain," Price said. "I guess even North Americans are too un-American for the senator."

"Hold, Stony."

There were voices on the lower level, from several directions. Lyons crept through the carpet of broken glass to peer down on the lower level, finding two groups of gunners in Army fatigues assembling in the courtyard below.

"Where is White Team?" one of them demanded. He was a tall, scrawny blond-haired man who was clearly in command. "Why isn't White Team here?"

"Hey, Buck!" a lone figure cried, rushing to join them. "White Team got ambushed—I'm pretty sure they bought it when the store blew."

"Ambushed by who?"

"That's the one that got away," Schwarz whispered at Lyons's shoulder.

"I don't know, Buck. First they went after me and Hill, and Hill got wasted and I started running. And then I was trying to warn the upper-level guys and they got gunned down right in front of me, and I thought they were hot on my ass, and then I heard them gunning back and forth with White Team up top until the store blew."

"Shit! They cops or what?"

"Not cops. They had SMGs, MP-5s, and that means special commandos or something."

There was a sudden chorus of malcontent among the killers in soldier garb, but they shut up when Buck ordered them to.

"It doesn't matter who they were, they must have bought it with White Team when the store blew. And it doesn't change our plans. Let's go do what we need to do, and we'll be home free in fifteen minutes."

Buck marched into the west wing without a backward glance, and his twenty-odd mercenaries followed quickly behind him.

"Stony, where are the blacksuits?" Lyons asked impatiently when they were out of earshot.

"Diverted to a landing on top of the north wing, to avoid the west wing, which is the Jackson Department Store. It's probably going to blow at any second."

"I don't think so," Lyons said. "That's where the colonel's mercenaries are headed. It figures into their escape."

"Stony, we saw yesterday how much these guys like to make distractions work for them," Schwarz said. "I'm betting they'll make a run for freedom at the moment of the blast,"

"Not if I can help it," Price shot back.

CHAPTER NINETEEN

The SWAT commander stopped and stared into the sky.

Who had called in the special ops and how had they gotten here this quick? It was definitely not a civilian or law-enforcement team arriving. The Chinook MH-47E, maneuvering quickly into a hover twenty feet over the earth, was the Special Forces variant of the big Boeing twin-rotor helicopter, equipped with a long list of avionics and defense electronics.

How did the special ops manage to arrive on the scene within a quarter hour of the first alarms?

Then he knew. The Feds had known this was coming.

When the special ops team began rappelling out of the hovering Chinook, so quickly and smoothly they made it look easy, the SWAT commander could see they were equipped with electronics and field gear. These were like pictures he saw in a *Time* magazine "Soldier of the Future" article. His SWAT team was going in naked compared to these guys.

"Commander."

The SWAT commander was a skilled leader, but he couldn't have ignored that voice if he tried. The man striding up to him had an air of authority that you could almost taste. It was like being in a phone booth with MacArthur.

"Yes, sir?"

"Pull your team out of there soonest," said the man in the slate-gray uniform and headset. "Then use them and all available law enforcement to get these people back."

The SWAT commander looked at the crowd of onlookers, fully five hundred yards from the structure and standing on the other side of the drive that ringed the mall.

"We tried. Surely they're not in danger that far—"

"We have no idea how much explosives are inside, but it might be enough to flatten a square quarter mile and send fragments in every direction. You know for a fact there won't be enough kinetic energy to wipe out all those civilians? You want the news to report that this city allowed hundreds of its people to get pummeled to death by flying debris?"

"No, sir."

"Do it, Commander."

Before the Stony Man Farm blacksuit commander turned away, the SWAT team leader was barking orders into his radio. The Chinook freed itself of the last of the blacksuits and their equipment, then ascended rapidly, putting distance between itself and the banal-looking Jackson Department Store.

Without need for further orders, the blacksuits took their positions behind abandoned cars in the parking lot, then waited for the signal.

The blacksuit commander asked for roll, and in fifteen seconds received check-ins from every individual, as well as the blacksuit pilots of the Chinook. They were ready.

"Let's put on a show," the blacksuit commander ordered. "In ten, nine, eight…"

WHEN THE HUGE helicopter began disgorging warriors, Jerome Buckley couldn't quite believe what he was seeing.

"How did they get here so fast?" he demanded. "It hasn't been fifteen minutes!"

"Shut up, Buck." Jam Shore, the commander, had a swiftness and a strength that didn't seem possible in a stick-figure of a man. He stared out the glass doors wordlessly, trying to think.

"They knew we were coming here, man. Those are special ops or something. They wouldn't have called in that kind of muscle without knowing something was happening."

Shore said nothing.

"We got a serious leak in the pipes, man, unless you got some other excuse for all the trouble we've run into here," Buckley moaned. "Either that or we got set up."

"Shut up, Buck!" Shore gritted, squinting through the glare on the dirty glass doors. "What are they doing now?"

There was an electric fizzing sound and then the shriek of a light-and-noise grenade going off in the middle of the hundred yards of no-man's land between the special ops team and the exterior of the department store. It was followed instantly by the burst of several fiery high-explosive rounds placed with precision fifty yards apart, then bursts of automatic rifle fire filling the gaps. Chunks and chips of asphalt and concrete, along with ricocheted rounds, pocked into the storefront and cracked against the glass.

Then the window-mounted machine gun on the port side of the Chinook came briefly to life, peppering the asphalt in a hundred-yard trail of small craters before falling silent. All the weapons were quiet. Not a single round had hit the doors directly.

"What was that for?" Buckley demanded.

"For show," Shore snapped. "They wanted to convince us not to leave the store via this exit." He nodded at the nearby Employees Only door, which led into the inventory storage area and the loading dock. Their escape vehicle was staged there—an armored panel truck. They had intended to send a fake radio message saying the van was full of escaping hostages. Then, as they pulled away from the building, they would blow the Jackson Department Store to kingdom come and speed off. There was a hidden garage nearby. In rehearsals it had taken them just twenty-eight seconds to park the truck, open the rear, pull out the ramps and drive away in a Ford Econoliner van that was inside the panel truck.

Buckley looked at Shore, then at the silent handful of mercenaries, with hollow eyes. "Oh, man. Oh, man. How'd they know our plan, Jam? Did Korl fuck us over or what?"

"We'll ask him later," Shore said. "We'll have to go out the back way and delay the first charge. We might still be able to use it for a distraction."

Shore led his agitated group back the way they had come, through the lower level of the department store.

It wasn't supposed to be like this. Not today's action. Not his life. He wasn't supposed to be running scared through Women's Fashions. Shore suddenly felt embarrassed and stupid to be where he was.

"We got double-crossed," Buckley was moaning. "Korl screwed us."

Shore didn't tell him to shut up again. He was beginning to think Buck was right. Shore had been a fool to go along with this scheme, no matter how well Korl planned it.

Yeah, it was too well-planned. Korl was no fool. This whole thing could go to hell and there wouldn't be a scrap of evidence to incriminate Warren Korl, or whoever it was Korl was working for.

Shore made two decisions. First, he'd fight like hell to get out of here because it would be a humiliation to die in a shopping mall. It would be the kind of thing the others, his kind of people, would laugh about, and that was unthinkable.

Decision two: if Shore went down, here and now, he'd find a way to implicate Colonel Korl. Give credit where the credit was due.

"THEY'RE COMING," Blancanales reported, squinting into the field glasses, their low-light capabilities giving him a crystal-clear, high-contrast perspective even with the mall lights dead. "There's a pair on the top level, hanging around the front of Jackson's."

The Able Team commando was using a concrete planter as cover. The thing was bigger than a hot tub and filled with soil. It had to weight half a ton and he couldn't have asked for better cover, with an unobstructed view of the Jackson Department Store top-level entrance and, through the glass rail, a good view of the lower-level entrance.

"We've got five, six of them down here," Lyons radioed from below. "Looks like they're watching for signs of trouble."

"Got a plan, Ironman?" Blancanales asked.

"Stop the bad guys and prevent a hundred million dollars in property damage."

"That's more of a goal than a strategy," Schwarz said conversationally. Four minutes of waiting had him edgy, and now they were just standing here watching the mercenaries move closer. Blancanales knew Schwarz would be ready to do something.

"Just keep them in the store," Lyons said.

Blancanales raised himself, threading the business end of the MP-5 through the decorative greenery. One of them was the tall, skinny blonde, the one called Shore. Number two was good old Buck, the one who had twice escaped Able Team.

Schwarz would really appreciate it if Blancanales left Buck for him, but that wasn't in the cards. When the pair abruptly bolted out the front of the Jackson Department Store they headed for the nearest cover they could find, and it was Blancanales's concrete planter just fifteen yards away. The Able Team commando stood and fired a burst that stitched Buck across the ribs and dropped his corpse hard on its face, while his M-16 scraped across the floor as if thrown.

Blancanales could have sworn he couldn't miss Shore, but the man reacted with a cheetah's on-the-run agility, virtually ducking the stream of bullets that came. The man made an erratic dodging pattern, dived and leaped back to his feet, then rolled into the entrance of the store and was behind the wall.

At that instant the battle erupted downstairs. Blancanales leaned over the rail and triggered a long blast into the line of mercenaries engaging Lyons and Schwarz. Three dropped before Blancanales spotted movement on his own level and cursed as he hit the deck, pulling to the side as he fell. He should have expected a lightning-fast reaction from Shore. The man was some sort of a gymnastic wonder.

The fraction of a second it took Blancanales to get behind the planter was a fraction too long, and there was a burning sensation in his scalp. He was jolted by an electric shock that numbed him instantly, so he hit the ground hard.

He shook off the blow and propelled himself angrily away from the floor, leaping to clear the end of the planter. He jammed the muzzle of the MP-5 through the narrow gap between the glass rail and the steel support and triggered a figure-eight blast that sent Shore scrambling out of sight again.

Then Blancanales felt the submachine gun chug to a stop. The glass rail just inches from his face shattered under a torrent of rounds from the lower level.

Blancanales leaned against the planter, catching his breath as he changed out the magazine on the MP-5. Got a little bit nuts there, Blancanales thought. Time to play it cool. Time to be the professional, because the other guys are professionals and they might eat you for lunch.

The gunfire below went silent, then came the rush when three mercenaries stormed out of the lower-level entrance of Jackson's with weapons blazing, closely tailed by a furiously limping fourth merc with a hideous leg wound. Their targets were Lyons's and Schwarz's hiding places.

Blancanales attracted their attention when he jumped into plain sight and cut down the man in the middle. When the fire turned on him, he dropped again. Then came the blast from Lyons's Atchisson. Blancanales felt it in the floor beneath him, and he was up again, finding just two bloodied survivors. A burst of 9 mm rounds from the MP-5 cut one of them from the shoulder to the hip. The last man standing was the one with the leg wound, and his final moment was spent in a kind of dementia as he sprayed automatic fire in every direction before another shotgun blast quieted him forever.

Blancanales triggered another warning shot across the front of the upper level, just to let his buddy Shore know the coast wasn't clear.

"Able One here. We've cleaned up the lower level."

"The main man is still alive and kicking, and inside the store," Blancanales responded. "Last I saw, he was at my entrance."

"Stony One here—I'm alerting the blacksuits," Price broke in. "He won't get out."

"Pol, it's up to you," Lyons said. "Negotiate. Get him to disable those charges."

Blancanales snorted grimly. He wanted to give Lyons a list of the things wrong with that plan, then he realized it was the only option, especially when he considered that there could very well be civilians inside these stores, hiding in fear for their lives.

"Shore!" he shouted.

Blancanales kept a hard eye on the entrance. Shore might respond with some more fancy footwork and a quick shot at Blancanales's head, which still burned from the round that had parted his hair.

"Shore, your men are dead. Time to give it up."

"Then what?" Shore shouted from just inside the entrance.

Blancanales tried not to even blink as he watched for movement.

"Then you go disable the charge inside that store, then all the other charges you've planted."

"What do I get out of it?" Shore demanded.

Pol was examining every word the man said. If his mind was anywhere near as lithe as his movements, he'd be looking for a way out, or trying to lull Blancanales before making a quick strike.

"You get to not get shot dead," Blancanales said. "After that it's up to somebody else to figure out if you're worth striking a deal over. Depends how much you know about Korl that we don't already know."

"Like who his boss is?" Shore replied.

"That we know."

"Then you know more than me, and I don't have much to bargain with, do I?"

"Rosario," Price said in his headset, "we may be running out of time."

"Shore, we both know we don't have time to write a treaty," Blancanales said, feeling the pressure building all around him. "You can live or die, and you have to make that decision." On sudden impulse he added, "But you're going to go down in history as one of the world's biggest chumps if you die in the Plus Sizes Lingerie Department."

"Fuck you!" Shore blurted.

Blancanales grimaced. He'd pushed Shore's button. "Your choice, Shore. Undo the bombs or become the Legendary Ladies' Wear Loser."

"I get the point," Shore said. "I'll do it."

"Good. Brief me."

"Two sets of charges. One in fifteen lockers at the north entrance, one here in the Jackson store. I've got the remote control and it detonates both charges, the north entrance first, the Jackson's store ten seconds later. I'm supposed to press the button at 12:00 p.m. They're booby-trapped, but I can disarm them from here."

"Do it."

There was a pause. "It's done."

"Slide out the weapon, then come out with the detonator held above your head in two fingers."

The M-16 slid across the floor and came to a halt.

The scrawny blonde stepped out, hands high, a small plastic device held in his fingers far above his head.

Blancanales covered him with the MP-5, ready for any sort of a trick.

The boom felt as though it came from the heart of the earth, distant and muffled, then there was the crack of the building breaking. Shore stared openmouthed at the remote control held over his head, the awful truth sinking in. Korl *had* betrayed them. The devices were programmed to detonate on schedule, with or without the signal from Shore's remote.

Blancanales glanced at his watch. Twelve noon. And four seconds.

The Able Team commando didn't give his prisoner another thought as he bolted, taking the escalators to the lower level in three giant leaps and racing away as the hail of debris from the north entrance filled the vast courtyard in a stinging cloud that had thankfully dropped its heaviest pieces. Blancanales couldn't care less about the flying fragments nipping at every inch of exposed skin as he fought furiously to put distance between himself and the Jackson's store. Then the flash of light behind him told Blancanales his time was up.

He launched himself bodily into the pool of foot-deep water, where the dancing fountains had once entertained shoppers. With a giant gasp he submerged and went fetal against the inside wall of the pool as the world outside turned to a river of fire.

CHAPTER TWENTY

The White House, Washington, D.C.

He hadn't believed it. He hadn't *allowed* himself to believe it. The President of the United States stared at the television monitor and felt the guilt.

The guilt came with the job. No matter how peripherally he was involved in the decision-making, it always hit him hard when people died because of the decision. Even when the decision had been right.

The first lady told him that his guilt was a sign of his compassion, but that didn't make it feel less painful.

The fire and smoke billowed out of two black craters, which looked even more horrible because the rest of the building was still standing and looked so normal. The Heartland Mall in the heartland of America was burning. How many innocent people were dead there?

What was more shocking was the realization that Hal Brognola and his team had been right: their hypothesis that this was the work of Franklin Jackson, a U.S. senator, had born hideous fruit.

"That's all you've got?" the President demanded as the FBI head began to wind down his briefing. "No suspects?"

"It just happened," the FBI man responded weakly.

"Baymont did not just happen."

"We haven't established that there is a definite link."

"Do *not* feed me PR," the President said hotly, then glared at the FBI man who knew enough to backpedal.

"There's almost certainly a link, but we haven't pinpointed it yet. We're watching various groups that would have cause—"

"You said that." The President cut him off abruptly and turned to his director of Homeland Security. "Do you have anything more?"

"No. The media was playing up the Saudi Arabian angle, even after the Baymont attack last night, but there's nothing to that theory. Everything I've seen points to isolationist extremists."

The President nodded, trying not to show his relief. The more verification he had for the Stony Man hypothesis, the more comfortable he'd feel when the time came to order a fix. "What leads you to that conclusion?"

"All the targets are non-U.S. in origin. The oil, obviously, started in the Middle East and was coming here. So were the container ships. The factory in Baymont was a lightning rod for nationalist and isolationist rhetoric—probably the most well-publicized symbol of foreign entities creating a perceived negative impact on U.S. jobs and economy. Not too long ago the prominent symbol was the Heartland Mall and Jackson Department Stores. This all points at an antiforeign business agenda."

"And I disagree," the FBI head added quickly. "We've got no intelligence on any organization with that agenda that also has this kind of funding and organizational skills."

"Just because you don't know about them doesn't mean they don't exist," the director responded.

"I'm sorry but you're wrong," the FBI head declared. "If they're this big and this wealthy, they *can't* have evaded us."

The President pondered that, then shook his head. "I don't share your confidence." He turned pointedly to the director. "Are you pursuing that angle?"

"Yes. I've got local law following a few leads, and the FBI is cooperating on several fronts."

"Taking resources away from what I feel would be a more productive avenue of investigation," the FBI head added.

The President nodded politely to the FBI head. "I'm afraid I have to agree with Homeland this time." He looked squarely at the director. "Let me know if you need further resources. I don't care who it is, I want this son of a bitch out of business."

The director's eyebrows came together, but then he nodded sharply. "Yes, Mr. President."

"SORRY IT WAS ROUGH for you in there," the director of Homeland Security said as they waited in the shade of a white veranda. The grounds of the White House were pleasant, cool and breezy, teeming with greenery.

The FBI head shrugged as his car pulled up. "I can roll with it. Next time it's just as likely to be you."

"Yeah."

The FBI guy took a step as his car door was opened by a White House Secret Service agent, then he stopped and stepped up close to the thoughtful director.

"What's he know that we don't?" the Fed said in a low voice.

The director shrugged and wouldn't meet his gaze. "More importantly, who told him, and why isn't he telling us?"

The FBI man frowned at the immaculate White House landscaping. "There were a hell of a lot of Justice guys on the ground in Cincinnati."

The director nodded. "Yeah. I think you should look into it."

The top man at the Federal Bureau of Investigation nodded. "I think I will."

Somewhere Over West Virginia

THE CHINOOK MH-47E swept overland, the pair of rotors thrumming powerfully. They were driven by a pair of Textron Lycoming T55-L-714 turboshaft engines that gave the Chinook the ability to perform heavy-lift tasks such as picking up tanks.

Right now the cargo was minuscule by comparison. Just some bruised, battered grunts, as dejected as a homeless mongrel in an alley.

Nobody said a word.

There was almost nothing to say. Not now. Not yet. Eventually they would study what had happened, every move, every detail. They would question every action, every decision, dispassionately studying their own behavior for a cause of the failure. Probably their analysis would determine that there was nothing they could have done to avert the catastrophe.

But right now the failure loomed large. They had gone to stop a terrorist act, and the terrorist act happened anyway. People—civilians, innocent bystanders—died.

All three of them had taken shrapnel cuts, and Blancanales looked as sunburned as Schwarz had after the Baymont blast. Pol's dark complexion became a rich brick-red after the water that had been protecting him reached near-boiling temperatures during the blast.

The blacksuits were unharmed. They were all alive, which was a small miracle, but it was tough to look at the glass half-full. Right now it was tough to even be angry. He should be enraged, energized with fury.

Lyons put his elbows on his knees and laced his fingers behind his neck, staring at the floor.

He didn't want to know how many people were still in the mall, hiding or trapped, when the bombs blew.

One dead civilian was too many.

Alang, India

"IT LOOKS LIKE a mass grave," Calvin James said.

The CIA agent, Paul Patel, assigned to serve as their liaison and guide, nodded grimly. "It is, in every sense of the word."

The city of Alang sat near the Bay of Khambaht, on a western peninsula jutting from the subcontinent into the Arabian Sea. It was here that the world sent its ships to die.

They came by the hundreds, the huge freighters and tankers and warships that were too dilapidated to maintain any longer. Even the occasional passenger cruise ship showed up. All of them came to be digested.

The ships were purchased by the Alang scrap barons, who paid a going rate of about $150 U.S. per ton. The doomed ship had arrived at this stretch of critically polluted beach during the high tides that came with the cycles of the moon, where ships were run aground into one of the two hundred and fifty huge slots accommodating vessels of fifty thousand tons or more. The ship was winched ashore and set upon by workers.

The CIA agent had said he would give men of Phoenix Force the "full-color tour," and directed the pilot to take a flight path over the beach, start to finish.

When they came upon the first ship, James thought it looked like the carcass of some impossibly big whale washed up on shore. It was a cargo vessel that had been winched and floated on the tide until its entire front half was out of the water. The hull was a mottled red and streaked with rust, adding to the illusion of some creature that died after suffering bloody wounds. A once-vibrant yellow image painted on the bow was now so faded James couldn't make it out at first, then he recognized the outlines of the four red stars and the Union Jack design of the flag of New Zealand.

"Like maggots eating a mouse," Patel said with a grunt.

The agent was of Indian ancestry himself, so James wasn't sure if the remark was racist or if it stemmed from the infamous Indian caste bigotry. Regardless, he had to admit that, from where he sat, the workers on the big cargo ship did look like maggots as they hurried the carcass through the process of corruption. There had to be hundreds of them swarming around the vessel, most of them operating acetylene torches that glimmered like stars. Others guided massive chunks of metal as they were lifted on crane wires and swung to the shore. Acres of excised girders, equipment and hull slabs were carpeting the shore, where more torches glittered in the hands of swarming drone workers. The front end of the vessel had already been chewed down almost to the keel.

Around it, the water was a black morass of drained petrochemicals, with foamy mounds of sludge collecting in the crevices. A haze of oily smoke blanketed the coast.

That was the first ship in the first slip, and then came another, and another. They were flying for many minutes over the endless, untidy row of ships.

"How many—" Gary Manning started to ask.

"They could top six hundred ships this year," the agent

said. "That's doubled from five years ago. The workforce reached more than seventy thousand last I heard."

"I think I read about this place," McCarter said. "Long time ago. Something about Greenpeace demonstrations."

The agent chuckled. "The environmentalists cruise off-shore every day and nobody cares—nobody in India, anyway. But it's a nightmare down there. There's spilled fuels and oil. There's all kinds of other chemicals coming out of those ships. Lead and mercury levels are sky-high in the water and the soil. Half the time the air is cloudy with asbestos. But working here is still better than starving."

As they finally came to the end of the long line of ships, James pointed to a small group of workers bearing a covered stretcher. They were wading through the muck alongside the skeletonized lower keel of a ship that was once huge, now nearly obliterated.

The CIA agent gave them a grimace. "The safety codes are as stringent as the pollution standards. The Alang workers have a saying—'One to one.' One man killed for every ship that's processed."

At the rear of the aircraft T. J. Hawkins said, disbelievingly, "Six hundred!"

DAVID MCCARTER assigned himself the task of walking the shore with the CIA agent. With his British accent he knew the Indian people might have an instant animosity toward him, but he would also seem less foreign than the Americans to the people of this untouristed end of India.

Paul Patel was stationed as a diplomat in the U.S. Embassy in Bombay.

"Hell, everybody knows I'm CIA," he said. "We just talk around it."

He had been born in the U.S., but just barely. His parents

risked the strenuous flight to Los Angeles when his mother was eight months' pregnant, and she gave birth within hours of landing.

"I appreciate all the effort," he told McCarter as they rode toward the shore. "I just wish they hadn't named me Paul. Paul Patel! It's like they couldn't decide if I should be Indian or American."

They arrived in front of an oversize shack, constructed mostly of scrap steel sheets welded together. A wheezing ship's air conditioner dominated the front entrance, where the elegant plaster arch from a long-gone cruise ship was wedged into the corroding walls. The windows were all scavenged view ports. The grounds were the same unclean soil that was everywhere along the shoreline, glistening with oil and too much poison to grow anything.

Patel smirked as McCarter took in the unlikely looking building. "Wait until you see the inside."

The interior of the building was truly bizarre—a vast, filthy cathedral. The wall-to-wall carpeting was made up of swathes of carpeting ripped from the floors of cruise ships and from captains' quarters on merchant marine vessels. Without regard to color or texture, they were secured to the floor with flat-head nails, creating an unpleasant patchwork. There were more ships' light fixtures than McCarter could count mounted on the walls and ceiling. Light-gauge exposed electrical wires were draped on nails and wedged into wall crevices. Most of the lamps were off, so that the vast interior was lit mostly by one massive, sooty crystal chandelier from some long-gone cruise ship ballroom. It was so big McCarter couldn't walk under it without lowering his head, so he went around.

Around the room, like rats in the shadows, a few administrative workers toiled under salvaged green banker's lamps at battered steel desks. One of them even had a computer, a huge tower extracted from a ship's bridge, and a young man was pecking DOS commands on the keyboard.

There were no interior walls or cubicle dividers in the building until they came to the rear, where Patel knocked, then opened the door into a reception room. The lighting here came from several standing lamps and was pleasant. The carpeting was one piece of dense beige. The receptionist's desk was small and somewhat worn, but looked as though it had been expensive when it was new, maybe thirty or forty years earlier.

The receptionist was half as old. She rose with a polite smile as she lowered the volume on the tiny desk television. "Good morning, Mr. Patel," she said in English.

"Good morning. We're here to see Wali. Let him know, will you, please."

"Certainly."

She spoke into the intercom on her desk, then hurried to the minikitchen in the corner to make tea. McCarter found himself propped in an extravagant, hand-carved chair with arms that curved into scrolls. The chair back swooped into a swirling top well above his head. The wood was gilded and well-preserved.

"It's a Louis the Fourteenth," Patel said matter-of-factly.

"Huh," McCarter responded, trying not to sound totally disinterested.

"I'm lying," Patel said a moment later, sighing. "It's a reproduction. But this entire suite of rooms was dismantled from an owner's office suite on an Italian cargo ship and rebuilt here. Walls, carpet, furnishings, everything. Quite an accomplishment."

"Yeah," McCarter said. "I'm flabbergasted."

Patel grinned. "That about sums it up."

McCarter had assumed the girl was the daughter of Aska Wali. Patel explained in a low voice she was his concubine. She somehow heard him over the television, which was turned up again, and flashed McCarter a vibrant smile. She was indeed a beautiful girl, McCarter thought, and she would probably be a very attractive woman—after she actually went through puberty.

Aska Wali was physically the polar opposite to his child paramour. He was corpulent and stooped, his spine bending under the constant stress of carrying a massive stomach. His office looked immaculate but it was permeated with his odor, and McCarter felt his eyes almost start to water at the assault on his senses when he shook the man's hand. The human stench made the polluted air of the scrap yard seem pleasant.

Wali waved at the chairs. "Please have a seat." He was actually trying to demonstrate good manners. McCarter didn't know if this situation could get weirder.

"I must say I'm impressed by all you've done," McCarter said, playing up his accent, giving a restrained wave at the walls.

Wali beamed. "There's no building like this anywhere in the world."

"I have never seen anything like it," McCarter agreed.

"Only in Alang could you even find all the parts for a building like this. It is one-of-a-kind." Wali was still grinning. Patel had said that a little flattery went a long way with Wali, and it was good advice. Wali was still smiling when he said, "So, Ambassador Patel says you want to take a look around this place."

Patel's glance told McCarter not to correct the title. Wali was clearly a man who desired status, and a man of status interacted with others of elevated status. Therefore, the Bombay embassy employee became an ambassador.

"You've seen the news reports about the sabotage of the oil tankers, I take it," McCarter said. "There have been several reports of a small cargo vessel in the vicinity of some of those tankers—an old Indonesian freighter named *Singep*. It was supposed to have been broken down here a year ago."

Wali put on a perturbed face. "Yes, and I have already shown papers on the *Singep* to your CIA and to Delhi officials. They made some rather insulting insinuations."

McCarter wondered how many times Wali had practiced the phrase "rather insulting insinuations." He smiled easily. "Director Wali, the CIA men who came here were just middle management. Not our top people. I apologize if they were insulting. We at the top level have been thinking through the problem. We think we know what happened, and we've come to look for new leads."

"You know what happened?" Wali asked. Even Paul Patel looked interested now.

"Here is how we see it," McCarter said. "Whoever planned to sabotage the oil tankers already had a certain kind of vessel that he intended to use for the job. He knew there would be an investigation, naturally, so he wanted to make sure the trail was hard to follow. So he hired someone here on your staff to watch for a vessel that was the same size and configuration as the vessel he already had. The *Singep* came to your facility and fit the bill."

Wali was frowning, and now he nodded cautiously.

"So you went ahead and broke up the *Singep,* but the other vessel was painted with the same markings. The people who did this even went to the trouble of painting the name onto the hull, then painting over it. But they painted over the name so poorly that, in bright sunlight, it could still be read. That way the trail led here, to Alang and to you."

"But I was not responsible," Wali protested.

"Of course not. But somebody in your shipyard is linked to whoever is responsible. That's why I would like to question some of your people."

"So Langley's not tying Wali to the ship anymore?" Patel suggested.

"No," McCarter said. "Think about it this way—if Wali was going to provide a ship to be used in the sabotage of the freighters, he would have removed the markings that linked it back to him. It would have been foolish not to. A man like you, Mr. Wali, would never have become the businessman you are today if you made such stupid mistakes."

Wali looked at Patel briefly, then his eyes danced to the walls, the ceiling, the desktop, everywhere except at McCarter's face.

"Yes," Wali said. "Of course that is true."

Of course it was, the Briton thought.

MCCARTER DRANK his tea like the manicured English gentleman he wasn't, one ankle propped stiffly over the other knee. He idly adjusted the buckle on his ankle-high riding boot.

The boots were from Italy but the soles had been modified in Virginia, by Cowboy Kissinger. Adjusting the buckle retracted the cover over an indentation in the sole. The bug was held inside by a mild adhesive until McCarter pressed his heel down. Then the tiny barbed hooks grabbed at the carpet fibers and the slight movements of his foot drove the tiny device deeper into the carpet.

After McCarter offered up a substantial fee "to cover your inconvenience," Wali was more than happy to allow him to question his workforce.

"You do know there's many thousands of them?" Wali said, laughing good-naturedly as his confidence came back. "But I hope you find the right man."

"I hope so, too."

McCARTER SPENT a few hours with Patel making a good show of questioning the ship breakers, asking for signs of sudden wealth among the workforce at the time that the *Singep* had been brought in for dismantling.

He felt like a fool. These men lived in poverty. They worked under the most deplorable, dangerous conditions for a few cents an hour because it was the only way to feed their families. No, they told him, none of their peers had been showing "signs of wealth."

When he asked if there had been any strange disappearances among the workforce during that time period, they were simply confused. People came and went all the time. It wasn't unusual for a co-worker to simply not show up one day. Maybe he moved on, hoping to find better pay in Ahmadabad or Rajkot. Maybe he became too sick from the poisoned air and water to work anymore—it happened all the time.

Driving back into Alang, Patel asked, "Is Langley really ready to take Wali off its list of conspirators because of the name on the ship?"

"Not for that reason," McCarter said. "Problem is, he's got too much money. It is much more likely that somebody working the shipyard simply passed on the physical details of the *Singep* and reincarnated her with a few cans of paint."

"So they don't think it was actually the *Singep* that was seen around the tankers," Patel said.

"With her name coming through the paint? That would be a bloody stupid thing to do."

Patel's mouth hardened. "It sure would."

HE HAD A PAIR of vodkas before the aircraft was even off the tarmac, and as soon as the Malay Air flight was airborne he was on the phone to the United States.

"It's Patel."

"Why are you calling?"

"There's trouble."

"Such as?"

"CIA, working with the backing of Delhi. They questioned Wali."

"What did you expect? He practically waved a flag and said come and get me. But it doesn't matter. The *Singep* won't be found. And Wali made it through Delhi's interrogation without cracking."

Patel was feeling frantic. Senator Jackson didn't get it. "You don't understand. This time they're really digging deep. I think they could uncover the operation."

"Even so," Jackson said coolly, "I've erased my tracks. I won't be exposed."

"I will!" Patel hissed.

"Then you had better make sure the operation isn't uncovered."

"What do you think I'm trying to do? We need to move the boat. Tonight is our only chance for another two weeks."

"The boat is safe. But don't worry, it is going to prove useful again. Tonight, in fact. As luck would have it, there's an unexpected target making its way through in the next eight hours. The *Singep* can get to it and send it to the bottom without even being seen."

Patel was aghast. "No. They'll track her for sure. It's too risky!"

"It's too rare an opportunity to pass up," Jackson replied. "Paul, you're overreacting. You're new to this venture, but I've been planning it a long time. Believe me when I say that the *Singep* will never be found."

CHAPTER TWENTY-ONE

Franklin Jackson was the laughingstock of the U.S. Senate, but a senator had certain privileges, provided for by law, even if he didn't have the respect of the rest of the Senate. These privileges included access to certain international intelligence reports—too important to trust the U.S. citizenry with, but after all not *that* important. Mostly it had to do with the comings and goings of high-profile political and business figures.

Jackson had long ago seen the potential value in such information. His awareness was now paying off.

This time the report wasn't about a political or a wealthy business leader, but about a pair of oil tankers that had left Iran just hours earlier.

In the Middle East the vitriolic exchange that started with the destruction of the oil tankers had continued unabated, never mind that subsequent attacks made it increasingly clear that the violence was not about one oil-producing nation trying to gain market dominance.

With amazing rapidity the war of words between Saudi Arabia and Iran escalated at a stampede pace. Iran and several other Middle Eastern oil-producing nations lost ships in the tanker attacks, but somehow Saudi Arabia, one of the biggest producers, was unscathed. Iran's thinly veiled suspicions had become blatant in the past twenty-four hours. Saudi Arabia and *only* Saudi Arabia had the motivation and the resources to pull off the attacks.

Now the Iranians had quietly launched two supertankers, with a massive supply of crude oil being sold to U.S. oil companies through a complicated series of legal maneuvers. While the world media wasn't told about the tankers, Iran had sent a clear message to the Saudis: if their U.S.-bound tanker twins came under attack, the Iranian government would hold the Saudis solely responsible and would consider the attacks an act of war.

This was what Jackson learned from his intelligence reports. Nothing top secret, but useful nonetheless. He knew precisely what time the tankers would move through the Gulf of Oman and into the Arabian Sea. When he plotted the course and checked the tide schedules, he was ecstatic to discover that the target was reachable. The *Singep* could slip out while the tide was rising, rendezvous with the Iranian tankers and take action.

It was a little risky, but he simply couldn't pass up the opportunity.

Alang

DAVID MCCARTER was halfway through his briefing when he revealed his suspicion.

"Paul Patel is as dirty as Aska Wali."

"What makes you say that, David?" Barbara Price asked.

"Nothing specific. It was his behavior. Whatever Wali is guilty of, Patel knows about it, but I don't think he's been in on it all along. Patel is very cool, very in control, but I think he's new to the Benedict Arnold role. His guilt was showing."

They had gathered in the sitting room of a hotel room suite in the small high-rent district of Alang, using a satellite phone connection to link with Stony Man Farm.

"He found out Wali was involved and agreed to steer the U.S. away for a fee?" Price suggested.

"A fee big enough to justify betraying his country and his allegiance to the CIA," McCarter said. "He was ready to believe my story about the Company not suspecting Wali. You could see how relieved he was."

"The CIA file on Patel shows fifteen years of service without a blemish," Price said. "Unless he's got a personal vendetta we don't know about, you'd expect it to take a lot of cash to make him turn traitor. Anyway, I'm not sure what that does for us. We've had translators listening in on Wali since you planted the bug, and we've learned nothing."

"There was no discussion about my visit?" McCarter asked.

"No. His phone calls were all business-related, and he spent a half hour involved in some office hanky-panky with his receptionist. She sounds…young."

"Bastard," McCarter said under his breath. "Stony, Patel is flying back to Bombay now. He'll be on the ground in half an hour and if I'm right about his complicity, he'll be the one who gets Wali to discuss their involvement. He's nervous, so he'll take extra precautions and call from home or a public phone."

"Well, there's a problem, David," Price said. "The bug's power is tiny. We were able to get a feed while you were wearing the retransmitter, but it's been off-line since you left the premises."

"We can put the retransmitter into place somewhere on the building," Hawkins piped in. "Better yet, we can get in and plant more bugs. Did the building look secure?"

McCarter laughed. "No. I doubt there would be anything on the premises that would be worth an electronic security system. But I wouldn't be surprised to find a junkyard dog."

"The entire facility works a seven-to-seven shift," Price said. "The place should be clearing out now. By the time you get down there you'll have the place mostly to yourselves."

"There'll be some sort of guard patrol," Rafael Encizo said. "Are we going to go taking out a bunch of night watchmen if they spot us?"

"No," McCarter said. "So we can't allow ourselves to be noticed."

THE BLACK INFLATABLE drifted on a surface of muck that rose and fell with the tide. Anywhere else the water would have curled under and broken on the shore, but along the shore of Alang the sea was suffocated under a thick soup of petrochemicals. Even after the work had stopped for the day the partially dismantled hulks dripped oil, fuel and sewage into the ocean.

Each time Manning and Encizo lifted their oars out of the water it seemed as if a thick, slimy skin clung to them, making them heavy. It was like rowing through mud. But the consistency of the water also made the raft virtually silent.

The descending ball of the sun disappeared behind the hulk of an old Russian cargo ship that was aground within sight of Aska Wali's patchwork headquarters. James took an oar and crouched on Manning's side of the raft to keep it from coming in contact with any part of the wreckage. Despite the ceramic mesh on top of the flat armor panels protecting the inflatable, they couldn't afford to allow a jagged scrap of metal to make a puncture. They beached on the oil-mud of the shore, tucked up against a four-yard-tall curved hull section. The shadows were dark, but the sun shone bright enough to make long shadows amid the piles of wreckage and sorted metal scrap.

Hawkins, James and McCarter left the inflatable, making their way through from cover to cover.

At a radio call from Encizo they halted, dwarfed beneath a mesh cage holding thousands of feet of steel pipe. Encizo gave them the position of an approaching patrol and they waited out the pair of watchmen, who were joking as they strolled on their rounds. The watchmen never saw the trio of black-clad figures that silently crossed the mud flats after they walked by.

McCarter powered up the narrow-profile retransmitter he had fixed underneath his body armor.

"Stony One," Price radioed. "We're getting a signal from the bug." She made a disgusted sound. "Wali's rutting again."

"It's good he's still on the premises in case he does get that call from Patel," McCarter said.

They reached the last of the stacked scrap and found themselves with a long stretch of open ground between them and Wali's headquarters, but there was no guard in sight and their careful examination showed them no sign of a security system. They covered the open ground in a quick jog and stepped into darkness again on the shadowed side of the building.

While McCarter stood guard on the ground, Hawkins and James scaled the side of the building, finding easy finger- and footholds in the putty-filled rivet holes where the hull pieces had once been joined and in the deep seams between them. Even without gear they were on the roof in seconds.

Hawkins quickly erected the permanent retransmitter, which consisted of a receiver tuned to the bug, feeding into a global satellite phone. From his backpack he extracted the Solardyne power pack, which was under thirty pounds even with the added field protection and camouflage panels. His main concern in setting it up was to make the solar panel invisible, even to workers on the deck of the huge ships parked nearby. With good sun the unit would provide 120 watt-hours of power every day. Even under the Alang haze it would be more than enough to keep the global phone running all day and provide enough charge to keep its battery pack running all night.

"Phoenix Five here," Hawkins radioed as he flipped the unit on and it automatically dialed out to the Stony Man Farm receiving number. "It's setting up. Let's see how it's working."

Back at Stony Man Farm the communication staff would make a quick diagnostic of the incoming signal.

"Stony One—it's loud and clear," Price reported. "We'll be listening in on Mr. Wali for as long as we need to."

That wasn't exactly true. The solar panel was designed to last for twenty years. The battery would keep going for more than 600 charge cycles, or more than a year and a half of daily cycling to keep the retransmitter going. But the bug that McCarter had planted would run out of power in just days.

Hawkins was hoping they'd find a reason to leave this foul-smelling junkyard a lot sooner than that.

"T.J., hit the deck."

Calvin James gave the alert in a low, almost calm voice, and Hawkins went down fast, cushioning his landing on the roof with his outstretched hands while he listened furiously for the report of weapons or a shout of alarm.

There was nothing.

James was flat on the roof, too, pulling out his field glasses.

"Cal?"

"Come here."

Hawkins crabbed silently to the roof edge, where the irregular wall panels protruded, and he pulled out his field glasses, peering into them in the same general direction as James.

"See the big one that looks like a tanker, maybe a half mile from us? The one in the middle."

Hawkins found it. There were a pair of what he took to be cargo ships, both partially dismantled, noses out of the water and leaning on their keels. Between them was the bulbous, rounded rear end of an ancient tanker, stained with corrosion along its seams and rivets.

"I see the boat, yeah," Hawkins said. "What about it?"

"I think I saw a crewman."

"Crew? As in somebody to sail the ship?"

"Yeah." James touched his radio and issued a report. "Whoever it was, he was definitely not a ship breaker. He was as blonde as I'm not, and he was in light clothing. I think he was drinking a beer."

"Beer?" Hawkins mouthed to James.

"Looked like it."

"Phoenix One here," McCarter reported from below. "I don't see Cal's Caucasian, but I do see some lights."

"Phoenix One, you going to check it out?"

"Yeah. I can't think of a good explanation for somebody to be there, let alone a non-Indian," McCarter said. "Definitely worth looking into."

"Plus," Hawkins said, "there might be beer."

HAWKINS AND JAMES were trapped on the roof when they heard a voice at ground level at the front of the building. They crawled to the front on their elbows and watched as a woman in a sari leisurely approached carrying a large basket under one arm and humming, occasionally singing a few words. She knocked and the front door was unlocked for her. Over the pervasive stench of the place, they could smell the rich aroma of hot food. A minute later the woman reemerged with an empty basket as well as Aska Wali's pubescent concubine. The woman and the girl chatted easily.

McCarter was watching from below, trying to figure out how he felt about Wali's little arrangement. Wali was a disgusting pig of a human being, but the girl and her mother seemed okay with their little prostitution-and-meals business. If it was keeping a poor family fed, was it a bad thing?

He made a disgusted sound as he radioed Hawkins and James to descend. The whole thing appalled him. He preferred his ethics devoid of dilemma.

The shadows were stretching across the mud, longer and darker, and the trio had an easy time reaching the inflatable. Manning and Encizo guided the raft into the open, then over the swell of the waves until they reached the three closely parked ships. They moved in tight against the first huge derelict, a cargo vessel from the late 1960s, and stayed against the hulk as they worked their way carefully around the rear end. The sun was gone. In this place of endless wreckage and destruction, the shadows of night were total at sea level even while the western sky, when they could see it, was still pale blue.

Still, the darkness was not sufficient to disguise the secret that was nestled between the two derelict cargo ships.

"Phoenix One here," McCarter radioed. "We just found the *Singep.*"

CHAPTER TWENTY-TWO

The *Singep* had been identified by name by witnesses at the originating points of three of the five fuel tankers that had originally burned. The description of the boat fit that of a registered Indonesian freighter that had been sent to the ship breakers in Alang, India, twelve months earlier. Aska Wali had reportedly scrapped it long ago.

The witnesses had all reported that the *Singep*'s name had been painted over with a flat white paint that, under direct sunlight, became translucent enough to make the name legible. The imperfectly hidden name had turned out to be an attention-getter. It made the boat memorable.

And here she was, right back in Alang. *Singep* was an ugly hag, well past retirement age, with chronic corrosion and her last complete paint job now peeling and flaking like an uncontrolled skin condition. She was small by the standards of shipping vessels that came after her, and it was her comparably slim girth that had allowed her to be slipped into the hiding place.

The hollow rear end of a long-gone oil tanker had been left on shore between the two cargo ships, and the *Singep* had been steered into the vast, empty shell, which covered more than half of her. Her own rear end protruded from the shell, but was hidden by the ships on either side.

"You can't see it from the shore, and from the water you would have to know what to look for. Otherwise it is just another hunk of junk," McCarter explained to Stony Man Farm in near whisper. "Her keel's in the mud, but it's high tide so she'll have enough water under her bow to get out. She could even go tonight."

Even as McCarter spoke he heard the sound of old metal as the water level rose and the ship's ancient hull groaned for the fifteen thousandth time, to the daily alteration in the sea level and the redistribution of pressure against its plates. The sound was close to human, filled with weariness.

"What was that?" Price asked.

"She's floating with the incoming tide," McCarter explained. "We're putting a tracker on her."

The inflatable nudged up against the hull and, while the others held the raft in place, Hawkins attached a tracking device in the highest hidden niche he could reach. The device had a long-life battery pack that dwarfed the actual unit. It would transmit GPS coordinates continually for weeks, so Stony would always know the *Singep*'s exact whereabouts.

But Phoenix Force's priority was to keep her from going anywhere at all.

At the first set of hull-mounted rungs McCarter sent up James and Encizo.

"This could be an intelligence windfall," the Phoenix Force leader reminded them as they left the raft. "But only if we leave survivors who can provide the intelligence."

The pair answered with quick nods and ascended into darkness. Manning and now Hawkins propelled the raft alongside the *Singep*'s waterline until the hollow black shell of the tanker engulfed them.

McCarter had thought they were in darkness before, but it was nothing compared to the cavernous interior of the tanker. The sky, the sea, and all around them was light-swallowing blackness. Only when he looked back, outside the tanker shell, could he see slight variations in the darkness that indicated some sort of barely definable illumination.

He put his hands on the hull to guide them and to keep them alongside the cargo vessel, then he felt the *Singep* tremble and move as if she were alive. There was another groan, this one more sonorous, agitating the water. McCarter heard a small splash not far away, then another, and a moment later felt a shower of grit against his face.

Hawkins spit quietly. "Rust. What's happening?"

"It's the tanker shell," Manning whispered. "The keel of the *Singep* was resting against it. The weight was hundreds of tons, and now the high tide is releasing it."

"Think the tanker will collapse?" Hawkins asked.

"Who knows?"

"Whoever parked the *Singep* inside it thought it would hold together," McCarter said. "Up we go, mates."

McCarter took the raft line with him as he ascended the next set of rungs, tying it when he was certain he was above the waterline. He sure as bloody hell didn't want to swim his way out of here.

He reached the rail and climbed over. Seconds later Hawkins and Manning were at his side. They found themselves on a canted deck, the walkway marked with tiny lights enclosed in plastic strips like the lights in aircraft aisles. Across the deck was a dark, low bridge.

Hawkins silently pointed. Manning and McCarter could see it: Aska Wali's headquarters building was visible through a narrow gash in the tanker shell. They were standing in the spot where James had spotted the Caucasian beer drinker a half hour ago.

There was a creak, and the deck leveled out by a degree or two. The near-invisible raising of the water was righting the massive bulk as if some supernatural force were bringing a monstrous creature back from the dead.

Then they felt something else through their feet. The engines, like the creature's heartbeat, suddenly thrummed back to life. The *Singep* was preparing to set sail.

JAMES AND ENCIZO followed the glowing strands of floor lights to a door leading belowdecks. A faint light leaked through. They heard the approach of footsteps and removed themselves into the darkness as the door swung open and two men emerged. They were in too much of a hurry to see the hidden commandos. Encizo lifted the first man off his feet with a sweep of his own foot, and before he crashed to the deck he was rendered unconscious with a gun barrel to his skull.

James used the second man's surprise against him. As he turned to see what was happening to his companion, the Phoenix Force commando used a hard twist of the man's right arm to take him down to the deck in a single movement while delivering a concussive blow across the face. The slight impact managed to echo like the sound of a gong. James's victim went limp.

As they were tightening disposable cuffs on the unconscious pair, James spotted a hand emerging from the interior blackness. It grabbed the door. He leaped for it and Encizo was inches behind him, but the door slammed and they heard the bolt slide into place. Behind it there was a shout, "Intruders! Lock down the ship!"

The lights came on.

THE DOOR to the deckhouse flew open at the instant the deck blazed with lights. McCarter squeezed out an immediate response, sending a sustained burst into the knot of gunners trying to push their way onto the deck. Three went down in an ugly pile before the others retreated.

More appeared on the far side of the deck cabin but met with unexpected resistance when Hawkins and Manning both unloaded on them, cutting down the leader and sending a wounded man flopping to the deck. There was a hasty retreat followed by shouted orders.

The ship's crew was organizing for repelling borders.

McCarter led the others aft into the cover of a rusted loading crane. The deck lights winked off.

They pulled on glasses, switching to night vision, and waited for an expected attack, but the deck remained empty.

The ship lurched. They felt the friction of the keel being dragged against the sea bottom, like one huge granite mass being dragged over another.

"The tide's not in enough," Manning said. "They'll rip her bottom out."

But the grinding decreased, and they could see the unnatural blackness of the interior of the tanker shell give way to the star-lit sky, hazy under the foul polluted air of Alang. The grinding ceased and the deck righted itself as the ship floated freely. The derelict cargo ships that made up the *Singep*'s hiding place fell away. It drifted in reverse, then the powerful screws turned in the other direction and the ship eased forward. Minutes later she was putting distance between herself and the shore.

CHAPTER TWENTY-THREE

The empty deck of the *Singep* began showing signs of life as an army of gunners moved toward them, easy targets when viewed through their night-vision glasses, but McCarter held his fire as a report came in from Encizo and James, now in position just beyond the bridge house.

They waited on the mercenaries, who became more confident as they searched the aft end of the ship without finding the commandos. They assumed their attackers had fled.

Then the Phoenix Force trio unleashed a withering blast of gunfire that mowed them down mercilessly. Amid the shouts of confusion, the four rearmost mercenaries retreated, bolting around the bridge house, only to slam into a wall of machine-gun fire delivered by Encizo and James. The last man standing thrust his hands into the air.

"Don't shoot!" he shouted as his weapon clattered to the deck.

With a scrape of wood on wood, a broad shutter was dragged open three stories above the deck and a bald, narrow-faced man in dark goggles poked his head out, extending his handgun toward his surrendering comrade. He squeezed the trigger twice in rapid succession before pulling in to avoid Phoenix Force's return fire.

The surrendering mercenary was dead, executed by his own teammate.

Encizo and James watched the third-story window swing open on their side of the deckhouse. They also saw a bald man in dark-lensed goggles crack off rounds at his own surviving teammates before their machine-gun bursts chased him inside.

The commandos found themselves standing in a killing ground. The deck was awash with blood and bodies. McCarter came into view and the team reunited amid the slaughter.

"Do you have any live ones?" Encizo asked.

"Not anymore, thanks to the man upstairs."

"Where's this ship headed?" James asked.

"That's an excellent question."

Stony Man Farm, Virginia

"THE CONSENSUS HERE is that they're headed to deep water to scuttle the ship," McCarter reported. "We forced their hand with our questioning this afternoon. They thought we were getting too close."

Barbara Price couldn't drag her eyes away from the display Aaron Kurtzman had pulled up for her. "I'm afraid you've got it wrong this time, Phoenix One," she said. "The *Singep* has a target. Based on your speed and heading, you're going to rendezvous with a pair of Iranian supertankers in under twenty minutes."

David McCarter said nothing for a moment.

"Phoenix One, they're going to blow the *Singep* and take the Iranian supertankers with them," Price reported. "You have got to get off the ship."

"Understood, Stony One. The crew must have an escape plan. We've already cleared enough seats to fit us on board the getaway vehicle, whatever it is."

Price looked at Kurtzman, both seeing each other's concern. "Listen, David," Price said urgently, "you haven't been watching the progression of events on this end like we have. If there's one thing we've learned from the behavior of the Jackson and Korl camp, it's that they consider their hired hands disposable. Remember how they wasted the watercraft mercenaries? Able saw them sacrifice their own men at the Baymont factory and at the shopping mall in Ohio. They simply don't care whether their own men live or die, and disposing of them has a lot of benefits for those at the top."

"It prevents leaks," McCarter said grimly, remembering the casual destruction of the teams on the Pacific islands. "And it's cheaper. They must be keeping the teams isolated to keep them ignorant of their comrades' fate."

"That's how we see it," Price said. "You have to assume that any escape route that the crew has is probably a trap. The opportunity to take down the Iranian tankers may be fortuitous in Jackson's eyes, but you can bet he planned all along to erase the *Singep* and her ship full of human liabilities in one fell swoop."

"Can you get us transport, Stony One?"

"No way. Not in twenty minutes."

"Can you warn the Iranians to take evasive action?"

"They're supertankers, Phoenix One," Price protested. "It takes them ten miles just to turn left. There's no way they can dodge the *Singep*, which has probably got a beefed-up power plant and no cargo to slow it down. If she wants to catch the supertankers, she will."

"So we have to stop the boat and get the hell out and do it all in twenty minutes," McCarter summarized.

"Seventeen," Price corrected.

"No problem, Stony One. We'll handle it."

Price smiled at McCarter's confidence. "I know you will, Phoenix One," she said.

But the smile left when she looked at Kurtzman and his eyes asked the big rhetorical question.

How would they pull it off?

If Phoenix Force failed, and the twin tankers blew, it just might be the cause of a new and bloody intra-Arab Middle Eastern conflict.

If Phoenix Force failed, they would be decimated just as surely as the tankers and the *Singep* herself.

And they had just seventeen—no, sixteen minutes.

It felt like a lifetime.

Arabian Sea

FIRST THINGS FIRST, David McCarter thought. Stop this ship. Render it inoperable and it can't destroy the Iranian tankers. Worry about escaping later.

"The screw," Manning declared abruptly. "That's the way to bring this ship to a halt. We just send in grenades until the prop gets bent."

"A bent screw will stop the ship for sure?"

"Yeah, the vibrations from a twisted prop will burn out the motor or shake the drive shaft until it warps and locks."

"Good," McCarter said. "Gary and Rafe, you're on it. The rest of us will try to find a way off."

MANNING AND ENCIZO jogged the length of the ship, and Manning secured a Kevlar line to the ship's railing without hesitation, looping it through a reinforced rung in his combat webbing and stepping over the rail. He walked down the rear of the hull until he reached its farthest protrusion and found himself dangling over the roiling wake, where the single powerful screw agitated the sea and drove the ship.

The big Canadian was confident when he'd suggested the idea, but now he wasn't so sure. The screw was below the water level, protected by the ocean. Could he actually land the round close enough to achieve real damage?

The answer was: he had to. But a single screw moving a cargo ship of this size had to be twenty feet or more in diameter. How could he miss?

Manning looped the twin lines over one wrist and pulled the pin on the first grenade, then released the pin, counted off three seconds and dropped the bomb. The high explosive fell away almost gently. It disappeared into the foam and a boiling white bulge formed on the ocean yards away, in the place they had been. The ship wasn't even nudged by the blast. Manning cursed under his breath. He was going to have to do a lot better than that. He primed the next grenade as he conjured a mental picture of the screw and its support. He didn't know enough about this ship to estimate the hull offset distance of the propellers.

As he released the grenade, it occurred to him that all he really needed to do was to damage the supports. If they warped, then the powerful turning of the blades would quickly wrench the whole thing off. With a last-second adjustment Manning sent the HE in a long, slow arc, putting it at the waterline where he hoped the supports were affixed.

Manning gritted his teeth when he realized what was about to happen, and buried his face in his arm as the HE hit the metal just above the waterline, then cracked open brilliantly inches above the wake. Even dangling far above it, the force of the blast reached Manning like a giant hand, smacking into him, and the Canadian commando flew sideways. The twin lines on his wrist dug into his flesh as he spun, knocked into the hull, then swung back to center. The rear of the ship met Manning like a skidding log truck meeting a moose on an icy Alberta highway.

Manning left planet Earth. It was momentary, but when he came back to full consciousness a half second later he found himself dangling by one arm over the furious ocean while his wrist uncurled from the twin wires. He started to slide as he grabbed for the wires with his free hand, and his fist locked around only one of them. His flesh burned as the Kevlar rope slipped through his fingers, and then the linkage locked on the line at his waist. Manning felt his crotch stop moving while his feet and head continued down until his skeletal system brought his entire one hundred and ninety pounds to a halt.

His spine bent farther than the designed specs allowed. He felt the chilling crunch of something grinding and breaking accompanied by a moment of excruciating deep-tissue pain, and he dangled like a broken puppet, looking at the South Asian constellations and facing his worst nightmare: paralysis.

Torture and death were preferable to a future of quadriplegia.

It took him just a heartbeat to figure out his arms still worked, and he dragged on the line until he was upright. He inhaled, exhaled and concentrated on the parts below the waist. The feet moved around, just like always, and now wasn't the time to test out the other extremities.

James shimmied down the line in a hurry as Manning dragged himself back to his grenade-tossing position. The concern showed in James's face.

"You okay?" he demanded.

"Yeah, fine," Manning shouted over the roar of the blades.

But he thought maybe he wasn't fine. He thought maybe he'd just been through the most frightening thirty seconds of his long career.

He grabbed another HE as James ascended the hump, then he flattened fast. A muffled retort of gunfire came from the deck. James pulled the MP-5 SD3 off his free shoulder and stretched it high in front of him. Rising awkwardly, he triggered a long burst before landing against the hull again. More automatic fire flew inches over his head.

"You hooked up to the rope?" Manning asked.

"Yeah, I can stay here all night."

James sprayed more 9 mm rounds around the deck and dropped as return fire came at him from at least two gunners.

"Need some help?" Manning called.

"Just stop the boat!"

"Hold on." Manning released, counted and tossed. Another careless throw, he cursed to himself, but the grenade dropped exactly where he wanted and burst just when he wanted it to.

It was like magic. The ship experienced a tremor and the smooth churning of the ocean became an angry frothing, inconsistent, as if several sea beasts of different sizes were battling viciously just below the surface. Something was bent out of shape.

The *Singep* didn't stop.

"What happened to the boat?" James shouted.

"I think I just pissed it off."

The railing an arm's reach above James took a powerful burst of gunfire that started and just didn't seem to stop, until the solid steel, incredibly, began perforating under the onslaught.

"*Somebody* is pissed!" James shouted as he retreated down the hull. "Hurry up and finish the job. They're gonna take out the line, and then we're SOL."

Manning had one HE left. It had to work because his smoke grenades weren't up to the job. He pulled the pin, watched the thing while he counted in his head, then tossed it away. It was swallowed by the chaos of water and darkness at sea level and he couldn't even guess how accurate it had been.

A weak swell of water was all Manning saw, and he bit out a vivid curse.

"Don't tell me you missed!" James exclaimed as the air filled with more autofire, as thick as swarming bees.

"I missed!" Manning shouted with bitter self-recrimination.

The *Singep* screeched, a mechanical warbling scream of immense metal stress that merged with the pounding of loose parts slamming violently into the hull. The wake not only wavered side to side, it was now thrashing up and down and the slashing propeller actually broke the surface momentarily before knifing into the sea again.

Manning hadn't missed.

"WE'RE IN TROUBLE!" Gary Manning shouted.

"Thanks for the update!" James retorted. They were hanging off the back end of an elderly cargo ship that was shaking as though it had palsy while at least four guys with automatic weapons tried to kill them by shooting a hole through the metal hull.

The Kevlar line supporting both Phoenix Force commandos was tied to a rung outside the rail, but the rail was now perforated and it was a miracle the line hadn't yet been hit.

"No, I mean we're really in trouble!" Manning said. "I blew a blade of the prop. It's out of balance and it's gonna fly apart any second, and guess who's in the way!"

"Well, we can't go up," James shouted as the entire rear end of the vessel began to rattle excessively.

"Then we go down!" Manning said.

"You first!"

James watched Manning float away into the darkness, then he was gone.

James unclipped the rope from his harness and extended his arms and legs, pushing off from the *Singep,* and found himself descending through blackness. When he looked down, the starlight reflection on the ocean was miles away, but it came at him at light speed and crashed into him brutally just as he straightened his body into a dive. That made the impact easier, but he arrowed deep through a chaos of bubbles. When he stopped descending, he found himself in absolute blackness.

Many men would have panicked in the claustrophobic blackness. Most men wouldn't have even known which direction to swim to get to the surface.

James had been through more water exercises and missions than he could count during his career with the U.S. Navy SEALs. Early in the program of Basic Underwater Demolition/SEAL training the want-to-be SEALs were taught to regard the water as a safe haven, not a place of danger. Despite the pain in his lungs, James found his way to the surface with smooth strokes, his mind already churning over his list of other problems.

He inhaled a huge restorative lung full of air and watched the group of gunners standing at the rear of the *Singep,* leaning over and trying to see the cause of the trembling affecting the ship. The whine of the cargo vessel's motor rose to a shrill pitch that sounded electronic and vibrated the very ocean. Then there was a crash as the screw spun apart and sent an eight-foot-long section of blade flying up and out, slashing through the rear hump of the vessel and planing through the hull before vanishing skyward. The upper torso of two of the gunners flew off, removed as neatly as with a guillotine.

"Cal?"

"Over here."

James was shedding his expendable gear as Manning swam alongside him with strong strokes. He tried his radio before thrusting it away and letting it sink. So much for waterproofing.

"Did you see that?" Manning asked, nodding at the ship.

"Yeah. Guess we took the smart way out."

"Yeah, you and me look like a pair of real geniuses right about now." Manning pulled his own radio set into position over his dripping head and brought it to life. "Phoenix Three here. Anybody reading this?"

Manning listened hard. James knew he wasn't getting a response. They observed the *Singep* drift to a halt although the engine noise was rising in pitch. Without the screw, it was spinning unimpeded, literally out of control. Then the whine was gone as the engine either locked up or was shut down.

"Phoenix Three here," Manning repeated. "Is anybody hearing me?"

Nobody was.

CHAPTER TWENTY-FOUR

Hawkins pressed his ear against the metal door and held up three fingers while clenching the handle. The pounding inside the deckhouse was unmistakably the sound of steps moving fast on stairs. He picked his moment, then counted on his fingers. Three, two, one… He yanked the door open a foot. Encizo, low to the ground in a crouch, tossed the grenade inside as the nearby figures turned frantically to fire on him. McCarter triggered a burst over Encizo's head. The door slammed shut and the commandos turned away, plugging their fingers into their ears.

The beams of illumination from the flash-bang grenade streaked through the deckhouse ports like spotlight beams, and the burst of noise sounded as if it alone could have burst the structure apart.

Then Hawkins yanked the door open again and this time Encizo tossed in a flare. It bounced off a corpse, downed by McCarter's submachine gun, and showed them a second figure writhing like a hooked worm on the floor. Down the stairs was a third man.

Encizo crossed the interior in a leap and fired, his rounds

nipping at the unshod heels of the hairless man in the sun-glasses, but the man disappeared.

"The bald guy's barefoot," Encizo said by way of explanation.

Hawkins shook his head in disgust. Baldy had preceded his companions without making enough noise for Hawkins to hear him. That was enough distance for him to avoid the incapacitating effects of the grenade. He couldn't have known they were going to try the trick with the flash-bang, could he?

McCarter lifted the deafened, blinded man into a sitting position and shouted into the side of his head. "Where's your escape boats?"

The man was still reeling from the assault and was trying to cower under his arms without appearing to have heard the question. McCarter nudged him in the gut with his weapon and shouted again, louder.

"All the way to the front," the man said weakly. "Lowest level at the front."

"Inside?" McCarter asked.

"We cut an escape door," the man explained.

McCarter started to stand, leaving the bewildered mercenary sitting there, then he crouched again. "I'm not going to cuff you," he said loudly, and he glanced at his watch. "Save yourself if you can. You've got eleven minutes until this ship blows."

The man stared around him, as if trying to find McCarter in his blindness to read his face. "The ship blows in an hour," he said.

"If I were you, mate, I'd have my arse off this ship in the eleven minutes."

HIS NAME WAS Ivan Kappa, but everybody called him Kappa the Cat.

He took off the goggles and looked around him as he ran,

and in the pitch-black interior of the lower level walkway, without a light source other than the tiny leaks coming from the deck above him, he saw it all. The openings in the steel grate floor. The rusty pipe rails. The peeling paint.

Kappa the Cat chuckled with relief. He had evaded the flash out of sheer luck and well-honed reflexes. With his condition the flash would have blinded him for good, not just for a few minutes.

He hated his light sensitivity when it first struck him. It had forced him out of Special Forces, which was the one and only place he had ever been a success. It had made him a night dweller, a vampire, the ultimate loner. Then he turned it to his advantage and became a highly specialized killer.

Kappa the Cat, they said, could see in the dark. He could sneak up on you and have the wire around your throat before you even knew you weren't alone.

Kappa hated the nickname at first. *Cat* meant pussy, right? Then he saw the fear that the name engendered.

Three years after leaving the Army he was enjoying life again and making good money for very little work, devoting himself in his free time to honing his skills. He'd learned many ways to make the darkness work for him, and learned to avoid the light that made his vision turn to clouds of painful red.

When Korl tracked him down, by accessing Kappa's classified military psychological records and FBI profile, Kappa thought the colonel was a joker.

Then Korl had laid it on the line. He had the perfect career opportunity for Kappa. Otherwise, Korl explained, the joint FBI-Army investigation of Kappa was going to have him arrested and prosecuted for multiple murders before Christmas.

Kappa took the job. Everything had gone swell until the special ops guys with the flash grenades got on board this stinking tub.

Hell, everything was still swell. It had been close, yeah, but he was still one hundred percent functional.

That was way more functional then anybody else he knew, especially down here in the dark.

"Kappa, it's Luther."

Kappa grabbed the radio on his belt. "Go ahead, Luther."

"There's a pair of them trying to climb down the back of the ship. We're going after them."

"What are they trying to do?" Kappa asked as he jogged.

"Unknown. Oh, shit! Kappa, they're tossing grenades at the props!"

That made him stop. He stood there in the darkness, suddenly frantic. "Stop them!" he shouted into the radio. "Get everybody to the back of the boat and wipe them out, understand? I don't care what it takes! We're fucked if we can't keep this tin can moving for another hour!"

"Understood, Kappa," said his second in command. Luther was competent, even if he wasn't the sharpest tool in the shed. How much brains could it take to shoot at those commandos until they were dead?

Kappa the Cat started jogging again. What Luther didn't know was that he was a dead man. The *Singep* would intercept the Iranian supertankers in about ten minutes. Navigation was tied into the ship's radar, and some creative manipulation of the control software was now going to make the *Singep* drive itself directly into the closer tanker. With luck the explosion would be sufficient to take out tanker No. 2, as well.

Kappa the Cat had a perfect score so far. He had succeeded at every task Korl had given him. Failure now—

The hull shuddered. The rumble of the engines turned to a stutter.

Kappa the Cat pursed his lips angrily, knowing his score was no longer perfect.

KAPPA SLIPPED into the small utility room and locked the door behind him, then yanked up the floor panels. He sat on the edge of the opening, then swung inside and pulled the floor panel back into place over his head. He released his grip, then Kappa dropped and was standing in utter darkness. He raised the heavy hatch that would make his secret entrance-way watertight.

The hatch had been removed from another part of the ship and welded into place by some of Aska Wali's miserable ship breakers, resulting in a floodable compartment.

Kappa loved this place. It was so well sealed that there was no light, none. Even he didn't have enough light to see by in this room. He had a tiny key chain flashlight dangling on his belt, powered by a single AA battery, and when he flipped it on, the yellow beam danced across the floor with his move-ments. It was more than sufficient for Kappa the Cat.

He checked the charge. A skinny rope of plastique had been adhered to the outer hull, making a twenty-foot square of steel that stood between his chamber and the ocean. Even without cargo weighing her down, this compartment was below the waterline.

Korl had assured Kappa that the escape plan would work. Kappa knew how Korl and that politician, Jackson, planned to matter-of-factly betray and murder the mercenaries they'd hired for their around-the-world campaign, so he was suspi-cious of the escape plan Korl hatched for him. Too extrava-gant.

But then Korl had come through with the escape vehicle.

Korl might destroy a human being without batting an eye, but there was no way he would toss out a piece of merchandise like this.

Kappa got inside.

"THIS IS AS FAR as we go," Hawkins said as he cranked on the wheel to open the hatch. The door swung inward and Hawkins saw moonlight.

"Hallelujah," Encizo muttered as they entered a large chamber filled with the chopped-off stumps of piping and ventilation ductwork. The former ventilation room was now packed with inflatable rafts packaged with their outboard motors. A crude opening had been burned into the outer hull and the jagged steel edges were coated with resin sealant so they would be smooth enough to pass the inflatables through without tearing them.

"Any contact with Cal and Gary?" McCarter asked Hawkins as he tried the radio again. He'd been calling out every fifteen seconds and not getting a reply.

"Negative."

"Bloody hell." McCarter pushed the frustration aside. He hated to leave the ship without his full team. On the other hand, they were incommunicado as long as they were buried this deep inside the steel hull. He could best serve James and Manning by getting outside and directing them to the chamber with the escape rafts. Or have them simply jump ship.

"The ship is stopping," Hawkins observed. "Listen to that!"

McCarter heard the distant engine noise rev to an unhealthy intensity.

"They did it," he said. "The prop's off, and the engine's got nothing to slow the ship down." He glanced at his watch. "Let's go."

They thrust two of the inflatables out the opening, one after another, yanking the cords as the packages dropped. The rafts broke open, righted themselves as they hit the water and were fully inflated in seconds. Encizo was poised to make the twenty-foot leap, so he could collect the floating gas tanks as they were tossed down, when the floor lurched. His feet left the ground and he bowled into Hawkins, who was already on his way to the ground.

"What the blazes—!" McCarter exclaimed, picking himself out from between a pair of knee-high duct stumps. He stroked a hand across a seeping cut on his face. It was minor and he ignored it.

The others joined him, grabbing for the door edges as the ship canted under their feet.

"That can't have been one of Manning's rounds," McCarter declared. "He's on the other end of this boat."

"Felt like it was just underneath us," Encizo said. "I think somebody blew out the hull."

"To sink the ship? It doesn't make sense."

"Not to sink the ship," Hawkins interjected. "Check it out."

They looked down, where they could make out a lip of steel plating curling up out of the waves just below the waterline. The ship settled another degree to starboard, and a huge belch of air came from the gap. It was followed by a black mass that widened as it emerged from the ship. In the darkness of night it was featureless, skimming so close beneath the Arabian Sea they could have jumped down and waded on top of it.

And it was getting away.

Hawkins popped a flare, held it, then launched it the moment the black mass rose above the waves. The submarine submerged again, as if startled.

He forced the image into his mind—every line, every detail of the craft.

"Let's get out of here," McCarter said.

Their rafts were gone, sunk by the blast. There were many more. They ejected another pair, then Encizo made his leap into the sea and grabbed at the heavy fuel containers that they had pushed out the door. By the time Hawkins and McCarter made the two-story leap into the ocean, Encizo had the outboard motor running and had tied a tow line on the second raft.

"Gary and Cal?" McCarter sputtered as he hoisted himself into the raft.

"I reached them," Encizo reported. "They're already in the drink."

He engaged the blades when Hawkins was just half in the raft, and McCarter had to yank him in by the collar when the acceleration threatened to pull him back into the water. They buzzed alongside the now-silent vessel. The engine was spent.

They heard shouts from the deck of the *Singep* as they left her behind, followed by a brief crack of gunfire, but they were already out of range.

"There," Hawkins said from behind his night-vision glasses, and he guided Encizo toward the swimming commandos. James and Manning looked as content as a pair of frat brothers taking a dip at Miami Beach during spring break.

"Care for a lift?" Hawkins asked as Encizo cut the engine and drifted the inflatables to the swimmers.

"Might as well," Manning said. "I'm getting a leg cramp."

McCarter stepped into the towed raft and started the motor, then hauled in his teammates.

"My watch says we're out of time," James said.

"Yeah, we're out of here, mates."

The lighter load in the two rafts allowed the outboards to produce better speed than if they had crowded into one, and McCarter and Encizo opened the throttles all the way.

"Check it out," Manning said, gesturing back to the west.

McCarter turned and saw the lights. Two sets of them, each on a vessel a few miles beyond the stalled *Singep*. The lights of each ship stretched over a vast length—they could only have been from something as huge as a supertanker. It was the twin oil tankers out of Iran, pushing their way through the Arabian Sea.

"Lucky bastards," McCarter said.

ON BOARD the leased Iranian supertanker the sleeping man stirred, then sat up.

Captain Adnan Amir muttered angrily to himself. He hadn't slept through the ringing of his alarm clock in twenty years. The brilliance of the sunlight through his curtained port told him it had to be well past his 5:00 a.m. wake-up time.

Then he saw that the alarm clock said it wasn't even three in the morning.

And the sunlight was shifting unnaturally, becoming noticeably dimmer. With dawning dread, Captain Amir stepped to the port and yanked at the curtains.

He was just in time to witness the final seconds of the brilliant fireball that had once been the cargo vessel *Singep*.

CHAPTER TWENTY-FIVE

Alang

It was an hour before dawn and the five figures that slumped around the table in McCarter's hotel room were as hang-dog weary as he had ever seen his team.

Too little sleep over the past several days. None at all in twenty-four hours. Then the battle on the *Singep*. But the final straw had come when they were still miles from the coast and their fuel ran out. From then on it had been nothing but hours of rowing to reach the coast of the peninsula. Phoenix Force was sapped.

Hawkins had sketched furiously in a field notebook throughout the night and when they reached the hotel he scanned his artwork and sent it to Stony Man Farm. The sketches were line drawings of the submersible they'd glimpsed just before the *Singep* exploded. It had been dark, the vehicle was black, and he had seen the thing for just seconds, which made him doubtful about the usefulness of his drawings.

Minutes later Kurtzman was transmitting schematics and

photos that displayed one submarine after another on the notebook computer that was the centerpiece of their communication with Stony.

Encizo grumbled as the images cycled. "Who'd have thought there were this many submarine models on the open market."

"The field's really opened up in the past few years," Kurtzman replied. "Lucky for us we can limit our search to the very smallest subs. Whatever you witnessed last night required a slim profile to get secreted inside the *Singep*'s hull and to get out again through the exit you saw."

"Stop there, Bear," McCarter said. "Go back one."

Hawkins had seen it, too. He had deliberately remained quiet. He wanted the others confirming his choice before he could lead them in any particular direction.

The image reversed to a photo of a dry-docked submersible standing on supports in front of a pair of smiling engineers.

"Got an overhead view of this one, Bear?" Encizo asked.

"Not a photo. Here's the schematic."

The photo was replaced by a full-screen image of detailed CAD drawing of the submarine with a slate-gray color scheme applied to give it a realistic look. The image rotated slowly until it stood end-up. Hawkins guided Kurtzman's adjustment of the image until it matched the profile of the boat they had seen hours ago on the Arabian Sea.

Hawkins had guessed the boat at under fifteen yards, stem to stern, and he placed it at maybe sixty tons, but he also estimated his own margin of error at up to twenty percent, which in his book turned his specifications into trash data.

But then again, the specifications of the sub Encizo and McCarter were stuck on looked close enough.

"Look at this," Encizo was saying, his finger pointing out

a detail in the top of the sub. "This must be a hatch, right? That's all I saw on top of the sub we saw."

"Yeah," McCarter agreed. "No conning tower or anything like that. And this looks right, too. This rifling or whatever." His fingers traced the barely visible channels that ran from the nose of the sub, along the side of the top. "T.J.?"

Hawkins nodded. "That's it. I'd swear that's the profile we saw. Bear, what are we looking at?"

"A picture of a ghost," Kurtzman replied. "That submersible is supposed to be dead and buried."

"Three sets of eyes are telling you it isn't," McCarter said.

"Which makes it even more interesting," Kurtzman stated. "I think you'd better tell us about this submarine."

"Okay, Phoenix, what you're looking at is the schematics of a MIL project that never was. Here's the short version— in 2001, a Navy contractor came up with a scheme to get itself inserted into a project that it had already been denied. It was pretty soon after the first test run of a specialized commando sub that is designed to piggyback on Virginia-class submarines. SEALs were supposed to be using them within the next year. The company in question had already been beat out in the awards phase as the primary contractor. They were involved in supplying some of the componentry, but after the first test run and budget forecasts, this firm decided they could do better than the main contractor and they had a lot of design costs to recoup, so they repitched their submarine to the Navy."

"The Navy doesn't back out of a project with a primary contractor unless the whole thing's falling apart," James observed.

"The idea wasn't to convince the Navy to abandon their primary contractor. The second company simply wanted more of their design components worked into the project, and the most effective way to demonstrate it was by actually piecing together the demo sub. It worked for them, too. The Navy ended up giving them a bigger share of the pie. And then the demo minisub was scrapped, according to the records."

"Looks like the records lied," McCarter said.

"Bear," Hawkins interjected, "why couldn't this just be a similar minisub? How different can one minisub be from another?"

"We're looking into that now," Kurtzman said. "It's the grooves along the surface that are the giveaway. The channels were designed for full-scale experimentation with channeling water around the hull to create a sound-polarizing effect. These are already some of the quietest submersibles in existence, but the thought was to mask the boat's noise to an even greater extent through the channeling. The shape of the grooves can be dynamically augmented during sub operation—hydraulic fill pieces move into and out of the grooves. It all happens automatically to create the quietest signature based on the speed and altitude of the sub."

"Did it work?" Hawkins asked.

"Inconsistently," Kurtzman said. "This particular technology was abandoned for other sound-mitigation techniques."

"So a sub with those channels was a one-of-a-kind," Encizo concluded.

"Yeah," Kurtzman replied. "Even if somebody appropriated the plans to the original demo sub and rebuilt it, there'd be no reason to waste expense on including those channels."

"Franklin Jackson?" McCarter asked.

Barbara Price came on the line. "I've just been checking into that. Jackson was on the board of directors of the company in question for nine months in 2001, before he became a Senate candidate. He made a lot of enemies and they booted him."

"The Man's going to tell you that's circumstantial evidence," McCarter said.

"The circumstantial evidence against Franklin Jackson is just about to overflow the septic tank," Price replied.

"So give us the details on the sub, Bear," Hawkins requested. "How does it compare to the SEAL sub that is actually supposed to see service?"

The differences, Kurtzman told them, were minimal. The sub in question was only slightly larger and heavier than the Navy version.

The Navy commando minisub designed to piggyback on U.S. Virginia-class submarines was a fifty-five-ton submersible with an operational range of 125-plus nautical miles. Direct-docking with the Virginia-class made coming and going easy. The minisubs were made to be piloted by commandos with minimal training, which meant their operation depended heavily on a navigation system using GPS augmented with nose-mounted and belly-mounted sonar sensors. A destination was typically preprogrammed, or the sub could be piloted with a joystick. Operation and diagnostics interface was ninety-nine-percent touch-screen controlled.

The sub was driven by specially mounted and enclosed pump-jet propulsors, providing better speed and maneuverability as well as low noise. The power source was a fuel cell using metal hydrides and liquid oxygen as a storage medium. The fuel cells gave the minisubs better range than standard batteries while providing the same low-noise characteristics of battery power.

"Here's the major difference on our sub," Kurtzman said. "It's got a much larger generator for recharging the fuel cells. The Navy designs use tiny rechargers, sometimes none at all. They depend on the host boat to get them juiced up."

"So ours is far more independent," James observed. "It's

going to have a cruising range way more than 125 miles, depending on how much diesel they've stowed aboard."

"Don't forget their floating gas station trick," McCarter added. "If they've got a long way to go, they could have staged floating refueling centers like we saw in Micronesia. Then their range is indefinite."

There was a moment of silence, then Hawkins asked, "Can you trace it, Stony?"

"We received a brief signal from one of the same satellite phones we traced in the South Pacific," Price responded. "It came nine minutes after the *Singep* exploded and was within two miles of the Iranian supertankers."

"We gotta hope he uses that phone exclusively for communications with home base," Hawkins said. "Stony, however they came by that boat, it couldn't have been cheap. Somebody got paid well to hand it over."

"So what do we do about it?" Encizo growled.

"We sleep," McCarter said. "We need it."

Ten minutes later they were all sleeping.

THE MINISUB SURFACED inside the remains of an Australian cargo ship. Kappa had arranged for the old hulk to be parked with its hind end over a depression in the seafloor. It gave him enough clearance to bring the minisub under the cargo ship, whose wide, flat underside had been opened with acetylene torches. A thirty-by-fifty-foot opening left him more than enough room to berth the sub.

Kappa the Cat had formed a good working relationship with Aska Wali. Wali had driven a hard bargain for the use of his ship-breaking facility, especially for the custom work Kappa had requested. Between the trio of hulls designed to provide the hiding place for the *Singep* and the eviscerated Australian hulk, Wali had claimed that twenty percent of his business was being idled. Kappa had demonstrated on paper how Wali could continue to operate his business at one hundred percent capacity. Wali had played dumb until Kappa had walked out the door.

Kappa paid more than he wanted to in the end. Not that it was his money. Still, Wali had ripped him off. That was a punishable offense. Kappa was almost happy when Wali started screwing things up. It gave him an excuse to mete out retribution.

First the Company man from the embassy in Bombay got involved. Kappa wasn't sure where the leak was but Wali was responsible.

Tonight was a worse offense. Wali had led some sort of special ops outfit right to the *Singep,* and the result had been a tremendous failure. The *Singep* missed its target. Never mind that the Iran tankers were a last-minute opportunity. It was still a failure.

Upon leaving the *Singep,* Kappa parked the minisub at a depth of forty feet. The exterior monitors showed the sea turning from black to white. Only after the flash of the blast had faded did he surface and search the sea around him.

Then he saw the tankers. Unscathed. Kappa was enraged.

The rest of his to-do list would have to wait. There was a new item on the list, and Aska Wali had number one priority.

THIS WAS Kappa's kind of place. Dark. There wasn't a single security light on the shore. He didn't have to put on the goggles until he closed in on Wali's bizarre headquarters building.

The ski goggles were Bolle models that could be fitted with prescription lenses. Kappa had located an optician with a business in specialized prescription eyewear such as dive masks, shooting glasses, motorcycle goggles, even gas masks.

Kappa's requests had pushed the envelope. He wanted his goggles fitted with electrochromic glass, with a thin coating on the surface that changes color and darkness when tiny electric voltages are applied.

At first the optician had insisted that photochromic lenses would fit the bill, but these lenses darkened automatically in bright light, and even the special grades didn't get extremely dark in bright sun. Kappa wanted control and he wanted full protection.

The goggles that were eventually manufactured for him included sensors to react to light intensity and to darken the glass automatically, along with a manual control. The Bolle ski goggle frames gave him complete eye coverage and they strapped around the back of his head. They wouldn't get knocked out of place. The electrochromic coating on the glass was powered with a tiny battery pack built into the glasses under the right eye.

Under the left eye was the computer chip to control the automatic darkening of the glass. It received input from a pair of photo-optic light sensors mounted on the front of the goggles above the glass, and it was defaulted to maintain a level of glass opacity that was safe for someone with Kappa's extreme sensitivity. One brilliant flash just might blind Kappa the Cat for life.

Kappa found himself using the belt-mounted manual override adjustment half the time, which he felt was a pain in the ass.

The problem was that ambient light picked up by the sensors never equated to the light at the spot where he was actually trying to look.

He was already thinking about a new pair of goggles with two sensors for each eye. He'd keep the ambient light sensor and add an automatic aim-and-adjust sensor. When he was looking at a particular point and needed a fine-tune on the darkening of the lens, he would hold down a switch to get a crosshairs display, center the crosshairs on what he wanted to see, then release the switch. The sensor would take a targeted light reading and balance it with the ambient for a new adjustment.

Now he adjusted the electrochromic lenses until they were so dark a normal person would see nothing. Kappa saw fine, scanning the grounds around Wali's shantytown mansion. He squinted hard as he examined the roofline and its scalding white floodlights. There was no watchman on duty.

Maybe Wali wasn't here.

Kappa chuckled. Wali would be here. He slept in his office six nights a week because the only alternative was to go home to his wife.

Kappa approached and hugged the building, then headed for a window he had scoped out weeks earlier on one of his visits to Wali. It was an old port window, large but in a corroded frame. The builders had torn the flimsy metal three times trying to bolt it to the wall. They'd given up and left it hanging by a single bolt. A generous caulking job kept the oily breeze from leaking inside.

Kappa used a razor blade knife to strip the caulk, then swung the window to the side and slithered inside.

He was in the main room, and it was quiet, though a tiny hiss of air came from the exposed ductwork overhead that led into Wali's office. The air-conditioning in the rest of the place had to have been turned off after hours. There were no lights, either. Kappa removed the goggles.

He crept through the darkness in bare feet, seeing into every black corner. Nobody worked like him. Kappa the Cat was one-of-a-kind.

He knew he was stroking himself, but after today's fuck-up he could use a little confidence building.

The door was unlocked. The receptionist's office was silent. The door to Wali's office was ajar, and he heard Wali's rasping snore. When he stepped inside, Kappa found that Wali wasn't alone.

It was one of the immigrant women. They came with their husbands and fathers by the tens of thousands to Alang. They were the poorest of the poor. You had to be desperate to accept work at Alang. The women, like the men, would do whatever needed doing to feed their families.

She sat up, naked and gaunt, when the door squeaked, and Kappa saw the darkness under her eyes and the pallor of her flesh. Young, but already beaten down by the world. A tired old woman before she turned twenty.

She reminded Kappa of a mother he had once had.

They communicated without words while Wali snored noisily. The suppressed handgun gave her a pretty good idea why Kappa had come, but she wasn't alarmed or afraid as she waited for him to decide whether he would kill her. She didn't even look terribly interested.

Kappa waved the gun when he could think of no good reason to kill her. She started for the door, but he stopped her with a gesture and stepped to the desk. He jimmied the drawer lock in seconds, one-handed, and tossed her an inch of Indian currency. Now she smiled, a thin hardening of her mouth, and left, dragging her sari. Kappa knew she'd keep her mouth shut.

He holstered the handgun, and by the time he heard the distant opening and closing of the door at the front of the building he had the garrote around Aska Wali's neck.

A gun, after all, would have been a quick death. Aska Wali deserved to suffer for a minute or five.

And suffer he did.

CHAPTER TWENTY-SIX

Chicago, Illinois, U.S.A.

"I thought all the foreign banks had their U.S. headquarters in New York," Hermann Schwarz said, gazing up at the big Michigan Avenue towers. "Does this make sense to you as a target, Pol?"

It was Carl Lyons who answered. "Think of it in terms of the economics."

Schwarz grimaced. "When we get to know each other a little better, I think you'll see economics isn't my strong point."

"You're not nearly as stupid as you look, act or talk, Gadgets," Lyons said as they strode up North Michigan. "Look at it from Jackson's point of view. He's accomplished a tremendous amount in just seventy-two hours." Lyons nodded at the newspaper boxes standing on the sidewalk against the building. The first box displayed the morning *Chicago Sun-Times* with the headline Foreign Firms Flee. The second box held the *Chicago Tribune,* which proclaimed, European/Asian Companies Pull Out Of U.S.

The stories proclaimed that unprecedented numbers of foreign corporations had been forced to abruptly close up shop in the past two days in the face of near-instantaneous fluctuations in insurance premiums on international businesses and on the loans that funded them. The businesses blamed a reactionary financial market.

"Christmas came early for Franklin Jackson," Schwarz said. "This is just what he was after. So why change course when everything's going swell?"

"He's not changing course, just expanding his realm of influence," Blancanales said. "He's done unprecedented damage to foreign manufacturing, product imports, oil imports. But they've all got overhead, property and inventory. The banking industry has only its people. The actual dollars are unreachable inside the global financial system."

Schwarz considered it. "So how does he drive out the foreign bankers?" Then he answered his own question. "By making them afraid to do business here."

Lyons was listening to his mobile phone when he brought them to a halt in front of the Banco de Mexico y España, which occupied an eleven-story North Michigan Avenue building. The first five floors were mostly retail—an ultra-high-end department store and spa and store management offices.

Schwarz had a bad feeling about this place.

"What do we do now?" he asked.

"We wait until something starts to happen," Lyons answered.

"Wait? Here? On the sidewalk?"

Stony Man Farm

"HOLD, ABLE."

Barbara Price switched her line and stabbed at the keyboard as if she were intent on cracking the plastic keys. There was a short ring, then she spoke sharply. "Hal."

"Barb?" Brognola said.

"Hal, what's going on? Do we have an assist or not?"

"I don't have an answer, Barb—"

"What's he waiting for?"

"Confirmation from Homeland Security," Brognola admitted sourly.

"Confirmation of what? Homeland isn't going to give him conformation, and you know it."

"I do know it, and I told the President."

"We're way ahead of Homeland and everybody else on the learning curve, Hal," Price insisted, feeling the heat rise to her face. "We've been a step ahead of Homeland and the Bureau and Langley since this thing started. Now we're allowing our men to go into unnecessary danger because of it?"

"The President isn't convinced there is danger—"

"The President didn't think there was danger in Micronesia, either," Price shot back. "He didn't think there was danger in Baymont and he didn't think there was danger at the Heartland Mall. What's going to convince him we know what we're talking about?"

"You know how politically delicate this thing is," Brognola replied.

Price felt the heat come to a boil. "The Man's in denial, and more people will die because of it. We put Able at risk twice and we're doing it again, this minute. After what Able's done for this country in the past two days, it's not a big sacrifice to send in some backup!"

"I've got another call coming in. Hold on, Barb."

Price heard the click of the connection being put on hold. She snapped the key that severed her connection and fell against the back of the chair, arms folded tight on her chest, and fumed.

Aaron Kurtzman was monitoring the infrequent blips of activity from the mercenary team. They were coalescing in the vicinity of the Chicago building, U.S. headquarters to the international bank. The Banco de Mexico y España, or BME, was based in Barcelona and in recent years had done more business out of its Mexico City offices than it did at home. In the past two years it had become a financial powerhouse in the U.S.

But the BME building was in the city. The military presence that Price wanted would be noticed. It would be big news even if there was no event.

But there would be an event. Price knew it. Her instincts had been right so far. When this event happened, it would be a lot better to have a force on hand to stabilize it quickly.

She glared at the screen showing a three-dimensional rendering of the Michigan Avenue location. There were icons for the most recent phone traces, and icons for the three members of Able Team. Nearby was a truckful of Stony Man Farm blacksuits, with two more of the commandos stationed atop nearby buildings.

Lyons, Blancanales and Schwarz were hanging around in front of the building, but she heard Kurtzman give them the okay to head inside. Their icons moved inside the building on the display. Their photo IDs got them through security and they headed up to the eighth floor, which was as high as they could go without passing through the high-security system.

"How's your control of the security and automation inside BME?" she called.

"Eighty percent, maybe," Kurtzman said without moving his intent gaze from his monitor across the room. "I can get them past the biometrics. What worries me is the human and the horns."

Kurtzman, with the help of Akira Tokaido, had hacked into the building's automation system using stolen security pass codes and cracks in the armor around the fire department emergency access overrides. There was an unexpected tricky problem—any time one of the codes was used the system was designed to trigger emergency evacuation alarms, if the alarms weren't already activated.

Able Team couldn't exactly make a clandestine entrance with the whooping of the evacuation horns announcing them. It would be just as bad if they were noticed by a set of human eyes when they entered .ae upper floors. Anybody who witnessed three strange men coming through the biometrics security system without a company official as chaperon would assume the worst immediately.

Tokaido had struggled to come up with a method of fooling the system into thinking the alarms were already sounding when they weren't. The system wasn't as tough to crack as it was poorly organized, with several incompatible systems customized to feed data into a command control, which was itself specially made for the bank building. Tokaido couldn't be sure he had found all the functions' paths amid the code clutter. Finally he had no choice but to break into the main system and change the programming itself to ignore all commands to start the emergency system. The system was so messy, so unstructured, he would never know if he was causing ripple-effect problems until they showed up, but it was his only option.

He plugged in the new code and recompiled the routine, Kurtzman looking over his shoulder. They held their breaths together as they monitored the system and the communications feed from Able Team.

"It looks okay for now, anyway," Kurtzman breathed.

Tokaido grabbed at the drawer under his desk and yanked out sticky notes. He scribbled something, then slapped his message on the bottom of the monitor.

Tokaido would have claimed the message was in English, not Japanese, but it was illegible to most readers of both languages. Kurtzman, with some experience at the task, deciphered the words "Put it back."

Tokaido grinned sheepishly. "When this is all done," he said, "I thought we ought to restore their burglar and fire alarms."

"Good thinking."

Chicago

THE FIRST FLOOR actually did hold a typical-looking bank lobby, with tellers and loan officers, but the tone was more serious than a bank catering to the general public. The patrons here were mostly Hispanic, mostly in two-thousand-dollar suits. The small stores filling the lower levels were the kind of establishments that sold two-thousand-dollar suits. There were spas and art galleries, and a small café.

"Where's the Radio Shack?" Schwarz muttered.

Their stolen IDs got them past the security guards and gave them access to the lower levels of the Banco de Mexico y España offices, where hundreds of BME employees and daily visitors made them anonymous.

Finally, through a circuitous route, they made it to the top level of the less secure floors and found the fire stairs entrance to the secure top floors. There was no way of knowing if anyone was on the other side of the door when they picked the exit-only lock.

"Stony, we're in place to try the biometrics," Lyons radioed.

"Stony Two here. We're ready," Aaron Kurtzman said, but he made it sound like a question.

Schwarz didn't like the sound of Kurtzman's lack of confidence. "Stony Two, you're not going to get us arrested, are you? I'll be really pissed if I spend the rest of this day in a Chicago lockup."

"We'll do our best."

Schwarz grimaced. "That's reassuring," he said off the air as he opened the panel on the security box set in the wall alongside the heavy-duty security doors.

The stairwell was cinder blocks and glossy white paint, and would have looked at home in any high school or office building in North America, which made the flashing lights and brushed stainless-steel surfaces of the biometrics reader look oddly out of place. The display was small and sealed behind a half inch of security glass.

"Oh," Schwarz said.

The others looked at him expectantly.

"No wonder Bear's got the maybes," Schwarz said gloomily as he examined the panel. "The banco's got quad-modal biometrics. This thing does a digital read on your voice, fingerprint, facial characteristics and pattern of lip movement, all at the same time."

"Able Three," Kurtzman said, "assume the position."

"I'm there," Schwarz said. His eyes scanned the unit, watching for signs of life other than the Ready message on the display and the flashing of all-go lights. If there were a security guard posted here he would have been watching those lights for a pattern that indicated a potential security breach. Unless the biometrics user knew to watch for those patterns, he'd still be standing at the panel when the guard moved in to apprehend him.

Schwarz wished he knew the pattern. Security guard or not, he'd like all the warning he could get if their cover was blown.

"Here we go, Able Three," Kurtzman reported. "Start her up."

Schwarz put his thumb on the small yellow panel, which glowed as it read his thumb print and initiated the check.

The display showed a new message: "Please speak your name and affiliation." At the same time there was a shifting of movement behind the eye-level dark glass panel, where the lens would focus on his face and lips for digital rendering and comparison. But surely there was more than one lens behind the glass, maneuvering independently…

"Bear, shut it down!" Schwarz shouted. "Freeze and shut up," he ordered Lyons and Blancanales, who were standing just behind him.

"Shutting down, Able Three," Kurtzman radioed tersely, and then he said nothing.

There was silence and stillness that seemed to go on forever. Schwarz couldn't tear his eyes from the polite message and the ominous patterns of blinking lights. How patient was this thing? How long would it wait for a response before calling in building security? Could Kurtzman even stop an identification operation that had already started?

The display message seemed to fade away, and then it came back with "Ready."

"Stony Two here. We shut it down."

"Did it collect any data?" Schwarz demanded.

"Not so far as we can tell—"

"Listen, Bear, this thing's got peripheral vision. It started scanning the lot of us."

"What?" Kurtzman almost shouted. "You sure?"

"I saw it happening. There's at least two extra video pickups back there, and the way they were focusing was not on me. They've got an auxiliary system hidden behind the first."

Stony Man Farm, Virginia

KURTZMAN SWORE under his breath.

"Hold, Able." He pivoted the wheelchair like a bar stool,

and found himself facing his entire senior staff. They looked at him worriedly from their stations.

"Give me something. Why didn't we know?" Kurtzman demanded.

"A separate data route, masquerading as ventilation system commands or something like that," Tokaido suggested.

"The system is untidy," Huntington Weathers said in a rumble. "Maybe that's no accident. There's all sorts of application activity that looks sloppy. We've got hundreds of lines of code that look like leftovers from old systems that were simply left there. Maybe we were fooled."

Tokaido shook his head. "There's tons of that stuff. It can't all be placed purposely to disguise other activity."

"'Course not," Carmen Delahunt said. "Which makes the actual camouflaged subroutines even tougher to see."

Kurtzman's neck was so tense that his head hardly moved when he nodded. "This system expects to be hacked."

"And expects to defeat the hackers," Wethers agreed. "If Gadgets had failed to notice the extra video, and if we hadn't had enough control to shut down the panel as fast as we did, the system would have scanned Carl and Rosario. Even if we made the system think Gadgets was somebody it knew, one or two independent remote systems would have sounded their own alarms."

"They've got to use redundant biometrics apps outside their own network," Tokaido added.

Kurtzman jumped on it. "Right. The system designers might disguise a data feed from us hackers, but there are two things they could not hide—not from us. One, extra biometrics analysis and comparison operations taking place on their internal software. Two, an extra, independent piece of biometrics software in this network."

"Bear?" Price asked on the intercom.

"Hold on, Barb," Kurtzman called.

"That meeting starts in seven minutes, Bear!"

"I know," he responded, then faced his audience. "How do we disable those redundant systems without setting off an alarm?"

"In seven minutes," Delahunt added thoughtfully.

"Search for activity across the network at the moment Able started the read," Tokaido stated excitedly. "Some sort of a message had to have gone out to prep the remote biometrics for an incoming data set. Figure out where it's going to. If the data set is formatted identically to the software we know about, we feed it the profiles we were planning to use for Carl and Pol."

Kurtzman nodded and issued a quick list of duties, then reported to Price as his team worked.

"Why not simply have Carl and Pol step out of the way when the biometrics start?" she demanded.

"The system will know if there are more people going through the security door than it thought were there originally."

Price sighed. "We're short on time, Aaron." Her voice had an almost pleading quality, an intimacy she shared with only those she was closest to, and only rarely.

Kurtzman felt the stiffness in his jaw become high-tension. He silently vowed not to let her down.

Chicago

THEY'D BEEN STANDING there, looking at one another like the Three Morose Stooges, but finally Schwarz heard Kurtzman declare, "Okay, Able, we've got it figured."

Kurtzman sounded full of confidence, and Schwarz knew it was an act. He could have made another crack about Kurtzman getting them arrested, but somehow things had changed.

"Affirmative," he replied without a trace of hesitation as

he positioned himself at the security panel. "Ready when you are, Stony Two."

"Proceed, Able Three."

Schwarz reached for the unit, paused to wipe his damp thumb on his shirt, then pressed it flat on the small yellow panel. He watched the dark glass and satisfied himself that there were indeed extra video pickups lurking behind it, focusing beyond him on his teammates. When prompted, he spoke the name of the employee he was impersonating. The name was Spanish. Schwarz couldn't possibly achieve an authentic accent, and he knew that shouldn't matter, but he found himself clenching his teeth as the system passed judgment.

Behind the scenes, Stony Man Farm was intercepting the data rendered by the system and sending a different set of data to be evaluated by the biometrics database. Somehow, Stony had also figured out how to nullify similar profiles being send by the auxiliary systems. How had they done that in just the last couple of minutes?

Accepted.

Like a politician, what the system said wasn't nearly as important as how it performed. Just because it claimed Schwarz passed muster didn't mean it really believed it, not until—

With a hum and a click, the door unlocked itself. Schwarz stepped down a narrow passage between a series of sensors and pushed the door.

He was inside. Stony had pulled it off. Schwarz started breathing again as Lyons and Blancanales went through the process and they stood together in the inner sanctum of Banco de Mexico y España.

"I feel like a jewel thief," Blancanales muttered.

Schwarz grinned. "Funny thing is, the cash is in a safe on the first floor. Up here they're protecting people and paperwork, not necessarily in that order."

Lyons reported when they had climbed to the top floor in the emergency stairway.

"Stony, we're in an alcove behind a fire door. There's a small window and we can see into the eleventh floor. This is as safe a place as any to pass the time."

"Understood, Able," Barbara Price answered. "The conference is supposed to start in two minutes, if I'm right about this one."

Lyons heard doubt in Price's voice. It spoke volumes. Price was as professional as they came, and she usually held her emotions in check when her teams were in the field. Lyons had worked with Price for a long time, under some of the most stressful situations imaginable, and the chord of submerged stress was like a ringing bell. She was more personally invested in this action, and she was rankled by the continued lack of support from above. The fact that Able was here alone, with just the blacksuits standing by to lend an assist, meant the Man had once again dismissed the Stony Man analysis of a target, even after their two bull's-eyes in Baymont and Cincinnati. To Price it was a slap in the face.

They'd been monitoring the movement of the phone call traces into Chicago. Less than an hour ago Price had been the one to identify this target. She had learned that BME conducted a monthly videoconference meeting for senior staff. It included executives of the bank in Barcelona, Chicago and Mexico City. It was the likeliest mark given Franklin Jackson's agenda, but their intelligence went just so far when trying to determine a target based only on the location of Colonel Korl's attack teams.

This was the downtown area of one of the biggest U.S. metropolitan cities. There were hundreds of companies here that did business internationally and that might meet Jackson's criteria as sinners against U.S. isolationism.

"Any movement from our friends with the phones?" Lyons asked.

"No trace of them in fifty-one minutes, so they could be anywhere by now."

"Able Three here," Schwarz radioed. "Has Bear got any clue about their method of entry?"

"No."

"How fast did he get into the building management network?"

"Just forty-three minutes ago."

Schwarz frowned.

"So between the last trace and the time Bear got access, Korl's team could have got inside themselves?" Blancanales asked.

Schwarz nodded. "Yeah. Without us knowing it."

CHAPTER TWENTY-SEVEN

Barcelona, Spain

Jorge Cabian looked at his watch, then looked at the television.

"The time on the TV is wrong," he stated flatly, turning to direct the question at a senior director seated at his right.

The man had become a senior director by knowing when to take responsibility for a problem, even if the problem had nothing to do with his sphere of operations and even when the problem was nonexistent. He was director of finance and had nothing to do with the maintenance of the videoconferencing equipment. He also knew that the system updated its time code from the corporate network, which updated itself several times a day from a European Union time server. It seemed unlikely that the time server was wrong and Cabian's watch was right.

Nevertheless, the senior director replied, "I'll have it fixed, Jorge."

Cabian was still irritated. He knew the man was giving him lip service. He knew it was his watch that was almost half a minute slow. On the four video displays he saw the board-rooms in the Chicago and Mexico City offices filling quickly, but at one minute until 10:00 a.m. North American Central Time there were still two empty seats in Mexico. One was filled just as the time code on the screen reached 10:00 a.m., and Cabian decided to cut the man some slack since he was bringing in millions of U.S. dollars' worth of new business.

The last seat was filled when the time code read 10:46 a.m. and Cabian gave a meaningful glare at his secretary, who interpreted exactly what was meant by it and made a quick note on her steno pad.

"Let's get started without *further* delay," Cabian announced loudly, trying to ignore the movement of the tiny camera perched atop the large screens. He spoke in Spanish. All meetings were conducted in Spanish. Only those who were fluent in true Spanish—not the gutter tongues of Latin America—rose to trusted positions under Jorge Cabian. "Also, I would like to dispense with the monthly reports as quickly as possible. Delmar, please start."

The director of Mexico City operations wasn't accustomed to launching immediately into his monthly summary, but he was a cool customer. You had to be to get anywhere up the corporate ladder that was propped up by Chairman and Director Cabian.

"This has been an excellent month for the Mexico office," the director began. The scattered microphones identified him as the speaker and the self-adjusting camera homed in on his voice automatically and quickly. In Barcelona the image on one of the pair of displays from Mexico City shifted into a close-up on the director. The system's preprogrammed video director even froze and faded the previous shot during the brief camera movement, then dissolved into the shot of the new speaker. It was as professional as any television camera work except it happened too fast. Cabian got jittery watching it. He tended to focus on the stationary shot on the first display, which showed a stationary shot of the entire Mexico meeting room.

The Mexico director of operations had been giving his report for a full minute before Cabian realized he hadn't heard a word of it. He tried to force his attention on the man, but his fears distracted him.

There had been a warning from the U.S., unofficial but definitely from some federal agency, practically begging him to cancel the meeting and to clear out his people. Cabian was a man who refused to be intimidated. More accurately, he refused to be manipulated. He didn't let anyone direct his actions. He'd told the U.S. ambassador who'd relayed the message that he wouldn't cancel the meeting under any circumstances. The Chicago office was one of the most secure nongovernment buildings in North America. Terrorists simply wouldn't—couldn't—get in.

But what if they did?

He glared at the image of the director, seeing the man's lips move without hearing what the man was saying. Something about landing a new account worth an annual eighty million U.S. if a certain problem could be overcome. Someone in the Chicago office asked a question, and the camera zeroed in on him with a jerk. The videoconferencing system in the Chicago office had been acting up for weeks, and it never seemed to get fixed properly.

There was a comment from someone in Mexico and the camera shifted abruptly to the new speaker, then the Mexico director spoke again and the camera zipped across the table to him. Cabian found himself experiencing a twinge of nausea.

His eyes were drawn to the wide-angle Chicago monitor.

He could see the door to the boardroom, out of focus but visible a few paces behind the executive sitting at the head of the conference table. That's where they would come from. Through that door. Was he going to see armed men come bursting through it at any minute?

No. He didn't believe it could happen. Not to him.

"...Mr. Cabian?"

The camera was lurching across the table in Chicago to focus on another director, who had asked him a question directly. Cabian had no clue what the question was about or even what was being discussed.

He turned his head to look at his secretary. The woman was a wonder, at work and in bed, almost psychic in her ability to meet his every need. Now she looked at him with mild confusion. She had never seen him preoccupied. None of them had.

Abruptly, Cabian's financial director broke in with a question of his own, and Cabian turned to the man, shocked. It had clearly been Cabian's turn to speak, and no one violated it, ever. Then Cabian realized the man had just saved him from embarrassment in front of his entire staff.

He'd have to think about how he could thank the man later, without admitting he had needed the assist.

There was a sharp sound from the audio system and Cabian started, only to see that it was from the Mexico display and was simply a man coughing. Despite his best efforts to stifle it, the camera focused on him, then shifted to another speaker, flicked back on the coughing man, back to the speaker. Cabian felt himself growing seasick, and his fear was escalating. He should never have allowed the meeting. What if the ambassador's fears were legitimate?

But could he do it without losing face? What would his people think if he stood up and canceled the rest of this meeting? How could he explain it without looking like a fool?

Then he heard the first blast.

The audio system registered the shot with extreme clarity. The autonomous camera on the Chicago display jerked wildly to the right and focused for a half second on the source of the noise—an arm and the extended muzzle of a suppressed rifle at the farthest extent of the camera's range of rotation. There was a gurgling cry and the camera swung wildly to the middle, focusing with a quick, expert image dissolve on the new business director as he choked, stumbling to his feet. As Cabian watched in horror, the man in the boardroom four thousand miles away grabbed at the bloody puncture in his throat and made hideous liquid sounds.

Shouts of surprise sent the automatic camera into spasms of movement and the screen blinked from one terrified face to another, then shot back to the wounded man as he crashed onto the table, tearing at his own bloodied throat in a desperate attempt to clear the ruined air passages. Two men were grabbing him, struggling to keep him from tearing his own flesh, but Cabian realized in a remote part of his brain that if they didn't allow the man to clear his throat of blockage he was going to suffocate in seconds.

On the wide-angle display Cabian saw the others in the Chicago conference room become still, facing something that was hidden from the cameras.

But Cabian knew what it was.

There was a burst of gunfire and Cabian clenched his entire body, but the shot had to have gone into the ceiling. The only reaction was that those helping the wounded director straightened and walked away.

The only sound in the Chicago office now was the thrashing of the dying director. He pounded the table with his head and hands, pushing notebooks and paperwork onto the floor while streaking the surface with rivers of blood, but unable to use his voice. As his movements became weaker he looked up, terror and agony written on his face, and he stared across the ocean at Jorge Cabian, as if he knew Cabian's pride and posture had led him to this agony.

When he died his eyes were still open, still staring into the tiny video camera, which lingered on the corpse because there was no other sound to attract its attention.

The Mexico City displays showed a riot of activity, with people shouting and scrambling in different directions, and Cabian realized there was chaos here in Barcelona, too.

"Silence." The order boomed out of Cabian like a roll of thunder. It was the cultivated voice of a commander and it brought instant peace to the meeting rooms in Barcelona and Mexico City. It was powerful enough even to get the attention of those who were facing a gunman in the offices in the U.S.

"What do you want?" he demanded. After a moment of silence, he tried again in English.

The off-screen voice of an American man answered, "What I want is your attention."

The camera swung wildly in the direction of the speaker but couldn't rotate far enough. It ended up focusing on the nearest terrified BME director and the muzzles of two guns.

Cabian couldn't keep the anger out of his voice. "You have it," he said.

Chicago

"ABLE, WE'VE GOT SIGNALS!" Price said suddenly. "Inside the building and on your floor. One in the meeting room, Number 2 on the east side of the building, Number 3 in the northeast corner."

"We're moving," Lyons reported as he led the way out of

their waiting place at the top of the emergency stairs, leaving behind the gym bags that had held their hardware. They jogged among the wide, richly appointed offices and heard the first burst of gunfire. Office workers were scrambling out of the glass-enclosed circular lobby that served as the reception area for the top-level executives.

A ripple of cries came from a gathering crowd at the sight of the armed commandos, but Lyons didn't take time to explain that they were the good guys.

"Get out!" he ordered.

The group fled, but a small mob of suits and uniforms gathered at the double oak doors—Lyons knew from the building schematics that this was the entrance to the boardroom. A gorilla of a security guard took a menacing step toward them, gripping a hefty Glock in two hands, not quite ready to bring the muzzle up from the floor.

"We're Justice Department," Lyons said quickly. The huge guard frowned, then decided the commandos would have simply gunned him down instead of feeding him a lie.

"What's going on in there?" Lyons demanded.

"We heard gunshots, then nothing," explained one of the suits. "We can't open the door."

"Two-inch-thick steel plate with a half-inch oak overlay inside and out. It's designed to be safe during a terrorist attack," the brute explained as if discussing baseball statistics, but his sneer showed he understood the irony. "Two stainless dead bolts and near airtight sealing with positive air pressure. We'll need plastique to get in."

"It's Mexico!" shouted a newcomer as he strode into the hallway with a mobile phone. "They're watching the whole thing over the video feed—they killed somebody in there!"

"Why? What do they want?" demanded the other suit.

"Talk it over downstairs," Lyons ordered. "You people get

this place evacuated. You," he said to the huge guard, "watch the door until everybody is off the floor, then go with them."

The brute backed away as the suits and the other security staff left the reception area and began shouting at the stragglers who had not yet had the sense to vacate the floor. The huge guard positioned himself in the wide-arched entranceway to the executive lobby.

"They're not coming out this way, are they?" he growled.

"I don't think so," Lyons said. "But don't bet your life on it."

The brute nodded thoughtfully, then his head snapped up as they heard the muffled storm of gunfire from beyond the vaultlike conference-room doors.

CHAPTER TWENTY-EIGHT

Barcelona, Spain

Jorge Cabian couldn't help sounding acrimonious. "You must want more than just to get my attention," he said to the unseen leader of the murderers in the U.S.

There was a rattle of paper. "Just as you have used Americans as pawns, now we use you as a pawn, foreigner."

My God, Cabian thought, he's reading a prepared statement.

"The U.S. has been the body upon which the foreign parasites have fattened. The fruit of our labor has been fed upon by the leeches from abroad. Our riches have been plundered for decades. We held out our hand to the world and every nation on earth abused our goodwill. Now the people of the Unites States are closing the open hands. Foreigners will no longer be allowed to profit at our expense. We are shutting the doors on international abuse of American generosity."

Cabian snorted. "Get your facts straight. This bank brings more gross dollars into the U.S. than out."

"The public-relations crap don't work no more, Cabian,"

the speaker said. Now that he was using his own words, he sounded like an uneducated, crass American from the Deep South. "You and yours have been playing with the numbers and spooning up lies to the people for long enough. We're full of it up to here. Here's what I think of your 'gross dollars.'"

Cabian tried to shout, but before a sound even left his throat he was drowned out by the bursts of suppressed gunfire.

The camera jittered around the room spasmodically, trying in vain to focus on the sudden cacophony. Noises came from everywhere as men and women screamed and crashed onto the tables and the floors. At every momentary lull in the sounds from dying human beings, the camera was pulled inexorably back to the source of suppressed gunfire, but all it could focus on were the vibrating muzzles and flashes.

Then the room was quiet again, and as the icy horror swelled inside him, Cabian saw nothing but corpses. They were all dead.

There was blurry movement very close to the wide-angle camera, and then a hand pulled something out from beneath the camera and held it for them to see. It was the DVD-R from the recorder on the videoconferencing unit, which automatically made a video record of every monthly meeting. The killers were taking a recording of the massacre.

What for? a part of Cabian's brain demanded.

But he knew. The media would never play it. Still, copies would travel around the world. Videotapes would be arriving in the offices of every firm doing business in the U.S., and every company that was considering it. Those who failed to get their own tape would see it on the Internet.

And it would go to the bank's customers. The U.S. customers would move their business, but foreign companies who did business in the U.S. would flee in terror. No one would want to risk the danger of the association.

Cabian couldn't help but admit the video would be an effective piece of public relations in and of itself.

The voice of the killer said, "Cabian, your business dealings in the United States of America have just been concluded."

The screens went black.

Chicago

THE TOP FLOORS had been gutted by the Spanish-Mexican bank when they purchased the building, with an eye toward creating a terrorist-proof environment. The boardroom was the safe zone on the executive level, with blast-proof walls, emergency power and oxygen supplies, and positive air pressure from both the building's and its own independent ventilation system. Occupants would be safe inside for hours from most bombs and fires, and they could ride out an atmospheric chemical or biological attack for more than four hours without being exposed to the agents. An extra fire door allowed for occupants to escape through an equally well-sealed corridor that took them across half the building.

The escape corridor was designed to be impassable from the outside, but the design had failed. Korl's mercenaries had clearly used it as their entrance. They'd leave that way, too, if the placement of mercenary guards was an indication.

Lyons spotted the first of them coming around the corner, where he was patrolling on guard duty. Before the Able Team leader got off his shot, Blancanales beat him to it, unleashing a burst from the MP-5 that ruined the wall after the mercenary made an instant retreat. Lyons bolted after him and triggered the Colt Python at the surprised-looking mercenary who had taken up a position of what he thought was safety.

The merc flung himself aside. His lightning reflexes saved his life for the second time in a half-dozen heartbeats, but that was more heartbeats than he still had coming. Lyons set his jaw with annoyance as he flung himself into the open, allowing himself to crash bodily into the far wall and exposing himself completely. Lyons had triggered the revolver twice. Two rounds took the mercenary in the head and chest and bloodied the textured ivory paint on the wall behind him.

The man was tenacious. He fought gravity, clinging to the wall, but it was a corpse's eyes that watched Rosario Blancanales appear, landing in a crouch and triggering the submachine gun at the end of the hall as a second gunner appeared with a radio held to his face. The distant gunner flopped down dead while his comrade slumped reluctantly to the floor.

Lyons sensed movement rushing past him and he whirled in time to see Schwarz cut down another gunner in the opposite hall.

"Guess there's more than Stony traced," Schwarz said.

"We should have expected that," Lyons responded. "Which door?"

Schwarz had studied the layout of the building for hours. The hall was wide, filled with antique furniture and oak doors, but he identified one of them without hesitation. "That one. That's where they'll come from."

"Let's set up—" Lyon's words were cut off when the door burst open as if kicked and a pair of back-to-back mercenaries stepped into the open, fingers on the triggers of their weapons, and the gunfire chased after Able Team like a swarm of hornets. Lyons leaped into the adjoining hall as Schwarz pulled into it like a tortoise withdrawing his vital parts into his shell, but Blancanales didn't join them.

He landed hard and triggered the MP-5 during the hour-long microsecond before the hail of rounds from the Calico M-961-A submachine gun chased him down. The flying streams of 9 mm rounds passed within inches of each other before Blancanales's burst made tatters of the gunner's chest. The Calico was flung onto the carpet and its owner pitched alongside it, but Blancanales's finger was locked on the trigger, hounding the second gunner as he bolted back into the escape corridor. The Able Team commando heard a wordless sound and saw blood fly from the mercenary's back just before he disappeared inside.

There were quick shouts of consultation that lasted just long enough for Blancanales to pull himself onto his knees, then a part of a man appeared, and the long seconds froze into a lifetime. The arm had a grenade; the face had a sneer. Blancanales swept his gun at the arm and triggered the magazine dry, but the arm vanished and the grenade was flying right at him.

He watched it come.

He could make an awkward leap back and to the side to get into the adjoining hall, but he'd never make it.

He could collapse on the floor and cover his head and hope that the burns and/or the flying shrapnel didn't destroy enough exposed flesh to kill him instantly.

That seemed unlikely.

But, what the hell, it wasn't as if he had a third option.

He fell flat again and never saw Lyons coming, so only Schwarz witnessed the maniac's gunplay. You'd have to be a maniac to step into the path of a flying grenade.

The Atchisson Assault 12 was at his shoulder and he fired it at the grenade as if it were a clay pigeon, then pulled an arm over his face and spun as the grenade, thrust away by the blast, clonked on the wall and detonated on the carpeting.

Schwarz watched the wall of fire thrust against Lyons,

sending him staggering backward but never taking him off his feet. The heat dissipated and the Able Team leader raised the shotgun again. Schwarz reached his side, wondering if Lyons was dead and staying stubbornly on his feet like the first dead gunner. But for a dead guy Lyons was moving fast, and when the figure in the door appeared with another grenade, Lyons fired before Schwarz. The Atchisson thundered and the arm transformed into a mangled red limb. The grenade plopped to the carpet, and shouts in the escape corridor were cut off by a fresh burst of fire.

Schwarz went on the offensive, half convinced that both his partners were too wounded to carry on. He moved to the entrance of the escape corridor, which extended from the rear of the BME corporate conference room. He opened fire at the figures at the end of the corridor. There were three of them still standing.

There was nowhere for them to hide from the extended submachine-gun fire and Schwarz watched his rounds cut across the chests of a pair of them, and they crashed into the figure behind them. He knew from their behavior that he'd hit body armor.

The last man pushed his way clear of the others, glaring at Schwarz through a clear face shield. His weapon was huge, like a clown's pistol.

Schwarz was convinced that everybody but him was insane. The guys he was working with had to be crazy to behave the way they did, and now this maniac was wielding a freaking grenade launcher inside a freaking blast-proof tunnel.

Schwarz kicked the door shut as the launcher fired. The door swung easily, but it felt so heavy it had to be armored. If it held, the entire blast of the incendiary round would be contained inside that corridor, and the three remaining mercenaries would be incinerated.

Then he heard the impact.

"Buckshot," he said out loud, and was surprised to find Blancanales and Lyons standing behind him. Neither of them looked dead.

The buckshot round nudged the door open again, and Schwarz herded the others back the way they'd come, finding cover. He had a feeling the maniac with the grenade launcher was going to try to clear his path.

The next 40 mm grenade sailed out of the escape corridor, hit the wall with a metallic clank, and an instant later burst. The hall filled with fire. Seconds later it was followed up with a fragmentation grenade. All they could do was stand there watching the intersecting hallway as the scorched walls were abraded by hundreds of deadly fléchettes. On the heels of the second grenade came a burst of automatic rifle fire that filled the hall and kept them where they were.

Lyons was reporting rapidly and quietly to Stony Man Farm.

"They're heading for the emergency exit, Stony," Lyons said.

"We're ready for it," Kurtzman replied on their open channel.

Schwarz flipped down a tiny extendible arm on his headset and edged to the corner, poking the small video pickup into the open and watching on the flip-down display. The three surviving mercenaries were backing down the hall, covering their trail with their weapons. The figure with the grenade launcher came to a halt, spotting the video pickup, and he grimaced sardonically.

Schwarz used the digital zoom to get up close and personal.

"Korl."

"What?" Lyons demanded, standing at his shoulder. "He's here?"

"Himself," Schwarz answered. "Able Three here, we have Colonel Korl, live and in person."

"Stony One here," Price replied quickly. "Let's take him."

"Ready when you say, Able," Kurtzman added.

There was a problem. Colonel Korl's companions had disappeared into the next corridor, heading for escape, but Korl was standing there, covering the trail with his clown-size pistol and holding the grimace as though he was waiting to have his picture taken.

Schwarz tried not to blink. He didn't want to miss the signal if the colonel decided to send another grenade at them, but there was no sign of an attack on the colonel's face. And there was no sign of hesitation, either. He was waiting and he had a reason for it, as if deliberately trying to foil Stony's scheme. But he couldn't know it. Could he?

Abruptly, Korl was gone, slipping after his compatriots. He'd be moving fast and Schwarz decided to give him three seconds, two, one—

"Able Three?" Kurtzman asked.

"Now, Bear!"

KORL BROUGHT HIMSELF to a sudden halt as the building filled with a fresh onslaught of whopping alarms, then cursed himself as the doors ahead of his last two enforcers slid suddenly into place and a series of red lights flashed on the panel.

The young brown-haired man, a recent dishonorable discharge from the Marines, gaped at the panel then whirled on Korl.

"Now they're gassing us!"

"No, they're not," Korl answered calmly.

"What do you mean? What's that supposed to tell you?" The has-been Marine was losing his cool.

Korl spent five seconds examining the display. "They've

hacked into the building. They told the system there's a chem-bio attack."

"And just why the fuck would they do that?"

"Did you happen to notice that we're locked in, asshole?" the second mercenary said through clenched jaws. The gunfire he had taken in the chest had broken at least one rib.

The ex-Marine's rage seeped out of him like blood trickling out of a sponge and he leaped to the sealed door, attacking it fervently as Korl and his wounded merc retraced their steps and entered one of the offices.

Korl touched a button on his phone and waited out the complicated connection procedure. It could take as long as three seconds, but it was worth it to have secure communications.

"Korl here," he reported. "We're making a rooftop exit."

"Understood," his mission communications replied. "Transport is on its way."

Korl yanked at the window, which opened less than two inches. The rubber safety stops had yellow decals marked with black text: Pull Up In An Emergency. Korl pulled up and the rubber piece fell to the floor.

Then Korl did nothing for five seconds. Under the circumstances it was an extremely long time to pause to think things over.

"Colonel?" the wounded mercenary asked, holding his chest and panting like a dying dog.

There was a shout from the hallway and the ex-Marine stormed in. "Were you just gonna leave me here?"

Korl grimaced. "I thought you were right behind us. I was just about to go fetch your fool ass."

The ex-Marine's wild eyes fell on the window. "Can we get out that way?"

"Secondary escape route," Korl stated. "A chopper will

land on the roof in forty-five seconds. Get the window. I'll help Dent."

Korl grasped the forearm of the wounded mercenary, who looked at the older man as if the ex-colonel had just felt him up. The merc yanked aside the window and leaped onto the tubular aluminum fire escape, scrambling up and out of sight.

Korl released the wounded merc as the sound of the helicopter reached them, growing rapidly louder.

"Colonel?"

"I'm testing a hypothesis," Korl growled. "Stay away from the window."

"We got to get out!"

"Not this way," Korl said. "Look."

The mercenary squinted at the building that backed against the BME headquarters.

"SWAT teams!"

"Chicago P.D. would never respond that fast. They're some kind of special ops."

The figures on the rooftop came running and immediately opened fire on the side of the building. The ex-Marine yelped vehemently and shouted for help, then fell silent.

The mercenary forgot the pain that was clouding his mind. "They knew we were going to try to get out this way?"

Korl held up the phone. "Not as secure as we thought."

"I thought it was impossible to listen in!"

"Maybe they simply traced the source. Maybe that's what they've been doing all along."

"So how the hell do we get out?"

Korl smiled savagely. "It's already taken care of."

SCHWARZ DIDN'T WASTE time with the video and it was a good thing he didn't. There was a quick shadow of movement that was gone. If he had been an eye blink later, he would have missed it.

"Stony here. We've got a new signal," Price radioed.

"Able Three here—where's it headed, Stony?"

"Nowhere, Able Three," Kurtzman reported. "It's right where it was last time. They must think the roof access is their only avenue of escape."

"No, they don't," Schwarz replied.

"What do you know, Gadgets?" Lyons demanded.

"I think it's a decoy."

Lyons frowned. "Let's find out."

Schwarz twisted the knob and kicked, then fell back to allow Blancanales egress, closely followed by Lyons. They swept the room and Blancanales inspected the only hiding place—under a desk hand-carved from honey-stained wood.

Schwarz strode in and grabbed the phone.

"Able, we just lost the signal," Price reported.

"It was us who turned it off," Blancanales reported. "Tell Bear they're on to him."

Schwarz led the way into the small alcove off the hallway where he had spotted the movement. They cleared the interior, finding themselves in a utility access area that was more closet than room. One bare bulb was yellow and dim.

"You sure this was where you saw them?" Lyons demanded.

"I'm not sure I saw anything," Schwarz responded testily.

"Sure you did, Gadgets," Blancanales said, thrusting an arm into a gaping black air vent and pulling in a handful of bright orange nylon material. "Emergency escape tube. The kind they use for getting people out of skyscrapers in fires. You control your descent speed with elbow pressure."

"Yeah. This is an unused elevator shaft I saw on the building plans. They were planning to develop it into their own emergency escape route after they moved the elevator closer to the front of the building. It only goes down to the fourth floor."

"We're not going this way—they made sure of that," Blancanales declared as the first wafts of smoke emerged then turned to a billow. "So what do we do?"

CHAPTER TWENTY-NINE

His name was Saemund Dane but only his mother called him Saemund. Nobody ever, *ever* made fun of his name—not after they learned what he did for a living.

"He kills people," his friends would explain to the jerk in the bar. There was always a jerk in a bar who thought Saemund was a hysterical name. "He's really good at it. He gets paid for doing it."

True enough. Saemund Dane was good at his job. He had natural talent and love for his country. That was who he worked for. Patriotism was the only rationale that would ever have permitted him to do what he did with a clean conscience.

Six months ago Dane was with the U.S. Marines, when he was recruited to rotate in to a non-Marine unit. He had asked questions and received answers that weren't perfectly satisfying. He was told that he wouldn't know the true nature of the agency he would be working for, or even its affiliation other than a suggestion of a tie to the Department of Justice. Dane would need to swear to keep everything he did learn about the agency and experience during his time there an absolute secret.

Dane was the rare kind of young man whose word was as good as gold, and he didn't make his decision lightly. He was intrigued, but made hesitant by inferences by the man who recruited him that this unnamed agency operated outside normal limits—as in outside the limits set forth by law and the Constitution. That opened the door to corruption. What if he was asked to kill innocent people?

In the end he'd elected to join Stony Man Farm and within weeks he'd known he had made a good decision. During the past six months the Sensitive Operations Group was instrumental in putting a halt to more than one horrendous international crisis—some, the rest of the world never even knew about.

The SOG broke the rules, but it achieved victories for the good of the nation and the world.

Most important to Saemund Dane was that the ethical core was strong. There was no corruption. The Farm was clean.

Perched on a window washer's mobile scaffold, Dane was more nervous than he had ever been since joining the blacksuits. It wasn't because he was descending the outside of a skyscraper at speeds faster than the unit was designed to travel, it was the nature of the target.

He found himself hoping he wouldn't have to shoot.

When they were three stories above the street, his companion brought the scaffold to a stop. The outside rail was draped with paint-stained blankets over the reinforced outer steel wall, giving them cover and protection. The two blacksuits kept an eye on the street. Perched across the street from the Banco de Mexico y España building, they had an unobstructed view of the eastern rear end as well as the north side, all the way out onto Michigan Avenue. Dane thought he even spotted a glimpse of Lake Michigan glimmering out there, but he didn't pull his eyes away from the scene in front of him.

What scared him were the people. Crowds of them. All over the place. Tourists and office workers and Chicago P.D. and joggers. Not one of them deserved to get shot dead because they happened to be in the vicinity of a mass murderer. Especially from friendly fire.

Dane felt guilty about thinking it: he hoped the bad guys went the other direction.

"Blacksuit Commander here. Blacksuit Four, I'm patching you through to Stony Base."

Dane looked questioningly at the other blacksuit, who was just as perplexed. Stony Base always relayed commands through the blacksuit commander except in field situations that created an immediate need for detailed communications.

"Stony One here, Blacksuit Four," mission controller Barbara Price said evenly but quickly. Her image appeared in Dane's mind immediately. She had a few years on him, but she was beautiful. And more intimidating than any CO in his eight years in the military.

"Blacksuit Four here," he managed to reply without hesitation.

"Give me your position relative to the BME building."

He told her as best he could. They weren't exactly coordinates.

"Get back up to the fourth floor," she ordered. "Start now."

"We're moving, Stony One," he said as his companion operated the controls.

The mission controller quickly described what to look for as they reached the level of the fourth floor. "I'm looking right at it, Stony One."

"That's where your target may exit the building."

Dane liked the new situation a little better. No civilians in the vicinity. Still, when the shooting started—

Price explained the identity of the perpetrators inside. "You're to fire tracker rounds only, Blacksuit Four," Price concluded.

Dane thought it was too good to be true. "Say again, Stony?"

"Fire the trackers only. Use no lethal munitions."

Dane almost grinned. Suddenly he was confident again. "Understood, Stony."

The other blacksuit commando had already prepared the airgun and he traded Dane for the Walther sniper rifle. Dane lined up his sights on the door and rehearsed a series of rapid shots at imaginary figures ascending the fire escape ladders.

Firing a tracer had challenges all its own. The CO_2 cartridge wasn't as powerful, and the projectile didn't develop the inertia to give it the accuracy of a sniper's round, even over the short fifty yards that separated Dane from the emergency exit. There was also the problem of anonymity.

Because for a tracker round to actually work, the target couldn't know he'd been shot.

"Be aware—here comes Able," the other blacksuit announced, then added, "at twelve o'clock."

SCHWARZ LOOKED straight down as his legs absorbed the shock, then pushed out again. As he descended at a breakneck pace he saw the pair of Stony Man blacksuits staged in the window washer's platform on the building across the street. One was staring at him, then the designated sniper looked up, dropped his mouth open in amazement and managed to turn his attention back to his target.

"Yeah, I can't quite believe it, either," Schwarz said out loud as his body was jolted by the next heavy landing against the exterior of the BME building. He slowed a little at the protestations from his shocked knees, but there wasn't time to make a leisurely descent.

He reached the sixth-floor level and quickly found a place for his feet on a wide window ledge, then locked down the Kevlar rope to his body armor, which served as a harness. As he grabbed for his weapon, the emergency exit below opened with a wrench of protesting metal. A mercenary swung his body out the exit and landed on the wall-mounted ladder.

Schwarz triggered the Beretta 93-R and sent a triburst of 9 mm shockers into the killer's leg and side just as the man released the catch on the ladder. The lower section telescoped toward the ground with a noisy rattle as the merc croaked in disbelief and fell after it, on his back, limp limbs flapping above him. He turned to a corpse when he crunched on the sidewalk, and an instant later the ladder clanged into its lowest position beside the body.

There were screams from the street level. A little civilian panic was a good thing, Schwarz thought. Now the people would clear out. A second mercenary jutted from the emergency exit and looked down at his fallen comrade, then figured out he had just done a very stupid thing. Schwarz didn't give the man time to correct his foolishness and squeezed the trigger again. The recoil from the three machine-fired rounds drove his aim up, despite his firm grip on the secondary handle under the barrel, but at least one of the 9 mm rounds punctured the mercenary. The figure went limp and slumped.

Schwarz didn't recognize either of the two dead gunmen. There was just Warren Korl and another mercenary still in action by the time Able Team had chased them off the top floor. That meant reinforcements had been waiting inside somewhere. Schwarz radioed the news to Stony for relay to Lyons and Blancanales.

The lifeless torso was jerked inside and replaced by a fast-moving gunner who seemed to know just where Schwarz was. The Able Team warrior found himself staring down the business end of a Calico submachine gun. He triggered a triburst fast and saw the rounds hammer at the brick building face inches from the gunner; a flash of blood appeared on the gunner's exposed wrists just before he fired his own brief burst.

Schwarz fired again but found his target pulling inside. He reloaded the 93-R, which devoured the Parabellum rounds fast when used in triburst mode. He risked a quick glance at the ground level. A few stupid civilians were still hanging around at the building corners, too fascinated to pull themselves away, and Schwarz simply wasn't going to risk using something less controllable than the handgun.

He slapped in the fresh magazine, once again giving himself a 20-round inventory to work with, and spotted the killer with the Calico pop out of the fire escape exit, twisting and triggering the submachine gun at the Able Team commando perched two stories above him. Schwarz was close enough to make it an awkward shot, and the mercenary didn't have the skills to pull it off fast enough to save his skin. The 93-R machine fired its three rounds in such rapid succession that the suppressed report blended into a single stuttering cough and a bloody crater opened up the gunner's chest. He deflated. The Calico floated away, clattering on the sidewalk below.

A hand grabbed the shirt of the dying man and yanked him inside, then the armored torso of Warren Korl jutted from the window on his back, so that he was facing directly up at Schwarz as he unleashed a barrage of rounds from an M-4 carbine. Schwarz triggered the handgun at the curved face plate, wrestling with the weapon as each triburst forced its aim away. There was a cracking impact and a flash of red and

Schwarz saw the colonel's head get knocked back. The face shield was suddenly a milky mask and there was a bloody wound showing on his neck where the face plate ended.

The impact had to have been like a blow with a club, but Korl managed to hold on to the M-4 and wriggle back into the building just as shouts and more shooting erupted from the inside. Schwarz heard the distinctive sound of Lyons's Atchisson.

"THAT'S HIM!" blurted the other Blacksuit.

"I know." Dane recognized his target even with the face shield in place. He peered through the scope of the weapon, distancing himself from the fact of the gun battle, planning his shot. He could see into the fire escape, and he could get a good shot if and when Colonel Korl retreated.

He saw the flash of a gunshot inside the building, then Korl stopped firing up at the Able Team commando. Korl was momentarily dazed. He'd been hit.

Korl had slid inside and gotten to his feet, and for a moment Dane had an open shot at his back.

"Now," Dane ordered.

He fired the airgun at the moment the other blacksuit unleashed a barrage of M-16 cover fire. The 5.56 mm rounds from the M-16 created a racket on the windowsill and the outside wall. Korl spun in place and ripped off the distorted face shield, returning fire.

Dane and his partner slouched behind the modular steel panels that served as the outside rail of the platform. Dane ignored the rattle of rounds hitting the metal just inches from his back and relived the moment he had fired the shot. He knew the shot was good and he had hit Korl with the round. But did the round snag in place? Had Korl felt the impact? Would the M-16 fire have distracted him enough to ignore any tug he might have felt?

Dane decided he preferred shooting bullets. There was more immediate gratification.

The pounding of the rounds from the M-4 stopped, and Dane sighted his weapon again at the window, searching for targets amid the flashes of gunfire and chaos of movement. The Zeiss six-power telescopic sight was almost too much magnification for the narrow distance between the buildings. He watched a rush of bodies surge across the window, then retreat again more slowly. The bloodied, enraged face of Korl passed in front of his scope momentarily, then Dane focused on a second man fighting at Korl's side.

It was another face he recognized.

"You son of a bitch," he muttered.

"Huh?" asked his companion, who hadn't fired his weapon into the chaos for fear of hitting a civilian or one of their own men.

Before Dane could grab his own sniper rifle there was a flurry of bodies exiting the fire escape, led by Warren Korl, who half fell the three stories, his bloodied hands barely gripping the ladder. He was followed by the man Dane knew, and then a third figure staggered onto the ladder, hunched over and holding his chest. The last man forced his body upright and bellowed in pain, but it was the only way he could bring his weapon in to play against the commando clinging to the side of the building on top of him.

The commando's triburst shoved the wounded gunner off the ladder before his own weapon could be fired. The body fell past his companions, who didn't give it a glance. Dane had his eyes on the other one, the one he knew.

The SOG commando on the wall, the one called Gadgets, unleashed a burst just as Korl's feet hit the ground and the former colonel tumbled down the sidewalk like a drunk. His only surviving comrade swung himself bodily into the narrow space between ladder and wall and allowed himself to fall the last three yards while he held the ladder only to keep himself in an upright position. When he hit the concrete, his body bent inside of the tight space, then he twisted into the open.

The blacksuit beside Dane triggered his M-16 and hit the last commando in the thighs, but he was running now and the hit had to have been a glancing blow, because the man only stumbled, never falling, before disappearing around the other side of the building.

There was a screech of distant brakes, then they glimpsed the colonel and the last mercenary darting into the next street and slinking into an alley.

"You son of a bitch," Dane repeated.

CHAPTER THIRTY

Alang

"I think you know why I came, Aska."

The words were followed by a small liquid sound. Maybe it was the smacking of lips. By this time Aska had surely lost his ability to breathe and was just seconds away from death.

"Aska," the voice said, "you made me look bad."

Something started pounding on the desk. Aska Wali was panicking. But the pounding stopped and the bug picked up the sound of something heavy falling to the floor. It took little imagination to picture Aska's corpse landing next to his office cot.

"That's all," Price said. "That was five minutes before you arrived."

"We got nothing, Stony One," McCarter admitted as he steered the SUV away from the shore. "We went through the place and found a jimmied window, but there was nothing else to prove a killer had been there. Except for the dead bloke with the garrote almost slicing his head off."

"Looks like Wali had a sleeping companion," Manning

added. "Can't tell you anything about her, except that she smelled bad and weighed a third as much as he did. She's not the killer, but she may have seen him or been involved somehow. From the impression on the bedclothes I would say she left when the killer got there or pretty soon before he did."

"We'll find her," McCarter said. "See what she has to tell us."

"You may not need to," Price said. "There's been a contact. We tracked a communication from the minisub while you were inside Wali's building—it wasn't a quarter mile from you."

"Why didn't you alert us, Stony One?" Hawkins asked.

"So you could do what, exactly, T.J.?" Price asked. "The contact came as the sub emerged from under one of the ships in Wali's stretch of the shore. You'd have been swimming pretty fast to catch it. Since it was on the surface when it departed, we got a infrared Image Intelligence satellite focused on the spot and managed to get snapshots of the minisub before it dived."

"You learn anything from the IMINT pics?" Encizo asked.

"No. We switched back to the Synthetic Aperture Radar satellite that we've been using for ocean surveillance, but the RORSAT was a waste of time. The backscatter from all the derelict ships created too much noise to see anything. Now we know why the sat pics of Alang in the archives are mostly daylight optic shots."

"So we don't know where the minisub is going next," Encizo said.

"No," Price admitted. "We don't."

"What about Paul Patel?"

"We're getting cooperation out of the CIA and the embassy staff, but they insist he's clean. We're going through official channels, so it's actually Justice making the request to Langley. Believe it or not, they're giving us the runaround."

"We don't have time for that," James protested. "Why don't we run around them?"

"Yeah, why not?" Price said.

Bombay

THE LIST of the great cities in the world must include Bombay.

Everything about Bombay was exaggerated, from its population to its history, from the vast scope of its cultural diversity to the massive breadth of negative karma rising from a population of millions of human beings living in some of the world's biggest slums.

The cultural and financial hub of the world's second-most populous country, Bombay was home to the Bharatiya Vidya Bhavan, the Palace of Indian Learning, promoting art and education. It was home to the Prince of Wales Museum of Western India. The incredibly prolific Indian motion picture industry was based in Bombay. Its learning centers include the University of Bombay, the Indian Institute of Technology, the Haffkine Institute for bacteriological research and the Tata Institute of Fundamental Research.

Greater Bombay long ago sprawled beyond Bombay Island and the other islands that once dotted the coast off the Konkan Coast. The islands were smothered beneath landfills and the inexorable mass of humanity. The mainland city couldn't contain the sprawl. The population spilled north until it reached the city of Thana, then kept going. Greater Bombay was home to more than eight million human beings in 1981. By 1991 the number was nearing ten million. By 2001 population estimates, if they realistically included the vast landscape of poor who huddled around the great polyglot metropolis, closed in on fifteen million.

David McCarter once heard somebody say that Bombay was like a smelly New York. The only thing wrong with that statement was the inference that New York didn't smell, too.

Salsette Avenue, he thought, could easily have been a street in New York City. Brownstone buildings lined this neat, quiet street. The trees were older than he was and spaced so that they shaded and cooled most of the walkways. Anything that gave even an illusion of cooling was welcome in Bombay, where the seasons went from hot and humid to hot and rainy.

Gaining access to the walk-up at 65 Salsette Avenue was ridiculously easy. Price had arranged it all while they were en route from Alang. They'd driven from Sahar International Airport to the office of a real-estate agent serving the high-rent districts around Netaji Subhas Road and Malabar Hill. McCarter had flashed his passport and was provided with the keys to a flat in the same building that was home to CIA Agent Paul Patel. The only snag came when the real-estate agent had realized McCarter was a Brit and had latched on to him for what might have been an hours-long chat. The agent was an expatriate Londoner himself. It had taken McCarter five long minutes just to get out the door. It was a near miss for the chatty agent, if only he had known how close McCarter was to rationalizing shooting him in cold blood just to escape.

McCarter and Encizo entered the building and made their way to the rented flat with the help of the doorman who greeted them by name from the list at his podium. Price's phone conversation with the real-estate agent told them the building was equipped with a "perfectly modern" alarm system that would alert the security staff if any burglar attempted to get into the building by any door or window—on the first or second floors. The doorman proudly affirmed that, yes, he was the "security staff" and that the neighborhood was so safe that the security system wasn't even needed during daylight hours.

McCarter and Encizo were reassured by the doorman's confidence. They could still hear the doorman's steps descending the marble stairs when they quietly crossed to Paul Patel's apartment door and opened it with the jiggle of a pick.

There were no electronics watching the flat. CIA or not, Patel didn't have much worth a burglar's effort, be he thief or spy. The furnishings were sparse. The tiny Godrej refrigerator was nearly empty. Only the bedroom looked lived in.

"This guy comes home to sleep and change clothes," Encizo observed. "We bug this place, and we're not going to hear anything but snores and zippers."

So they planted most of the bugs in his clothes, using fat syringes to drive the barbed ends of the tiny electronic devices into the underside of his lapels. The devices were too small to broadcast far and a retransmitter would have to be set up anywhere they hoped to get a signal out.

The problem was solved four hours later. It was ten o'clock when Patel arrived at his flat, ten-twenty when the sound of sloppy snoring came over the receiver in the rented apartment. Hawkins and James had relieved McCarter and Encizo, and it was James who undertook the breaking-and-entering task. He jimmied the door, entered Patel's apartment and found his mobile phone charging in a stand on a small table inside the front door. He opened the phone with a tiny, stainless-steel screwdriver and placed the electronics package inside. The package circumvented the encryption on the phone by simply sending the information to a second mobile transceiver number, which was then relayed automatically on a standard phone line to Stony Man Farm. The sophisticated Bombay mobile phone system was essentially being forced to work with them instead of using its encryption against them.

James replaced the shell of the phone and dialed a local Bombay telephone number. When he heard the "okay" signal, he hung up and put the phone back in its charge base.

Hawkins listened hard while James was gone and never even heard a break in the rhythm of Patel's breathing.

"I could have watched TV on his couch and he wouldn't have known I was there," James reported on the radio when he was back. McCarter and the others were taking up residence at a nearby hotel to minimize the risk of being spotted by Patel in his building. "I'm guessing he had a quart of Scotch for dinner."

"How'd the plant go, Cal?" McCarter asked.

"No problem. The retransmitter is in place. Stony?"

"Communications ran a diagnostic on your test call," Price responded. "They got a clear signal. We should be able to monitor every call he makes."

"Stony One, is our friend Paul known to have a drinking habit?" McCarter asked.

"Negative," Price responded. "There's nothing in the official records, anyway. But he would know about Wali's murder by now, and I'll bet he eased the stress with a drink or five."

"Maybe he thinks he's next," Hawkins offered.

"He just might be," Price agreed.

Stony Man Farm

THE WAITING WAS mercifully short, thanks to the time of day difference between India and the United States. The incoming call prodded the Stony Man Farm communications software awake before it even rang the phone on the hall table in the Salsette Avenue flat.

The phone rang six times before CIA Agent Paul Patel had stumbled to it and thumbed the button. Before Patel even said hello the Stony Man Farm electronics was zeroing in on the East Coast U.S. source of the call.

Every word of the conversation was recorded digitally. These recordings were later compared repeatedly to positively identify the speaker, using every voiceprint protocol known to be reliable to the global intelligence community.

It was as positive a voiceprint identification as could be made.

Then the audio was analyzed again, this time for the microscopically small glitches and changes in recording noise and background sound that might point to a recording assembled out of existing audio archives. No evidence of fraud was found.

Finally a digital analysis dissected the voiceprint of the speaker in search of the unavoidable lack of natural inflection that would prove the conversation was generated using a voiceprint-replicating system. No matter how good the software and the replication algorithms, no computer-made voice could create speech that was natural enough to fool another computer.

"This seems like overkill," Tokaido muttered at one point.

"We can't have too much evidence," Kurtzman said. "We're not trying to convince a court of law. The jury is the Man, and he's a lot tougher than any twelve of our peers."

Tokaido keyed in a new set of protocols and ran another analysis, and the voice of Senator Franklin Jackson came from the speaker yet again.

"You're my man in India now, Paul."

Paul Patel responded, his voice heavy with sleep and thick with the aftereffects of alcohol. "What's that supposed to mean?"

"What I mean is, Aska Wali was charged with certain responsibilities in that part of the world and now he's out of the picture. I need you to take over."

"I don't think so, Senator. I'm not sympathetic to your cause."

"I do think so, Agent Patel."

"What about the goons that offed Wali? Let them do your work."

"The goon has already left India. He's got more important tasks to complete. You'll be strictly an errand boy."

"Forget it."

"I will not forget it, Agent Patel. And I can always have my goon pay a visit to Bombay."

Silence.

"I didn't bargain for this."

"What did you think would happen when you cut yourself in for a share of Wali's cash? Did you think you'd drop some hints and get a big payoff and never suffer any comebacks? It doesn't work that way. Not when you work with me."

"Just tell me what you want me to do, Senator."

"Here's the problem, Agent Patel. All around me people are fucking up. Aska Wali fucked up, and then my Asia-based goon fucked up by not seeing it. One of those mistakes was nearly fatal to me and my undertaking. My people are being hounded on two continents. I've got a serious intelligence leak somewhere, and the dogs are closing in on my ass."

"So you want to drag me down with you?"

"I simply want you to lead the dogs up the wrong trail."

BROGNOLA WAS BRIEFED by Price, then lingered in the War Room to reread the reports—all of them. When he was face-to-face with the President the next time, he was going to have to have his ducks in a very straight row.

The body count was rising. Senator Jackson and his operations commander, Colonel Korl, showed with every orchestrated action that they didn't care who they killed. They wiped out civilians and their own men without compunction. It was a kind of ruthlessness that Brognola had witnessed before, but usually it came from the minds of religious zealots. Was Jackson that kind of a fanatic?

When Brognola realized he wasn't alone, he looked up. It was Kurtzman, in his wheelchair just inside the door, looking tired. The chain of events of the past few days had been relentless and every man and woman on the Farm payroll was sleep-deprived.

Kurtzman leaned back into the wheelchair, peering into the ceiling of the War Room, as if contemplative.

"There have always been men obsessed with insane plans for mass murder," Brognola announced with an antacid dissolving between his teeth. "I don't know why I'm unsettled to learn there's a maniac like this in the top ranks of the U.S. government."

"I'm not surprised at all," Kurtzman said. "We've seen them before. It's the risk you take when you allow the people to select one of their own to take on positions of power. Anybody with a message that resonates with the citizens can garner the vote."

"That's a pessimistic attitude," Brognola grumbled.

Kurtzman sat up straight. "I didn't mean to say I think democracy is a failure, Hal. But there are flaws in the system. The people are collectively intelligent enough to keep dangerous people from attaining positions of power most of the time. Jackson has shown his true colors, and his political career won't survive another election even if we fail to stop him now."

Brognola said thoughtfully, "Yeah, Aaron, but this guy is so *thoroughly* flawed. He's a mass murderer. If *he* can be elected to the Senate, does that mean he could have been elected to the presidency, with a few extra years of self-restraint?"

Kurtzman considered that silently.

"There might be somebody out there like that right now," Brognola continued. "Maybe he's a state governor. Maybe he's already a damned senator. He's keeping his dark side under control and he's got a better grip on himself than Senator Jackson. He's waiting to show his true colors until he's got a stronger position. Until he's got the *strongest* position."

"Now who's being a pessimist?" Kurtzman asked.

"Maybe a realist. The problem is, if this hypothetical power player is so good that he fools everybody else then he'll fool me, and us, and we'll become his tools. He'll send the Farm to do his dirty work. He'll be smart enough to choose our projects carefully, so that we do what he wants without alerting us to his true motives."

"It is a grim possibility. How do we avoid it?"

"Start doing background checks on elected officials?" Brognola asked.

"We already do that, constantly," Kurtzman replied. "Besides, the man you're describing would have been under such tight self-control he may have revealed nothing about his hidden…flaws, in word or action, throughout his career."

Brognola nodded. "I'm not saying I have the answers. I'm just saying we need to be on the lookout. It probably won't happen."

"It probably won't," Kurtzman agreed, but he sounded as though he had more to say.

Brognola felt burdened with negativity, and he didn't want to discuss it further. He got to his feet, trying to avoid thinking about the presidential election. "I'm due in Washington. Keep me informed."

"About?"

"Just keep me informed."

CHAPTER THIRTY-ONE

Cowboy Kissinger was immersed in his own thoughts as he peered into the high-resolution display, oblivious to the comings and goings of his staff. On the screen what looked like a microscopic photograph of an insect's appendage was actually the etched surface of a bullet of unusually small caliber.

Kissinger liked what he saw. The projectile was more of a dart than a bullet, but could be fired like a bullet. Using proton-beam chiseling to engrave a specific texture on its micromillimeter-thick platinum plating, Kissinger hoped it would reach rotation speeds many times that achieved by conventional and even specialty munitions. The theory was that the right texture combined with the right spin speed would create gyroscopic and air-movement characteristics to make a bullet that self-corrected for the pull of gravity and the interference of the atmosphere. He hardly even admitted it to himself, but there might even be the capability of creating rounds with programmable flight paths.

Imagine a weapon that would fire with pinpoint accuracy around a corner or over a hill, and inexpensive enough that you could equip every soldier.

It was just a pet theory that he played with off and on, and his interest was spurred by the minisub that Phoenix Force had observed in India with its textured hull designed to reduce noise.

His computer modeling showed him he was on the right track in terms of the shape and texture of the projectile. Advances in proton-beam chiseling in microscopic manufacturing applications had made the rifling of prototypes feasible.

Everything was there—except the gun to fire it. That, he was still working on. How could he possibly propel this oversize sewing needle hard enough, while spinning it fast enough? No way a compressed-air charge would accomplish it.

He looked at his watch as Kurtzman rolled inside the armory.

"We need to find that sub," Kurtzman blurted. He had no time for pleasantries.

"What happened to your global phone-tracking capability?"

"They got wise in Chicago. The minisub called home from Alang, and we have to assume he got the word to switch to another communications channel."

"I assume you're trying to trace it."

"We've appropriated a big chunk of Signal Intelligence satellite resources just for that purpose and we're combing every other possible communications channel. Even with the SIGINTs it's a needle in a bunch of haystacks. It's likely that even if we stumble over their communications we won't know it."

"They're not going to give you the convenient point of reference they did the first time," Kissinger remarked.

"Yeah."

"What about air reconnaissance? Navy search vessels?"

"Not with our hands tied. We'd call out every ship in that part of the world if we could, and it would take that kind of coverage to find a spy sub. But the powers that be don't think it would be a good idea." Kurtzman shook his head. "I don't have time to tell you the whole sad story, Cowboy. Can you help?"

Kissinger tapped his chin with his finger, then tapped at the keyboard to clear the screen and brought up a map of the Arabian Sea. He indicated the screen at the point well off the west coast of the Indian subcontinent where Phoenix Force had disabled the *Singep* and saved the twin Iranian petroleum supertankers from destruction.

"How much of a head start?"

Kurtzman looked at his watch. "Sixteen minutes."

Kissinger looked up quickly. "What?"

"Our last trace was in the water off Alang. The minisub returned to perform a little cold-blooded murder. Phoenix is on the scene as we speak, but they were too late to catch the minisub. The last call out was sixteen minutes ago."

Kissinger's face fought to hold back the grin.

Kurtzman sat up straighter. "You know a way."

"I know a way. But it'll piss off the U.S. Navy."

"Like I care."

"You'll need to call in some serious favors to make it happen."

"Enough disclaimers. Tell me."

Kissinger told him.

Arabian Sea

"WHOEVER YOU PEOPLE are, you sure know how to piss off the U.S. Navy."

"Yeah, well, the Navy can stand in line," replied the

scrawny man who was now flying the MH-53E and relegating the Navy pilot to the role of copilot. On his own freaking helicopter! It wasn't right.

But the tall, skinny guy was being good-natured about it, the Navy pilot decided.

"So what gives? You guys Secret Service or something?"

"We're men in black. It's a federal agency."

"You're shittin' me." It was almost a question. The Navy pilot stared until the guy gave him a friendly smile.

"Yeah, I am." Before the Navy pilot could probe further, the guy continued. "And if you learn any more than that, you'll have to be neutralized as an intelligence risk."

"Oh."

Jack Grimaldi couldn't tell if the Navy man believed him or not. This pilot, Grimaldi decided, wasn't the brightest porchlight on the block, but whatever worked to keep the man's mouth shut. Grimaldi deemed it wise to reinforce the point. "Not me, you understand," Grimaldi added conversationally. "It's the guy in back. He's the hard-ass."

The pilot furled his brow. "Not the hombre from Abilene?"

"Him."

"Whoa," the pilot breathed. "Who would have thought?"

Grimaldi watched his position closely and finally opened the intercom to the rear of the huge Sea Dragon. "T.J., three minutes until we're at the starting mark. How's the hardware?"

"Functional, I guess," Hawkins said. "We'll be ready."

Stony Man pilot Jack Grimaldi made minute adjustments to the course, enjoying the thrum of the big aircraft as it flashed over the Arabian Sea.

The MH-53E Sea Dragon was the Navy's Airborne Mine Countermeasures helicopter, a Sikorsky behemoth that in sheer size and power was the largest vertical takeoff/landing—VTOL—craft ever made with the exception of the Russian Rostvertol Mi-26 Halo and the Mi-6 Hook.

The primary role for the MH-53E AMCM helicopter was to sweep for and neutralize mines, also seeing a lot of duty marking channels and even towing watercraft.

The Sea Dragon had three power plants driving the seven blades of its primary rotor and the four blades on the tail. The General Electric T64-GE-419 engines produced a standard peak of 4,380 horsepower at 14,280 rpm. In emergency situations its engine's contingency elevated up to 5,000 horsepower for two minutes.

She was designed for tough working conditions. The separators on the engine air intakes removed particles of sand, dust or sea spray. Contamination could reduce drive power, but with the separators the Sea Dragon operated efficiently even when she was hovering low over the ocean, such as during sea rescue or troop deployment.

The power plant trio allowed the helicopter to transport vehicles, or fifty-plus passengers, or more than twenty litters when in a Medevac role—any cargo weighing up to 33,000 pounds. It could tow up to 25,000 pounds.

Grimaldi loved the big beast for her massive muscle, but not the high level of automation. Any thirteen-year-old kid could have operated the Sea Dragon under normal circumstances—from what Grimaldi understood about the computer skills of today's teenagers. Right now the cruise control was keeping her on a straight line heading north by northeast within sight of the coast of the peninsula that hung like an extra toe off the side of the Indian subcontinent.

"Ready, T.J.," Grimaldi announced as they approached the target coordinates. "In three, two, one."

In the vast rear compartment of the Sea Dragon, instead

of fifty-five troops or twenty emergency medical evacuation litters, there was just Thomas Jackson Hawkins and a workstation inside a hardened cabinet. The riveted steel computer desk looked as though it could survive being rolled down a mountain.

Hawkins monitored the display, feeling almost as unnecessary a human component as Grimaldi in the cockpit.

"You making sense of this, Bear?" he asked.

"Negative, T.J.," Kurtzman admitted via the speaker. "But the computer is. Here come the first results."

Hawkins watched in fascination as the images opened up on his screen in small windows. The corpses of sunken ships, digitally realized in their current state of decomposition. To Hawkins it was like using some sort of video electronics to see the corpses while you drove through a cemetery at Autobahn speeds.

The device was the U.S. Navy's ALMDS, or Airborne Laser Mine Detection System. The technology had been under development since the late 1990s, but the unit mounted on the Sea Dragon was one of only a half dozen prototypes currently in use. The prototypes were field-testing the latest developments in the technology, and regular production for widespread U.S. Navy user wouldn't happen until 2005.

The ALMDS was encased in a pod mounted on the belly of the helicopter, where an extremely fast laser scanned the ocean underneath the aircraft and made a digital topographic rendering of the ocean floor and any solid objects lying there—even when the Sea Dragon was traveling this fast.

Speed was a major benefit of the ALMDS. The swath of real estate covered in a single sweep, and the speed of the sweep, was exponentially faster than other technologies for hunting beneath the waves. In human terms the analysis was instant—the ALMDS identified the telltale straight edges and other too perfect geometries that denoted man-made objects.

The software was designed to specifically track mines, even identify them by likely country of origin and age. The system even ranked their potential threat based on their position, assumed stability and proximity to known traffic routes.

The ALMDS was also turning out to be the most effective shipwreck finder ever created. All it took was a few programming additions to add wreck-identification capability to the system, which functioned invisibly behind the scenes during mine-sweeping exercises, and it managed to locate shipwrecks too numerous to catalog. Even ancient sunken wrecks had been inadvertently located when the ALMDS happened to sweep during a period when the tide brushed away a top layer of the sandy seafloor and briefly exposed old hull timbers.

The tiny windows that Hawkins began seeing were all man-made items, but none of them were what the system was looking for. The specifications of the submarine that had fled the *Singep* had been loaded into it. None of these items came close. The software displayed them as a courtesy to its human operators. Pretty pictures to keep the humans amused.

Hawkins wasn't amused. The shore of Alang was like a battlefield, the collapsing corpses strewed everywhere. Maybe they were castoffs the ship breakers had purchased then scuttled when they realized the scrap value was less than the cost of dismantling. Some were hulks that had been hauled into Alang by their owners—or hijackers—only to have their hopes of a hefty payoff dashed.

Many of the computer-imaged hulks were real wrecks, not scuttles. A coldly color-rendered tragedy. Many of them were graves after all, Hawkins observed.

If it hadn't been for Cowboy's sudden interest in submersible craft, they wouldn't have even come this far. Kissinger was intrigued by his research into the identification of the prototype sub. That led him into a more or less aimless surf through the classified data on the disposition of other recent technology prototypes. He had come across the information about the newest test generation of ALMDS currently in the field.

Nothing new to Kissinger. The units had been actively under development since 1999. He remembered thinking that the availability of the units for Navy use created a unique opportunity for corruption: any Navy commander with an ALMDS unit could conceivably have the unit search for valuable wrecks. He made a mental note: in a few years, when the ALMDS went into widespread use, he was going to search for Navy officers who started or partnered in ocean salvage businesses.

Then he was distracted by the concept of the texturing used on the surface of the minisub. Sure, it hadn't worked, but he'd received some electronic files recently from a Berkeley professor conducting ballistics studies on munitions with specialized rifling and unusual caliber.

He hadn't given the ALMDS another thought until Kurtzman showed up asking for a way to find the renegade sub.

The sub pilot had made a serious mistake in returning to Alang. He'd given Stony Man Farm one last trace, putting the minisub in the waters at Alang just before and after the death of Aska Wali.

The vital factor was the tides. They were high this time of the month, but high tide had come and gone around the time the *Singep* left. The sub pilot had been forced to contend with shallows, and in the stretch of shore where Aska Wali's ship-breaking business thrived, that meant steering through a meandering series of channels, carved in the mud by the currents.

The sub pilot knew the channels. He never would have made it to shore if he hadn't. But it had to have been slow going on the way in, and slower on the way out.

That was two hours ago. The sub could have covered a lot of distance since then, but she couldn't outrun the Sea Dragon and the ALMDS. Between the two of them they devoured Arabian Sea real estate.

"Hey!" Hawkins was on his feet without knowing it, grabbing the mouse to pause the automatic progression of the tiled images and backtracking screens. "Bear, did you see it?"

"No. What did I miss?"

"I'd swear it was a sub. Hold on." Hawkins finally reached the screen he was after and read out the target code to Kurtzman.

"I've got it, T.J. It *is* a sub. How did the system miss it?"

Hawkins shook his head. "Wait, Bear, the system didn't miss it. It's too big to be our minisub."

In fact, the longer Hawkins looked at the blocky rendering on his expanded window, the stranger the cigar-shaped profile looked.

"What's wrong with this picture?" he asked Kurtzman.

"It looks like a relic," Kurtzman suggested. "Like an antique."

"And it's lying on its side," Hawkins added. "That protrusion on the right is a turret cluster."

"You're right."

Hawkins glared at the table of target details provided by the ALMDS. Included in the specifications was a field for the speed of the vessel, ascertained by the system when it made an automatic second reading on the target after identifying it as man-made. As with all the shipwrecks, ALMDS declared that the target was moving at 0.0 km/h.

In the field for Probable Identification was the designation *Unknown*. But Hawkins thought maybe the shape looked familiar. He had a bizarre sensation, as though unexpectedly meeting a distant relative for the first time, whose picture he's seen in the family albums all his life.

"The shipwreck databases have nothing marked at these coordinates," Kurtzman said. "It's long dead, whatever it is."

"Yeah," Hawkins breathed. "Hey, Bear, could you make a save of all the data on this target for me?"

"Uh, sure. I see no security problems with that, as long as you keep it to yourself. Mind if I ask why?"

Hawkins was deep in his own thoughts, but then he answered. "I ever tell you any of the stories I learned from my grandfather?"

"Yeah. He kind of collected military tall tales, didn't he?"

"Yeah. Military legends, he called them," Hawkins said. "And you know, a couple of them have turned out to be true. It just took fifty years for the proof to come to light."

There was an extended pause that stretched between the two sides of the world. Tentatively Kurtzman asked, "Did we just find evidence of a military legend, T.J.?"

Hawkins was nodding, growing a strange grin. "Bear," he said, "I think we did."

He didn't say any more about it. It wasn't the kind of thing he wanted to discuss on a global communications link. He did keep the screen open, however, and glanced at it again from time to time as the morning wore on.

The MH-53E Sea Dragon flew in a tight spherical path that increased in size and length. The route was designed to best locate the sub without allowing it to slip past by traveling from one search path into a previous path at an opportune moment. Unless Stony seriously underestimated the speed of the sub, they should find it here, and find it here soon.

There was another possibility: instead of moving into the Arabian Sea after extricating itself from the shoreline at Alang, the sub could have retreated north, deeper into the Bay of Khambaht. That seemed unlikely.

In broad terms Stony Man Farm knew the intention of the crew of the sub: create terror and destruction to help the cause of American isolationism. Price and Kurtzman were of the opinion that the Bay of Khambaht didn't present targets likely to further that cause. Hawkins had to agree.

So the sub had to be out here somewhere, in the vast Arabian Sea.

But where?

There was a stack of plastic-wrapped hoagies in the refrigerator and they were calling Hawkins's name. He was halfway across the vast, empty interior when the computer beeped softly.

Hawkins forgot the hoagies.

Bombay, India

DAVID MCCARTER NODDED at the woman in the suit who was unlocking the wooden door to her second-floor flat with an antique brass key. Her outfit was tailored to look like a conservative corporate uniform while accentuating her svelte limbs and the swell of her breasts. She had the gleam in her eye. Man or woman, McCarter thought, the aggressive corporate types all had that twinkle.

The uniform was strictly boardroom. The pale complexion told McCarter that she was originally from someplace closer to his part of the world than this one. She gazed levelly at him, a smile playing at the corners of her mouth. Both of them liked what they saw.

"Good afternoon," he said politely.

"Good afternoon," she replied in a drawl that was part

Georgia sweetness, part Dallas ambition. "What are you doing in my building and why haven't you stopped by for a drink?"

"I didn't know I was invited."

"You," she said, emphasizing each word, "are invited."

"I'll keep it in mind."

"Why not now?" She twisted the key in the lock to prove she was serious.

"I'd love to," he said, and he meant it, "but I have an appointment with Paul Patel upstairs."

"Not for romance, I hope?"

"No, for violence."

She watched him walk on with eyes that positively flashed. Somehow she knew he wasn't kidding, and it put her off balance. But she recovered before he was out of sight.

"British," she called, "when you're done with the violence upstairs, why don't you come give me a knock."

McCarter wasn't sure what she had in mind exactly, but he wasn't going to have the chance to find out, either. Unless his visit to Paul Patel was a total bust.

He couldn't afford for it to be a bust.

Manning was on watch in the nearby apartment. He spotted McCarter on the stairs through the peephole and opened the door with a question mark on his face.

"Good afternoon." McCarter smiled with all his teeth.

Manning's question mark weighed down the skin on his forehead until it wrinkled. "Sorry, I thought you were somebody else."

"I'm visiting a mate," McCarter said, nodding at Patel's door. "We'll have a talk. Share stories. Why don't you listen in, give me a hand if it comes to that."

Manning tried to picture any circumstance in which Paul Patel could overpower David McCarter. "Yeah, right."

"You never know."

"I'll be there if you need me."

McCarter knocked on the door. He heard footsteps and the scraping of the door chain. As the dead bolt was withdrawn, the Phoenix Force leader reached under his summer-weight linen blazer and withdrew the handgun. He flipped on the laser-aiming module and when the door opened, he planted the tiny red dots in the middle of Patel's chest.

"Good afternoon," McCarter said once again with proper courtesy.

Paul Patel saw murder in the commando's eyes and knew he had been found out. The blood drained from his face and he almost passed out. The highball glass left his lifeless fingers and shattered.

"You going to arrest me?"

"Sorry, mate, that's too much paperwork for me," McCarter explained. "Somebody official will be around to collect you shortly."

"Who?" Patel croaked.

"Maybe the embassy heavies. Maybe their on-call doctor with a big plastic body bag."

Patel stumbled back and sank onto the couch, shivering in the thick heat that was like a Louisiana Fourth of July. He ran his fingers through his hair.

"Might as well come on in," McCarter announced, and Manning arrived a moment later.

Patel glared at the audio recorder Manning brought with him.

"You've got me bugged?"

"You got it. We recorded a few chats between you and your senator friend in the U.S."

Patel sat up straight. "I'll tell you everything. All of it. All I want is immunity."

"I'm not making any deals, mate," McCarter said. "I don't want to know everything. Just a few important facts. If you fail to tell me, then as far as I am concerned you are complicit in mass murder. That means you don't deserve to live yourself."

Patel believed the man was sincere. He began to talk.

Rockford, Illinois

IT WAS the second-largest city in Illinois and often dubbed one of the least livable big cities in the U.S. Warren Korl cared only that it had a decent-size airport. He couldn't get away fast enough. He used a convenience store calling card to pay for his call in an airport phone booth.

"It's me."

"Why are you calling me on this line?" the senator demanded.

"They've been tracking us through our mobile phones. This line will be safe for a few seconds. I'll call you at home on the cutout line in fifteen minutes."

"I can't leave the office now!"

"In fifteen minutes," Korl insisted, then he hung up.

Stony Man Farm

"HOW ARE WE doing?" Kurtzman demanded.

"You know how many pay phones there are at the Rockford airport?" Akira Tokaido complained, grinding on pink gum. "Who'd have thought people in Rockford had anybody to call?"

"How about the house?"

"All I can find is three regular phone lines," Delahunt said. "I can tap into any of them, but it would be foolish to route a call through security channels then feed the signal into an open line."

"We've got to get in one way or another, people," Kurtzman declared as the clock on his PC display inexorably counted down the seconds. He was getting nowhere himself.

With Korl wise to their previous tracking methods, they had to find some way to get themselves back into the communications loop. The tracer the blacksuit sniper had managed to adhere to Korl would tell them where he was and allow them to listen in if they were able to keep a retransmitter in his vicinity.

A blacksuit tracking team with a retransmitter had found the signal in Chicago, but it was almost too late. Just as it faded into static, the blacksuits had gone after it. They had clung to the feeble signal tenaciously, finally closing the gap and tailing it out of the city. A handful of blacksuits in the Rockford airport were keeping in close proximity to Korl. But what would happen when he got on an aircraft?

"I'm in," Tokaido announced. "I've got access to the switching systems of all the companies with pay phone concessions. The call will come through one of them. Then we match the audio from the bug to pinpoint it. Should take a few seconds of speech to do it—no more."

"I'll be ready to trace the call," Delahunt said.

"Hunt?"

"I am ready, Aaron," rumbled Huntington Wethers, who was monitoring a variety of nonstandard communications channels. A voice call, they all knew, could be disguised inside any sort of a digital link, from cable TV to the automatic monitoring system used to read the water meter. Jackson and his operation had shown its versatility in this field.

The bug was feeding them the ambient sound of an airport interior and the minutes now dragged. To Aaron Kurtzman's chagrin, Korl ended up waiting a full twenty minutes before placing his call to the senator at his home in Arlington. The first words out of his mouth were, "How do we know this line is secure?"

"Don't worry about it. It's secure. My people went to great lengths to make sure of it."

"That's what you said about the satellite phones we were using before."

"Colonel, I know enough about the encryption to be sure it wasn't hacked."

"You're a naive asshole, Senator," Korl replied. "I figured it out. They didn't break the encryption, and they didn't have to. All they had to do was identify what the encrypted communications looked like and then track down satellite communications that use them."

"I—I don't think they could do that—"

"Well, they did it. That encryption that you said was really special and unique, well, you know what? It was so special that it led the goddamned special ops right to us every time we used it! What really burns me is that you chewed my ass about having a leak."

"You don't know that's how they traced you—"

"I do know! I watched it happen! Have you any idea what has happened to my standing army since we started working for you, Senator? Do you know how many men walked away from the spic bank fiasco? Two! Including me."

There was a long sigh. "Jesus."

"They're gonna ID those bodies real fast, and then somebody is going to start linking those names to Colonel Warren Korl, U.S. Army, Retired, if they haven't done it already."

Silence.

"I'm giving you a fair warning, Senator. If I get nailed, the first name out of my mouth is Franklin Jackson. Even if everybody hates you, you're still a federal elected official and that's a big enough of a fish to buy me a reduced sentence."

"If you think they're closing in on you, then it's time to bow out, Colonel."

"If I thought that I'd be long gone. I'll finish the job. I got a bunch of men out there who been workin' hard to put this job together, and I'm not gonna let them down if I don't have to. We'll do what's required of us. By morning we'll be on vacation."

"What about the other man who escaped the bank with you."

"He's beat up. I put him in bed at his momma's house, and she'll care for him."

"He'll have to be taken care of, just like the others."

"Consider it taken care of."

"I THINK IT'S A TEXT TAG attached to binary code, but I can't even determine the character set," Huntington Wethers explained, showing the others the digital information he was trying to get a handle on.

Akira Tokaido grinned and the grin kept growing. "Sneaky," he said.

"You know about it?" Kurtzman asked.

"I know about it. Mind if I sit here for a minute?"

Wethers got up graciously. "Be my guest."

Tokaido's fingers pecked the keys until he had pulled up a word processing program that converted the indecipherable text data.

"It's not encrypted. It's just a proprietary character set used by a Japanese communications satellite operator. Our senator friend is running one of their new satellite dishes. They're very cool. You get broadband from a dish that's like eighteen inches. I heard there was a test system in place for

the U.S. to run broadband off these little dishes with existing satellite protocols. That's what Jackson is using. The encryption is just your average commercial security measures."

A minute later Tokaido said, "We're in. We'll hear it all.
If he used it for data, we'll see that, too."

Kurtzman was suddenly smiling with relief. "Senator
Jackson is gonna learn the hard way not to take political
gifts."

CHAPTER THIRTY-TWO

Stony Man Farm, Virginia

"Senator Jackson has been in touch with Colonel Korl twice more in the last three hours. The transcripts are here." Barbara Price laid her hand on the stacks of paper and the envelope containing a CD copy of the audio. "He clearly implicates himself and Colonel Korl. Repeatedly, by name and by title. We have a signed confession from the CIA agent in the U.S. Embassy at Bombay. He names Jackson and Korl."

Brognola nodded. "It's about all you could ask for."

"There's more. We have one of the Korl mercenaries in custody."

"How?"

"A stroke of sheer luck, but the credit goes to the sharp eyes of Saemund Dane, one of the blacksuit snipers."

"I've never met him but I reviewed his file. He's top-notch."

"In every department. He's the one who placed the bug on Colonel Korl. While he was at it he happened to see the face of the man who escaped the BME building with Korl—it was someone he recalled meeting during joint special ops training exercises a year ago. Get this—Dane knew the guy's name, rank and serial number. He's one of those quiet genius types. He can recite the same particulars for any commanding officer he's ever had and every Marine he's ever worked closely with. The man in question rubbed Dane the wrong way. He knew the guy was trouble when they first met and took the initiative of committing his information to memory, then never thought about the guy again until he saw his face through the scope in Chicago.

"Korl mentions in one of the transcripts that the man was wounded and recovering at his mother's house. Sure enough, we found him in the bedroom he grew up in in Champaign, Illinois. His military career ended unhappily eight months ago."

"What's being done with him?"

"Dane volunteered to baby-sit him at the nearest hospital along with a few other blacksuits. Dane convinced the man to spill his guts. He says he'll deliver a signed confession from the guy in under an hour. It'll name Korl and Jackson. As far as I'm concerned, it's icing on the cake. We already have incontrovertible evidence against the senator."

"I agree."

"Will it convince the President?"

"I don't know the answer to that."

Price sighed and worried the red ballpoint pen in her hands.

"Paul Patel told us how Jackson plans to use the stolen minisub?" Brognola asked.

"Yes. T.J. already tracked it down and showed it to be on a course into Bombay," Price said. "Quite frankly, looking at it from Franklin Jackson's perspective, Bombay is a perfect target."

"Because?" Brognola prodded. He thought the Stony Man Farm mission controller looked uncomfortable, even jittery. Price got to her feet and paced as she talked.

"India's biggest export customer is the United States, and the single biggest shipping source for those goods is Bombay. Chemicals, jewelry and cut gems, cotton clothes and textiles, hand-worked leather and other crafts, tea, engineered components. It's all produced on the Indian subcontinent for the U.S. markets and most of it goes through Bombay. Also, India has the most potential for growth because of the rapid development of its manufacturing infrastructure and the fact its people are so poor. Their labor rates are unbeatable and will be for decades to come."

"Have you people been able to narrow it down to a more specific target?"

Price leaned over the conference table. "Yes, Hal. *Bombay.*"

Brognola glared at her. "The entire city? How?"

Price thrust a heavyweight paper map onto the table. It was a geophysical survey of Bombay, marked with indecipherable red pencil lines.

"You know anything about the physical makeup of the city?"

"I've been there. I got the basic tourist-class Bombay history during a cocktail reception at the Prince of Wales Museum. If I remember correctly, it used to be seven islands that have been turned into a peninsula through massive landfills."

"Right. That's key to the targets Franklin Jackson has chosen. Targets—plural. Chosen for the purpose of halting India's export business to the United States."

"Seems unlikely," Brognola said.

"It won't after I explain it, Hal," Price said, sounding weary. "Target Number 1, Mumbai Harbor. It's the busiest port in India. The crew in the minisub will first sabotage a predetermined list of ships. Their intention is to plant explosives up and down the harbor and detonate them in series to create a catastrophic conflagration that will span the docks. They're targeting incoming tankers and ship refueling centers."

"They'd need a hell of a lot of explosives."

"Not really. Even without knowing the details, Paul Patel gave us enough of the plan to extrapolate a strategy for virtually wiping out the harbor. There is a massive amount of flammable material in this stretch of waterway. There are accidents and fires all the time, but they're isolated relative to all the facilities. With some creative explosives, the fire can be spread from end to end."

"To what end?"

"Close down shipments out of Bombay."

"There are other ports in India. What good will it do Jackson to force the Indians to launch their import business from elsewhere on the subcontinent?"

Price shook her head. "There are no other ports in India that can be—"

"Sure there are. Calcutta is one of the biggest ports in the world. Madras is huge."

"And unusable. We're not talking about a developed country, Hal. If the U.S. lost Houston it would be a tragedy, but we'd be able to accommodate the shipping needs out of New Orleans, but only because we've got a transportation system in place to handle the movement of the cargo hundreds of miles out of the way. India doesn't. Their rail system is overburdened and poorly maintained, and there are no roads that can carry even a quarter of the Mumbai cargoes three hundred miles to Madras. Let alone to Calcutta. That's more than eight hundred miles away."

"So you project economic devastation for Bombay?" Brognola said.

"The impact would be felt by those who are lowest on the economic scale," Price explained. "The ones who actually make the clothes and harvest the cotton and assemble the goods. They'll lose their jobs, and they're the ones who can least afford to. The result will be mass starvation. Even if half the people flee the city, it will leave five million starving human beings in the vicinity. The relief agencies have never had to deal with a crisis as huge."

"How long to rebuild the Mumbai shipping facility or a replacement elsewhere in the vicinity?" Brognola asked.

"With international aid and the help of the U.S. Corps of Army Engineers, they could have a new shipping facility operating at fifty percent within twelve months, assuming they dredged Back Bay and made it the new shipping center. A more likely alternative would be to expand the shipping facilities at Ahmadabad and construct a highway system to enable transport of goods from Bombay to Ahmadabad. Our estimates show they could restore shipping capability to seventy-five percent of its current levels after just nine months."

"Which makes the target seem less and less attractive to Franklin Jackson," Brognola stated. "He's not interested in slowing down the pace of foreign commerce with the U.S. He wants it eradicated. All his efforts have been geared toward putting a stop to it."

"You haven't heard the rest of his plan."

Hal Brognola looked up from the Bombay map he had been studying. There were questions ringing in his head, every one of which called into doubt this scheme of shutting down Bombay shipping. It was too wild, too big. Too politically incorrect. Something harsh cut through his doubts, and it was the strange coldness in the voice of Barbara Price.

She had a rare mettle. She had strength, resolve, courage

and intelligence he couldn't guess at. When she showed him her soft side, it was a rare thing. Right now she was trying to keep it inside, but he knew he was witnessing subsurface emotion. Was it fear?

"What?" he said.

"Jackson's plan calls for the minisub crew to steal a series of chemical containers from a docked ship before the fires are ignited. The containers will simply be dumped into the water, then divers will mount flotation devices to bring the containers to neutral buoyancy. The sub hooks on and tows the containers away."

"Tows them where?"

"Here." She ran her finger along the map, around the tip of the peninsula, following an inlet from the Arabian Sea that opened north of Madh Beach and extended northwest. Then a channel of the inlet jutted off at a right angle, taking it deep inland.

"Dahisar Creek?"

"One of its names. It was formed by landfill and ends here, at the base of one of the former islands, very near the Kanheri Caves. The caves are just off the tip of the creek, and a few miles from Tulsi Lake and Vihar Lake. We've already checked out this body of water. What information we can get tells us it is deep enough to allow the sub to get through. Some places just barely. The containers in tow will be smaller than the sub, so they'll make it through.

"They stage the containers anywhere along this section of the creek," she continued matter-of-factly. "A few hours later the units rise to the surface and RDX explosives detonate with force sufficient to vaporize the chemical contents of the containers. The effluent cloud spreads inland on the breeze traveling off the Arabian Sea. The deposit is widespread, but the real targets are the lakes and reservoirs."

She tapped her finger on the blue shapes on the map, one after another.

"Bombay's water supply," she pointed out. "Seventy-five percent of Bombay's water passes through reservoirs on Worli Hill, Malabar Hill, Raoli, Pali Hill, several others. Depending on the prevailing winds during the forty minutes after the blast, all the reservoirs could be poisoned. The Bhandup Water Treatment Plant would definitely be contaminated. It's the largest water treatment facility in Asia. Bombay uses more than six hundred million gallons of water a day and five hundred million of those gallons go through Bhandup."

Brognola silently digested the impact of the red circles Price was scribbling, one after another, until the map was pocked with bloody marks.

"It gets worse," she added almost conversationally. "The reservoirs and the treatment plant are self-cleaning in a way. They could be made safe again. Not the lakes. They collect monsoon water and distribute it to the city. By itself the lake at Bhatsa provides close to half of Bombay's daily water usage. There's virtually no chance it would escape contamination. Upper Vaitarna Lake and Modak Sagar would probably be contaminated, as well. Those three lakes altogether provide most of the water needed to keep ten million people alive."

She was done. She fell into her chair again and crossed her arms, staring him down. The emotion she had been struggling to contain was buried again, deep. Her eyes held nothing except a brutal cold.

He hadn't realized. He simply hadn't comprehended the lengths that Jackson would go to. It still seemed impossibly heartless.

"I've got details," Price said. "You want to know about

missing shipping containers of C-4? Each one, sixteen British tons. You want to hear about how the location of these containers was kept secret, but was known to Senate committees studying disposal legislation? You want a list of names from that committee?"

"What are the chances it would destroy the contamination agent?"

"If it were biological, maybe, but not chemical. You can bet Jackson's plans take the distribution method into account. He hasn't made a stupid mistake yet. We think the minisub will go after a shipment of methyl isocyanate."

Brognola swallowed that one unpleasantly. The Indian people had suffered one of the great industrial tragedies of all time when the accidental release of the same chemical killed and injured thousands of people near Bhopal in 1984.

"When it settles in the lakes the toxicity will essentially take up residence there. The slow drainage of the water will remove some of it, but when the next monsoon season refills the lakes, the toxicity will spread again to next year's drinking supply," Price continued relentlessly. "We project the contamination to have an instantaneous lethal effect on tens or hundreds of thousands of Bombay residents—we are talking about one of the most densely populated parcels of land on the planet. Acute exposure will come from drinking the contaminated water—the people will have no choice but to drink contaminated water—and will kill thousands more.

"Chronic exposure—exposure over the coming years— will bring the death toll well into the millions, because MIC is carcinogenic. And it is phytotoxic, so what little agriculture is carried out using Bombay's water supply will be killed off, as well as ninety percent of the plant life in the greater metropolitan area."

She was looking at him expectantly. "I need some support from you here, Hal. I need you on our side again."

"Barb," he said, "I've been behind you every step of the way."

"You've been playing politician."

"It's a delicate political situation. Yeah, I had to finesse the powers that be. You want to know where we'd be standing if I didn't?"

"Maybe a million lives wouldn't be standing on the brink if we could have acted faster," she retorted.

"Wrong. Because we'd have been censured. If there's a single hard lesson I've learned, it's that you don't rub the fur the wrong way on the back of a political animal. 'Cause it'll always turn around and bite your hand off."

"I know—"

"You need to trust that I'm dealing with Washington as well as they can be dealt with."

Price considered this statement, then swallowed a throatful of vitriol and spoke patiently. "Hal, I see where you're coming from. Now see where I am. Where we are. The Farm, and Able and Phoenix. We've proved our case. We've delivered the goods on Senator Franklin Jackson, and the evidence isn't circumstantial. It's not subjective. You're walking the line and I appreciate why, but now you need to choose a side."

Hal Brognola heard the words and understood the meaning while the rational part of himself stepped back, watching these two old friends converse.

How had this become a moment of uncertainty? Why was this a turning point—a fork in the road or an unspoken commitment? Brognola was confused, which was a rare enough thing, but right now he wasn't even sure what to be confused about. There were personality dynamics that he didn't understand.

Was Price, intentionally or subconsciously, speaking for them all—the entire senior staff of Stony Man Farm?

"It boils down to this, Hal—we need aggressive backup. We need it now. We need you to be aggressive enough to deliver it."

He was slightly stung at the implication that he was less than aggressive, although he knew that wasn't what she was trying to say. "I get the message. I agree with you. You've nailed Jackson and there's no excuse for excusing him any longer, whether he's a senator or not. Here's the thing, Barb— and you already know this—I can't make guarantees. The President of the United States is his own man. There's no assurance he'll give us the backup you want."

Price nodded, eyes down, pulling the map toward her and staring at it on the tabletop for a long moment. Brognola felt the temperature drop by twenty degrees.

"I won't let it happen," she said to the map of the city of Bombay. "I won't let a million men, women and children die if I can stop it. I'll call in whatever help I can get. I'll hack into every intelligence system on the planet to get their attention. I'll go on the news networks. I'll flop out every political secret I know. And if we all go to jail because of it, so what?" She looked up, and she tapped the map. "All that would be a small price to pay."

HAL BROGNOLA SAT at the table in the Stony Man Farm War Room, by himself but not alone. The map was there, and somehow the scrap of paper off some computer plotter was potent with the lives it represented.

Of course Brognola was a man who valued human life, but even a value that strong could become submerged beneath the murky waves of nonsense of political maneuvering.

Politics. Mentally he spit the word.

The administration feared the Farm because the Farm was a fearsome weapon—the same reason it used the Farm. This time the Farm was being used too close to home. Against one of its own. A politician.

It was time, Hal Brognola decided, for the Man to stop being overcautious and to start being effective.

He needed to make his case plainly. He would pull out the veiled threats if he had to. A President who failed to act aggressively to save so many lives would be reviled by the world.

That was the kind of persuasion a President understood.

Brognola thumbed the number on his mobile phone and left the farmhouse, waving to the waiting crew to get his helicopter ready for departure.

"No," he shouted under the downwash. "Two hours is no good. I'll be at the White House in forty minutes."

CHAPTER THIRTY-THREE

Arlington, Virginia

THE AIDE HAD COME to the house wearing her sailor jacket at the specific request of Senator Franklin Jackson. He'd also asked for the braids that made her look even younger than she was. It turned out that the little miss from a small town fifty-three miles outside Atlanta was just the medicine the senator needed, more than happy to help him work out his stress with some strenuous play and then volunteering to give him a body rub that had gone on now for more than half an hour.

There was a buzz from the phone on the desk, and she swung off to fetch it for him. The senator was face-first on the floor and limp with relaxation.

"Everything okay?" He paused. "Hey, you still there?" Another pause. "Fine. Report again in an hour."

He thumbed the phone off.

Seattle, Washington

COLONEL WARREN KORL hung up the pay phone outside the car rental office and stared at the thing in his hand. He had been reaching for his wallet while reporting in to Jackson and had found the hard, metallic object covered in needlelike barbs. The points were buried deep into the fabric of his jacket, almost inside the pocket. The positioning was almost perfect. It was the least likely place for him to have found the thing.

It was a bug. A goddamn bug!

The discovery had brought him to a mental standstill just as the senator answered, but Korl had recovered fast. Jackson hadn't known there was anything wrong. Korl had some decision making to do.

It had to have been shot at him. The only time it could have happened was at the bank building. The jacket was reversible and he had turned it inside out, changing it from a dark slate color to a warm brown. The bug was on the inside. It had to have been fired at him at the bank.

It was a small device. He wasn't up to speed on the latest technology, but he was pretty damned sure it was too small to have the power to send far. It would need a receiver or a retransmitter in close proximity to get the message anywhere. But to accomplish that they would have to know where he was.

Then he saw the pair on the bench, not five paces from where he stood. They looked as if they were discussing their route. So where was their rental car? The service personnel were standing around with nothing to do. No customers and no pending rentals. So what was the pair on the bench waiting for?

He knew the look. Short-cropped hair and the muscular jawline that came from a prime level of fitness. These guys were operatives of some kind. The bag that sat between them had the retransmitter. There was no doubt in his mind.

But how had they tracked him all the way to Seattle? Had

he been so distracted he had failed to notice a tail on the way out of Chicago and all the way to the Rockford airport? Of course, if they observed him taking the Seattle flight it would have been easy enough to arrange for another tail to pick him up when he landed.

Korl thought furiously. Had he or the senator said anything to signal their target? He didn't think so. No. He was sure of it.

So all he had to do was lose these guys.

First he had to get the upper hand with these bastards, whoever they were.

Stony Man Farm, Virginia

"THIS IS KORL TALKING to you. Whoever's the smart-ass who put the microphone on my clothes, I know you can hear me."

Kurtzman sped into the room at the urgent call from the communications technician.

"The first thing I want from you is some acknowledgment," the voice of Colonel Korl said through the speaker.

Kurtzman grabbed the phone and poked out an extension. "Barb—!"

"I hear it. I'm on my way."

"I think I would like you pieces of shit to do a little monkeying around for me," Korl said.

Price sped through the door seconds later and stooped to listen.

"What I think I want first is for the ugly one with the green jacket to get up and take the jacket off. I want to see what he's carrying."

"He's not bluffing. He's found the device," the communications specialist said. "From the levels I'm getting, it looks like he's talking right into it."

"I think you know what I'm capable of doing, friends. I

think you know I've already got something planned for this city. Here's the deal. You do what I say. You do it, or I take the munitions and start blowing up playgrounds and grade schools."

Kurtzman and Price looked at each other.

"Now I want Ugly Man to get to his feet and take off his green jacket. You think you can take me into custody? I'll tell you that I already got a contingency in place. I mean it, friends."

"Does he mean it?" Kurtzman asked.

"I think he's bluffing," Price said. "But I'm not taking the chance."

She got on the line and issued her orders to the two blacksuits.

Seattle

KORL STAYED in the phone booth while the special ops monkey did his trick. He stood and removed his jacket. The holster under his arm was there, as plain as day.

Dammit. Korl had been harboring a shred of hope that he was wrong, but the hope vanished. Now he was convinced that they—whoever they were—were right on his tail. How did they get so close?

A plan came to him. He assessed it for flaws. It was basic, but maybe it would be good enough. He issued his orders.

The agents did as commanded. They entered the car-rental agency and a few minutes later emerged with a rental agreement and a set of keys. They strolled down the aisle looking for their car.

When they had pulled out of the lot and turned on the road to the interstate, Korl dropped the bug on the floor of the phone booth and smashed it with his heel.

He jogged to his own rental and swerved around to the rear of the lot, finding the service entrance and barreling through.

Ten minutes later he pulled in front of the run-down four-flat where one of his Seattle contacts lived. The man was a lowlife, not to be trusted, but he'd serve his purpose this time. Korl took no chances. He stripped down to his boxers and put on a baggy shirt and greasy blue jeans that belonged to his contact. The man watched him incredulously.

"Give me your keys," Korl said. "I'll trade you for the Chrysler."

Korl left in a nine-year-old compact Ford that threatened to die out at every stop, but he felt safer. Leaving behind everything he'd had with him—except his handgun—made him confident he wasn't carrying any more bugs.

As he drove in circles, doubling back again and again, he analyzed the chain of events that led the FBI, or whoever it was, to him. He already knew they had been tracking him by the flawed "encrypted" phone. They had to have tailed him out of Chicago to Rockford, then had another team ready to tail him on the ground in Seattle.

But he wasn't being followed now.

It was dusk, and it was time to get back into the game.

THE SUN WAS DOWN. The immaculately landscaped avenues of the industrial complex were quiet. Even most of the late workers had gone home for the day. The only signs of life were in the fenced-in enclosure around the Hilo All Products Importing Corporation grounds, where the security guards, always in pairs, stopped at the employee picnic tables to drink coffee between rounds.

Blancanales had counted four pairs of guards, all walking a different route. They never got to stop for more than five minutes at a time. HAPI Corp ran a tightly guarded ship.

"It's not going to do them any good," Hermann Schwarz muttered.

Blancanales shook his head, saying nothing. Lyons had his eyes glued to the night-vision binoculars and was as still as a statue.

"They're just sitting there."

"They don't want to start the show without the colonel," Schwarz said.

They had taken their position more than two hours ago, climbing onto a roof of a secondary storage facility that overlooked the hundreds of acres of asphalt stretching behind the vast box that was HAPI Corp's main distribution warehouse. It was difficult to imagine the hundreds of trucks that would be needed to actually make use of a lot that was this huge. Since the lot was excavated at a shallow angle that descended to the dockside warehouse, it was surrounded on both sides by concrete retaining walls that heightened to more than twenty feet.

The place was all but deserted, and it stayed silent for so long they began to doubt the reliability of Stony's intelligence.

Price insisted that this was the target. "We got it right out of the mouth of Jackson himself," she insisted. Nobody argued the point.

Then the mercenaries showed up. They came in pairs, creeping through whatever darkness they could find. Able Team stood there and watched them get into position.

"Able One here, I'd sure like to know when we can get this show on the road. I see no reason to wait for the colonel to put in a appearance." Lyons had radioed the same opinion four times so far.

"Keep it in your jeans, Able One."

"What are we waiting for, Stony?"

Stony Man Farm

BARBARA PRICE WAS about as keyed up as she ever became. She had been waiting for the call from Hal Brognola for longer than she had dreamed possible. He had to have been kept waiting by the President.

She didn't want to tell Carl Lyons what they were waiting for. It would insult him, even if it was common sense.

They were waiting for help.

But with every empty minute it looked as if the help wasn't coming.

What she didn't understand yet was what Colonel Korl was waiting on. They knew he was close. Surely he was prepared to strike the facility. What was keeping him?

HAPI Corp was an obvious target for Franklin Jackson. The company was based in Japan but it brought goods into the U.S. from all over Asia. It had started as a joint venture between Japanese consumer goods firms, which had increasingly moved their manufacturing outside Japan in the last decade to save costs. Pooling their shipments allowed them to achieve economies of scale without the markup charged by shipping firms. Now the joint venture was shipping and distributing billions of dollars worth of Asian products to U.S. retailers.

Eleven percent of the products now sold by the stores that Franklin Jackson once owned was shipped in here. The retail dollar value was in the billions. No single business concern had benefited from Jackson's humiliating mistakes more than HAPI Corp.

"Barb, there's a ship coming into the HAPI facility," Kurtzman said over the intercom.

"Since when?" she demanded. "There's nothing scheduled."

"It's an old Chinese freighter called *People's Pride*. The manifest says it's carrying 'commodity stock' for HAPI distribution. They have a standing contract to buy leftover shipping space at rock-bottom prices on Seattle-bound ships. By 'leftover' in this case, they mean five thousand tons of goods. Uh-oh."

"Uh-oh what?"

"Hold on." Price heard Kurtzman and Tokaido consulting quietly, then Kurtzman spoke over the intercom to her again. "The manifest uses a Japanese colloquialism for fireworks. She's bringing in illegal fireworks under the guise of legal consumer products."

"It composes the entire shipment?"

"Looks like it," Kurtzman said. "Five thousand tons is a lot of illegal fireworks."

"Able One here, Stony," Carl Lyons radioed. "Something is happening here. We've got people starting to show up. Looks like warehouse staff."

"How many, Able One?" Price asked.

"We've got maybe forty so far."

Price pictured it all, vividly. How ironically symbolic for Franklin Jackson. Destroy an Asian company bringing in illegal fireworks for the U.S. Fourth of July.

Short of sinking the ship they came in on, destroying five thousand tons of fireworks would destroy the entire facility and every human being in it.

Washington, D.C.

A PRESIDENTIAL MEETING with visiting diplomats had gone on forever. Hal Brognola hadn't been patient. If he wasn't a high-ranking Justice official, the Secret Service would have taken him into custody.

Now, after all the waiting, he was just sitting here, staring at the walls of the Oval Office while the Man skimmed the reports.

The phone in his breast pocket started to silently vibrate again. The three-pulse signal told him it was from the Farm.

He didn't answer it. Again.

The Man suddenly let the report fall to the desktop and rubbed his forehead with his thumb and finger.

"We've delayed too long as it is, Mr. President," Brognola said finally.

"You're right. There's no denying Jackson's culpability any longer."

Silence.

"Tell me this, Hal. How sure—I mean *sure*—are you about the targets in Bombay?"

"We're relying on a few facts and the testimony of one man. Paul Patel. We know the minisub exists. We know Jackson has the funds to pull it off. We know he's murderous enough. We know the C-4 is missing."

Brognola watched the Man weigh this information and knew he wasn't buying into it. Which meant Brognola would have to use blackmail and threaten to expose the plot to the media. If that happened, the President would be forced to martial a huge response to the Bombay threat. Of course, Brognola would likely be out of a job and the Farm—

"We can't risk it."

"Mr. President?" Brognola said.

"We can't risk it being true. We can't put all those lives on the line. I'll order a full-scale response to the actions in Bombay and Seattle. I'll give you military support. I'll call the Indian prime minister myself to get immediate cooperation."

It took Hal Brognola a long moment to register the fact that the President of the United States, despite the possible political repercussions, was about to do the right thing.

CHAPTER THIRTY-FOUR

Seattle

"We've reached the *People's Pride,* and we can't convince her captain to delay docking at the HAPI facility," Price said.

"Coast Guard?" Lyons demanded.

"On their way. ETA ten minutes. The ship docks in four."

"We're on it, Stony," Lyons said.

He turned to his partners. "There's no way we're gonna stop the ship from docking. We have to stop the colonel from getting to the ship."

"So?" Blancanales said. "Let's stop him."

"He's probably bringing part of a shipment of C-4 that's gone missing from DOD inventories. A lot of it. Maybe tons."

"So?" Schwarz said. "We'll be gentle."

"Right," Lyons said. "My guess is the explosives aren't here yet."

"Otherwise, why the mercenaries gathering at the gate?" Blancanales added.

"So let's remove the mercenaries," Schwarz said. "With them we don't have to be gentle."

Bombay

"STONY, THERE'S GOT TO BE a hundred ships tied up in Mumbai," McCarter complained. "Most of them are cargo vessels of one kind or another. We don't even know what to look for."

"We're trying to track down the chemical carriers," Kurtzman responded.

"I'm guessing the Indian port authority doesn't have real-time systems online with ships and their manifests," Hawkins said from the passenger seat.

McCarter nodded in agreement. He felt useless, driving the small boat back and forth down the length of the Mumbai docks, looking for trouble. In the blackness of night they could see nothing. A major shipment hijacking could be happening under their noses, and they'd never know. Investigating every docked ship on foot would have taken hundreds of man hours.

So they were essentially standing around with their thumbs up their noses waiting for something to happen. For the fourth time they passed the boat with Encizo at the wheel. James was up front and Manning was glowering in back.

McCarter knew how he felt.

"Got something, Phoenix One," Kurtzman radioed unexpectedly. "We went in through the back door and raided the expediter schedules of companies who get chemical deliveries out of India. There's a Mexican garden products company expecting a shipment of methyl isocyanate that's supposed to leave India tomorrow—today your time."

Kurtzman provided the slip number, and McCarter called for Encizo to join them. The two high-speed boats, unofficially borrowed from the U.S. Navy, were black-hulled for clandestine operations. These 50 mph watercraft were originally designed for counterterrorism insertions and now saw regular use by SEAL teams and other special ops outfits.

The ship in question was dappled with severe pale security lights, and the night was filled with the vibration of its idling engines. At the water level the illumination glimmered in a sickly rainbow on the twisting fingers of floating oil and spilled fuel. Lights off, using the auxiliary electric motors for silent running, the twin watercraft went unnoticed by the guard duty on the ship.

"Anything?" McCarter asked.

"Hard to tell," Hawkins said, glaring at the instrument in his hands, which fed enhanced audio signals to the Texan's headset earphones while the software identified the sounds it knew. Under ideal conditions it could ID and enumerate everything from dolphins to close-proximity rebreather users. "The engine noise is confusing the reading. It's having trouble distinguishing other sound sources."

"Sonar?"

"Not good for close readings. If the minisub is here, it's too close to the seafloor and the wharf supports."

"Hey." Calvin James stood, pointing off the rear end of the boat.

A foot-long scrap of wood planking floated on the surface.

"Yeah?" McCarter asked.

"It wasn't there a minute ago," James explained.

A fist-size burst of bubbles surfaced under an oily sheen and popped lazily.

"Let's check it out," McCarter said. "Cal. Gary."

"We're on it," James said. In seconds he and Manning had removed their dark shirts. Underneath, their chests and necks were painted as dark as their faces. Even James used oily cosmetics to camouflage the sheen of his brown skin. They shrugged into the underwater breathing apparatus harness, the big CO_2 scrubbers and the oxygen tanks.

"Think twice before using that," Encizo reminded Manning as he snapped the underwater flashlight to his belt.

They had been briefed by Stony One about the man who Paul Patel had said was commanding the Indian arm of the Jackson-Korl campaign of terror. He was Kappa the Cat, real name Ivan Kappa. He had been a Ranger with an exemplary record except for suspected use of barbiturates and amphetamines to combat insomnia. He finally overdosed. The cocktail of chemicals found in his bloodstream included prescription-strength sleeping pills and phenothiazine-class antipsychotics with a street reputation for boosting sleeping pill performance. They were also blamed for causing the breakdown of the macula, the light-sensitive part of the retina, in a small number of users.

While recovering from his overdose Kappa had been diagnosed with exudative, or "wet" macular degeneration. The growth of new blood vessels beneath the retina was killing retinal cells. The therapy employed on Kappa combined the injection of a drug called Visudyne, which was activated in the retina with a laser directed into the eyes. The therapy stabilized his vision and he was lucky to get away with just a few minor blind spots.

Kappa was found to have retained ninety percent of his vision. His real problem was light sensitivity, which kept him behind dark glasses during the day. It was enough to keep him out of the Rangers, even without the drug conviction.

FBI files showed his light sensitivity was probably getting worse, as he was never seen without a pair of custom-made ski goggles that covered his eyes completely and could be darkened to accommodate light levels.

All the Phoenix Force commandos remembered their

glimpse of the nearly bald figure in the ski goggles who had assassinated his own men aboard the *Singep,* then escaped down the stairs into the bowels of the ship just before the minisub fled. There was little doubt Kappa the Cat would be commanding the minisub. He might even be alone. There was no evidence that any other mercenaries had survived the *Singep.*

James and Manning turned on the night-vision lenses mounted under their masks and slipped into the water noiselessly.

The Mk 25 was the standard-issue, closed-circuit oxygen underwater breathing apparatus for U.S. Navy combat swimmers. The Mk 25 Mod 0 type offered the least in terms of thermal protection, but also the best user mobility. In India's tepid seawater, cold wasn't a worry. Their biggest concern was the danger inherent in the closed-circuit oxygen rebreathers, but Calvin James was an old pro.

James had gone meticulously through the Mk 25 Mod 0 predive checklist. He had inspected the oxygen bottle pressure and the soda lime canister packing several times. It might be overkill for a shallow dive that was expected to last just a few minutes, but James never shortchanged the preparation phase of a dive.

Using the rebreather, exhaled breath from the diver was directed through the material in the soda lime canister, which absorbed the carbon dioxide before the air passed again into the breathing channel. This allowed the air circulation to be completely contained and no bubbles rose from the unit to give away the diver's presence.

The lack of bubbles and light made the sea close in around them. It was a claustrophobe's nightmare. Even the glimmer of movement made visible by the low-light glasses didn't help much.

When they were at a depth of ten feet, the surface above them became just a shimmer of multicolored oily streaks and vague shapes of the high-speed boats. At twenty feet there was only a ceiling of blackness.

James glanced at his dive buddy, who was a ghostly phantom even though he was within arm's reach. Manning wasn't at home in the water the way James was, but he gave the okay sign.

Shimmering in the imperfect low-light display, the hull of the docked shipping vessel loomed out of the darkness, covered in slime and strands of sea growth like a giant's decaying corpse.

Something tapped James on the leg. The thing bounced against his oxygen bottle, then wobbled up in front of his face, and the two of them watched it head for the surface. It was another chunk of a wooden packing pallet, freshly broken.

They descended straight down, until a shape swam out of the darkness. It looked like a backyard propane tank that had scuba gear lashed to it, three on each side. Hovering ten feet above it, they could just make out the big letters that covered the canister with a danger message in many different languages. Around the tank was the broken remains of the wooden crate that had cushioned it during transport.

James pointed, and they moved along the tank until they spied its linkage to the next tank, and the next. They were sitting on the pallet bottom of their shipping containers, which were sinking into the muck of the ocean floor.

Then they saw a diver, working without a light source. James and Manning would have called the seafloor completely dark, but there was enough ambient illumination for Kappa the Cat to do his work. This was one of the few opportunities he had for working without protective eyewear. He had on a standard scuba mask and was breathing through his own rebreather unit.

James and Manning were bringing their weapons into play, but Kappa made a startled move and peered into a device strapped to his forearm. He swung his head wildly in their direction, but James knew even a man like Kappa couldn't have seen him and Manning—they were at least eight yards away. But it didn't matter if he could see them or not—Kappa grabbed at his belt for the handle attached to a line as James and Manning triggered their underwater flare guns. James turned off the night-vision display and for a fraction of a second he was immersed in total blackness, then the twin flares filled the bottom of the ocean with light.

In a heartbeat James took in the entire scene laid out in front of them. He could see the train of canisters linked to a tow-chain sprouting like an umbilical cord from the belly of the minisub.

Kappa's line passed through a conduit into an open hatch on top of the sub. Some sort of winch inside the hatch hauled Kappa in it at a reckless speed.

The diver had his arm over his goggles, and he didn't see or didn't care when the winch pulled him into the side of the sub violently. The man groped with one arm for the hatch. When he found it, he pulled his swim fins up under his body and straightened, descending inside.

Another pair of painfully brilliant flares rocketed through the water, and one of them bounced into the hatch just before it pulled closed. The second flare began a twisting dance in the twin jets of water as the water inside the hatch was replaced with air in an emergency exchange.

The minisub bobbed up a few feet from the abrupt buoyancy change, dragging the first canister up with it, then the sub's rear end descended again and the two commandos heard the clank of metal.

IVAN KAPPA COLLAPSED when the water drained from the dive chamber, then felt the heat of the flare burning into the flesh of his hand like a blowtorch. He found the door to the interior and unlatched it, collapsing into the minisub's interior and slamming the door behind him.

The savage hiss of the flare was muted. Cautiously, Kappa removed his arm from in front of his eyes.

It didn't help. He couldn't see. His vision was a swirl of lightning streaks generated by fresh trauma to the nerves of his retinas.

He had left the minisub without his eye gear. It was dark and he was forty feet down—he had never dreamed he would be exposed to a light source, let alone be trapped in the coffin-like hatch with the inescapable phosphorous brilliance of an underwater flare. The light was like nails driving into his eyeballs. The flare was gone, but the nails were lodged deep in his skull.

He groped for the seat and collapsed into it, then fumbled over the controls.

He didn't need to see to operate the minisub. He knew the location of every control. It was designed to operate more easily than a fishing boat. It even had the automatic pilot already programmed for the journey ahead.

Ivan Kappa started the diesel engine—no need to bother with the stealthy electric motors—and punched the remote control to initiate the inflation of the canister floats.

He would do this job, and along the way maybe he'd see his vision start to come back.

THEIR DIVE LIGHTS were now on and strong strokes carried them to the minisub. Manning grabbed at a rear diving plane and pulled one of the explosive packs from its mounting on his shoulder. Manning had assembled the packs carefully—

just enough high pressure to destroy the diving planes and props, paralyzing the minisub, but not enough to shock the nearby chemical-containing canisters.

James was moving with powerful strokes for the hatch when he heard the rumble of the engine and spotted a fraction of movement out of the corner of his eye. He twisted and kicked violently against the ocean water, changing his trajectory and sending his body into Manning's with the inertia of an enraged killer whale.

Manning grunted and lost his mouthpiece, bubbles bursting around the pair of them as the props went into a frenzy. James propelled them down and away with all the strength he could muster. When they reached the gelatinous muck of the seafloor, he reinserted Manning's mouthpiece.

The minisub was fishtailing as her prop speed drove higher and the weight of the chemical canisters anchored her to the bottom. The rear swung in their direction, and immense power of the sub's power plant hit them with an invisible tidal wave. James was forced down and away, and felt his body plowing up mud.

The force was gone an instant later and the clear water became a cloud of mud that engulfed him, but not before he spotted the movement of the canisters as their flotation pillows inflated. He reached blindly into the murk that engulfed him and felt some part of Gary Manning's UBA harness. He muscled the pair of them into the water flow and out of the mud.

The cloud changed from filthy brown to shimmering pink.

Manning, James realized, hadn't escaped the prop. James felt the fear. It didn't come often. He wouldn't let it affect his actions, but he couldn't escape the one thought, How could a human body make contact with those spinning blades and survive?

Yet the big Canadian commando was conscious, and he

still held the mouthpiece in his teeth. One hand had an iron lock on his left biceps and the ugly strands of blood flowed from between his fingers. The glaze on his eyes was apparent, despite the mask.

James grabbed at the custom accessory pack on the front of the CO2 scrubber. Even through the haze of shock Manning knew what James meant to do. The wounded commando shook his head. He wanted to stay and assist!

James stabbed at the emergency button, which glowed red and sent out the high-powered radio beacon tied into the Miniature Underwater GPS Receiver. The MUGR could be allowed to float on the surface as a GPS antenna, but James didn't release it. He'd send Manning to surface with it, and it would sound an alarm in the headsets of the commandos on the surface as well as on the monitors at Stony Man Farm, a half a planet away.

James snatched the bright stainless-steel ring from the chest pack, and a belch of bubbles appeared at Manning's shoulders as the orange pillows inflated.

Manning grimaced and tried to shrug, but then he was rising up, carried by the emergency floater that would thrust him face-first from the water even if he lost consciousness.

The blood cloud billowed behind him, and as he disappeared into the blackness James witnessed the train of canisters lunge forward, settle and lunge again. They were inflating fast, too. The billowing balloons had lightened the load substantially in the last sixty seconds and it wouldn't be long before the sub would find the strength to drag them off.

James couldn't let that happen.

CHAPTER THIRTY-FIVE

Seattle

Carl Lyons strolled across the vast asphalt lot like a man without a mission.

He held his jacket draped over one shoulder, looked at the sky and took an imaginary wedge of chewing tobacco out of his pocket. He stuffed it into his lip and sucked on it while making easy time.

He was being scrutinized by two men with automatic weapons. At any moment they could have taken him out with an easy shot. His acting had to be good.

When he got close enough, he began to whistle as he leaned against the retaining wall that kept the higher level of decorative garden from collapsing onto the employee parking lot. By that time he was out of their field of vision, but they were stationed just overhead.

He dropped the coat and took a leap that carried him four feet up the wall, where he grabbed the safety railing and hauled himself up to it, then laid the Atchisson Assault 12 on the bare metal. The gunner pair was too surprised to know what to do at first.

"Evening," Lyons said.

The nearer man figured he had a chance. He was good, he was fast, and he needed just inches of movement to put his target into the line of fire of his M-14. The carbine shifted onto Lyons and the Able Team leader fired. The shotgun blast shredded his assailant's arm to the bone and tore the flesh off his face. The second man was blocked from most of the buckshot and screamed when he found the side of his head flayed. The Atchisson thundered a second time and the scream stopped.

THAT WAS THE SIGNAL Schwarz had been waiting for. He emerged from behind a house-size garbage compressor and found himself looking a the backs of three more mercenaries. Stationed here, they had an unobscured view of most of the huge exterior. Their entire attention was on the distant gunshots.

"Hey!"

One of them actually had the presence of mind to have his weapon ready when he turned, and Schwarz aimed for the only exposed flesh he saw. His burst of 5.56 mm shockers cut through the merc's throat, then Schwarz turned the M-16 A-2 on his companions. The quick sweep of fire shoved them around without finding a gap in the armor and Schwarz gave up, jumping behind the garbage crusher. He thumbed an anti-personnel buckshot round into the 40 mm M-203 grenade launcher mounted under the barrel of the M-16 A-2.

It was vicious, but Schwarz felt no compassion for Colonel Korl's enforcement staff.

They didn't even have a cause. They killed innocent people for a freaking paycheck.

They were the worst kind of murderer.

Schwarz stepped out. They were ready for him, but he was

faster. The 40 mm round changed the M-203 into a shotgun, and from just five paces it was devastating, sandblasting the flesh from their hands and heads. The pair was dead before they dropped to the ground in an untidy heap.

AT THE SOUND of the buckshot grenade, one of Blancanales's targets ran into the open.

"There he is!" shouted a towering, meaty mercenary with a distended jawline. He made his short carbine look like a toy gun. He yanked the weapon to gut level and triggered a blast up at the overlook. "Dammit!" the merc shouted.

Blancanales took that to mean Schwarz had evaded his gunfire and that was all the trouble the Human Chin was gonna give his friend Gadgets. He rose to his knees atop a storage building and sneered at the surprised reaction from the killer below. Blancanales squeezed off a burst, but the mercenary wasn't as stupid as he looked, and he proved it by taking flight. The Able Team commando led him in his sights and fired another burst that caught the mercenary in the side of the head. The man tumbled hard, and Blancanales swore he felt a tremor.

He flattened and crawled on his elbows to the side of the building that looked out onto the guard shack. There was a uniformed guard inside, slumped against the wall. Where were the other two gunners?

"Able One here," Lyons radioed. "They're right below you, Pol."

"Can you flush them for me, Ironman?"

"We'll see."

There was a report of gunfire from the darkness of a decorative copse of trees on the far side of the lot. It was hundreds of yards away—not a likely shot from the big Colt revolver, but the mercenaries below weren't taking their chances. They tramped noisily around the side of the building. They didn't realize they had escaped into danger.

Blancanales jumped to his feet and unleashed a vicious onslaught, but his prey almost stumbled into a drop-off. They flung themselves off the edge. The Able Team commando didn't know if he had hit either of them.

Then he saw the truck.

His gunfire brought it to a halt with a chirp of breaks. It sat in the open, idling on the dark street. The faceless driver and camouflaged commando regarded one another across a hundred yards of emptiness, trying to read each other in the dark.

It was a short semi trailer without markings. Could be anybody, Blancanales thought. Could be somebody hired to pick up a shipment of Chinese-made toaster ovens.

But Blancanales knew, somehow, that the man at the wheel was Colonel Warren Korl.

The diesel engine sputtered and the rig lurched forward and flashed its lights, then Blancanales saw the pair from the guard shack jump to their feet and send a barrage of fire at his rooftop. Blancanales returned fire and fell, but not before the blow crunched into his gut like a tire iron.

He fell flat and fought for breath, then heard the footsteps on his rooftop. His clenched body refused to obey his commands and, just as he found himself capable of gasping for air, the tissue damage blinded him again.

Then there was a gunshot just above him. Blancanales realized that whoever had joined him up here was shooting at the gunners below, and he forced his eyes to focus.

"The truck, Gadgets," he gasped.

"It's coming. Shit, Ironman!"

Blancanales pushed himself upright and saw the unmistakable figure of Lyons stepping off the ledge and plummeting to the parking lot, landing in a run, bolting to the front gate as the semi picked up speed and aimed itself at the gates. The truck slammed into it and the concrete uprights crumbled, the steel crossbars curling around the truck like another grille.

The rig didn't slow and Lyons stared it down, almost sneering. When it was in range, he pulled the Atchisson to his shoulder and fired. The front tire flattened and the truck swerved hard. Lyons fired again and the front windshield went opaque. The truck's weight carried it inexorably forward and it jackknifed, tires screeching and vibrating as they slid sideways on the asphalt and bore down inexorably on one running man with a shotgun.

Blancanales's excruciating pain had ceased to be as he lived the impossibly long seconds of uncertainty. Lyons sprinted like a track star and still the semi came at him, tires smoking and exploding one after another, the bare rims scarring the asphalt, the immense inertia battling furiously against friction and gravity.

The Able Team leader reached the end of the line. He was at the wall. He became airborne, spread-eagle, then he caught the wall with his outstretched arms. Blancanales saw his legs pushing his upper half up and over the safety rail, and he collapsed among the trees and the bodies of the men he had shot dead.

The rig's front end screeched to a stop and the rear end of the trailer whipped into the wall right where Lyons was, as if it aimed for him, the rear corner folding noisily. The concrete buckled, the rail bursting out of its sockets. The small decorative garden atop the retaining wall was flattened like an old Chrysler inside a crusher.

Then the night was silent.

"Able Three here," Schwarz said into the radio, unable to

tear his eyes off the distant scene of ruin. "You read me, Able One?"

Nothing. Blancanales forced himself to breathe, and with every fill of his lungs a grinding sensation made him aware of loose parts.

"Able Three here," Schwarz said. "Love to hear from you, Able One."

Silence.

"Hey, Carl! Speak up, you moody miserable son of a bitch!"

Everybody here is dead, Blancanales thought. Everybody except me and Gadgets.

But the night proved him wrong. The shattered windshield of the big rig left its frame with a series of vicious kicks from the inside, then a bloodied figure appeared behind the wheel.

The diesel engine sputtered and struggled to life, the gears engaged with the grinding of metal, and it inched forward, dragging itself painfully out of its jackknifed pose and wobbling on flattened tires. The bloody figure of Warren Korl was at the wheel.

The night echoed with the long whistle of the arriving cargo ship as it slowed for docking just beyond the vast warehouse.

"He's gonna circle and head back in," Schwarz said in disbelief. "Hey, Colonel! Hey!"

Korl's eyes were vividly white for a moment against his gleaming, bloodied face, then he dived for cover behind the dashboard in time to avoid the burst of rounds that Schwarz fired, aiming high to cover the extra distance and praying for a lucky strike. Korl was steering from the floor and the rig turned, limping to the warehouse.

Blancanales felt wounded. Sick. And sad. A holocaust was about to occur, and he didn't see how it could be stopped.

Then the obvious answer came to him.

Schwarz triggered a long burst from a fresh magazine, trying in vain to score a hit through the window of the rig. But Blancanales took his own weapon and forced himself up onto his feet, then somehow made himself take the long step onto the neighboring rooftop.

"Stay back, Gadgets!" he called over his shoulder.

"Hey, Pol—?"

Blancanales didn't have the strength or the time to explain.

Bombay, India

"HERE HE IS!" Rafael Encizo barked, lunging over the side of the boat like the hydraulic arm on a piece of heavy machinery, coming up with the big, limp body of Gary Manning.

Encizo felt as if he were landing a marlin after a long competition—huge, heavy, and completely without fight. Manning dangled in his arms, as soggy as a dishrag, and the Cuban draped him carefully on the floor.

Encizo found himself covered in blood and traced it with his eyes to the wound. It looked like something very sharp had cut the man's arm half off.

Encizo clamped hard on the wound as the others gathered around him. Without wasted motion, the wound was cleaned, closed and sealed inside an emergency pressure bandage.

Encizo couldn't tear his eyes away from his friend. Gary Manning was staring at the sky through slitted eyes, his flesh as sickly white as the fish that rotted belly-up in the wharf muck.

"Where's Cal?" somebody asked.

CALVIN JAMES tore away the air hose. The inflatable leaked air bubbles momentarily, then sealed itself. James forced his fingers into the protective steel mesh and wrenched it off, then slashed at the inflatable with his dive knife. The plastic was extra thick, but it gave way to the sharp point of the blade. There were four, long, self-sealing partitions, and he fought savagely to penetrate each one of them, but at last they lost their air and the inflatable was useless.

One down. Five to go. Then six more on each of four more canisters in the train. He had started on the first canister, the one linked directly to the belly of the minisub. If he neutralized its buoyancy, would it anchor the minisub to the bottom?

The other cars in the train were clearing the bottom as James released the gas from the final balloon on the right side of his canister. The canister flopped onto its side and James clawed over the top, tearing at another balloon cage as he felt the flotilla inexorably rise. The remaining balloons on his canister were filling themselves to capacity, and the stretched material surrendered more easily to his dive knife.

Finally the last flotation device released its air. It seemed he'd been working for hours, but the watch on his tac board said it was just four minutes since they had chased Kappa into the minisub, just three minutes since he had watched Manning ascend in a river of blood.

The canister moved forward and James clung to it, feeling their speed increase. James allowed himself to be carried to the end of the first canister, tied up on the linkage, then gave himself some slack and inched along the second cylinder.

Then he saw the boulder protruding from the seafloor, as big as a ranch house in the suburbs, complete with a pointed roof. The minisub and its train of deadly cylinders would have cleared it—except that now the low-slung cylinder James had sabotaged dangled too low.

By the time James saw the rock, he had less than two seconds to brace himself for the impact.

CHAPTER THIRTY-SIX

Seattle

Blancanales saw lightning flashes when he made the leap to the next rooftop. Something sharp was cutting things up inside his chest. If there was a bone fragment in there worming its way—

He just needed half a minute more.

The diesel rig was complaining as it strained to accelerate despite the sloppy masses of rubber on its rims. As it was, Blancanales couldn't believe Korl was coaxing so much speed out of the vehicle. There was no time left. If the worst happened, it had to happen now.

The worst-case scenario was a distinct possibility.

Blancanales put the high-explosive 40 mm round into the breech of the M-203 grenade launcher mounted under his assault rifle, then brought it up high. Hitting the spot on the ground just in front of the accelerating rig seemed an impossible shot on that vast sea of asphalt. There was no time to think it through. No time to line up a careful shot. There was no time left for anything.

He triggered the weapon.

The moment he fired, he knew that the worst-case scenario had happened. His aim was off. The round wouldn't hit in front of the rig. It would hit the rig itself.

He should get into cover, but there was no cover. He couldn't move anymore. His body was screaming. It was broken. He wasn't going anywhere.

Then something very close swooped out of the darkness, plowed into Blancanales and bodily propelled him away from his last brief image of his HE round detonating atop the trailer. There was a flash of an explosion, but by then he was falling off the other side of the building. He landed hard on his back, briefly seeing the stars in the night sky.

Blancanales didn't see those stars vanish a moment later in the brilliance of white fire. He had gone away, descending deep into his own, personal darkness.

Bombay

THE CANISTER of concentrated poison bounced off the boulder with a deafening clang that vibrated Calvin James down to the skeleton, filling his head with instant, throbbing pain. He found himself flopping on the end of his tether like a vicious fish fighting on the hook. He grabbed the rope, pulling himself close to the container to avoid the tearing fingers of the increasing current.

Somehow the canister hadn't ruptured from the impact. Even a tiny trickle of methyl isocyanate would have killed him.

But the impact had banged a realization into him. When he and Manning sent the flare into the hatch with Kappa the Cat, it had done what they'd intended it to do. The light had overloaded his ultrasensitive macula. He was blind.

But the fool was still trying to carry out his mission. He had engaged the automatic guidance system, but it hadn't taken the dangling cargo into account.

James knew he couldn't let Kappa the Cat go on, or eventually he was going to smash one of the canisters open. The minisub wasn't designed for towing, but it was going fast enough that James would very soon be torn off—or battered to a pulp.

He had to stop the sub and he had to do it now, whatever it took.

James clawed his way around the dangling canister, finding a precarious handhold on the welded rim where he had ripped away one of the steel mesh inflatables, and dragged himself along it until he reached the belly of the minisub. In the chaotic flashes of his dive light he found the steel linkage that joined the canister and the sub. He placed the explosive.

It was just what Gary Manning had instructed him not to do.

"We want to disable the minisub without compromising the chemical canister integrity," Manning had explained carefully as they'd prepared for the dive. That seemed like days ago.

Sorry, Gary, James thought.

He had no other choice. No way could he reach the rear diving plane, which was where Manning intended to plant the charges. If James tried it, he'd simply get sucked in and chopped to pieces in the whirling props and that would be that.

He activated the detonator. The red light came on, then he positioned his feet against the hull and cut the line, forcing himself down and away from the minisub and using every energy reserve to stroke against the powerful pull of the rotating propellers. For a moment he was caught in a maelstrom of current, then he found himself drifting beneath the towed train of canisters.

He was breathing hard. Could he be running out of air? The tac board, with its compass, depth gauge and watch, still insisted that an amazingly short time had passed since he'd sent his wounded friend back to the surface.

His hand poised over the MUGR release. The unit had a tracer, but he wouldn't activate it. He wouldn't summon his teammates to their death. James was certain that the water all around him was about to become virulent poison. But he waited anyway. No sense in killing himself with the explosion.

Finally he was tired of it all. It was time to end the threat. He grabbed the transmitter and pressed the button.

"WHOA—SOMETHING just exploded," Hawkins reported, staring into the sonar. "He did it. James blew the sub."

"Where?" McCarter demanded.

Hawkins looked at him sharply. McCarter said nothing more. They couldn't go there. There was no point in racing to the scene of the blast. If even one of the canisters leaked, then James was a dead man. They would be, too.

"So why are we just sitting here?" Manning demanded from a rear floor, where he was wrestling with Encizo to be allowed to sit up.

McCarter didn't answer. Manning won the battle, but when he was sitting up he didn't say anything more. The four of them stared into the open ocean and the distant lights of Elphanta Island.

Hawkins had his attention on the chem-bio sensors. Despite an amazing degree of pollution, nothing set off the alarms.

Then something beeped. Hawkins's eyes danced across the controls, looking for the source of the alert.

It was the tracer on the floating antenna from Phoenix Four's Miniature Underwater GPS Receiver.

Somewhere out there, Calvin James was alive.

CHAPTER THIRTY-SEVEN

Stony Man Farm, Virginia, U.S.A.

Somewhere on the other side of the world, aboard a U.S. Navy vessel, Gary Manning was undergoing emergency surgery to repair serious deep tissue lacerations to the upper arm. There could be permanent nerve damage.

Somewhere in a Seattle hospital were two bruised and battered men without official identities, hovering at the bedside of another John Doe who looked as though he had been thrown off a building. Which he had.

"Carl will live. Gadgets suffered burns and concussion, but he'll pull through."

Barbara Price didn't look at Hal Brognola. The big Fed hunkered down miserably at the other end of the War Room table.

"Rosario?"

Price just shrugged.

"What's wrong with him?"

"What's not?"

He didn't push it.

"Help came," she said finally. "But it came too late. We had hundreds of U.S. troops pouring into the port at Mumbai and all they could do was mop up. They located the explosives scattered throughout the port. They retrieved the canisters. They raised the minisub. But they weren't any help to us."

"What about Kappa?" Brognola asked.

"He was still inside the wreckage when it came up. He apparently survived the explosion that disabled the sub, but the hull was warped and the hatch jammed. He must have panicked. He broke most of his fingers trying to open it. Eventually the interior filled with seawater and he drowned."

"What's the situation in Seattle?"

"HAPI Corp is going to need a shitload of landfill before they can put in a new parking lot. When the truck blew, it made a crater so deep there was seawater seeping into it. But they got off lucky. They experienced just one human casualty, a front gate guard. All the rest of the dead were Korl's men."

"What about Korl himself?"

"Incinerated. There's not a speck of him left."

Brognola fought for words. Finally he said, "You know I did my best, Barb." He thought he sounded pathetic.

Price looked up. "I know you did, Hal. I know you played the game as best you could. But the other players didn't come through when they should have. The other players didn't have the guts to take a risk to help us. Not until they were forced into play, and by then it didn't matter. We were sacrificed on their political game board."

"Barb—"

Her chair scraped and she was on her feet. "And you know what, Hal? I'm sick and tired of *my* players being sacrificed."

Seattle, Washington

TWO OF THEM had gauze turbans. They sat on either side of the comatose figure in a mass of post-op bandages. They had been there for hours, mostly watching the news networks as they reported over and over on the bizarre events of the past eighteen hours. Senator Franklin Jackson was dead of a self-inflicted gunshot wound, just minutes after the first media broadcast of an audio tape implicating him as the mastermind behind a string of terror attacks around the world.

The television didn't have any meaning to the gauze-wrapped pair. All they really cared about was seeing some sign of life from the lifeless, electronically monitored lump on the mattress.

Neither of them had spoken in more than an hour when Carl Lyons said, "You know, I heard you call me a moody, miserable son of a bitch."

Schwarz glared across the bed. "I did not."

"On the radio. After the truck hit the wall."

"You were hallucinating."

"I know what I heard."

"I didn't say it."

They were silent for another minute, then Lyons growled, "If Politician ever wakes up, he'll settle this."

There was a groan from the figure under the blankets. They heard something that sounded like words spoken through a throat filled with gravel.

"Leave me out of it."

TAKE 'EM FREE
2 action-packed novels plus a mystery bonus
NO RISK
NO OBLIGATION TO BUY